WHO SHOT THE WATER BUFFALO?

WHO SHOT THE WATER BUFFALO?

KEN BABBS

THE OVERLOOK PRESS
NEW YORK, NY

This edition first published in paperback in the United States in 2012 by
The Overlook Press, Peter Mayer Publishers, Inc.
141 Wooster Street
New York, NY 10012
www.overlookpress.com
For bulk and special sales, please contact sales@overlookny.com

Library of Congress Cataloging-in-Publication Data

Babbs, Ken.
Who shot the water buffalo? : a novel / Ken Babbs.
p. cm.
1. Helicopter pilots—Vietnam—Fiction. 2. United States. Marine Corps—Fiction. 3. Vietnam War, 1961-1975—Fiction. I. Title.
PS3602.A225W48 2011 813'.6—dc22 2010052011

Design and typeformatting by Bernard Schleifer
Printed in the United States of America
1 3 5 7 9 10 8 6 4 2
ISBN 978 1 59020 733-8

For the men and their families of HMM-163
(Marine Medium Helicopter Squadron-163)
The Ridgerunners
1961–1963

"So let us not talk falsely now.
The hour is getting late."

—Bob Dylan

I
THE STATES

1960-1961

Getting Ready

"He crowned thy good
—He told me He would—
with brotherhood . . ."
—Brother Ray

1. Sparks Flying

I'm all shot up, Doc . . . it was a trap . . . no one expected a heavy machine gun . . . we headed for it like filings to a magnet . . . I came into the zone hard, dropped the chopper to let the ARVNs out and everything went to shit . . . the windshield blew apart . . . my shoulder was all torn up, a real mess, Doc . . . there's a curse on that shoulder . . . the same exact one I fucked up in flight school . . . there I was, tooling along on my Lambretta motor scooter cheerfully whistling the Marine Corps Hymn, headed for my early-morning celestial navigation class . . . learn to steer by the stars . . . at the time I was steering one handed and swerved to avoid a child and fell out of bed, ha ha, except it wasn't a child, Doc, it was a little fucking perro *Chihuahua come yapping out from behind a car and sunk its teeth in the front tire . . . sent the evil creature flapping around the fender and catapaulted me off the scooter onto the rough asphalt, peeling the skin off my shoulder, shirt, skin, and all, peeled me right down to the very cherry red meat . . . but be dogged if I was going to let that dog and scooter act throw me off schedule like it was the end of daylight savings time . . . fall behind, get it, Doc? . . . I wasn't going to fall behind in my flight school classes . . . I had to keep up with Cochran . . . no way was he going to leave me behind . . . I drove that scooter on a flat tire to the BOQ and borrowed a fresh shirt, cleaned myself up, and made it to class on time, giving Cochran a nod as I slipped into my seat . . . so you see right there it all comes back to Cochran, Doc . . . he's the reason, the genesis and the comeuppance, this is all his fault, that damned Cochran . . .*

He's a big bruiser of a guy, muscular back straining against his Marine Corps shirt. He's got a motor scooter by the seat and handle bars and, letting loose a deep grunt, hefts the stubby Lambretta into the guts of a dumpster.

I'm standing on the sidewalk outside the Admin Building of the Pensacola Naval Air Station where I've just checked in for flight school. My mouth is twisted between shock and mirth. The big bruiser turns, sees the what the fuck look on my face, scowls, and says, "I've had it with that son of a bitch. Fooled me for the last time."

He steps forward and looks me over. I'm five nine and wiry. He's six two and solid. Tufts of hair stick out of his sleeves and peek from beneath his shirt collar. Black bristles cover the backs of his hands.

"Fooled you how?" I say, standing tall as I can.

"It starts right up on the first try, runs like a top, then double crosses you when you least expect it. Then it won't start at all, no matter how many times you try." He smiles meanly. "Not any more." He wipes his hands back and forth and, with a look of disgust, flings his hands apart. "I'm shunt of it."

"I guess you wouldn't mind if I took it off your hands?"

"No, why would I mind?" He smiles broadly, showing gleaming white pearlies.

"You gonna give me a hand getting it out of the dumpster?"

"You shitting me? You want it, you rescue it."

I climb into the dumpster, hoist one end of the scooter up on the edge and push it over. I climb out, set the scooter on its stand, turn the key, give it some gas and tromp down on the starter. The motor coughs, catches and winds up to a high-pitched whine.

I look at the previous owner and give him a grin. He whips off his fore-and-aft cap, makes to throw it on the ground, thinks better of it, comes over and hops on the back. The scooter sinks to the ground.

"You'll see, she'll break your heart, too. Onward."

"Where to?"

"The O Club, where else. The sun is over the yardarm someplace in the world. Time for a drink."

I gun the motor, pop the clutch and we lumber off like a waddling duck, tail dragging, sparks flying.

The officers club is a regal affair, brick wings on either side of a white colonnaded portico that leads into a large foyer with paintings of naval aircraft on the walls. A door on the left opens into the big dining room, the door on the right into the O club.

We're wearing our winter uniforms, long-sleeve shirts and tie, gold 2nd Lieutenant bars on the collars, fore-and-aft caps in our hands. You wear your hat in the bar and the bartender bangs a big bell and the offender buys drinks for all. It's February and there's a whiff of spring in the Florida Panhandle. President Kennedy's been in office for a month and the country's bubbling on a wave of enthusiasm.

We click glasses. "Well this is a fortuitous meeting, for me anyways," I tell Cochran, thinking of the scooter. "How'd you get in this man's outfit, anyway?"

He swirls his glass on the bar top, making wet circular patterns. He was, he says, an obstreperous child in a Youngstown, Ohio family firmly ensconced in the movie-theater business, actually a front for nefarious gangster activities. Pinball machines with cash payoffs, slot machines in back rooms, card games, small-time action with big-time mannerisms of gangster fascinations as they divvied up the spoils. Meanwhile at home all was light and cheer, his tall Irish mother a willowy, graceful contrast to her dark stocky Greek husband—the two boys a curious amalgam: Cochran, the elder, tall and massive with all the hair, the same upbeat, outgoing personality as his mother; his younger brother, a shorter glowering replica of their papi.

"Makes my cow-raising ranch life in Locos, Texas sound pretty ordinary in comparison," I tell him, but I enliven my telling with accounts of Mexican adventures at my grandmother's house across the border and high spirited barbecues at our ranch this side of the border; *vaqueros* busting broncs in the corral, long rides through chapparal rounding up the herd, hot branding irons and the smell of burnt hair and flesh, the hissing and smoking of coffee dregs thrown in the fire. My mother was a lovely, high-born, University of Texas belle who couldn't abide the isolation of the ranch. My rough-hewn Texan father, full of cowboy wisdom and laconic frontier bluster, wasn't exactly a social live wire.

"When Daddy enlisted in the Army in World War Two, Mother took advantage of his being gone and went back to her family in Austin where she got a divorce. With my mother gone, *mi abuela* and I wandered back and forth across the Rio Grande, and I spent almost as much time at her old home in Mexico as I did on the ranch. When I was high-school age Daddy sent me to the Texas Military Academy. After that I attended college at Texas Military Institute."

"Yeah, good old college," Cochran says. "It kept me from working in the movie theater, and Air Force ROTC kept me out of the draft. Unfortunately, I got caught with my hand in the department files the night before the ROTC final. They booted me out of ROTC and college both. I signed up for Marine Officer Candidate School and completed the program before my folks got wind of what went down."

"I got my commision when I finished TMI. I was lined up to go in the Army. Four generations of soldiers on my father's side of the family and I had to go against the grain and choose the Marine Corps. Daddy didn't know about it until he saw me in my Marine Corps uniform. Talk about your busted pride. I thought he'd choke, but he swallowed the bitter pill."

"Thank God for these gold bars on the collars," Cochran says. "The fact I was an officer in the Marines is what kept my father, brother, and the Youngstown gangsters from pulverising me for spoiling the family name by getting kicked out of college. If they had their way they'd have turned me into a punchy popcorn vendor in one of Youngstown's skidrow movie theaters."

"We've settled our respective family hashes and now, here we are." Me, Tom Huckelbee.

"Yes, here we are." Him, Mike Cochran.

We click glasses and stare morosely into the mirror behind the bar.

"I've led quite a peripatetic existence," I say, talking to the mirror.

"You have?" Cochran turns and looks me over. "How cosmopolitan. First time I've ever heard anyone use that word outside of a book. How do you spell that? And don't say T-H-A-T."

"C-O-S-M-O" I begin.

"No, you ninny," Cochran interrupts. "Peripatetic."

I know what he means. Avoidance syndrome. Spelling's never been my *fuerte de align*, not my strong suit. I picture the word in my mind.

"P-E-R-A-P-A-T-E-T-I-C," I spell.

"That's P-E-R-E," Cochran says. "You're perepathetic."

"Oh yeah? I got a ten-spot says I'm right and you're wrong."

The bartender settles the beef with a dictionary. Words over easy. On the rocks. We're both wrong. I gallantly acknowledge my error, but I don't have to pay up, for his spelling goof has nullified the bet.

"I'll get this round," Cochran says, the soul of generosity. "Aside from your illiteracy," he continues, "how do you like living on base in the BOQ?"

"If you're implying I'm illiterate, I've got another ten-spot that says both my parents were married. I hate the BOQ. Why?"

"No bet. You've probably got the papers to prove it. Whaddaya say we get a pad off-base?"

"Sounds good to me, where?"

Cochran pulls a scrap of paper out of his pocket. "Charming two-bedroom, one-bath bungalow on the beach two miles from base," he reads.

"Let's do it."

We drink up and go outside. Cochran watches as I hop on the scooter and slam my foot on the kick starter. Nothing. I try again. Not even a whimper. Again, then more kicks, faster and faster, until finally, thoroughly fed up, I get off and kick the scooter and knock it on its side.

"No good sagebrush-eating bitch," I yell at the inert machine.

"Can I give it a try?" Cochran asks.

"Be my guest." I fold my arms and step aside.

"If I start it can I keep it?"

I narrow my eyes. Does he know something I don't? I shrug. Why not.

He sets the Lambretta upright, balances on the seat, takes a deep breath, slams his foot on the kick starter, nurses the gas and the no-good piece of shit coughs to life.

He turns to me with a big grin. "All in the way you breathe," he says. "Calm, collected."

"Breathe this," I say, blowing acrid gin and tonic in his face. I climb on the back and we putter off the base toward the beach, tail scraping, sparks flying.

The pad is a small house overlooking Pensacola Bay. Our landlord, retired Admiral Hiram B. Jenkins III, and his Southern, high-bred, white-haired wife, Matilde, live in a sprawling house with a screened-in porch. The house sits atop a stone foundation lapped by the waves.

They invite Cochran and me to dinner. Dress whites with swords. The Admiral's uniform drips with epaulets, horn piping and medals. His wife is adorned in a white lace evening dress. Her powdered bosom heaves and she rolls her eyes languidly.

"So nice you all could come. We don't have many guests since the children are grown." She pats her eye with a hanky.

The Admiral slaps his knee. "Oh for Christ's sake, Matilde. Don't bore the men with family matters. Come along, officers, onto the bridge." He swings open the floor-to-ceiling glass-paned doors. We step onto the screened-in porch.

"Bit of a wind," the Admiral declares.

The Bay is whipped into froth. Spray splatters our uniforms.

"Ah, bracing." He twirls a knob on his shortwave radio.

"Sqrzzd . . . storm warnings along the Gulf Coast . . . possibility of Hurricane Ed turning west . . . bawkzzg . . ."

"Reminds me of the typhoons we faced in the Sea of Japan."

Admiral Jenkins adroitly lights a cigar in the howling wind. He offers us the humidor. I go through a pack of matches. Cochran fares no better.

"Yas, bows to the sea. Take them head on."

A breaker explodes against the foundation. Salt water smacks the screen.

"Come take a look at my battle paintings."

He splashes through a puddle and leads us inside. His wife is polishing the crystal with a linen napkin.

"Ah deahly love to bring out the china and crystal and silver for this splendid occasion. We entertain so rarely these days."

The dishes and goblets and ranks of silverware on the huge table gleam as brightly as her smile. Place settings are laid out on a lace tablecloth, *qué elegante.* Out of the wind, I light my cigar.

"I say, Mistah Cochran," Matilde coaxes. "Will you all come assist a helpless female?" Cochran glances at the Admiral.

"Go ahead, lad. Mister Huckelbee can join me in the main cabin."

The Admiral escorts me to his bedroom. Mrs. Jenkins and Cochran go in the other room. The Admiral closes the door.

"Now you mustn't breathe a word of this to the Missus. She's not allowed any alcohol. The doctor made her swear off when he realized she was rapidly becoming totally dependent."

"You have my confidence, sir."

He opens a sideboard. The shelves are loaded with booze. Glasses and ice on the counter. We mix big drinks and gulp them down. His battle paintings hang on the walls. Cruisers belch fire. Japanese ships turn stern up. Sailors swim through burning oil. Planes drop torpedoes.

Transports blow in half. My head's a swirl of choppy seas and stiff drinks. We stagger back to the wardroom.

Cochran and Mrs. Jenkins waltz out of her cabin. Cochran's eyes are big. I blink mine, fuzzily. We head again for the flying bridge, out on the porch.

"Sqrzak . . . Hurricane Ed nears Pensacola coast . . . immediate evacuation recommended all dwellings near shore . . ."

"Evacuate hell," the Admiral roars. "We didn't evacuate for the typhoons and we won't evacuate now. Mister Cochran, front and center."

He leads Mike toward his bedroom-cabin. Mrs. Jenkins looks up from her polishing.

"Oh, Mistah Huckelbee, will you all be a dear and help me for just a tiny second?"

"Why surely, ma'am."

She closes her bedroom door and puts a shushing finger to her lips. She takes my hand. I lean forward. Every Southern gentleman knows age is no obstacle to love. She brushes me off with a wink and a laugh.

"Silly thing. At my age I'd need a purse string before I could give a man any satisfaction."

She opens her closet. Peeks around her shoulder. "You mustn't breathe a word of this to the Admiral. The doctor has put him on a strict, no-drink diet. His liver is practically holes."

The wall of her closet is lined with bottles. She pulls out a little tray of glasses and ice. We mix two stiff ones and belt them down. She hands me a stack of napkins. Her eyes are cocked but she doesn't forget to close the closet.

Cochran and the Admiral come out of the main cabin. Cochran's face is skewed.

"Fantastic collection, sir."

"Too stuffy!" the Admiral roars. "We need air." He throws open the veranda doors. Wind lifts the table cloth.

"Oh my precious crystal!" Mrs. Jenkins shrieks. She spreads her arms across the table like a hen covering her chicks. A cloud of powder rises fron her chest.

"Getting some real weather now," Admiral Jenkins bellows. His medals flap. A huge wave smacks the screen. Water runs into the house.

"Frzzdllk . . . forced evacuation of all houses on Pensacola Bay . . . Awcczk . . ."

Red flashing lights appear in the drive. A sheriff's deputy raps on the door. Water pours off his slicker.

"Better move out, sir. Hurricane's expected to hit right along here."

"Nonsense. I've stood on the bridge through typhoons that would make this dinky storm look as piddling as an April shower. I didn't abandon ship then and I won't now."

"All right, all right. I give ya yer warning." He retreats into the rain, muttering, "Yah wanna stay, no hair offa my goddamned scrotum. Dumb farts wanna die, let 'em . . ."

I look at Cochran. His goofy grin curls toward his ear.

"Shay, Admiral," he slurs. "Has Mister Huckelbee seen your giant conch yet?"

"By God! I'm glad you mentioned that. I don't believe he has. Come along, my boy."

I follow him dutifully, as a good junior officer would, duty before dishonor and all that.

"Oh, Mister Cochran," Matilde trills. "Could you give me a teensy weensy hand for just a teeny weeny bit?"

We cross and recross the wardroom, cabin to cabin, drink to drink. The Admiral opens the outside doors, lets the wind through, by God. The curtains stand out straight, sheets to the wind. The tablecloth flaps, a sail gone to luff. Mrs. Jenkins tips the lid off the silver serving platter. It flies across the room. The Admiral serves us up. One pork chop each. Speared to the plates. Twelve peas per plate, squashed down. Tiny wedge of lettuce, slithering. Smidgen of roquefort. Mrs. Jenkins waves matches at the drenched candles. We wipe our faces with sopping napkins.

"I declare, gentlemen. I'm having the worst time. Won't one of you all assist me in finding some dry linen?"

Cochran wavers after her toward the bedroom.

"By damn, Huckelbee," Admiral Jenkins fumes. "You haven't had a chance to look at my Samurai sword."

We pour cognacs and sweet liqueurs. Smoke cigars and drink mocha java. The electricity goes out. A storm lantern dips and sways from the ceiling. Pensacola Bay pours into the house. We pile the crystal, china and silver on the table and wrap the tablecloth around everything. Mrs. Jenkins huddles over the pile, cooing: "There there, my babies, I won't let anything happen to you."

The Admiral paces, his chest braced against the gale. "'43, or was it '44? The bridge was shot away and water coming over the gunn'lls, but we kept going."

Cochran and I sit numbly. Our watersoaked cigars are losing their leaves. We cup our chins in our hands.

"Wake up!" the Admiral orders. "No sleeping on watch."

"Yessir." We blink away the salt spray.

"Now say you're flying off a carrier in a single-seat attack jet armed with a 500-pound bomb."

The house shakes with a tremendous blast of wind.

"You have searched for an enemy ship without success. Now, low on fuel, you're headed back to the carrier when you spot a white ship marked plainly with red crosses. Obviously a hospital ship. Got that?"

We nod and grin.

"Suddenly your commander calls on the radio and tells you to drop your bombs on the hospital ship."

"Believe tha's against the rules of war, sir," Cochran mumbles.

"He has secret information that it's a disguised enemy missile ship with its weapons zeroed in on your carrier. He gives you a direct order: *Drop your five hundred pounder down the smokestack*. What do you do?"

"Ah, that's a tough one," I say. "Can I take some time to think it over."

"No time! You're almost out of fuel. You have to decide now or you won't make it back to the ship."

Cochran smashes his fist on the table.

"Y'God, I'd drop the bomb!" he bellows.

"You would?" I'm surprised to hear that.

The Admiral beams. "That's my boy."

Mrs. Jenkins sobs over her family treasures. "My precious crystal. I won't let them hurt you."

The house shakes. Flying spray lashes the Admiral's face. He wipes it off with his sleeve.

"But," says Cochran, biting down on the cigar. "I'd miss." The cigar shreds to pieces. Bits cling in brown patches to his white jacket. He spits the cigar out.

The Admiral glares. "All right, smartass," he roars. "See if you can get out of this one. What if you're ordered to drop a nuclear weapon on a town?"

"I'd never have that problem, sir."

"And why is that?"

"I'm going into helicopters."

"You are?" the Admiral and I cry in unison.

"They don't drop bombs," Cochran mumbles.

What a shocking admission. Aspiring pilots are supposed to want to fly jets, the hotter the better. Studliness is at stake. Only low-grade, lousy-aptitude pilots fly choppers. But looky here, blustering and sopping though he may be, my man Cochran is telling a by-God Admiral he's volunteering for the slow, plodding, wacky-dacky eggbeaters.

Well, if that's the way the winds blow, I'll sail the course too. I stand up and draw my sword. "I'm going into choppers myself." I swing my sword grandly.

The Admiral slashes with his Samurai, sparks flying. Mine clangs to the floor.

"Pansy ants!" the Admiral yells. "I shoulda known." He flails with his sword.

Cochran and I dive under the table.

"Hiram!" his wife shrieks. "Don't injure the china."

She leaps on the pile to keep it from sliding off.

"Guess that's the last of our trips to the private staterooms," Cochran says morosely.

"And just what *was* going on in there?" the Admiral yells at Matilde. "It wasn't drinking?"

"Oh, no sir," we all scream in unison.

He stalks onto the porch.

"Frzzk . . . eye of hurricane expected at . . ."

"Eye my ass!" He gives the radio a swipe with the sword, sends it crashing, sparks flying. "Bring your worst. We weathered thirteen in a row, each one stronger than the last."

The radio dies in a gurgle of sea water. Mrs. Jenkins moans over the table. The wind stills and the rain stops. Cochran and I slink outside into the calm of Hurricane Ed's eye. We wade through knee-deep water to our little house and fall over one another piling up furniture and nailing blankets across the broken windows. Hurricane Ed heads west to give Mobile a good licking. A red sun rims the horizon. I give Cochran a baleful look.

"Helicopters, huh?"

His eyes are as red as the sun. They flash sudden fire.

"You better believe it, numbnuts. Helly chopters don' carry no Fat Man."

"*Lo entiendo. Que risa, pendejo,* I get it . . . Funnier'n shit, dumb ass."

We never sample the Admiral's sideboard again, but it doesn't matter to us. Flight school takes up all our time. I'm lousy enough a pilot the chopper-flying decision probably saves my life. Not that it's all that easy to fly. Too confusing.

Work the stick with your right hand, the collective with your left hand. The collective is a device that sits alongside your leg. It's got a twist throttle on the end like the motor scooter so that's one thing I'm used to. Up the collective, down the collective—sounds like a corny commie capitalist argument, but when you pull the collective up, up you go, when you push it down—not so fast there—down you go.

Never let go of the stick! The chopper flops crazily, gyrates wildly, spiraling toward its doom, until, pouncing jackrabbit fast, the instructor grabs the stick and straightens things out. He's dealt with this student fuckup before. Rudder pedals keep the bird flying straight ahead and are used to turn the helicopter in circles when you're hovering. Hovering, another helicopter peculiarity.

Left hand on the collective, twisting, lifting and lowering, right hand on the stick, forward, right, left, backward, feet pushing on the rudder pedals, left foot, right foot—is it any wonder I'm confused?

The saving grace of the chopper is its slow speed. Goof, you've got time to correct. For Cochran it's not a problem. He not only loves to fly the chopper, he's good at it, too.

To him, the man plus the machine equals the bird. Soar like a gull. Hover like a hummingbird. Plummet like a hawk. Brake like a duck. Roost like a grouse landing on her nest of eggs. He graduates number one in the class. I bring up the rear. He's not so great with the scooter. I get it back the next time it won't start and take the beast to the shop for an easy fix. A bolt holding the carburetor to the intake manifold is loose.

Our orders are the same: report to Medium Helicopter Squadron 188 at The Marine Corps Air Facility in Santa Ana, California. I sell the Lambretta to an incoming flight school student. Cochran checks the base bulletin board and finds a 1952 Pontiac Chieftain, a green two-door hydramatic with a flathead six, fender skirts, windshield visor, wide whitewall tires, one major scrape along the side, a steal at two hundred and fifty bucks. We load our gear in the back seat and head out for the Coast, rear-end sagging, tailpipe dragging, sparks flying.

2. What's In A Name

Sheee-eeet fire, Doc, you ain't doing me any more good than a rattler running fangs up and down my shoulder blade . . . rat-tat-tatting machine gun banging chopper blades thumping and flashing lights going off like a pinball machine . . . whose fault is it, Doc? . . . I know . . . the San Andreas Fault . . . Teutonic plates shifting, or something like that . . . no, wrong continent . . . but any place you cut it, it's a mess . . . been that way for centuries . . . lowland tribes fighting mountain tribes . . . then it's French Indochina until the Japanese take over . . . here come the Frogs again, hippity hop hippity hop they get in deep, knee deep . . . hey, there's rubber plantations to drool over . . . not on our patch, says Ho Chi Minh . . . he's a dirty commie, Doc, a member in good standing of the Red Horde and a sneaky bastard, too, the young Ho . . . Marines are Gung Ho, does that mean we're related? . . . no no . . . what do you get when you combine a penis and a potato, Doc? . . . that's right, a dictator, and that's Ho . . . he forces the Frogs into making a stand, winner take all, and even with surreptitious help from the U. S. of A., the French surrender . . . Vietnam gets partitioned . . . reds in the north, republic in the south . . . Ho is a unification guy, he's rattling his saber . . . the democratic regime in the south is shaky, Doc . . . how do I know?

. . . it's like the thermos, Doc, you know how a thermos keeps something cold, cold? . . . and something hot, hot? . . . how do it know? . . . by absorption . . . ha ha . . . but we're dealing with reality here, Doc . . . there was a buildup going on . . . new meat fed into the hopper . . . more pilots to fly the chopper . . . what better training ground than California . . . open up your golden thighs, Californy here we come . . .

Unending sunshine. Hot days, balmy nights. A half hour drive from the helicopter base to Laguna Beach, much better happy hour bars than our club on the base. Luscious single women come from miles around to meet handsome virile blowtorch drivers while eggbeater pilots hide in the corners and gawk and drool. Or tell a lie. There I was, honey, doing a reverse Immelman at the bottom of an inverted loop, you know, where your only recourse is to swap ends, and the G suit is pumping massive gobs of blood into my thighs, gave me an erection you can't believe, it's lasted a week. She arches her eyebrows, "Inverted loop my ass," and flounces over to squeeze a jet jock's bicep, "Oh, it's so big." Crash and burn, scorned and reviled, retreat the better form of valor, we slink chagrined and shamefaced back to the base.

Which is a former blimp base from World War Two, just off the I-5 on a sprawling flat hunk of land surrounded by orange groves. Two cavernous hangars dominate the skyline. Plenty of room inside for the squadron's twenty-four choppers. Maintenance bays. Wooden offices and a ready room where the pilots gather for briefings and, after training flights, kill time reading paperbacks, playing board games, and conducting spelling bees.

The all new HMM-188 is a mixture of experienced pilots from the group pool and new blood from the training command. We newbies have to be assimilated and brought up to snuff. Our teachers are the older lieutenants with thousands of flying hours under their belts. Having snuck through flight school by the thin skin of my wet-with-sweat pants—"Ya kin teach a monkey to fly, Huckelbee, but it takes a man to fly the plane and not have the plane fly him"—now out in the fleet, I have to get acquainted with a bigger, meaner bird: the UH-34D, the Dawg. Pilots perched high in front, and below them, an open belly capable of holding twelve fully equipped Marines, me wondering if this nine cylinder, clattering assemblage of engine, transmission and hydraulic systems driving a twenty-foot, four-bladed rotor will fall to pieces under my anxious hands. Scary at first. Just saying Dawg gives me the willies, but what's in a name? A helicopter by any other name would clatter as loud.

The presence of another pilot in the cockpit preserves life and sanity. It takes a while but I pass the checkpoints in sequence, and thanks to mastering the coordinated movements of hand, feet, eye and brain that it takes to do a full autorotation—where you back off throttle and bottom the collective, the engine and tranny disengage, the blades provide enough lift to glide to the ground, you pull up on the collective and settle gently onto terra firma—I'm qualified to be an HAC, a Helicopter Aircraft Commander.

I'm paired with Cochran a lot. Due no doubt to the influence of Lieutenant Carl Emmett, the schedules officer. Emmett is square-jawed, burr-headed, son of Germanic stock, bred and born in Milwaukee, and he brooks no shit, for not only is he a superb pilot, he has the self-assurance of never having been proved wrong, no matter what the subject.

We're walking along the flight line, heading toward the choppers, a clear morning with the sun's rays bouncing off the orange trees, Emmett giving us the straight skinny: "The underboost will tear up the engine as much as an overboost." I look at Cochran, mouth, *what?* but before he can hip me to lugging the engine, six burly Marines in combat gear grab Cochran and Emmett and me by the arms and hustle us into the back of a 6-by-6 truck where we're thrown to the floor with our hands tied behind our backs.

We've been warned about this—escape and evasion training. Get dropped off in the boonies, live off the land, make it to a designated pickup point and get choppered back to base or—and this is the hairy part—get captured and thrown into a rat-infested prison to undergo intensive brainwashing and interrogation.

After a long drive they sit us up, relieve us of our wallets, cut the plastic cuffs and kick us out.

"The rescue chopper will be at the pickup point at 0600 in five days," a tough-looking grunt yells. "See you there. If you make it."

He kicks out a box of supplies. His raucous laugh is the last thing we hear. Then we're alone in the midst of scrubby bushes sticking out of the sandy ground. Clear sky and hot sun overhead. Cochran checks the map, shades his eyes and looks around the horizon.

"We'll go this way," he says, and strides off.

"Hold it," Emmett yells. "The pickup point's the other direction."

"That's the whole idea," Cochran calls back. "They'll have that area blanketed. They'll never look for us up there." He points to a ridge. "I don't know about you but I'm not up for that brainwashing interrogation resistance training."

We've heard all about it. No one in the squadron has ever made it to the pickup point. They've all been captured and come back full of horror stories of being locked in a tiny windowless hut with a bare dirt floor, hole in the corner for bodily evacuation, sleep deprivation with ceaseless Chinese music clanging and a bright light that never goes out, interrupted by screaming interrogations: "you talk or we rip out one eye, then—"

I follow Cochran and, after a short wait, Emmett comes grumbling along.

"This isn't going to work," he says, "but we've got to stick together."

It's not much different for me than being out on the range with the cattle. The grunts gave us two canteens of water each, and survival knives and matches and a bag of rock-hard C-ration crackers and dried soup, so we know if we ration everything we'll be okay foodwise.

"Just like boy scouts," Cochran says, ambling along, top half of his flight suit tied around his waist, T-shirt wrapped around his head, body soaking up the sun.

"How do you expect to cook the soup?" Emmett wants to know. "They'll spot the smoke."

Cochran scratches his chest. "Good question. Where's that boy scout manual?"

"Oh God, put your shirt back on," Emmett says. "You look like a half-assed gorilla doesn't even know that half from a hole in the ground."

"I can cook the soup," I say, deflecting an oncoming fray. "We'll use dry twigs and make a small, smokeless fire, early in the morning when the fog will cover it."

"Where'd you come up with that?" Emmett growls.

"Old cowboy and Indian trick I read in a Clarence Mulford novel," I tell him, and, never having heard of Mulford, the Hopalong Cassidy creator, Emmett shuts up.

We mosey along the ridge and follow it for a couple of days, then circle around to get behind the pickup spot, the theory being they won't expect us coming from that direction. We pick our way between big boulders that are scattered around the hill. Cochran stops short and holds out his hand, no farther. I peek around him. Emmett crowds alongside. A big rattlesnake is sunning itself on top of a flat rock.

"Whoa. Fresh meat," Cochran says.

"No way. Stay away from that thing," Emmett says.

I start cutting a branch off a tree with my survival knife.

"Go over there and get him to strike," I tell Cochran. His eyes get big. "Use a stick or something. Don't get near him."

"No!" Emmett bellows. "It's not worth it."

Too late. The blood is up. Cochran waves a stick, the snake lets out a loud crackling rattle and lunges. I jam the fork of branch down on his neck and hold him, fat body thrashing, tail whipping.

"Don't just stand there," I yell. "Slice off his head."

The fat is in the fire and the shit has hit the fan and Emmett rises to the mark. One fast cut with his survival knife and the snake is ours. The thrashing and our hearts slow at the same time. Cochran picks the rattler up by its tail. It's as long as he is tall.

When morning comes I have a small fire going that doesn't make any smoke. Cochran has skinned and gutted the snake. The rattle is tied to his belt with a piece of vine.

"We can lay it in the fire to cook it," Emmett says.

"No way, we'll cook it like hot dogs."

Cochran cuts off a chunk and spears it with a sharpened stick.

"Who died and left you boss?" Emmett growls.

"Hey, who's fucking this puppy?"

Before Emmett gets his dander up too high I say, "Better this way. You don't want to get any ashes on the meat. That's gritty shit. What you might call abradant." I spear a chunk and stick it over the fire.

"How do you spell that?" Cochran says.

"G-R-I-T—" I start in, but he interrupts, "You know what I mean, wiseass," so I spell it for him and he doesn't argue; there's another point for me in the neverending spelling bee.

We're blowing on the hot dripping chunks and nibbling at the edges, so Emmett, snarling and grumpy, gives in and starts roasting a piece on a stick.

One of the rules of the training exercise is we're not to have any contact with the natives. A river runs along the far edge of the training area and while we're using a shoelace and a bent paper clip to try and catch a fish, a boat floats past with two locals aboard. Cochran hails them, and after a short palaver, he gets us to empty our pockets and pool the change we've got left after our captors confiscated our wallets. Emmett bitches about breaking the rules, but the snake is history and he's as hungry as we are. Cochran buys a small sack of grits and a bucket of lard from the fishermen and we are relishing eating a good meal before we head out on a speed run to the pickup spot.

We build a fire and start cooking.

The smell of the grits and the lard is driving us nuts but Cochran insists we can't eat until it is completely cooked, otherwise we'll be swelly belly and hobbling like goats with the cramps. Emmett has put up with being outvoted every time there's a conflict long enough. This is beyond democracy.

"Hell with you, you fucking gorilla. I'm going to eat those grits and eat them right now."

He sticks his knife in the bucket and jams a mouthful down. Then gulps the glop until he is full. Cochran and I wait until the grits are cooked and lick up what's left.

At dawn's light we spring from our hidey-hole and sprint for the chopper, a shitting, farting, belching, puking run for Emmett, but he is determined to make it in spite of his stomach being swole up like a pregnant sow. With the make-believe enemy Marine grunts chasing close behind, Emmett collapses after us into the chopper and we settle aboard and return to the base to the cheers of the welcoming pilots and the grumbles of the disgruntled grunts, irked they didn't get a chance to work us over in the POW camp.

"It was touch and glow there for a while," Cochran says, "but Grits here sucked it up and we were able to come home allee allee in free."

What's in a name? A Grits by any other name would swell as much.

"No thanks to you, you fucking gorilla," Emmett grouses.

"Hey, where's my rattle?" Cochran says, feeling around his belt. Everyone laughs.

"Your baby rattle?" One of the pilots says.

"No, from the rattlesnake we killed and ate . . ." He eyeballs Emmett. "Grits, did you? . . ."

Emmett won't have any of it, he's still cramped up, shakes his head and turns away. Cochran eyes him, suspicious, but lets it go. Now that we're back on base, Emmett is again the experienced pilot, we're the newbies.

Emmett is an all-American American. Always ready to give a quick coach's halftime pep talk to the squadron, his topic the threat of the Red Horde—they win in Korea, they win in Southeast Asia, next thing you know it's the Phillipines, then Hawaii and finally, San Francisco, raping and brainwashing and fathering a new horde of commie bastards.

Not on Emmett's watch, and he figures hard, clean, dynamic team play will win the war against the Red Horde just as it won the big games in high school and college.

He subscribes to congressional reports so he can keep track of movie stars and authors and members of Red front activities. He keeps a list of Commie publications in his desk drawer in order to hip the pilots to them and warn them not to buy or read them. As squadron training officer I figure I can use his info in a lecture, spice up the training schedule with some *bueno saludable,* good healthy hate. I ask Emmett for some names and addresses of pertinent publications.

"Are you crazy? The FBI keeps close tabs on people who order those things. They'll put you on their suspect list."

"I'm getting the material to use *against* the Red Horde. You have to know them to defeat them."

"Write the FBI first. Tell them what you're doing. That way you'll be covered."

"He's right," Cochran tells me, putting down his newspaper. "That's the way the feds keep tabs, through those orders. But they're slicker than you think. They've got a much better way of keeping track."

"How's that?" says Emmett, suspicious.

"Simple. The FBI runs the publishing houses that print the Red Horde magazines and newspapers."

"Ah, bullshit, you don't know what you're talking about."

"Oh yeah? What could be simpler? They print the stuff then investigate everyone who orders the rags. At the small cost of running the presses which they already use to print wanted posters, they keep their fingers on a whole bunch of subverts."

Cochran gives me a knowing wave. "Sure, Huck, write the FBI. They'll send you everything you need."

Emmett turns away in disgust. "You're so full of shit your eyes are as brown as your hairy gorilla ass."

What's in a name? A gorilla by any other name would be as hairy.

We turn to squadron maneuvers en masse, including a deployment in Yuma, Arizona, where we fly all day and play poker all night. On the way home we're ordered to sit down at March Air Force base on the desert side of the Santa Ana Range to wait for a coastal storm to lift. Six sections of four choppers, flying in the squadron vee, we break and form into one line and land on the runway.

When we're parked, the pilots and crew chiefs get out and begin their card games and bullshit sessions. A hot desert wind whips across the field, picking up dirt and tufts of dry weeds and splattering the cards with sand. The squadron Operations Officer, Captain Beamus, stands with his back to the biting wind.

Captain Beamus is a strict, squared-away banty rooster, shorter than even my sawed-off frame. A former ground pounder, he maintains the rigid posture that prevails in the ranks of the Marines in the trenches, and it is his duty to impart their discipline, excellence of character and impeccable appearance to a loosey-goosey gaggle of ill-bred, slovenly, joke-a-billy helicopter pilots.

He turns to Emmett, his number-two man: "Let's get over to windward, out of this dust."

"That's not windward," I say. "That's leeward."

He keeps walking. Cochran stands behind me. He nudges me in the ribs.

"He's ignoring you. He can hear alright."

"Leeward!" I holler.

Beamus keeps walking, unperturbed. You *abeza estupidez,* crud-head. I'll make damn sure you hear. I yell in his ear: "LEEward, not windward!"

Captain Beamus stops, his back to me. Cochran's laugh swirls in the wind. Emmett stares. I grab my baseball cap and am about to beat Captain Beamus on the back of his head when he turns and skewers me with an icy glare.

"Just what the hell do you think you're doing, Lieutenant?"

"Ah, I didn't think you heard me, sir." Twisting my hat in my hands.

"I don't find it necessary to reply to every inanity uttered behind my back. You have something to say, say it to my face. Do I have to spell that out?"

"Yes, sir, I mean"—spine snapping straight, thumbs along pants leg, heels clack together—"roger that, that's a rajah, suh!"

He strides away. I slap on my hat and search for Cochran. I find him behind a chopper, pretending to inspect the wheel.

"Where's your tire gauge, grease gorilla?" I snarl.

Cochran grins. "I knew he could hear you."

"Lapsong Chung say man who pull trick on friend fall flat on his own face."

"Oh yeah? Who he who say dat? Some black sheep in the Confucius family?"

"Older ancestor, recently unearthed in an archeology excavation. Chinese government's not sure whether to embrace or disparage him. You better take his message to heart."

Cochran throws up his hairy arms in mock innocence. "Not even Lapsong Chung would associate me with such explosive, back-head, hat-beating behavior. You better rajah that, mister, or you'll be in deep doo-doo with the Rajah."

What's in a name? A rajah by any other name would rule the same.

Nicknames come about in unplanned and unexpected ways. Our skipper, Lt. Colonel Arthur Rappler, is stern visaged and a hard worker, meticulous to the extreme. Lean and boney, fingers yellowed from nicotine, his dark eyes are set back in his skull. His rare smiles are thin grins.

He flew fighters in the Big One and the Police Action. The Korean War's end brought his combat flying to a halt and he was ordered to a helicopter squadron for retraining in the slower, dual-piloted choppers. Now he's the top man of his own squadron and he's determined to whip us into the best flying outfit in the entire Wing.

After our desert deployment in Yuma he has us flying so much we're broke before the end of the fiscal quarter, gas funds bouncing around the bottom of the money barrel like loose marbles.

"Slash the training hops to the minimum," he orders. "Don't cut them off completely though. One of the other squadrons might insinuate we mismanaged our funds."

Every morning we rush to the flight line to get airborne before Rajah Beamus runs into the C.O.'s office and slaps his tally sheet on the desk.

"Sir. Spotted it just in time. We've exceeded our allotment for this week."

Lt. Col. Rappler scowls. "I'll take care of it. You're excused."

The C.O. picks up the phone to the line shack. "I don't give a shit if they have already started engines. Get those pilots back in here. The launch is cancelled."

I meet Cochran rambling back from the flight line,

"What happened?" I ask, "Run out of gas?"

"Got thumped by the hammer."

The hammer strikes indiscriminately. A hand-scrawled notice appears on the bulletin board: "All loose change spilled out of pockets will be contributed to the fuel fund. By authority of THE HAMMER." The acetate schedules board is splashed with a grease pencil message: "Everything cancelled. Go home. Write your Congressman." Signed, "THE HAMMER."

It's all bullshit, and we keep flying, just not as much.

The next day, Cochran and I are making a practice instrument landing into El Toro and hear on the radio that an A-4D just flamed out on its approach to the field and crashed in an orange grove. The pilot ejected and landed alongside a dirt road. His wingman is orbiting overhead. We're diverted to pick up the downed pilot.

Cochran calls the orbiting jet on the radio, "Marine jet, this is Yankee Victor Three Seven approaching your position."

"Roger, Yankee Victor, have you in sight."

"Hey, Gordo," Cochran exclaims. "Is that you?"

"Roger that."

Cochran gives me a big grin and says over the intercom, "Buddy of mine I went through officer candidate school with."

He keys the radio button. "Okay Gordo, we have the pilot in sight. Now don't let those stovepipe jocks give you any static about idle radio chatter, we're all in this crotch, er, Corps, together.

Two clicks on the mike button is Gordo's response.

We set down next to the pilot. He gets in the belly and we fly him to El Toro and let him out on the flight line, next to his ready room.

That night at the El Toro O Club we're treated to free drinks by the fighter-bomber squadron.

"So did they give you any shit about me yakking with you on the radio?" Cochran asks Gordo.

"They tried to but I shut them up by saying it wasn't me doing the yakking, it was those chopper assholes."

Two days later, Lt. Col. Rappler discovers a footprint on his chair. The chair is the seat from the jet that crashed on approach to El Toro. In appreciation for our picking up the pilot, the jet jock's C.O. gave us the ejection seat and the Skipper had it installed in the ready room, front row, center seat.

The footprint in the chair is covered with dust. Someone wrote a word in the dust with his finger: HAMMER. Lt. Col. Rappler wipes the seat clean. He rubs his hands and gazes at the chair.

"Now that's pretty good. Yep, the man who did it has a darned fine sense of humor. That's the sort of person I like to have around to keep up the squadron morale."

He eyes the room, scanning every face.

"I'd appreciate having that man drop around my office. I figure he's a valuable asset to the outfit, maybe even ripe for a slot in career and welfare."

His lips tighten. A twitch. It's his grin. We laugh, out of relief. No one drops around his office.

Instead, the next morning, at eye level, in gray navy ship paint, directly in front of Lt. Col. Rappler's ejection seat, a claw-hammer, caught in the act of striking, is drawn on the lectern. And underneath, printed in block letters, the words: "THE FLIGHT OF THE HAMMER."

Lt. Col. Rappler contemplates the artwork for a few minutes, then amiably addresses the squadron: "Say, this Hammer nickname is the kind of thing that holds a squadron together. Unites it into a real tight group."

Again the thin grin. Then a dark scowl. "Let's level with one another. I know what this crap is all about, but I don't mind. I thought I made myself clear on that point. I tell you what, though. Let's keep it in the family. No one else would understand. It will be our squadron's secret. And we'll keep the choppers in the air. We'll find the money somewhere."

Give the dude his due. He changes the squadron nickname from the Flying Eights to the Hammering Eights.

We spend two weeks aboard an aircraft carrier making practice heliborne landings off the California coast. Two drag-ass weeks that start ominously poor right from the get-go when, because there are more pilots than choppers, some of us have to ride out to the carrier as passengers.

Belly riders. The lowest of the low. The ignominy. To have righteously earned the wings and then not be allowed to fly. No wonder tempers are in torment. And whom, that's right, whom do we blame?

Captain Beamus, that's who. The Rajah. Because he's the Operations Officer, he makes out the list of who flies and who rides. That cock of the walk, struttin' with his shoulders back, chest out, hup two, hup two, like a ground-pounding drill sergeant instead of a Marine officer aviator. A hardass. A Marine's Marine. Sticks with the regs like a martinet. Lives alone, no dame, no pain. Abides by *mas el stricto*, military code. And you better do the same, Mistah!

His uniforms are hand tailored. His creased trousers break over spitshined shoes. A vertically rodded spine snaps him upright like he's got a coat rack stuck up his ass. Coming from an old military family myself, I can appreciate the squared-away officer. The sight of a master player titillates my jowls, my hair bristles like a hog's, my eyes glare like wrestlers' facing off, replicas of scowls. Captain Beamus can dig the compatriotism. Else why does he continuously make the effort to set me straight?

"You know, Huckelbee, you're a bright boy. It's too bad you don't apply yourself instead of fooling around with your little spelling bees."

Ha ha. Force a laugh. Burned me there. Very clever, Captain. Spelling bees. Rhymes with Huckelbees. He's a poet but doesn't know it. Although his shoes show it. They're spitshined. He doesn't fool me though. I know his game. He's trying to undo the undue influence of that crude, unmilitary, crass, obnoxious and disrespectful bastard, Cochran. Before he can apply any more pressure on me, Captain Beamus gets suckered by the grunts.

Because of his prior ground time, the Rajah feels like he's particularly tight with the Pathfinders, the Marines who live below decks, the troops we carry ashore during mock landing exercises. They convince Captain Beamus that if he were truly a Marine, a real Marine, he would have a Marine haircut, not one of those aviator's excuses for a haircut. Too long. Too unkempt. And the only one who can correct this situation is their very own battalion barber. Can't trust an important job like that to a sailor.

"Not too short, boys."

He sits in a chair in the troop compartment. A sheet is draped around his neck. "Leave a little for the ladies to run their fingers through."

What he really means is, leave me enough to comb over my bald spot.

"Sure thing, Cap'n."

The electric clippers hum and buzz. The barber steps back and appraises his artistry. The infantry officers whistle in appreciation. Sneaking a peek from outside the door, we snortle into our hands. True to his word, the barber left a little something: a monk's tonsure around his dome. The Pathfinders turn Captain Beamus loose unknowing and unawares. Normal curiosity and a glimmer of suspicion sends him scurrying through the innards of the ship seeking a mirror before anyone sees him.

The passageways are painted sea-green. A petroleum smell lingers. Blowers hum. Captain Beamus's face is covered with a film of greasy sweat. After checking himself in the mirror he almost makes it home free but is caught rounding the corner of the wardroom by four squadron pilots who were lounging in the coffee mess, swilling java and passing scuttlebutt.

"Why, sink the Titanic, if it isn't Captain Beamus."

"Isn't he the rough looking customer?"

"Gruntish, I'd say."

"I do believe, sirrah, you've proved once and for all that it takes a born aviator to ride herd on the Pathfinders."

Captain Beamus doesn't dawdle to bandy.

"As you *were*, gentlemen!"

He lays low the rest of the shipboard deployment and, with no one to tell him differently, his assistant, Lieutenant Emmett, copies the same schedule going ashore that we used coming aboard. Same pilots and same belly riders, and we take Emmett's act of laziness straight to our prickling, overheated hearts.

We stew in the waiting room, awaiting the call to man planes. Our spirits are low, at the level of earth mortals whom pilots look down upon with disgust from their lofty cockpit seats. The senior officers have been called to the flight deck to preflight the birds and start engines.

The squawk box roars: *Ready room one, this is flight deck control. Passengers man your aircraft.*

We bound from our chairs. Brawl out of the ready room. Metal outcroppings grab at our baggage. Dogs and switches snatch at our clothing. Low hatches swat at our heads. We press on and brawl out onto the hangar deck. Skid to a stop in front of the huge, deck-edge elevator. The railing around the elevator is up, holding us back.

The railing drops. Before we can run onto the elevator the squawk box blurts again: *Passengers return to the ready room. Number seven chopper having difficulty starting.* The railing goes back up.

"By God," Cochran shouts. "They called us and now they're going to get us."

He jumps over the railing onto the elevator just as a wailing air horn blast its warning: going up!

Not the gentle wheeze of a respected hotel elevator. This heavy-duty airplane lifter launches Cochran and flips him over the railing. He tumbles over our heads in a backward somersault and lands on his feet. "What're you standing there for?" he asks over his shoulder. "We have to go back to the ready room."

I catch up with him and clap him on the back.

"What timing," I exclaim. "To know the exact instant."

His shoulders droop. He eyes the other pilots and shrugs. "Yeah, I had to plan it perfectly. Come on. Let's get below so we're ready when they call us out again."

"I shoulda guessed. You didn't look a bit surprised. That was the tip-off."

He stops and faces me. "I give you credit for more brains than the rest of these sheep, Tomas. Those things happen all the time. You can't fool around being surprised. You have to jump the surprise and drive it to the top."

When the call comes, we walk up and board the choppers resignedly, and, later in the day, after we land at the base, the Hammer chews our asses because the choppers were kept standing on the flight deck, engines running and blades turning, while the belly riders dragged ass into their seats. Made the whole squadron look bad.

The next morning, before the skipper arrives for the all-pilots meeting, Cochran stands up to make an announcement. His five o'clock shadowed face is a mask of anticipation.

"Now that we've finished our training and we're the Group Ready

Squadron, it's time to throw a party. Our own private affair. Hammering Eights only."

"Where?" someone yells.

"The Long Beach Naval Air Station Officers Club. And if you've got any objections, forget it. I've already reserved the bar. The manager has promised happy hour prices the entire evening."

3. Reaches of Freedom's Frontier

I know what they say, Doc . . . tough it out . . . stiff upper lip . . . bite the bullet . . . chew the leather . . . steel rod up the spine . . . they can say it, Doc . . . and as number four in a line of old military men, I know I'm supposed to believe it, but no matter how hard I pretend . . . that shit doesn't work . . . Great Grandaddy, a private, charged up San Juan Hill with the Rough Riders . . . Grandaddy, a corporal, drove a truck from Calais to the front in World War One . . . Daddy, a sergeant, patrolled an oil pipeline in New Guinea in World War Two . . . and to think, me, an officer, the only one to get all shot up . . . what do they say to that, Doc?. . . all's we have left from their military wisdom is letters writ with thick fingers in an awkward hand . . . Grandaddy writes he is a boy no more, that he is going on his upward years and done his duty . . . he says to tell all them cowboys down on the ranch it won't be long until he's back and will show them how to do squad right and stand at attention and drill and hand pack inspection and rifle cleaning and police up . . . and only then can they go to Barney's Bar and party . . . only then . . .

Daddy writes about a beach party . . . Carlos, the Cuban-born guitar player . . . native servants in white blousy shirts and colored skirts

. . . fuzzie wuzzies in fuzzy wuzzy garb . . . goat meat on a stick . . . moon through the palms . . . Malays singing Pistol Packing Mama *. . . everyone claps and yells "bagoo" and the party degenerates into dancing and caterwauling around the fire . . . stagger to the water's edge, throw up and pass out . . . the Captain proclaims before he keels over, "You don't respect me as an officer, do you?" . . . just goes to show you, Doc, no matter what your rank you can't buck the party system . . . whatever party's in power: dance party, cocktail party, dinner party, tea party . . . the more the costumes change, the more the parties stay the same . . . you can take that to the bank, Doc . . . the fog bank . . . it's rolling in . . . off the ocean and onto shore . . . lights glow in the mist . . . the outline of a building . . .*

The Long Beach Officers Club. A green and white striped awning covers the walk to the front door. A doorman in a resplendant uniform beckons us in. A sign on an easel announces LADIES BINGO NIGHT in huge letters. Below it, in tiny script: *HMM-188 Squadron Party In The Bar.*

My enthusiasm bubbles like ocean froth. "Not what you'd call top billing," I exult. "But at least we made the marquee."

I extend my elbow. "Shall we join the soiree, m'dear?"

Rosey fluffs her bright-red hair and takes my arm. "Yes, since I'm escorted by the Marquis de Soiree." Her freckled skin glistens in the artificial light. Emerald flecks shine in her eyes. An elementary school teacher, tonight she's far enough removed from the kids and PTA she can cut loose and howl. A combo blasts in the corner of the room. Couples belly up to the polished mahogany bar. Drinks cover the tables. "Let's shake everything," Rosey shrieks over the din. The band hits it hard: *I stole a kiss, and then another.* Rosey bumps and grinds onto the floor. *I didn't mean to take it further.* You'd think she was the one who'd been at sea for two weeks. She closes her eyes, and turns it loose. *I saw you when you kissed my daughter.* Her breasts rise and dip to the lyrics. *Wed her right now, or face a slaughter.* I head for the bar. *One mint julep was the cause of it all.*

Cochran stalks in with his date. Her sleek, black dress shows more cleavage than a tunnel blasted into Baldy. A blue and white bouffant perches on her head. Her teeth sparkle like they've been polished with an electric buffer. I angle over to meet her.

"Yas," she gushes, holding my hand with the slightest squeeze of thumb and forefinger, "but it was only a bit part, nothing really."

"You gotta be kidding. A Hollywood movie?'

"I was also offered a job dancing in *Carthage in Flame*, but I couldn't afford the trip to Italy. Half the cast paid their own way, you know."

Cochran prods her. "Come on, Katrinka, before he finds out you're hashing at Lou's Lunch House to pay the rent until the next big part."

He steers her toward the bar, one hand on her elbow. His other holds a big wooden pole wrapped in brown paper. I wallow in their wake, whiffing *odor de flores.*

Cochran stops for another introduction. Captain Beamus of all people. The band rips into another song: *He's a mean motah scootah and a bad go-gettah.* The Rajah nods politely and extends his hand. *He's the toughest man there is alive*. Katrinka is tall enough to eat peanuts off his head. *He's the king of the jungle jive.*

"What a *divine* wig," Katrinka gushes. "Where did you have it done? Maxine does all my work. Have you tried her?"

Captain Beamus puffs up. *He got a big ugly club and a head fulla hair.* Buttons strain. His eyes shoot darts. *Like great big lions and a grizzly bear.* Eyebrows jiggle up and down, beating time to the throbbing vein in his forehead. *Look at that cave man go.*

"Wig? What wig?"

There he goes. Alley-Oop, oop, oop, oop-oop.

"Why it's nothing to be ashamed of, darling. You don't think for a minute this upsweep is all *mine*, do you?

She trills an obbligato of laughter. Musses Captain Beamus's hair. The hairpiece slips awry. Her laugh ripples up and down the octaves.

"Not bad at all . . ." she trills. Lifts the wig. "Except . . ." Plops it on his silver-dollar spot. "For *that*! . . ." Warbles a soprano shriek. "I *love* it . . ." Hugs his head and presses her breasts tightly against his throat. A red flash rockets up his face. Cochran spins Katrinka away. Captain Beamus pats his hair into place. I grab Cochran's arm.

"Did you put her up to that, or is she for real?"

Cochran winks. He raises the paper-covered pole to keep from bashing a pilot in the head.

"Why, Huck, you have an evil mind. Come along, dear."

He leads his date through the mob, leaving me to round up Rosey. Displeased wives, knowing what hungover louts they'll have for husbands tomorrow morning, scowl from corner tables. Rosey rubs her shoulders, elbows and fragile decolletage against my twangy tweed. A glass crashes to the floor and creates an instant pond. Shouts and laughter. Pilots stomp and jump in a happy circle. "Can't hold 'em, can't drink 'em!" The Marines have landed and the situation is well in hand. A trumpet blasts a loud fanfare. Everyone turns. Cochran stands on the stage. He waves the paper-covered pole and signals for quiet.

"All right," Cochran shouts. "We've finished the training phase and have completed carrier qualifications. The squadron is prepared for action. Gentlemen—let them take us when they may."

A cheer fills the room. Lieutenant Rob Jacobs throws his glass at the fake fireplace fastened to the wall. The brick-painted plastic breaks in two. The glass falls to the floor, intact. Not missing a beat, Cochran continues: "To commemorate this auspicious occasion, I've put together something to represent our squadron pride, something that will go forward with us from this day on. Will Lieutenant Colonel Rappler come forward?"

The C.O. is dubious, very dubious. Nevertheless, he walks through the crowd and hops up on the stage. His rear end sags a bit but his stance is upright and steady. He grins thinly. Cochran clutches the Hammer's shoulder and pulls him close.

"Sir! On behalf of the squadron officers, I would like to present you with this symbol of the devotion, bravery and the highest level of performance you have inspired in us all. A small but meaningful gesture, one that should impress upon you our willingness to follow you to the farthest reaches of freedom's frontier."

He turns the Hammer loose and holds out the long wooden pole.

"For you, sir."

The Hammer rips off the paper and uncovers a polished wooden staff topped by a flag and pennant. He unrolls the flag. A scarlet background with a golden border. In the middle of the red field a winged golden claw hammer, poised in flight, ready to strike. The long fringed pennant is covered with scarlet letters emblazoned on a golden field: THE HAMMERING EIGHTS.

The pilots slap one another's backs. Climb on chairs and whistle and clap. The Hammer shouts over the bedlam, "Men, you don't know how much I appreciate . . ."

The pilots swarm forward, sweep him off his feet and hoist him on their shoulders and parade him around the room. The flag flaps. The pennant trails. The gyrating pole threatens the lights.

"Never been anything like it," the Hammer shouts. "Best damn squadron ever. Never a finer group of men. Now dammit! Put me down."

He sticks the pole behind the bar, and drapes the flag and pennant across the mirror. Invites Cochran and me and our dates to join him at his table. Shakes Cochran's hand, congratulating him.

"It's nothing, sir. Let me be of greater service. I'll get a round of drinks."

Cochran hustles away without taking anybody's orders. The Hammer snares me with his deep-set eyes.

"Get me two screwdrivers, Huckelbee."

"Yes sir, two screwdrivers coming up. Back in a mo, pet." I give Rosey a peck.

"*G-Two*," a faintly audible call drifts across the room.

"Two screwdrivers," I yell. The whippet-like bartender—hair slicked back, pencil-thin mustache on his upper lip—pours a shot, adds mix, throws in ice, swoops down the bar, hands off the drink, scoops up the change, throws it in the bell-ringing cash register and rushes past me.

"Two screwdrivers," I shout. His dark look twists into an ugly scowl. He doesn't stop.

"Service with a smile," Cochran yells. It stops the man short. He juts his chin across the mahogany.

"Can't you see I'm busy?"

"Why yes, it is rather crowded."

The bartender slams Cochran's drinks on the bar. Cochran reaches in his pocket and counts out a handful of change.

"There you go, my man, right on the old kisser."

"Kisser your ass." The bartender's lips suck tightly against his teeth. He hurls the change behind him. The coins splatter against the beer cases.

"Thank you kindly," Cochran says, picking up his drinks. "Oh, say, how's about serving my buddy down the bar there? He's been waiting a long time."

"Please." I raise my finger.

A stately woman in a sequin-covered dress elbows in beside me. "Pardon me," she interrupts. She smiles at the bartender. "It's getting quite warm in the bingo parlor. Would you mind bringing me a glass of water? And put a little ice in it, please."

"Water!" The bartender throws his hands in the air. "Now I've heard everything. Can't you see I'm the only one working? That damned cocktail waitress never showed up. You want water, lady? Go right over there." He points across the room. "All the water you can drink. Fresh out of the fountain."

"Well!" She steps back, indignant. "I've never been talked to like that in my life."

"Don't feel bad," I say. "I've been talked to like that plenty of times."

"You, young man," she says, giving me the look she'd reserved for the bartender, "are not married to an Admiral." She flounces back to the bingo game.

What's the difference, neither one of us got served. I square my shoulders. Pound on the bar.

"You rude son of a bitch," I holler. "Bring me my drinks."

The bartender heaves himself up on the bar and hollers in my face: "What did you call me, mister? Say it again."

"I said, 'Two screwdrivers, please.'"

"Mac, you've been giving me a bad time all night and I'm warning you, one more word and you're cut off."

I shake my head sadly. "Sorry, but I'm an officer and a respected customer. You can't cut me off."

"The hell I can't—"

"Huckelbee, where are those screwdrivers?" The Hammer's voice jars me back to my mission.

"All right, cut the crap and bring me two screwdrivers."

"That does it, wise guy. You're cut off. No more drinks."

Cochran takes my arm. "Don't bug the poor fellow," he tells me. "You're going about this all wrong. Be nice to the man."

He turns to the bartender and gives him a big smile. "Now, how's about doing the job you're paid for and bring us two screwdrivers, friend?"

"You too," the bartender yells, pointing a vindictive finger. "You're the other one. No more for you either."

"Oh no you don't," Cochran yells back. "You grabbed the wrong cat by the tail this time."

The band ramps up the volume. *We gonna romp and tromp till midnight.* Women turn and stare. Men peer over their drinks. The bingo players look in from the other room.

"Wait a minute, just what seems to be the problem here?"

The Hammer has arrived. He will settle this amicably, fairly for both sides. *We gonna fuss and fight till daylight.*

Cochran and the bartender and I assail him simultaneously: "Won't serve us drinks . . . they've been obnoxious . . . swearing . . . insulted an Admiral's wife . . . nasty name calling . . . gonna cut us off . . ."

"Wait a minute, wait a minute," the Hammer says.

Cochran and I clap our mouths shut, leaving the bartender shouting: ". . . and before you Marines came in here this was a decent, respectable Navy place." *We gonna break out all the windows.*

"What's that you say?" the Hammer shouts back. "Listen, Mister, these are my men. This is my squadron. You have any trouble with them, you tell me. I'll take care of it. But you leave my men alone, understand?" *We gonna kick down all the doors.*

The bartender curls his lips, unintimidated. "Who you think you're talking to, Mac? I ain't one of your Gyrene toadies. I cut them off, and now I'm cutting you off. Any more static and I cut the whole party off."

The Hammer leers. *We gonna pitch a wang dang doodle all night long.*

"You don't have the balls."

"Party's over, boys." The bartender slaps his hand on the bar, missing the Hammer's nose by inches.

"You cheap screw," the Hammer yells. "I'll come across that bar and chew you into pieces small enough to spit through a brick wall."

"Try it and I'll split your head open far enough to drive a Mack truck through."

The Hammer raises his leg to get a knee up. The bartender picks up a forty-ounce bottle of Seagram's VO. Cochran gives the Hammer a boost and he flies over the bar. The bartender swings but I intercept his blow with a beer bottle. Whiskey and broken glass shower the bar. The squadron pilots charge with a roar. Rosey clutches my sleeve. Cochran reaches across the bar and grabs the bartender by the front of his white jacket. The Hammer staggers to his feet. He aims the flagpole like a spear at the bartender's chest. The bartender slips out of his jacket and flees down the bar, skids around the corner and makes for the door, the Hammer hot behind. Cochran and I cut the bartender off. Rosey, hanging onto my sleeve, whips behind me like a Chinese dragon's tail at a New Year's parade. The bartender veers out of our trap and dashes into the bingo parlor with the Hammer, Cochran, me, Rosey, Katrinka and the rest of the squadron in hot pursuit.

"*O-Sixty Three*," the bingo announcer's voice carries over the noise.

"Mister Bingham," the bartender yells. "Help. They're after me, I'm outnumbered."

He cuts around a table and runs for the stage. The Hammer swipes at him with the flagpole. The pennant swoops across the upswept hair of the lady players. They screech and duck. Cochran dives for the bartender's legs, but the skinny lout vaults onto the stage and escapes. I trip over Cochran and sprawl against the platform. Rosey smacks into me, then Katrinka, and we roll in a tangle of arms and legs and breasts and bright red hair and fluffy pompadour. The Hammer jerks to a halt, the flag pole pointed toward the bingo announcer, the bartender hiding behind his back.

The announcer looks at the marker in his hand.

"*B-Three, B-Three, please fill in B-Three on your cards.* Say, Harry," he says to his assistant, "take over for a minute, will you?"

He turns to the bartender, "Would you mind unclinging yourself from my back? And," he daintily pushes the flagpole away with a finger, "can't you point that thing another direction?"

"*N-Thirty Six, fill in N-Thirty Six.*"

Cochran and Rosey and Katrinka and I stagger to our feet. Katrinka's pompadour is falling apart in octopus-leg tendrils. Her strapless dress is skewered sideways, a breast exposed. She stuffs it back in. Cochran tugs at his tie and pulls it off. His shirt buttons pop. Rosey's emerald-green eyes sparkle with excitement.

"Oh, Huck, you were wonderful." She clings to my arm, squeezing me with her goodies. The Hammer sets the flagpole upright. Stands at attention.

"Lieutenant Colonel Arthur Rappler, Commanding Officer, Marine Medium Helicopter Squadron number One Hundred and

Eighty-Eight reporting a severe dereliction of duty on the part of that poor excuse of a bartender hiding behind your coat tails."

The bartender bunches his fists, "You and me, buddy," he snarls. "Not yer whole damned pack."

The bachelor pilots are casing the bingo ladies, ready for any sign of testiness.

"*G-Forty Eight, please fill in G-Forty Eight.*"

"Now, now, I'm sure it's a simple misunderstanding."

"Misunderstanding, hell. That bartender's got to go, and go now."

"They're cut off, boss. You can see how crazy they are. Any more drinking and the club's a goner."

"Let's talk it over in my office, gentlemen, shall we, so the ladies can continue their game?"

"*O-Sixty Five, please fill in O-65.*"

The manager walks down off the stage.

"BINGO! BINGO!" a female voice calls.

We follow the manager. The flagpole charts our course across the room. The Hammer and the bartender yell in the manager's opposite ears. Rosey hangs onto my arm. The flotilla suddenly veers and stops. The Admiral's wife pokes her finger in the manager's chest.

"BINGO!" she cries. "I have a bingo."

The manager closes his eyes. He opens them and flutters his lids. "I'm sure you do, madam. Take your card to the platform and have it validated."

"Don't think for a minute you're going to cheat me out of my bingo with all these shenanigans." She waves her card at him and heads for the platform. The pilots scatter and give her an unobstructed path. The manager steers the Hammer to his office. "Right this way, sir."

"Insult to the squadron . . . to the Marine Corps," the Hammer is saying.

The manager's eyes widen. "My God! All of you?" We squeeze in. The flagpole threatens the lights.

"Now, gentlemen, please, won't one of you explain?"

"Officers!" the Hammer shouts. "Every one of these men officers. And that bartender! Either he goes or I write a letter."

"Not tonight," the manager protests. "I can't possibly let him go tonight. Oh no. We're much too busy for that. He's the only man I could get."

The bartender crosses his arms and gloats.

"Then I write the letter. And not only that, I'll pull my squadron out of here and you won't have any need for a bartender—"

"Let 'em go," the bartender hollers. "I kicked them out already."

"Tomorrow," the manager pleads. "Can't we settle this tomorrow?"

The shouting, banging and shuffling drowns out a persistent ringing. Captain Beamus picks up the phone, holds a finger in his ear, nods, and pokes the Hammer in the back. The Hammer wheels around.

"Phone call, sir. Group Commander."

"Who? Colonel Strammond?"

The name elicits immediate silence from everyone. The Hammer takes the phone and listens. He snaps to attention.

"Yes, sir. I understand, sir. Right away, sir. You can count on the Hammering Eights."

He hangs up, turns and stares through the crowd, out the window, across the docks, over the masts of the ships; across the breakwall and ocean, to the distant horizon and the steamy lands far beyond.

"I promise," the manager repeats, squeezing his hands together. "I'll take care of it first thing in the morning."

The Hammer rouses from his revery. "Too late! We're leaving."

"*Leaving?*" the manager cries in anguish.

"*Leaving*?" we howl angrily.

"*Leaving!*" the bartender laughs triumphantly.

"That's right. Squadron recall. Everyone back to the base."

The Hammer hands Cochran the flagpole and marches out of the office. Cochran strides behind. The band breaks into song: *Dontcha treat me this away.* The flag and pennant unfurl in the breeze of the brisk pace. Katrinka flounces next to Cochran. *I'll be back on my feet some day.* The rest fall into two marching ranks. Rosey and I are the last ones out. *Don't care if you do, it's understood.* I grab a drink off a table and slug it down. Survey the empty room. Chairs askew. Floor littered with broken glass and spilled booze. *You ain't got no money you just ain't no good.*

"We'll be back," I shout, punctuating my promise with a crystalline crash. I kick the broken shards. "Marines! You want 'em? You got 'em!" *Hit the road Jack, and don't you come back no more.*

Half an hour later, with the women waiting outside in the cars, the pilots muster in the ready room. The new squadron flag stands alongside Old Glory, next to the acetate schedules board. The murmuring questions and rumors hush as the Hammer mounts the podium. He grips the sides of the lectern. His knuckles are strained, his mouth grim.

"This is it, men. We've worked and trained hard these past few months preparing ourselves, and now that the call has come, we are ready."

He pauses and sizes up every man among us. Damned if he can't zero in on a fella. I lean forward to catch his words.

"A friendly nation is under attack by the Red Horde. They have asked for our help and President Kennedy has responded. Pack your gear. We're going to Vietnam."

II
VIETNAM

Summer, 1962

Soc Trang
The Delta

"We went in like boy scouts . . ."

Shu Fly pie and apple pan dowdy
Makes your eyes light up and your lips say howdy

---

4. Keeps the Manly Juices Flowing

Come on, Doc, straighten things out, will you . . . confusion abounds . . . Vietnam . . . its meaning lies hidden like an artichoke heart . . . layer under layer . . . brown swarthies topped by French polyglot Legionnaires hidden beneath Japanese Yallerbellees flanked on the left with red pagan Kali . . . on the right is orange Buddha and, intertwined 'mongst all, the Catholic crucifixation . . . they, the Papists, control the government in South Vietnam . . . the atheist communists control North Vietnam . . . and now the unholy want to topple the holy . . . is it a holy war or a civil war . . . during the day the government agents tell the villagers to be true to them . . . at night the North Vietnamese agents tell the village leaders, you join up with us . . . if they don't, the Cong kill them . . . nothing civil about that . . . and what are your secret revelations, Señor Huckelbee . . . did you look down on the pope's nose or consider it a delicacy . . . forgive me Daddy, for I have sinned . . . I gave the turkey sacrament to the dog under the table . . . would you consider that blasphemy . . . hardly . . . nary a leaf on our family tree ever turned nose up against Papacy . . . not in hardscrabble Texas . . . and certainly not in Mexico . . . nor Vietnam neither . . . where Catholicism rules . . . or ostensibly so . . .

Kyrie eléison, miserere nobis: *Lord have mercy on us* . . . Pilots in camouflaged flight suits covered with bulky flak vests kneel on a mesh landing pad. *Qui tollis peccata mundi: Thou hast takest away the sins of the world* . . . The priest wears a surplice and carries a prayer book. He waves his free hand in blessing. *Miserere nobis: Have mercy upon us, we who are under the bullet* . . .

In Saigon, IV Corps American advisor Colonel Angus Bomar smokes his pipe like a thoughtful professor. Jabs a red stickpin into a wall-sized map where red circles pinpoint VC strongholds. Ho Chi Minh's picture is a punctured bullseye.

"Tide's turning, men. Best defense is a good offense. Strategic hamlets make the difference." He rotates his pipe. Fires a stickpin into the map. "Send a team in where she hit, boys. *Chieu hoi*."

His staff joins in chorus, "*Chieu hoi, chieu hoi*, defect defect."

Deum de Deo, lumen de lunine, Deum verum de Deo vero: God of light, very God of very God . . . "Goddamnit, I said add fifty and fire for effect," an airborne American artillery spotter screams over the radio. "He dropped fifty."

"Affirm, Gumshoe," a weary sergeant on the ground acknowledges. "Turn the dial this way," he patiently instructs an Army of Vietnam soldier. The ARVN looks sixteen; he's probably thirty-two. His hand clutches the elevation knob of a U.S. Army 105-mm howitzer.

Et iterum venturus est cum gloria judicare vivos et mortuos: *And he shall come again with glory to judge both the living and the dead* . . . Sneaky Petes, Special Forces troopers, slither through the mountain jungle. Montagnard tribesmen lead the way. Their eyes probe for buried stakes, tips covered with human excrement, sharp enough to penetrate a GI boot. Break the skin, hello infection. Goodbye locomotion. The VC know a man lame is more trouble than a man dead.

Confiteor unum baptisma in remissionem peccatorum: *I acknowledge one baptism for the remission of sins*. Baptism of fire. Eleven thousand American advisors move pins in maps. Spot artillery shots. Fly support missions in goony birds and two-seater T-28 trainers converted to fighter-bombers. Teach the disassembly and detailed nomenclature of the Browning .30-caliber air-cooled light machine gun: strip off the cover plate, hold it in the air, name it and pause while the Vietnamese instructor translates to thirty new Vietnamese instructors squatting inside a grass hut. Seven more weeks and each instructor will teach the same thing to thirty more instructors.

Operate a field radio relay station. Advise a South Vietnamese ranger battalion. Build a strategic hamlet in the Seven Peaks area. Lead a patrol out of Mang Buk. Fly with the modern Marine Expeditionary Force, code named Shu Fly: a helicopter squadron and its supporting units based at Soc Trang, Ba Xuyen Province in the middle of the Mekong Delta, 85 miles southwest of Saigon, 20 miles from the coast.

Agnus Dei qui tollis peccata mundi, dona nobis pacem: O Lamb of God who takest away the sins of the world, grant us thy peace. Under the bullets flying like motherfuckers on full auto going off so loud you can't hear the screaming, "Die, Dillinger, die . . . eat lead, Pretty Boy Floyd . . . take that, Capone . . ." up and down the line, spraying the canal and arcing into the sky until the magazines are empty and we drop the tommy guns and grin like kids at Christmas. We're testing the left-over weapons stored in arsenals since the First World War. They gave us .45-caliber Thompson submachine guns with the 500-round cylinder magazines you blow off all at once. You can't hold the gun steady, it recoils up and to the left no matter how hard you try to shoot straight and we're supposed to carry these in the choppers? Shades of G men and 1920s gangsters and the St. Valentine's massacre.

Fun's over, we give the Gunny the guns and go back to the tents, walking past the portable showers and water heater and water tank pumped full from the canal and treated heavily with chemicals; showers run a couple of hours a day, naked men with slithery butts and sudsupped crotches, how ribald can you be, but who's to see? VC maybe, eyeballing through binocs, "Look at the size of that." In metric, of course. Until the flight surgeon has canvas sides hung around the showers. We waltz past the big concrete-sided hangar, open to the front, a building left over from the former WWII Japanese air base. Next up is the mess hall, one of the few brick buildings, and then the rows of tents where we bunk, six to a tent, walls and ceilings shored with two-by-fours, tent flaps tied up on the sides to let in whatever air is moving.

We sit on the porch, chew the shit, slurp cold drinks in our mess cups.

"How's about some of them horse ovaries, Huck?" Cochran asks, forcing me up to get out the cheese and crackers.

When we're filled up, half drunk, talked out, we hit the rack, swelter under mosquito netting, sweat soaking through our skivvies.

I sit upright in bed. The canvas cot lurches. Diesel generators roar.

Lights from the concrete hangar throw an eerie glow across the sky. A monsoon breeze ripples the tent. The parachute hanging from the roof billows and waves.

The screech that woke me keens again. I wasn't dreaming. Reach for the flashlight with one hand, my .38 with the other. Shoot blind or chance the light? I hit the button. The beam spotlights two rats. Fangs bared. Jaws slathering. Hydrophobic. Black-button eyes. Red at the rims.

"Git, you bastards." I sight along the barrel. The light goes out. Corrosion's killed it. My stomach flip-flops. This damn climate. The light wavers and reappears. The rats are gone. Back to their dugouts under the floorboards. The scavenging bastards. Prowl the tents at night. Eat the crackers and sardines scattered among the liquor glasses and ashtrays. Traps and poisons don't bother them. Can't kill the rats how we supposed to stop the VC? *Owww*, a cramp ties up my guts. The wind whirls and the tent shakes. A spasm yanks my intestines. Here it comes. The first hard drops spank the tent roof. I rip the mosquito netting off, hit the deck in my bare feet, and tear outside into a smacking wall of rain rushing in on the wind.

I skid around the corner and run between the tents. Water pours over my eyes into my nose and mouth. I grip my tortured stomach. Squeeze guts *el memo*, you goofball, gotta make it. *Whoops*. There go the legs. I hit the mud face first. Ah, what's the use? I'll jes' lie here and squeeze this soft goo with my fingers, rub my face in the glop and die of nausea and dysentery.

Shouldn'ta said that. My stomach tightens. I twist into a corkscrew and clutch the Saint Christopher Rosey gave me along with the lingeringest kiss in mammary-pressure history. Choice time, body-boo. Either get up and get moving or let it loose right here. Yep. Abandon all decorum, mateys. Shovel me up with *la basura* in the morning. Dump me in the canal with the rest of the trash so the tide can flush me out to sea.

No no, can't have that. Very unprofessional, Huckelbee. Is this the surrender of the hot dog eager beaver who left the note on the Ready Room bulletin board: *Anytime, day or night, call on tent number four when there's an emergency flight.* Well, I'm getting the call now, all bowels, man your instruments, be ready for broadside fusilade, *muy fortissimo*.

Nemmine that, I can make it. Jes' let me crawl down this leetle ol' path, shit, flashlight gone, forget it. I know this route by heart. Ah, at last, there they are. Those sweet havens of mercy. Three screened-in huts atop a little hill. I'm gonna make it. An' on dah turd day he rose again, a rose arose a rose. By any other name she'd still be a. One hand on his belly, the other squeezing his ass, he staggers to his throne. A wooden box covers a deep pit, three lids cover three holes. Smoke wafts from the lids. Someone throw a cigarette in there and catch the paper on fire? This is too damn hot. I gotta get outta here . . . out the door and downwind to the Staff NCO head. In the night, who's to know? Screen door slams shut, pulled closed by a concrete block counterweight.

Relief at last. Hold yer head and think about your reward. The clean skivvy award. Never qualify. Jes' look at these mud-covered drawers draped around my ankles. I'm a mess. Fittin' for dis place. An' that smell. *Wheeoh*. El Smoko de Crappo. What about that fire upwind? Now I remember. Doc Eversham, the flight surgeon, isn't satisfied that the Soc Trang camp laborers dip the goop with buckets from the pits every three weeks, then take the honey home for their gardens. No, he's also gotta dump in gasoline and burn out, so he claims, those tropical bugs. He alternates the huts so there's always two available. Lotta good it's done. The bugs live on, everyone's got the runs.

A wet plop sops my back. Sit and get wet or go outside and get wet. The seat's already warm. Why move? Wipe the mud off my watch. Almost five in the a.m. Been here five months. Come to bring the lowly denizens out of the 13th century and into modern times. Portable USMC on land, sea and in the air: portable electricity, portable showers, portable toilets and potable water from the portable water-filtration system.

Must maintain a modicum of civilized concessions, white man' s burden and all that, even though we're melting pot multicolored. And quite comfortable, too. A tent for a home. Mosquito netting. Well-stocked fridge, thanks to the weekly Air Force booze flights. Gin and tonics after flying. For the fevah, of course. Barter across the fence with ARVN troops guarding the airstrip. VC promised to destroy the field before fall. Maybe. Meanwhile, eat French cheese on English crackers, pleasant hors d'oeuvres before the evening charbroiled Yankee steaks.

We weren't always so casual. When we first got here and the ARVNs took pot shots at night, everyone poured out of the tents in response, and the enlisted men took up defensive positions around the choppers. The pilots milled sleepily in the ready room tent, until word came to secure, false alarm.

Now at the sound of a night shot, the most anyone does is turn over in bed or swat a mosquito snuck through the netting. Jaded already. And the tour's not even half over, *tsk tsk*, cluck a tongue. Lay on some remorse. About boy scouts gone native. Counter remorse with optimism. The ol' Esprit de Corps is still strong. It's kept us from going balmy and turning on one another completely. Kept us working the job. Flying the helicopters. Deliver the goods. Short on money. Short on spare parts. Short on a clear-cut policy. Say, now that you mention it, what the hell are we doing here? You already answered it, dolt. Flying those helicopters. Supplies to the outposts. Wounded to the hospitals. Troops to the landing zones. Keeps the manly juices flowing. Sounds exciting. But right now it's not so great. Ease off, boy. Don't let your physical miseries give birth to pizzant thoughts.

In the sliver of light showing on the horizon the choppers look like grasshoppers squatting with folded wings. A sentry walks past. His silhouette shimmers. Very impressionistic through the bug screen. Make that pointillistic. Seurat, I believe. Or was it Renault? My memory's gone to rot like the rest of my body. Someday it will be over and I can retire to that great outhouse in the sky where the fixtures are solid gold, the flushers never rust, the paper is dry and the stool's always solid.

Till then, remember, lad, you're part of adventure. That's a man's lot. But in this case not sought. More like sot. Ha ha. Thank God for a fleeting moment of enlightenment. But then I always feel a bit religious after a good crap. The door creaks open and slams shut. One of the tent-mates. He scratches the welts on his arm, lowers his pants and sits.

"Turn that arm into a mosquito feedbag didya?" I mutter.

"I let it dangle out the netting. The itching woke me up. I moved and so did my innards. How much time we got?"

"None."

"Blah."

He leans over and concentrates. His face contorts. Gives his teen-looking countenance an aged strain. When the Air Force jet ferrying us to Vietnam crossed the International Date Line, Lieutenant Ben Benson slapped a flaming orange HMM-188 Hammering Eights baseball cap on his head and settled back to enjoy the flight now that he was officially in the Orient, never telling a soul how he found time to have the lower edge of the ball cap embroidered with Chinese characters and the words Japan, Okinawa, China and Vietnam; and centered between the words, a large-lettered, single block name: BEN-SAN.

He's been called Ben-San ever since. A short, merry fella with lit-up eyes, a turned-up nose and a light brown crew cut, he treats everyone like an intimate member of his family. Wide open, he seeks immediate rapport, maybe a result of his parents' divorce when he was a year old and he and his two sisters had to move in with Grandma and Grandpa in the back of his mom's beauty parlor two blocks off the main street of Cornhill, Nebraska.

"What do you think of a girl that goes down on you?" Ben-Ṣan asks out of the blue.

Jesus. There's a subject for early-morning heavy-head talk. Not enough I gotta submit to emboweled indecency, I have to participate in sex-act dialogue, too?

Ben-San's just come off a week of R and R in Japan where he fell in love with a girl named Yoshika. A bar girl but she has designs on working some day in a beauty parlor. He ought to know something about the beauty parlor thing.

"This got something to do with your girlfriend?"

"Yeah," he says. "I don't know what to think. It's 'cause she was having her period."

I tune out. Let the rain hitting the roof console me. His words fade in and out.

". . . all over me like a monkey on a banana . . . so hot I let her go . . . didn't think about afterwards."

Yas, me boy, real life doesn't provide a handy movie fade at the end of the scene.

"A good stiff drink helps take the edge off those sticklish situations," I mutter.

Ben-San moans. "I can't get it out of my mind."

"Say what? Ninety-nine guys out of a hundred would be overjoyed."

"It's worse than you think. I made the mistake of telling my mom about Yoshika in a letter."

"You told your mom? Good God, Ben-San. I know you get purty openly disgustingly personal in your conversations but isn't that a bit over the line?"

"If I had known the stink Mom would raise I'd never have mentioned Yoshika. Say, you don't think I told her about . . . ?"

"What else you talking about?"

"Christ love me for an idiot, I'm not completely off my rocker. It's because Yoshika is from Japan is what's got my mother upset."

"What the hell she think, you're going to get married?"

"I don't see how we can now."

"Now? You mean never. You can't even consider it."

"Not you too, Huck. You're not prejudiced like that, are you?"

"Prejudice, smejudice. No one in this godforsaken hellhole can think of getting married."

"I suppose you're right, I just wish I could get her off my mind. Can't sleep. I'm shot." He pulls up his drawers. "One of these mornings I'm going to ground myself so I can sleep in."

"Wouldn't do any good. They'd make you the duty officer and you'd have to spend the day in the ready room tent."

"Blah." He slaps his cap in his hand, puts it on and goes out the door. "See you at the briefing."

Better pull myself together. Scram out of here before the morning crowd rushes in. Where's that TP? Soggy as a wet sponge. Ya don't wipe here, bro, ya wash. Legs, do yer stuff. Back to the tent. Rain's slacked off. We'll fly today. Lucky us. There's a light in Doc Eversham's. No need to knock.

"Hey, Doc, you up?"

"Good morning, Huckelbee. God, you look like a hog that's been wallowing in the mire."

"Took a header on the way to the head. Say, you got any powerful stomach medicine? I can't keep anything in me."

Doc Eversham smiles behind his pipe. Sharp Ivy Leaguer, he's amused by the constant variety of interesting ailments that crop up in these awkward field conditions. He brushes his unmilitarily long hair across the top of his head. His white smock is spotless and wrinkle free. He motions me into his office, a screened-off portion of his tent.

"Let's see, you had the Kaopectate and the half-strength codeine. What about these?" He holds up a bottle of green pills.

"No good, Doc. I took the whole bottle and it hasn't helped. I'm desperate. Give me your strongest medicine."

"Hmm, from the looks of you, maybe I'd better. But this is a one-shot binder. I don't want you to mention it to anyone else. These are for the extreme cases."

"My lips are sealed. I'm counting on you to help on the other end."

He pulls aside a little curtain. A fat safe sits on the floor. He twiddles the dial and swings the door open. I peek inside. The safe is loaded with jars of clear liquid. Grain alcohol, one-hundred-percent pure. A box full of pill bottles sits on the jars. Doc Eversham takes out one of the pill bottles and closes the safe. He shakes out a pill. It's tiny and yellow, with a shiny brittle covering.

"Take it now," Doc says. "If this doesn't work nothing will."

I put it on my tongue. Bitter. Swallow it with a cup of water the Doc hands me. "God, what is it?"

"Opium."

No wonder he wants it kept quiet. And in pill form, too. I always thought you shoved a plug of it up your ass.

"Mum's the word, Doc. Say, hadn't I better ground myself?"

"You'll be a little woozy for an hour, but then it'll go away. You'll be able to fly."

"Okey-dokey. Thanks a million."

I head out of his tent, and when I glance back, the Doc's looking at the little bottle. I slither down the path. A cup bangs against a metal mess gear plate, the first indication of the rush to chow. I slip through the back of our tent, drop my muddy skivvies and go out on the porch to wash up. Brush the dead bugs out of the aluminum washing pan. Shake the five-gallon water cans. Wouldn't ya know it? All empty. Up to me to replenish the water from the camp's water system.

Some water system. The same pipe that runs the showers ends at a spigot next to the mess hall. There's always a crowd around the spigot. Our tent is situated in a prime location. We have a water buffalo parked at the end of our tent row. The water buffalo is a 500-gallon tanker trailer, filled and towed to the end of our tent row every couple of days. For the senior officers only, but we sneak our water from the water buffalo, too; not strictly kosher but beats waiting in line at the mess hall spigot.

Whoever in our tent empties the last can has to fill them all. When the cans get low everyone uses the water sparingly until the last container is emptied. Looks like it's my turn. The water buffalo's parked between the ready room tent and the skipper's tent. He rates a personal shower. Two fifty-five gallon drums atop a wooden roof. Filled by enlisted men. Bucket by bucket from the water buffalo. Heated by the sun. Pull the chain, the water gushes out. Lap of luxury. I'm tempted to step in and use the old man's shower. Naw. No sense tormenting him. Don't bug the heavies. Not unless I'd like a hammer to the head. Fill your five gallon cans from the water buffalo and be happy you got that, boy. Trudge through the sludge. Back to the tent porch for a whore bath. Two spits and a square of toilet paper. I squint into the mirror. A round ugly face stares back. Nose flared and flattened against a fat upper lip. Bristly stubble covers my chin. A few blond hairs patter like dew on my cheeks.

Where's that steel helmet? They are issued to everyone. A John Wayne wash basin. Over at the mess hall kerosene water heaters are stuck in garbage cans. Wash your mess gear in them. First can soapy, next two clear, good source of hot water for shaving. I fill my helmet. *Slip slap* razor up and down my cheeks, looks like a curved pagoda roof the way the razor swirls through the lather.

Say, that pill does have a bit of a wiggle to it. I grab my utility cap, and step off the porch, ready to test my stomach with some food. Lt. Col. Arthur Rappler, the Hammer, trudges through the gloomy morning. His black leather pistol belt engraved with cattle brands and crossed pistols rides over his butt and under his gut like a rain-slicked highway curving around aging hills. He glares coldly.

"Good morning, sir," I stammer, throwing a salute.

He returns it and walks past. What's the matter with him? Got the RA? Red ass? Good thing I didn't use his shower. Better dawdle a while till he's out of sight. Across the path the Vietnamese laborers are already on the job. They squat and pass around a big bamboo pipe in front of a half-finished brick building. A new BOQ, part of a permanent camp being constructed for an Army chopper squadron. The Army operates in the mountainous northern half of SVN while we're restricted to the lowland south. Soon, we'll exchange camps, but before rushing into any hornswoggled horse trade, the Army sent a Major to Soc Trang on an inspection trip and sure enough, after checking out our tent city, it's no deal. We're not up to their snuff. They've got a permanent camp on the coast at Da Nang. The officers live four to a room in buildings, not tents. Overhead fans keep the air circulating. If they're still too hot they can go to the beach and cool off. The town next to the base is open and well explored by the soldiers. Think they'll trade all that for a compound of tents, mud, binjo ditches, field showers and a hot, fly-ridden mess hall?

No way, Jose. The facilities are being constructed to make the Army's stay here more like their northern home. Soon as the work is done we'll exchange places. There'll be a change in the weather. A change in me. I can smell that sweet sea breeze now. No, it's Old Spice. Wafting ahead of its bearer.

Major Bert "Pappy" Lurnt, the squadron Exec. He must have doused himself good. Raindrops roll off him like he was oiled. A florid scarred face provides a cobblestone foundation for his mottled nose. Born and reared in the Arkansas Ozarks, he's a canny dirt sage, full of the wisdom of the cracker barrel store, and he never lets anyone forget it with his corncob pipe, slow drawl, saggy drawers and whiskey thirst.

He's put enough years in the Corps, he could retire any time he wants. A fifty-four-year-old Major, he knows he'll never go any higher, but to hear him talk he's got nothing to lose. Every year from here on is gravy. Sounds as if worry couldn't penetrate his smiling shield or disrupt his farm-boy aplomb, but appearances are deceiving. He doesn't like tilted wheels. The minute a stressful situation comes up he shakes, chain smokes and looks around for help. He finds absolutely no comfort from the Hammer. The C.O. plays on his taut nerve strings like a jazz bass player orchestrating a rhythmic hell. I've got a feeling this is one of those moments. He's having a tough time lighting his cigarette.

He looks me up and down. Shuffles his feet and coughs nervously. Throws the matches in the mud.

"Goddamnit, Huckelbee. Everyone else is going along with the program. Why can't you?"

"How's that, sir?" I sift through the old bean, attempt to pin down a fuckup I can't recall.

"I just saw the Skipper and the first thing he said was, 'That damn Huckelbee. He'll do anything to aggravate me.' Why do you want to rile him up? Just makes it hard on me."

"What did I—?"

"Don't interrupt. Back in Arkansas, the hogs roll in the mud and then it bakes on them in the hot sun and gets so heavy they can't hardly move so they rub themselves raw getting it all off, except for a big ball on their tails they can't get at, and you got to break up those balls with a hammer. Now, why don't you save us both a lot of trouble and put a bar on your cap? You don't want a hammer breaking your balls do you?"

Unlike the Major's, my utility cap has no rank insignia pinned to the front. Our normal working non-flying uniform is T-shirts and utility trousers. With no one wearing utility jackets the only way the men can identify the officers is by the rank insignia on our hats. After being together a year and a half you'd think everyone would know one another and their rank, but even here in this stinking Delta, where we work fourteen hours a day and fall into exhausted sleep at night, we must observe the uniform regs.

"I'm with you, sir. I'll put the bar on my cap."

"Good." He sighs. "Now for Chrissake be on time for the briefing. And drag that big galoot Cochran with you." He slouches off, muttering, "Those shavetails, slippery as an Arkansas sidewinder. I need a prod rod to keep those rapscallions in line."

I go in the tent and put on my flight suit. Rank and name are sewn on, now I'm kosher. Trade my utility hat for my Hammering Eights ball cap.

"Come on Cochran," I yell. "Rise and shine. Time's a-wasting."

I don't wait for his answer. I hit the trail to breakfast. Typical. First I was early. Now I'm practically late. Mind a blur. Pill goofy. The officer's section of the mess hall is almost deserted. Eager beavers have already departed for the ready room tent to copy aircraft assignments and lay out their flight gear and survival equipment.

Rob Jacobs, a low-slung, lumbering lieutenant is still eating. A good-natured guy from the heartland of the Iowa cornfields, he slurps down his eggs and potatoes as fast as he can shovel them in. What do you do with all that corn in Iowa, Rob? We eat what we can and what we can't we can. A comical braggart, he never talks about the shooting war going on around us.

"Well, Rob, packing in the chow I see."

"Gotta fill up here, Huck. Once we leave it's C-rats in the chopper."

He pats his hair. The son of a retired Army Colonel, he flunked out of West Point and bounced around three different colleges before applying for and being accepted into the Marine Aviation Cadet flight training program.

He swipes the last of the egg and pops the toast into his wide mouth. He grins at me.

"How about this, Huck. Think it will fit?"

He holds up a big apple. I don't bother to answer, too busy gulping down my own breakfast.

"All right. Watch."

He sticks the apple between his teeth. Chomps down. Swirls of shiny skin pulsate and glisten, both his and the apple's.

"That's real good, Rob. You better check with the Guinness book of records. You might have a new one."

His eyes bug out. The apple is stuck. His jaws are locked and he can't get the apple in or out. A mess tray bangs on the table like a Chinese gong. Cochran flops down at the table.

Rob Jacobs is clawing, his fingernails are digging, he's dislodging chunks of pulp. The cords of his neck bulge. Cochran leans over and stares him in the eye. Rob pleads wordlessly like a begging dog, muffling grunts, waving arms.

"Don't fret, son," Cochran says soothingly.

He lays a hairybacked hand on top of Rob Jacobs's head. Then raps him on the jaw. The apple parts neatly. Half vanishes into Rob's mouth. The other half falls to the floor and rocks gently, a half-moon Chinese junk rocking on the wavery floor. An opium pill is the junk of the Chinese.

"Don't forget to chew," Cochran says. "Carefully." Cochran sits down and begins wolfing his eggs. "You ready for that poker game tonight?"

Rob Jacobs doesn't answer. He runs out of the mess hall and we hear him spitting outside.

"Funny thing about that guy," Cochran says through a mouthful of food. "He's going farther and farther out with that big mouth business. This place is getting to him but he won't admit it.

Cochran swills his coffee and glances at his watch. "Plenty of time. Funny, I couldn't sleep this morning. Must have that game on my mind. Tonight I clean up." He smiles at my seeming indifference.

Cochran wipes the last of the egg and potatoes out of his mess plate. Glances around the mess hall.

"There's another pigeon I'd like to pluck."

One side of Cochran's face twitches. His eye tics. I'd think I was seeing things if I weren't already used to his tic trick. He developed it during the poker games. Whenever he bluffed, his eye would start ticing and pretty soon everyone knew he was bluffing. He'd been losing steadily—using the tic to set them up—and tonight he is ready to pounce, already practicing his tic.

"Yes," I say. "The time has come. The clock is ticking."

"Ha ha, very funny."

His eye twitches toward the other table where Captain Beamus sits drinking his coffee. The Rajah chews his lower lip, his mind cataloging the millions of details the ops officer has to sift and sort before a big operation.

"Hey, Rajah," Cochran yells. "What's on the agenda today? Troopers or supplies?" Captain Beamus glances at Cochran, and looks away.

"Good thing you don't get up this early every day," I mutter. "Talk about getting off on the wrong foot."

Captain Beamus goes out and bangs his metal coffee cup against a garbage can. Cochran bangs his cup on the table, clangs bouncing in my head echo like a decaying whistle. That pill's still at work.

"Shitfire, Huck. I thought you were keeping track of the time and here you are dreaming like a horny college boy. Let's make it."

He grabs his Hammering Eight's ball cap, whacks me on the shoulder, and sprints out the mess hall. We swish our mess gear in and out of the water, quick stop at the tent to throw the tin plates on the floor, snatch flak vests and pistol belts, and skid down the slick path into the ready room tent chanting, "Here, here, here," as the Hammer rises to brief the mission.

5. Lost A Bird Gained A Bird

Jumping Jehosaphat Doc, can't you give me something for the goddamn pain . . . or am I to wallow like a stuck hog in his mire and bleed till I puke my guts and chew off a finger . . . open the door let the wind whip in hot and dry off the sodden paddies . . . we've been issued flak vests and pants, and even though they are hot and uncomfortable, we wear the damned things even when wandering around the choppers parked at outlying airfields . . . or while checking out the marketplace in the nearby ville . . . next thing we know the ARVN Generals, green-tinted sunglasses beaming on us with envious glances, tell their American adviser, Hey we need flak suits, too, and in the blink of a Pentagon eye, 50,000 of them are sent to Vietnam and distributed to the soldiers . . . one day, when flying alongside a road, we see a mile-long line of ARVNs, encased in their personal flak jacket and pants, sweat pouring off the poor fuckers in the hundred-and-ten-degree heat . . . one of the soldiers tears off the American-made shit, throws the garb into the ditch, and then everyone starts ditching the heavy gear . . . no sooner are they free of the hateful things, than here comes an army of civilians to gather up the flak vests and pants and scurry home with their loot to put them to use . . . building materials maybe, keep the walls from being punctured with bullet holes . . . the smell of rotting vegetation primordial goo belches like thousands of years of decay sucked straight into my lungs . . . stink coming off me rank as any man shot to shit, no matter what his rank . . . who's responsible for this mess, Doc . . . and don't say, as it was in the beginning so it shall be in the end . . . give me more than that, Doc, if you're up to the challenge . . . or is the responsibility too overwhelming? . . .

The Hammer's a responsible man. Because of his ability to respond, you think? That'd be response-ability, I s'pose. You gotta admit the C.O.'s a hard working guy. Leads every mission. Racks up more flight time than anyone else. And his concerns don't stop there. He personally attends to every detail that goes into an operation. Attends the Vietnam planning and briefing conference at Tan San Nhut airport in Saigon. Overflies the mission area in an L-19 spotter plane. Pinpoints the landing site on the charts. Ensures that the flight arrives over the troop pickup point at the right time. Figures how long it takes to fly from there to the zone. Plans the routes of entrance and retirement. Coordinates the close air support. Plans the times for reveille, breakfast, briefing and takeoff. And finally, when all the details have been reviewed with the operations section, he conducts the morning briefing. He's worn down, eyebagged, nerves raw, but he pulls himself together, standing quietly, a moment of suspense, before he speaks.

"There's scuttlebutt that some of you aren't happy that I have decided that only those pilots who have qualified as section leaders will sign for the aircraft, those with the most time and experience."

Means some of us are stuck in the copilot seat. The HAC, the Helicopter Aircraft Commander, is the pilot who signs for the helicopter, and the one responsible for whatever happens to the bird. As the Pope is infallible in matters pertaining to religion, the HAC is infallible in all matters pertaining to his chopper. The copilot is his subordinate.

"I've had Lieutenant Emmett pair you according to rank. The senior man signs for the aircraft."

Emmett smiles from his position in front of the schedules board. Takes some fancy juggling on his part to keep the old junior-senior ploy afloat. He's a team player though. You can count on that. Fullback's body. Pile-driving legs. Determined gleam in the eye. Who wants to get on the wrong side of Grits? Cross him and fly with the heavies. No thanks.

"You also realize," the Hammer continues, "there will be continual flight checks whenever we have the opportunity—give you junior men a chance to qualify as section leaders."

Who gives a rat's ass? Let the HAC take the rap if something goes wrong. There's been a bit of grousing by the copilots I must admit. Put the mixture handle forward yourself, sir, your fucking arm ain't broke, and don't throw me no bones, minor gripes, considering.

"Any questions?" The Hammer pauses and looks around.

"Yessir." Captain Beamus stands up. "Could we have an update on our official role here, sir? Some of the men think we should be allowed to fire on the zones as we go in."

The hawks are eager. They want this to be a full-bore shooting war. Emmett talks it up all the time. The Red Horde is not just South Vietnam's enemy but our enemy, too, and their advance must be halted and the only way to do that is blast them back into the hovels from whence they sprung. Keep it tight, go in low and hot, heads up all the way, backs pressed into the backs of the seats, shoulder straps snug, guns going off on full auto. Pooty piddlin' war, but it's the only one we've got, so let's make the most of it.

The Hammer pauses to collect his thoughts, and then lays it on the line: "We are here strictly in an advisory capacity. No shooting unless fired upon. Our job is not to attack this country's enemy, but to support the government in its fight against the Viet Cong."

The dreaded VC. They pop out of canals and mangrove swamps, hit quick, capture guns and radios, disappear, then play hidee seekee with the ARVNs chasing them down like angry housewives *stomp stomp* gonna kill those fucking *cucarachas*, but *too late too late* they're gone, escaped between the baseboard and wall, the paddy and the dike. Those

M-60 machine guns in the bellies of our choppers are dying to spit fire, why have 'em if we can't use 'em? And now we have M-14 automatic rifles with us in the cockpit.

"The main thing is, I don't want any of our people getting hurt."

Not even a slight flesh wound? Maybe on the face, a scar of war? A ticket into politics, and that's where the power lies, not thirty years seeking a General's star. I can see it now: WOUNDED VET FOR JUDGE splashed on billboards and across headlines in Bordertown, Texas, the cowfolks dumbfounded by the sight of a veteran with a purple heart on.

"An all-out shooting war might appeal to some of you but Washington doesn't want it and neither do I. Be ready for anything. Climb out fast, fly at least fifteen hundred feet, above small arms range. If you have to go lower, keep your airspeed up and make constant heading changes, no sense in being an easy target."

Those first tracers lacing the paddy LZ do raise an aversion to a tidy war wound. First emergency evac with three wounded ARVNs trailing entrails is enough to discourage thoughts of a scar. First round zinging through the metal skin of the chopper raises the hair on the back of my neck and fills me with a total hatred toward unseen strangers trying to kill a friendly, short, ugly Texican who wishes them no harm.

We're running at the max. High speeds. Heavy loads. Hard on the Dawg. Mud and rain. A testing ground for tactics and weapons. Huge accumulation of American money and gear. A shitty job but somebody's got to do it. Time will tell all tales but, as the feller said, looking at his house swallowed by the ground, "Looks like we're pissing our goodies into a sinkhole."

I'm flying copilot with Cochran who's already made section leader, strictly on the basis of his superior flying ability, which even his fiercest detractors can't deny. The first inkling of daylight is showing on the horizon when we walk out to the flight line. The rain has let up and a mist hangs over the paddies. A rotten smell wafts from the water. Sergeant Soonto, our crew chief, has a big smile on his face as he waits at the chopper. He's Samoan, with a mug that looks like Rocky Graziano worked it over, but he's so tough he'd never go down, even if pummeled by the champ.

"Bird all ready, sir," he says.

I kiss the Saint Christopher medal Rosey gave me, and climb in the Dawg and start running through the check list. "Rotor brake on. Radio master on. Fuel on. Emmett must be in a good mood, putting us together," I tell Cochran over the intercom.

"Yep, he thinks he's gonna clean up in that poker game tonight. Still doesn't know I've been stringing him along. Mixture idle cut off. External power on. Collective down."

Cochran hits the starter and the gas-fired eleven-hundred-horse radial engine belches blue smoke out of the exhaust. "Steady on fourteen hundred RPM, oil pressure good, instruments okay. Rotor brake off."

The blades wind up and settle into their familiar rhythm.

"All set down there, Soonto?"

The crew chief clicks his mike. Chocks clear. Tap the brakes. Shoulder harnesses locked. We roll forward into the number-six slot.

"Hammer Flight ready for takeoff," the Hammer says over the radio.

He lifts off and we follow him aloft, six sections, four choppers each. Cochran and I are flying wing on Pappy Lurnt. His bird is a black silhouette against a red background as the first rays of sunlight streak across the sky.

When we reach altitude Cochran says, "Take it a while, Huck, I'll see what I can raise on the AM band." He picks up an English speaking voice. "Hot shit, Hanoi Hannah."

Her voice is prim and meticulous. "Just as the gruesome Japanese emperor worshippers of World War Two had to drink cup after cup of hot sake for their ancestors' sakes before launching kamikaze flights, the barbaric American Marines leaving Soc Trang airfield this morning gorged on human livers ripped from valiant Vietnamese women and children in order to work themselves into a killing frenzy and ensnare our freedom-loving people into their materialistic slavery . . ."

"The nerve," Cochran interrupts. "To think of such a thing. Having to *ensnare* anyone into materialistic slavery."

"Yeah almost as bad as her inability to complete her sentence."

". . . it is still not too late, Marines, to come to the aid of the Vietnamese freedom fighters and defend our people and country from the atrocities performed by the Army of South Vietnamese troops under orders from the capitalistic puppet ruler Diem, that traitor to the people of Vietnam who lives in an opulent mansion on his Mekong River estate, outside the occupied capitol of Saigon where the orders from the imperialists are broadcast through the puppet's mouth in lies that cost our people dearly in every hamlet overrun by ARVN thugs machine-gunning women and children, their cries heard world-wide by all people of the common bond begging you Marines to abandon your misled generals and join us on that day when all men and women will stand side by side as equals and free peoples commonly joined in the peaceful struggle against the true enemies of mankind: hunger and want; and now a song by one of your favorite groups, the Shirelles. *Take my love with you to any port or foreign shore . . .*"

"And on and on she goes," Cochran says. "VC say it goddamn be *their* way, ARVN say goddamn no, *ours.*"

"Maybe we're playing it wrong," I say. "We should bomb them with goods. New refrigerators, motorcycles, tape recorders, TVs, all the prime stuff."

"I do believe you are showing signs of wisdom, massuh Huckelbee, but it isn't the American way to hand over our precious commodities. No, what we want to do is bomb them with money."

"Yes. Greenbacks falling from the sky. Then they could buy our precious commodities."

"That's right. Ensnare them into materialistic slavery. They'll be just like us" *. . . for I'll be true to you soldier boy . . .*

"Close it up," The Hammer cuts in over the radio. "We're going down for the pickup. You're straggling, number seven."

"*Click click,*" someone keys his mike, a flagrant breach of proper radio procedure.

"That wasn't me," Rob Jacobs radios.

Ben-San, flying co-pilot with Pappy Lurnt, waves. Is he the mysterious clicker? We fall into column and angle toward a packed clay runway sitting next to a dirt road.

"Relief is near," I say over the intercom.

"What relief?"

"Shade from the broiling sun."

Heat waves shimmer across the water-soaked land.

"You call that Vietnamese pop stand shade?"

The runway, a hummock of elongated clay, looks like a turd floating in water. A thatched roof, open-sided hut sits at one end. We land and park in a row and wait with our rotors spinning.

The Hammer comes up on the radio. "Troops are still a quarter mile away."

Figures. The way they take their time, no wonder the Cong always disappear before we get there.

"Shut them down," the Hammer orders. "Looks like we'll be here awhile."

We kill the engine and set the rotor brake and climb down. Everyone heads in a straggly pack to the pop stand. Forget the American type geedunk and glups. The pop is tepid, the *ba muoi ba* "33" beer laced with formaldahyde. The snacks are left over from French colonial days. We cluster together in as much shade as we can find. The Hammer strides over.

"All right," he says, "any more of that mike clicking business and you'll be on the flight line every night practicing proper radio procedure."

Kapow! Kapow! Two shots startle out. *Dios mio,* holy shit. We split in all directions. *Don't bunch up. One round can get us all.* I sprawl beneath the pop stand. *Kapow!* I peek around the corner. Cochran stands out in the open, on the edge of the runway, pointing his pistol across the paddy water.

"What you got?" I yell.

Kapow! Kapow! The water spurts fifty yards away. Cochran lowers his .38, pops the cylinder and ejects the empty casings.

I sprint over to his side. "What was it?"

He pulls bullets from his bandolier and shoves them into the pistol.

"I've been carrying this damned thing around so long I've built up an uncontrollable urge to shoot at something. When I saw those ducks I couldn't resist."

"You were shooting at ducks?"

"Yeah, missed the fuckers. They flew away over the dike."

"Ducks," I growl. The rest of the pilots stand in a semicircle, muttering to one another, "Ducks, ducks, for the sweet mothering Jesus, Cochran."

"Be kind to your web-footed friends," a pilot sings. Others join in: "For a duck may be somebody's mother . . ."

The Hammer stomps up, quieting everyone. He snatches Cochran's pistol and holds it out to Captain Beamus.

"Confiscate this man's weapon. Lieutenant Cochran won't be allowed to carry a firearm until he learns the proper responsibility for its use."

Beamus shoves the pistol inside his flak vest. The Hammer faces the pilots and looks them over with a grim face.

"Let this be a lesson. I've noticed a certain laxness in your professional bearing and it's bound to affect performance. Don't let it go any further. The ARVN troops will be here in a few minutes. There will also be South Vietnamese dignitaries flying in to assess the success of the mission. They want to make this a showcase operation. The area will be alive with reporters and TV people. I have no doubt of our ability to uphold our end. Keep your minds on the job and stay out of trouble."

He spreads a map out on the ground. We crouch around it and look down at the positions circled in red: the landing zones, a few klicks apart. Supposedly behind VC lines. For a week Air Force pilots have been looking for that line but so far there's been no contact. Today we'll go deeper into Indian country, see what we can flush out.

We break up the meeting and head for the choppers. The ARVNs march in on the road that connects the strip to the neighboring village. Their steel pots hang low on their heads. They carry live chickens, and ducks strapped to their packs in mesh bags. They walk hand in hand and whistle and sing. No wonder the Cong can hear them coming.

We fire up and as soon as the troops are aboard we pour on the turns and head for the zone, radio blaring . . . *asked your mama for fifteen cents* . .

The scuddy clouds have blown clear and the zone lies ahead. Cochran leans into the straps and turns up the radio . . . *see an elephant jump the fence* . . . Two-seater American T-28s, prop-driven trainers converted to fighter bombers, flash by, Vietnamese pilot in front, American advisor in the rear seat. They rake the zone with machine guns, pull up, bombs gouge craters in the mud . . . *jumped so high he touched the sky* . . . Cochran pushes the nose over and we roar in, rotor head vibrating, wind zinging, Rufus Thomas singing . . . *never got back till the Fourth of July* . . .

"What the hell's that?" I yell.

Bullets splatter the water as we flare over the rice paddy . . . *walking the dog* . . . stitchings from automatic weapons sewing holes across the smooth surface. I grab the M-14.

"We're pilots, not gunners," Cochran bellows. "Ride the controls."

He's walking the Dawg across the paddy, raising a geyser below us . . . *just a-walking the dog* . . . The transmission screams as we hover over the water. The ARVN squad leader, a grizzled veteran, jumps out and disappears in six feet of water leaving a bubble and protruding rifle barrel. Soonto grabs the barrel and hauls the NCO back aboard. Cochran adds power and noses forward to a clay dike where he sits down on solid ground.

"Kick the bastards out," he orders.

Another dike sits thirty yards to our left. Bushes and trees line its banks. My ears are attuned to every strange zing and splat, anything different from the familiar yowl and yammer of the chopper. Geysers spout in front of us.

"Over there," Cochran shouts. "Drill the bastard."

I riddle the mound with a long burst. The chopper skips and dances, Cochran lifts and turns the chopper so Soonto can cut loose with the M-60. The ARVNs are squatting on the ground, blasting the bushes. Cochran wraps on throttle and we surge off the dike, flash across the trees and climb, last one out.

"Eat lead, you butt-ugly mud fuckers," I give the foiliate another burst. The magazine empty, I stick the rifle between the seats. Eyes closed I can still see the dancing geysers.

I look over at Cochran and key the intercom. "For a peace-loving maverick you were a mighty bloodthirsty cheerleader back there. Thought we were here to fly not to fight."

"That peacenik bullshit is only good to a certain point. Those motherfuckers were shooting at us. Take it a while, mister buttuglio. My hands are sweating like a bitch."

The bird is light and free under my slippery hands. My knotted stomach loosens, matching the rotor head vibes, dampened at cruise rpm . . . *if you don't know how to do it* . . . I join up on Pappy Lurnt, our section leader . . . *I'll show you how to walk the dog* . . .

Pappy interrupts the song: "Second section, I'm setting down. Circle and cover me."

I follow him down in a cockscrew descent and watch the major land on a hummock. He clambers from the cockpit, struggles out of his flight suit, leans his hands against the chopper and squats, holding his gear out of the mud. Arkansas razorback, he gotta go he gotta go. A flat-bottomed skiff skims across the paddy on the other side of the hummock, three black-clad men poling for all they're worth.

"They must think Pappy landed to go after them," I tell Cochran.

"If they only knew, they'd be after him, catch him with his pants down."

"I'll give them a what for."

I kick the stick over, drop the collective and dive for the skiff. The men abandon the boat. Two of them run through the knee-deep water into the cover of the brush. The third hightails it across the paddy. Muddy ringlets mark his trail. I sight in on the back of his head and build up airspeed, then level off. I'll flatten the bastard with one of the wheels. The surface ripples under the rotor wash and the rice stalks sway in the blast of air. The water explodes in shuddering bursts in front of the man and he dives into the muck.

I yank back the stick, honk on the power and rise off the water.

"Who's shooting?"

"Ben-San," Cochran answers. "He opened up on the guy."

Another couple of yards and we'd have been in the line of fire. Cochran grins like a Cheshire.

"You'd have let me splat that guy's brains all over the chopper, wouldn't you," I snarl.

"If that's what you wanted, killer. Everyone's gotta decide for himself. I already blew my cool today. Just hope I can stick with flying from now on, not gunning."

"Yeah, right, advisory capacity only—"

"Get back here," Pappy Lurnt cuts in. "Just 'cause a man's gotta answer the call of nature doesn't mean you can go skylarking all over the place. Join on me."

I bank to the rendezvous and we head over the water-quilted landscape and return to the landing strip for another pickup.

"Skipper's down," a call comes in on the radio. A white plume of smoke rises a half mile away. "He's okay. Took a round in the transmission. His wingman picked him up. They're leaving the chopper, we'll get it later."

All day long, ARVNs are picked up and flown to the zone. We stop at a temporary airstrip to refuel from big black bladders squatting on the ground. Not bothering to shut down the engines, we heat C-rats on the hot manifolds and eat while the tanks are topped, then head back to the zone, which looks like a football stadium parking lot so much crap has been hauled in and laid about, with supply types scurrying and bigwigs arriving, the press shooting pictures and scribbling in notebooks.

The Viet Cong tried to surround Father Wong's village but the ARVNs surrounded the Cong instead. Many dead is the report, with the remainder fleeing in sampans. The ARVNs are elated. Catching or killing a single VC is memorable but today's work is worth the visit from the Secretary of Defense. Orbiting overhead, we can see a dozen huts burning. The rest of the ville is still intact. We land and shut down, and Cochran and I follow the crowd to a bare spot on the edge of the village.

Dead VC are piled on top of a mound, bodies bloody and mangled, all with the same signature: a bullet in the back of the head. It's a staged photo op and the cameramen are busily shooting, burning ammo in the propaganda war. A prisoner stands by himself, hands tied behind his back.

"North Vietnamese," an American voice says. I step closer to hear better. "He's an adviser," the American says. "He had a one piastre bill in his pocket. That's their code sign."

A voice from the past. Vern Battles, my old high school nemesis. King shit of Texas Military Academy, he never could stand it when I tackled him in football practice, me just a sophomore and him a big stud senior. They ran sweep right and Vern Battles blindsided me and my shoulder popped out. Now we're bosom buddies, hand shaking and back slapping, in this shit together, ancient animosities forgotten in the rush of meeting and exchanging histories. He's the American adviser to the ARVNs we're hauling, and it's a bitch of a job, he says, the Vietnamese battalion commander does everything his own way, ignores Battles, who is always exhorting the ARVNs to attack, attack, attack.

Thin and stoop-shouldered from backpacking the PRC-10 radio, Battles nevertheless looks like he just got off the parade ground. Khakis starched with razor creases, even his floppy jungle hat is blocked to fit his head at a rakish angle. The only thing he loves better than his job—fighting, swearing, running, advising, leading—is talking about it.

And I'm eating it up, nodding, grinning like an idiot, agreeing with everything he says. Cut them off at the nuts, break the bastards' legs, yes yes, we're a couple of idiots gone completely bonkers. He'd like to take it to the Cong, destroy those fuckers, but he's frustrated, the ARVNs can't or won't understand him, his interpreter speaks French but no English, Battles speaks no French and only a little Vietnamese. Misunderstandings all the way around and Battles figures it's on purpose so they don't have to do anything he says.

The prisoner stands stiff and glaring. Battles motions him to crouch down and when he doesn't move, Battles knocks him to his knees. The prisoner looks straight ahead, emotionless. Cochran walks up, takes a package of C-rat cigarettes out of his pocket and puts one in the prisoner's mouth. The VC spits it into Cochran's face.

"You Americans are soft," he says. "That's why we'll defeat you in this war."

Cochran picks the prisoner up by his neck with one hand, and holds him off the ground. He shakes out another cigarette, drops the pack, sticks his finger in the VC's mouth and jams the cigarette in. He pulls out a lighter and fires it off.

"Not soft, man. Kind, maybe, but not soft."

He drops the VC to the ground.

Emmett shakes his head. "Great, Cochran, just great. The summation of our mission as only a gorilla can state it."

Cochran's smile is glued.

"That's enough," Battles says. "Let the ARVNs work him over. We kicked ass today. Great body count. Gotta go, battalion is moving out."

He slaps my shoulder, hikes the PRC-10 radio up on his back. The radio is called a prick ten, perfect for Battles, a prick to the tenth degree.

"Crazy war, huh? Good seeing you, Huckelbee. You guys are doing a terrific job with those choppers."

He doesn't have a clue, same old turd. "Break a leg," I yell. He doesn't turn. Raises his arm. *De superioridad moral*, what you might call a self-righteous jerk.

A short, beaming-faced man, wearing green khakis and a steel helmet atop his rounded dome, steps forward. He bows slightly and smiles.

"I am Father Wong and this is my parish." He motions towards the huts. "And these are my parishioners." He nods at the villagers gathered around.

He and two hundred Chinese immigrants fled their homeland ahead of the Red Horde, he tells us, and now, once again, they are beset by the godless communists determined to wipe them out.

"By all that's holy those atheists aren't chasing me any farther. Here I stay." Sticks his Staff of God into the ground. "On this mud flat I built my church." A grass shack sitting high atop big mud bricks that keep the building dry during the floods.

The Diem government is all Catholic so Father Wong gets the backing and supplies he needs. President Kennedy is Catholic, too. The Pope has an ear cocked. The story of Father Wong and his village is picked up by the American press and before a pilgrim can shake his chalice, Father Wong has his own fort, private army, American cash, a fervent following and the Father Wong song. Right on cue the village kids raise their voices:

Father Wong
And his throng
Two hundred strong
Fight the Cong
Who are wrong
Beat the gong
Say so long
Cong are gone.

Father Wong smiles proudly. Half medieval Jesuit, half warrior-fighter, half priest, half counselor, half terrifier, he brandishes the wrath of the padre's guns in this world and the wrath of the Catholic God in the other.

"They thought they'd wipe us out," he says. "VC burn huts, rape women, steal rice, pigs, chickens, ducks and snakes and then go to edge of village and cook the meat, drink sacramental wine and have big party, give us the finger.

"Ha ha. Not on my patch. I buy three one-oh-six millimeter reckless rifles in Saigon and hide them in church and in reflecting red and orange and gold flaked sun setting on canals blow them apart and wreck their party with antipersonnel projectiles blast them into the darkness from which they came.

"Not that it has deterred the Cong," he admits. "They have big reward on my head but we are stronger all the time with more weapons and better training and we go in the field ourselves and hunt them down but we aren't totally barbaric." He shakes his head piously. "We try to rehabilitate prisoners, teach them catechism, give them chance to join Army of Christ."

We nod obsequiously and follow him around the village, yas, Father Wong, yas, doing a grand job, just grand, WHAT THE HELL IS THAT?

I'm face to face with a black shriveled head stuck on a pole in the middle of the village square. Its eyes are bugged and protruding, tongue black and swollen, pushing out of cracked peeling lips.

"One of the men we rehabilitated. He went back over and was captured again, raiding and looting. Unfortunately he died in the fighting, burned in the hut he torched. A shame, really."

Ben-San steps forward. He's brazen, reckless, going to outdo Cochran. Pulls out a cigarette and jams it between the charred lips.

"Get a picture of this," Ben-San says, posing.

Whoa, I'm thinking. Better kill those prints. What if Mom, apple pie and pasteurized-vitamin-D whole milk ever saw the sons of our evangelical heartland indulging in such gruesome pranks?

"Ah, what's so atrocious about a man smoking?" Ben-San says.

Everyone shuffles their feet. This is too much over the top. Pappy Lurnt breaks the tension. "Mount up, Gyrenes, it's time to book on out of here."

"Don't you mean boogie on out of here?" Ben-San says.

"You shavetails don't understand Old Corps talk. Used to be when you went on liberty you signed out in the book. We don't sign out any more but we still book, so haul your asses and on the double."

An hour later, silhouetted against a brilliantly colored sunset we approach the field at Soc Trang, daisy chaining toward the runway in a mad bucking whip, fighting turbulence and rotor wash, the men below watching us arrive safely so they can feed us, purify the water, fire up the showers and work on the choppers all night so we can get up before dawn the next morning and repeat the ball-busting experience all over again.

We stagger into the ready room tent and drop our gear on the floor, everyone pushing and shoving for space. In the middle of the melee Captain Beamus steps up on the podium and yells, "All right, who shot the water buffalo?"

Cochran's head jerks up.

"The water buffalo? . . . Oh no . . . did someone actually . . . ?"

"That's right. Emptied a whole magazine."

Cochran charges through the flight gear, scattering hard hats, flak vests and knee boards. He grabs my arm. "Get the buckets . . . the water cans. . ." Hustles me out of the tent. "Quick, Huck . . . the water cans . . . quick."

I envision holes in the sides, water pouring out, long trips to the mess hall spigot, carrying water cans all the way. I run back to our tent, grab two cans, and rush to the water buffalo only to find Cochran muttering and cursing. Too late, I think, the water's all gone.

I take a closer look and, miraculously, there are no holes in the water buffalo. I open the tap and water gushes sparkling onto the ground.

"Just like this fucking war," Cochran says, shaking his head. "Man says one thing he means another. Someone else hears him he gets a completely different take. Everything's totally fucked. I'm getting so I can't tell *what's* real any more."

We drag back to the ready room tent. Captain Beamus continues his harangue. One of the crew chiefs shot a water buffalo while we were going into the zone. Maybe a good case for righteous indignation for him but it doesn't mean shit to us after the anxiety of losing our private water buffalo.

The other pilots know we've been filling our cans from the water buffalo while they have to wait in line at the mess hall spigot. Payback time. They laugh and point and grab their crotches, high five, do a fake circle jerk, then break into a shuffle, slap legs, click fingers above their heads, chant, "Who-ah shot-ah dah wa-tah buffalo? Hey! Who-ah shot-ah dah wa-tah buffalo? Hey!"

"All right, knock that shit off," Pappy Lurnt hollers. "We got more important stuff going on here. You know, we left the skipper's chopper out there but I'm happy to say although we lost a bird we also gained a bird."

He holds up two silver eagle insginias.

"Just got word the skipper's promotion came through. He's a full bird colonel now."

The Hammer walks forward. Major Lurnt pins the eagles on the colonel's flight suit and steps back and gives him a salute. In the midst of the scattered applause and muted huzzahs Cochran and I grab our flight gear and hustle out of the tent.

6. Prepare for the Retreat

Come on, Doc, cool me down here, I've got a hole in my shoulder bigger than a shotgun blast . . . hawks and doves . . . to shoot or not to shoot . . . some say yea some say nay . . . "It's all bull roar," says Daddy . . . shoot at the flock or shoot at the bird . . . one is nay one is yea . . . the moment comes you decide the way . . . you can't be of two minds . . . indecision will get you every time . . . a hunter has to be of one mind . . . they looked so cute, Doc, like little kittens with bushy tails and black and white stripes so I jumped down in the garbage hole to pet them and they stuck their tails in the air and let loose a smell that made me sick and my eyes cry and I got out of there and ran howling and crying to the house and Abuela *grabbed me before I got to the door and tore my clothes off and put me in a tub and poured in tomato juice and water and soaped and scrubbed me and covered me with a towel and made me sit on the steps in the sun while she picked up my clothes with a stick and threw them in the garbage pit and covered everything with dirt . . . yas, Daddy, I've heard that bull roar . . . tie a bull's scrotum to a long piece of hide and whirl it around your head and listen to the bull roar . . . learn to do it son and when that time comes, whatever is in the way won't work against you, remember that, son . . . looney tunes bizarro gazarro, Doc . . . right hand doesn't know the left hand exists, Doc . . . in one side of the mouth all hail and high water . . . out the other side all doom and gloom . . . blow hot or blow cold but never blow lukewarm, not if you're a hunter . . .*

He's a hunter sniffing the air, blood on the wind, his back up, stalking, the thrill of the kill, and, like the guy who's been down so long everything looks up to him, after a shower and a steak barbecued on grills next to the mess hall, Cochran is ready for the poker game.

Rubbing his hands, grinning and smirking, working on the tic, poking me in the ribs, smacking his lips, Cochran bounces on his size twelves, bopping between the tents toward our destination: Grits Emmett's tent.

Cochran pauses, squares his shoulders, composes his features into a bland blend of calm and bends down to enter the tent, then he stops, huddled over. He motions with his hand for me to stay back and watches the action inside a moment before turning and, going *shhh* with his finger to his lips, draws me away into the darkness. He pulls me along by the arm, slowly, then faster, and, as soon as we get out of earshot, lets loose:

"Shit piss corruption snot, seventeen assholes tied in a knot, I can't believe it!"

"What the hell are you so all-fired het-up about. Whyn't we go in there?"

The light from the hangar casts a garish glow across his cragged face, black brows twisted, mouth grimaced.

"The table's full," he snarls. "Every chair taken. No place for us, Huck, no room at the inn." He laughs bitterly. "Emmett, Jacobs, Ben-San, Beamus, the chickens ripe for plucking, they're all there, but instead of us, they've dragged in the good doctor who knows as much about poker as a proctologist does about the Peloponnesian War."

"Peloponnesian, huh? That's profound. How do you spell Peloponnesian by the way."

"Shut up. I know the warriors beat up on the eggheads and that's good enough for me."

"Wait a minute. You think they set it up like that or just got tired of waiting? You were taking your own sweet time getting there."

He hunches and slouches and paces. Damned if he doesn't look like a gorilla, with his face scrunched, eyes narrowed, mouth curved down and arms dangling.

"Don't be so damned naïve. Of course they set us up. All this time I thought I was playing them along they've been conspiring against me. Ha. Think they've got the last laugh, do they?"

"Ah, for Christ's sakes, let it go. In this crazy mixed-up mess one little poker game doesn't mean a hill of beans."

"Play that tune somewhere else, Sam the man. Ah, what do we have here?"

He stops and looks at two fire-fighting backpacks sitting next to the hangar. Metal cans with short hoses and nozzles; you pump them up, they spit out a fifteen-foot stream of water powerful enough to knock down a blazing wooden wall.

"Just what the good doctor ordered," Cochran says, slipping his arm into a shoulder strap and hefting a can onto his back. "You grab the other one."

"I've got a *muy malo* feeling about this."

"You got a real bad feeling about everything. I'm feeling better, doctor. Come on."

We slink back to the tents, talking over the plan. Cochran will sneak around back and I'll stay in front. I'll watch through the flap and when I see him let fly I do the same. We pump up the pressure as we're walking.

I kneel down and look in at the game. A light hangs over the table illuminating the cards and the money and the players. Emmett's back is to me and Rob Jacobs sits next to him. Then Ben-San. On the other side Captain Beamus and the Doc sit beside each other. Rob Jacobs is a religious freak and Emmett is bugging him about it, an obvious ploy to distract him from the cards.

"How can you possibly reconcile gambling and religion?" Emmett asks, blowing smoke from a big cigar.

"Life is a gamble," Jacobs replies happily. "Fate deals the hands and faith steers you straight through the game."

"Roger that," Ben-San says. "Ante up. Five-card stud, nothing wild."

Emmett shows an ace and opens with five dollars. Cards are dealt face up around the table and everyone folds except Rob Jacobs, showing a pair of sixes.

"See your five and raise another ten," Rob says.

The tip of Cochran's nozzle peeks through the flap.

"Call and raise you another ten," Emmett says.

Jacobs taps his hole card.

"I'm reminded of the time," he says, "Jesus was walking through a crowd and a woman suffering from her period for thirteen years without interruption couldn't fight through the crowd to touch Him."

"Play cards," Emmett says.

Rob Jacobs looks at Emmett's aces, tilts the corner of his hole card and peeks at it. He drops the corner and smiles.

"The woman dropped to her knees," Rob says, "scurried between the people's legs and managed to touch the hem of Christ's robe as He walked by."

"Shit or get off the pot," Emmett roars.

"When I decide to pay that's when I'll play," Rob Jacobs says calmly. He picks up a ten spot and waves it. "Not before."

My hand tightens on the nozzle. The smoke from Emmett's cigar swirls around the light like a dragon's breath.

"She was instantly cured," Jacobs says, pointing with his ten dollar bill. "As she fell to the ground in a swoon Jesus stopped and turned. 'Who touched me?' Her heart froze. 'I, Lord.' He looked at her and smiled. 'Go in peace. Give thanks at the temple.' He walked on. 'But how?' Peter asked when he caught, catching up. 'How did you know?' 'I felt virtue go out from me,' Jesus told him. 'I wanted to see who it went out to.'"

"Oh Christ on a cross," Emmett yells. "You calling or not?"

"I'm thinking," Jacobs says. "If he felt virtue go out of Him and knew how it was used, that means He had no healing power in or of Himself but acted strictly as a cosmic valve through which power benevolently flowed, and whenever anyone touched Him with urgent need the valve automatically opened. Get it?"

"I'll get you by the nuts if you don't shut up and . . ."

"I call," Ron Jacobs interrupts. "What you got?"

Emmett reaches to flip over his hole card and the table explodes in a blast of water that sends cards and money flying. Emmett turns to look and I splatter his cigar. The doctor sits dumbfounded. Captain Beamus dives for the deck. Cochran blasts Rob Jacobs and sends him spinning. The chairs go flying. We rake the tent up and down and side to side. The light gets hosed and blows out, throwing everything into darkness.

"What the fuck? You sons of bitches. I'll kill your asses!" Emmett yells and stomps drown the noise of the gushing water.

Water pressure gone, I scram out of there, Cochran right behind me. Panting and laughing we drop the backpacks against the hangar wall and then hear them crashing through the tent rows, screaming for revenge.

"Uh-oh,"Cochran says. "We're cut off. We'll never make it back to our tent."

"Okay, so what's the plan?"

"I was so intent on the attack I didn't prepare for the retreat. Let's get out of this light."

We cut around the hangar and into the shadow. A jeep sits on the road, engine idling. Sergeant Soonto ambles out the backdoor of the hangar. A big smile lights up his face.

"Lieutenants. What brings you out this fine evening?"

"Exactly what I was going to ask you," Cochran says. "You aren't going anywhere in that jeep are you?"

"Yes, sir. I'm heading into the ville to buy fresh vegetables at the market. Someone makes the run every night."

"Would you like some company?"

"Sure, hop aboard. What's all the noise about?"

"Ah, some rats got into the cheese and crackers in one of the tents and they're hunting them down. Pay them no mind. Let's head out."

He jumps in the front next to Soonto. I hop in the back and we slink down in the seats. Soonto gives us a puzzled look.

"Just drive," Cochran says. "If they see us they'll want to come along."

We go past the ARVN sentry lounging at the gate, rifle held casually at his side, our protection from the Cong. Cochran sits up.

"Well, what do you think?" he asks. "Did Grits have that ace in the hole or not?"

"Probably, but question is, did Jacobs have another six?"

"I doubt it, otherwise he'd have bumped him again."

"We'll never know now."

"No, we don't know nothing about no poker game. We been in town all evening, right, Soonto?"

"Whatever you say, Lieutenant."

The ville is dark in the outskirts of town. As we go in deeper, lights glow from open doors and windows. Soonto drives into the middle of a dirt-packed square and parks. Shops line one side, an open-air market on the other and, in between, a tavern with tables and chairs set up in front.

Soonto cuts the engine and jumps out. Kids come running and scurrying, hands outstretched, voices shrill. Loudspeakers blare tinkly clangy songs, adding to the din.

Locals stand arguing, excited, cutting loose with hysterical jabber and squawk. Neon signs flicker. Banners proclaiming the arrival of the new moon droop in the listless air, thick with the smell of *nuoc mam* fish sauce poured over rice. Young girls giggle and point at the jeep. Yellow bulbs hang from shredded wires, attracting moths, mosquitos and flies that have abandoned the binjo ditch for the warmth of the light.

We follow Soonto to a table.

"Beer. Beer. *Ba muoi ba*, Beer 33," he hollers.

A boy comes out of the tavern. He carries a tray of the formaldehyde-laced brew.

"Ice," Soonto bellows with a grin. The boy rushes off, returns with tall glasses loaded with ice cubes.

"Local ice?" I ask.

Soonto nods. "They bring it in every day by sampan. Damned if I know from where. Ice is like heat. It kills all the bugs. Just don't drink the water and you'll be all right."

Cochran raises his eyebrows. That's not the way Doc Eversham put it. He says bugs live in the ice. What the hell. We pour the beer over the ice and drink fast before it has a chance to melt and infect us all.

"That's right," Soonto reassures us. "If it melts it dilutes the beer, can't have that."

The beer picks things up. High piercing voices join in on the tinny-sounding songs blaring out of the loudspeakers. Soonto is well-known in the ville. All the kids come over and hit him for cash. Shoe shine. Peanuts. Hard candy. Sure, sure. We take it all in, one big blast.

"Where's my number one?" Soonto bellows. "Where's my lady?"

A boy scurries off.

"I've been teaching her English," Soonto confides. "She's picking it up pretty good."

A woman dressed in silk pants and a long shirt, her mouth stained with betel juice, her demeanor regal, walks up to the table.

"These are Marines from the air base," Soonto says. "They have come to visit your town."

She smiles and nods. Cochran nods in reply. I give her a wave.

"Welcome," she says. "Mister Soonto is a good friend."

She motions and another tray of beer and ice-filled glasses appear.

"Would you like to join us?" Cochran asks.

"Oh, no. Mister Soonto and I must do his . . ." She searches for the word.

"Shopping," Soonto says. "The supplies."

"Ah, supplies, yes."

Soonto stands up. "I'll be back in a while. You Lieutenants enjoy yourselves."

The beers keep coming. The noise and lights and people swirl. We're flush, pockets full of money we saved for the poker game, and we throw American bills on the table, no piasters on hand.

A young woman approaches. She smiles and taps Cochran on the shoulder.

"Oh, howdy, ma'am, can I buy you a beer?"

She shakes her head and gestures with her hand.

"Huh? What's she want, Huck?"

"You, I'd say."

Cochran is suddenly fumble bumbled, unsure. "Well, hell, why not?"

He lurches to his feet. The lady beckons to me.

"What? Me? You mean, me, too? Both of us? *Ay Jesus,* oh, lordy."

She smiles and nods. Whoa, boy, we're living right, now. A little sloshed, but what the hell.

She leads us into a room at the side of the restaurant. It is cool and dark with a table and chairs. She indicates that I should wait and leads Cochran into another room.

I sit down and reach for a beer. I can either count the number of bamboo poles holding up the walls or else strike up a conversation with the lizard hanging on the ceiling or maybe count to a hundred backwards, make sure another beer won't poke a hole in the crystalline puddle that used to be my mind. No, I'll just sit here and peer through my fingers and turn those flies that are doubled up back into singletons, maybe grab one out of the air with chopsticks . . . now where are those chopsticks, there's always chopsticks . . .

She reappears, not looking so chipper, goes to a tub in the corner, pulls her dress over her head and lays it on a chair and scoops a handful of water into her crotch. She grimaces. I'm getting my first full-bore look at a naked feminine body in way too many days to be the slightest bit cool. She catches my shit-eating grin, gives me a wan smile and shakes her head. "Too big," she says, and splashes more water, dries herself, puts on her dress and comes over and takes me by the hand. Cochran walks out, buckling his belt with a sheepish grin.

"Go gittem, Tiger."

Once again the dress slips over her head, her body is small, lithe, brown, with perfect breasts, a rounded belly, sparse bush and tight tush, oh my constricting throat but I gotta look *ay Jesus* she is helping me with my clothes oh what a wonder, she spreads her wings and envelopes me *ay Jesus* Rosie and Mommy and Auntie and Teacher too and all my loves and all my lovelies and all my beauties who have brought me to where love gushes and love explodes . . . a hand pokes me in the shoulder, insistent, poke poke, wha? Where did I go where was that place where I was lost where are my pants?

I stumble out to the table.

"How much did you give her?" Cochran asks, pulling on a beer.

"I don't know, twenty, maybe? . . ."

"Whew, great night for—"

"Hey, Lieutenants!" Soonto calls. "We gotta skate, it's getting late."

The jeep is piled with crates of cabbages and leeks and lettuce and tomatoes and bamboo sprouts and lemons and sacks of rice and sides of water buffalo meat. There's no room in the seats so Cochran and I sit on the front fenders, Soonto loops a rope around us and we lurch off top heavy and swaying to shouts and laughter, kids running alongside slapping the jeep, one false move and over we'll go spilling our cargo into the canal where we'll be trapped below water with Soonto gazing mournfully at the cabbages as black shapes rise and swallow the veggies as the jeep trundles through the night its headlights leading the way home.

The base is dark, the only signs of life two sleepy mess cooks come to unload the jeep. They untie the rope and we tumble to the ground. Soonto looks us over.

"You going to make it, Lieutenants?"

"When duty calls we will answer," Cochran says, struggling to his feet. He trips over me. "Stand by to repel boarders. Sergeant Soonto, assume the command. Lieutenant Huckelbee and I will be in our quarters."

"Aye aye, sir."

Soonto salutes, a big grin across his face.

"Carry on and much obliged. Scouting mission deemed total success, and no need to file a report but if you're asked you might say we left a little earlier than scheduled."

"You got it, sir."

Arms interlocked we weave toward the tents. An ominous shape looms out of the dark. Cochran pulls up and yanks me back.

"Halt!" he calls. "Who goes there? What's the password. Repeat your general orders."

"Don't give me any of that shit, you fucking gorilla. I knew you'd have to come out of your hidey hole eventually."

"Well kiss my grits if it isn't our esteemed colleague, Lieutenant Emmett. To what or to whom do we owe this honor at this late hour?"

"You know well goddamn well why I'm here. The whole camp's on your case now, you rat-turd fuckup."

"I beg your pardon. Have you been drinking, Mister Grits? Does he seem rational to you, Tomas?"

"Not really. What's the beef, Grits?"

"Nice," he says. "As if you have no idea at all what's gone down. Just where the hell were you? You didn't show up for our poker game after bending everyone's ear for a week how you were going to clean our clocks?"

"Sorry about that," Cochran says. "By the time I got showered and changed I was still so bummed out about making a jackass of myself over that water buffalo mess I didn't have the heart to face anyone."

"Yeah," I say, "and when we saw Soonto heading for town on the supply run we decided to go along, get out of Dodge."

Inexplicably, Emmett begins laughing. He holds his side and grabs a tent pole for support. "Town?" he splutters. "Town? No one's allowed to go to town at night. No one's even allowed past the perimeter."

"Shhh, keep it down," Cochran says. "You don't want to get Soonto in trouble. He didn't want us to go."

"Yeah, right. I suppose next you stole a chopper and flew to Saigon?"

Cochran puts his hand to his heart, his sensibilites wounded.

"I can't believe it. An officer and supposed gentleman, refusing to believe the word of another. Come on Tomas, this conversation is terminated."

"No, wait, you can't . . ." Emmett splutters, but Cochran and I brush past him and make it to our tent without tripping over our feet and once inside fall to the plank floor holding our hands over our mouths.

"Some of us take this mission seriously," Emmett rails from outside. "We're not here for the fucking around."

Cochran fumbles around in the dark. "Get your dop kit," he whispers. "We're blowing this pop stand."

Shaving kits in hand we sneak out the back of the tent. All around us flashlights are clicking on, accompanied by grumblings and shouts, "What the fuck is going on . . . knock that shit off, will ya . . ." A rifle fires over in the enlisted men's area. I follow Cochran, tripping over tent pegs.

"I didn't realize we raised such a shit storm," Cochran says. He slides along the back of the tents to the ready room. "We're not on the flight schedule today. Let's see what else is available."

He walks up to the front of the ready room tent and looks at the schedule board.

"Here's an open slot," he says. "No one is signed up for R and R today. Let's grab it."

R and R. A flight out and back on the supply plane with an overnight stop in a foreign town. Anybody not flying that day can sign up. A gust of wind skips across the runway. The tent billows, the side flaps rise and through the openings vast vistas beckon from the other side of the concertina wire, from across flooded fields, the sand dunes, and the ocean: Hong Kong, Manila, Bangkok, Tokyo, alluring fleshpots replete with hotels, clean sheets, civilized food and drink and friendly companionship. *Oooph,* Cochran jabs me in the ribs.

"Wake up, dolt, you can sleep on the plane." He writes our names in the R and R slot on the acetate board.

"There, we're covered. Let's vamoose, cowboy."

We slip out of the ready room tent and over to the airstrip. Lights flash and voices call out. Something is going on back in the enlisted men's area. Ahead of us a big gray shape sits on the edge of the runway. Vehicles are clustered around it and men move in and out. We go around to the back of the plane and up the ramp. Cochran grabs a seat along the bulkhead and I slump down next to him. The ramp rises and closes. There's a whine outside, the APU coming on, followed by the engines turning. Cochran has a big grin on his face.

"Just the ticket," Cochran says. "Grab some shuteye. We'll be there before you know it."

7. Escaped By The Four Skins

Lighten up, Doc, you need a softer touch with that needle . . . my girl Rosey could show you how to be gentle . . . like the night in the guard shack in California when I was the duty officer, staying up all night in the guard shack . . . Rosey sneaks in with a cup of coffee and we tussle on the couch, best two out of three and I'd have taken her except the enlisted man making the rounds surprises us and my offical retort is to ask him for his eleventh general order and when he says he only knows ten I hip him to the eleventh: never disturb an officer locked in amorous conduct . . . and the surly fella turns me in the next day . . . if I ever catch him with a dirty gun I'll short-arm the fucker just like Daddy told me they did to each other in New Guinea . . . what's irrational at home is perfectly normal overseas . . . Daddy comes on like a wealthy know-it-all philosopher but we never had any oil under our dusty scrub-grass ranch although we did harvest a few dollars they paid us to sink a dry hole before they realized it was a worthless endeavor . . . and did they apologize? . . . no, it was like when Marion Morrison, the most famous Hollywood Marine of all, said, "Never apologize, Pilgrim, it's a sign of weakness" . . . you don't have to punish yourself for your mistakes, Son, other people will do it for you . . . I know, Daddy, they are waiting in line . . . that thin line between sanity and insanity and I've crossed it, Doc . . . can't even tell time, not when time lies around like ground fog on a wispy morning . . . what did the seer say, I can't see him so good . . . oh yeah . . . when you're in an insane situation the only way to keep your sanity is to act crazy . . . who's acting, Doc . . . this is for real . . . and reality has wore me out, Doc . . . I need a rest . . .

R and R. Rest and Relaxation. Rehabilitation and Reclamation. Romping and Ratfucking. A necessity for hot-shot pilots burning themselves out on the steady diet of "Fly and drink and to hell with the Victor Charley" attitude we 'Mericans so easily develop in the tropics.

As soon as we get off the supply shuttle we grab a taxi and head straight for Tokyo center, splashing through puddles, half blinded by a driving rain. Ugly scars cover our gaunt taxi driver's arms and face.

"I wonder if he got burned from the bomb?" I ask Cochran.

"More likely a car wreck," Cochran says grimly.

Tiny cars and smaller motorcycles weave in and out of the traffic. Taxicabs dart and squirm in orgiastic frenzies. Brakes screech like frightened rabbits. Gnarly pines peek between buildings. A chrysanthemum blooms on a doorstep. Bamboo stalks poke up between buildings. Old folks *clack clack* on sandals with wooden *klok-klok* soles. Kids flap the streets in go-aheads. The ghost of Fat Man haunts the pachinko parlors and bombards their balls with gamma rays.

On every wall, billboard, subway sign, and shop front, flourescent posters entice customers into movie theaters and pachinko parlors with all the *hace lo correcto* savoir-faire of a hundred-car freight train working the Kyoto grade.

"Far out artful stuff," Cochran yells, bouncing on the taxi seat. "Let's send some home, one for every Bay Front apartment."

We skid into Four Corners. A bulbous traffic light sits in the center of the intersection. Monstrous lights blink and signal. Street creeps ply their trade.

"We'll hire us a local yokel to print obscene words on statues and posters," Cochran continues gleefully, "and dig the wiggle of his secret giggle when an American buys the art and hangs it in his house. Someone who can read the language will eventually visit and reveal the secret and the obscene word-writer will have avenged his country for us having dropped the bomb."

"Stop it," I yell. "You're throwing a paranoid slant on things. The streets are already full of enough scurrying, diabolic, conspiring, devious maniacs running to catch trains, delivering goods and signing contracts."

"Right, it's up to us to foil them."

"I'm with you."

The cab bangs into the curb. Cochran pays the driver. I get out in the pouring rain and survey the scene.

Are the citizens really staring accusingly at our pallid skin, our dark hair and the pink on our flushed cheeks? I tuck in my chin, keep my arms close to my sides and mince-step down the sidewalk, avoiding contact. But not Cochran, the crazy bull Yank.

Swinging his arms and splashing through the puddles, he snarls out the side of his mouth, "Don't let these little bastards intimidate you. They'll give you the biotah fish eye the minute you think that you're responsible for their misery."

Too wet to argue, I lead the way into the 500 Club, patronized by officers only, and owned by T. Harry, a Japanese in honorably good standing with police; six, eight years running the same place, no trouble. Sign says drinks two hundred yen—sixty cents, stateside prices. Girls clean dependable Jo-Sans with up-to-date hospital cards, no danger from infection like street creeps hanging around Four Corners or MTO.

Cochran slaps the bar and bellows across the room in his lusty, bossy profundo voice, "Hey, innkeeper, bring a *combat* warrior a drink."

Cochran looks like hell, disheveled and soaking wet. I look as bad, but not so imposing, and I'm determined to make up for Cochran's loutishness with silver-tongued loquacity, although my not-so-svelte clothes are lacking the necessary clout.

"Yes, my man," I say to the bartender, "a soothing libation, if you please."

The bar is an east-west rendezvous, a cocktail lounge you'd find in San Francisco, Dallas or New Orleans, with a teak bar, knee-high formica-topped tables and soft low chairs. A longhair combo sings Del Shannon lyrics: *As I walk along I wonder what went wrong, with our love, a love that was so strong.*

"Drinks, bartender!" Cochran yells again, thumbing his nose at my attempt to placate the guy. "Two thirsty men here!"

He's decidedly feisty, not acting like the lowly helicopter pilot that jet jocks normally hold in flying contempt. Three of the superior beings stand at the bar, peer sideways at us, glitters of anger from behind their aviator glasses, burr heads bristling. Mouths muttering. "You don't think you low and slow chop-chops gonna shore up Diem's regime do you? The Prez better get some heat into this fray, and that's us, Jack!"

Cochran and I give them the razzberry. We are, after all, the ones flying nine-piston, egg-beating, hole-drilling troop and cargo platforms into heavy-fire LZs. Eat rotor wash, stovepipe jockeys. The jet pilots turn their backs, ignore these cretins. They down their drinks and leave in search of a better place, where they can be properly appreciated.

And as I still walk on, I think of the things we've done together, while our hearts were young.

"Hey, innkeeper, bring the drinks over here," Cochran bellows again. He leads the way to a table.

The bartender pours a smidgeon of water into a glass half full of scotch and hands it to a misshapen American in a rumpled business suit, with dark war-zone bags under his eyes and a beachhead spare tire around his middle. Spare Tire takes a swig and mutters, "Aw them fucking pilots, been in Vietnam, got shot at, think they're the only heroes in the world. Well, I'll tell you something. They should have been at Mama Toko's place in Pusan the night the MPs busted the joint when we was ganging up on the ROKS and the MPs beat Hogan across the kidneys with their night sticks and he threw up all over the MPs' starched khaki tunics. Got the shit kicked out of us. There was some combat for yah."

A tall, stoop-shouldered American with horn-rimmed glasses dangling on the end of a hook-opener nose winces at the story. He sidles past Spare Tire and looks at us sideways through the horns, then over the rims. He coughs. His huge Adam's apple bobs up and down like a cork float.

"Ah, pardon me" he says. "I couldn't help but overhear. Is it true you're stationed in Vietnam?"

Cochran glances at me. I shrug. Go for it.

"Look at my hands," Cochran says. "Shaking like a rotor blade out of track. You *did* say you're buying?"

"Yeah, sure." The string bean waves vaguely at the bartender. "It's rough there, huh?"

"I'll say rough. You ever lie in bed at night, feel something rustling in your gear, shrug it off as a rat or varmint, then turn on your flashlight and spotlight a sneaky Pete infiltrating the camp and stabbing the boys in their sleep?"

The string bean's face pales. My turn. I rise from my chair.

"We're looking down the barrels of their twenty mike-mikes, mortars explode over our heads, choppers crash like rocks, but we bore on in, those bastards can't stop us. We overwhelm them with our strength, outmaneuver them with our equipment, outfox them with our smarts, destroy them with our superior firepower—"

"—and it's rough, man, rough," Cochran interrupts. "Nerves are frayed."

The tall stranger nods. "The reason I'm concerned is I've got orders to Vietnam. Not as a combatant. I'm a doctor. Doctor Hollenden, and I feel this is a grave mistake. Do you have to carry pistols all the time?"

"Everywhere. Didn't I tell you about the infiltrators?"

"But I've never fired a pistol before."

Cochran shakes his head resignedly. "Time you learned, Doc. Time you learned. Remember, it's you or them."

"Yeah," Spare Tire intones. "You or them. First one to the bar wins."

I'm a-walkin' in the rain, tears are fallin' and I feel the pain, wishin' you were here by me, to end this misery.

Cochran lets it slide, our drinks have arrived. We slug them down and signal for another round. Cochran smiles at a plump, bleached blond. She springs onto his lap. Her flowery, off-the-shoulder dress barely covers her abundant breasts. Twin cheeks burst the seams of the filmy material clinging to her rear.

"My name Yaeko-Sue," the fulsome wench says with a slight lisp. Hints of expectations to come. Doc Hollenden falls into a chair. Sucks his glass dry. Waves for another. I raise my finger, *me too*. Yaeko-Sue bangs Cochran on the arms and chest. She thinks he's insulting her when he laughs at her awkward English. He gives her a big slurping kiss. She shrieks and slaps his face, a love tap. The place and pace have picked up. Jo-Sans cuddle their men. Busy gals, talking, sipping cokes and orange drinks, you like? Oh sure, me like. Most of the drink money goes to T. Harry, a smidgeon to the girl. If I no got a yen for her, I no pay the yen for her. Tough way to make a living.

Cochran's discovered a new nub to rub. A well-dressed gent, native businessman from the looks of him. He sits at the bar and stares at Cochran in gold-toothed amusement. Cochran catches him and smiles back.

"What say, pard?" Cochran calls across the room. "Have a drink? On me? No speakee. Tough shittee."

"On the contrary," the gent replies in excellent English. "I'd be delighted."

Cochran gives a big guffaw. "All *right!*" he bellows. "Thought you didn't catch me there."

"Yes, I understood quite clearly. I find a great deal of pleasure in talking to the different American types I encounter."

"I bet," says Cochran. He takes a big swig and bangs his glass on the table. "So what do you think of these American types?"

"I enjoy them. They are very interesting. It's a good thing, I think, that they come here and see a little of the fear and terror they have unleashed on the world."

The gent smiles and sips his drink. He casually allows his sleeve to fall, exposing his forearm, scarred from the wrist to the elbow.

"What do you think of our city?" he asks Cochran.

"Oh, I don't know. We've only seen this area and that's mighty impressive."

"You think so?" the gent says, smiling.

"Yeah, it's a real shithole, just what you'd expect after your damn fool sneak attack that kicked off the last big war."

I sit up straight. Now it's coming, right here, right now, the big bang theory brought to life, exploding in the bar, blown up, blown out like the movie, *Hiroshima Mon Amour*, lovers in bed intercut with shots of Fat Man exploding. But no, everyone remains calm, inscrutably so.

"And what do you do, my friend?" the gent asks, sweet as a budding rose.

Cochran tosses back his drink. "I fly B-29s, friend."

The gent backhands his glass and sends it flying across the bar. It crashes against the back shelf and smashes into tinkling shards. The bartender sighs and picks up his rag.

And I wonder— why, why she ran away, yes, and I wonder, where she will stay, my little runaway.

Cochran smiles warmly at Yaeko-Sue and nuzzles her cheek. Yaeko-Sue shrieks and smacks Cochran two hard hits on the chest.

"You no scrape me you ape."

"That's Gorilla, not ape." He stands up and Yaeko-Sue falls on the floor. Her scream is louder than her shriek.

"Now what?" a smooth voice interjects.

The hush that follows would give credance to the silence at the bottom of a three-thousand-foot mine.

A rotund, butter-melting, smiling man, slick-haired and dressed impeccably in a three-piece, pin-striped suit, bows to the room. None other than the famous T. Harry. What an honor. The king descended from his throne to mingle with the masses.

Yaeko-Sue blushes and genuflects like a nun blessed by a priest. In this joint his dick would be the appropriate tool. Dewy drops of pre-come lubricant splashing the faithful's upturned face. Forget that. This is for real.

Cochran's poised. I'm ready. Yaeko-Sue, trembling like a leaf in a timorous breeze, is what keeps us from exploding. She's on the hot spot and not us. Cochran goes conciliatory.

"It was off the plane and straight to the club," he says, rubbing his whiskers. "So naturally we're a bit on the ripe side. No harm intended."

"And none taken," T. Harry replies unctiously. "You'll accept my offer of a round of drinks? On the house, of course. A small appreciation for the great sacrifice you are making in that ugly affair down south."

Cochran gives him the raised eyebrow. I leap into the breach.

"To be sure, oh gracious benevolent host with the most. A thousand haiku of gratitude graffitied on subway walls all over Tokyo," bowing and dipping in blatant obeisance. Don't wanna play ball with T-Harry, too strong, immovable, steel-hard, you'd get the bat up the old ass. No no, forget that.

T. Harry makes a small bow and glides silently to the bar.

"Nicely done," Cochran tells me, "but I wouldn't make a habit out of it, if I were you. You may be in the Orient but seems to me you're not *doing* the Orient. Keeps you out of trouble maybe, but you shouldn't go against your natural desires."

"Don't you be lecturing me, wiseass. I'm the one got us out of that little jam, not you."

"So true. But now that we've been blessed and sanctified by the high muckity-muck, let's get down to business."

He's determined to fill the hourglass with as much of himself as he can, laying his vulnerability lovingly on the line until we get back on the plane and return to Vietnam. Doc Hollenden, still going full bore, has been taken in tow by Yaeko-Sue.

"Plenty more where she came from," Cochran orates magnaminously. "You know the Ko birds. You can hear their trilling calls for miles. There's Heroko, Teroko, Yosuko, Heidiko, and all the rest of the Ko family that comes under fire when the R and R boys go Ko hunting. Yas," he continues, downing his scotch rocket. "It's a sport made famous on world-wide TV. You've seen it on Sunday afternoons, heard the wild, lingering sound of the Ko bird floating over the wind-rustled habu grass: 'Hey, Yank, you buy me a drink?'"

Yaeko-Sue punches him soundly. Doc Hollenden grins vapidly and drapes his arm across Yaeko's back. I signal for another round. Yaeko swills two quick watery drinks in a swirl of giggles. She's laughing so hard she has trouble stuffing the drink receipts down the front of her dress and Cochran sticks in his hand to help her out. She dissolves in a rubbery welter of shrieks and guffaws. The entire Ko flock chirrups to her side.

At the far end of the bar, T. Harry leans over the bar, seemingly unconcerned, talking in a low voice to the scar-armed businessman. From the looks of his glare, Scar Arm's animosity hasn't abated. Might be a good time to blow this hole, I'm thinking. Cochran claps me on the shoulder.

"We're going to the beach. Yaeko-Sue knows a private spot where officers can let down their hair, be themselves, not like the uptight squares you see around here. Har har. Grab you a girl."

"Forget it. I'll go stag."

"None of that, me boy. Tonight it's stud, not stag."

He drags me to a booth where Spare Tire, pretty much looped into insensibility, is sitting with a Ko girl. Spare Tire waves a fancy zippo lighter somewhere near the vicinity of the girl's face. She dips and bobs, trying to get her cigarette to coincide with the lighter.

"May I?" Cochran asks. He plucks the lighter out of Spare Tire's hand. "Nice piece of hardware."

"Looks like a miniature flashlight," I say.

"No, it's a mental detector." He sticks it next to my temple. "Too bad. All blank. Nothing there."

"Let me see that thing." I grab it out of his hand and peer closely. Light blue. Push button. I shake it. "No wonder you didn't get a reading. It's out of batteries." I throw it back. He catches it on the fly. "We'll see about that." Holds it to his temple. A sheet of flame courses across his scalp. The girls scream. His hair curls and fizzles. I douse the fire with my drink. Smoke fills the booth. Cochran holds the still-lit lighter under the Ko girl's cigarette. She jumps back and falls out of the booth. Cochran shakes his head in sympathy. Flakes of hair fall to the floor.

"Oh well, can't win them all. Better she quit smoking anyhow."

"Shay, tha's pretty good," Spare Tire says. "Le's see you do it again."

"Some other time, Pop."

Yaeko-Sue helps the girl up, talking rapidly in her ear. Then Yaeko-Sue turns to me. "You in luck. This is Heroko-Betty. She will give up all nighter at Tokyo hotel with this drunk man to go for moonlight swim with you."

Heroko-Betty is as thin as a willowy reed. Decked out head to toe in skintight leather. Short raven hair. Lips a crimson smear. Skin like a white shroud. She looks at me demurely.

"You not believe Heroko-Betty, but I was married to American jet jock killed in plane crash. I have twelve-year-old son lives with my mama and papa in Osaka. 500 Club help me save money to buy dress shop. Three days a week I take sewing lessons and in only two years can look for my shop."

She droops languid eyes.

Cochran prods me from behind. "Can the gab. Let's make it."

Spare Tire lurches to his feet. "Hey! Where you think you're going?"

"No time to talk, Pop."

We head for the door. Scar Arm barrels across the room to cut us off and we arrive at the door in a dead heat. Scar Arm grabs Heroko-Betty by the wrist and it turns into a tug of war, me pulling from one side, Scar Arm from the other. Cochran and Yaeko-Sue throw their weight into the fray and we pull Scar Arm out on the sidewalk. He holds on grimly.

"I put plenty money in this club," he shouts at Heroko-Betty. "You work for T. Harry and me. You owe us many years yet."

Cochran flags down a taxi.

"If you not come back, you through. Dogs will lick your bones in gutter."

The door booms open and Doc Hollenden flies out. He bangs into Scar Arm and knocks him into the gutter. Heroko-Betty's sleeve goes with him. She screams and lunges for it but I pull her back.

T. Harry stands at the open door, his great bulk silhouetted in the light.

"You western barbarians act like street creeps, you can join your street creep friends. Hey, where you girls think you're going?"

The taxi sprays a sheet of water across the front of T. Harry's seven hundred dollar suit. Cochran opens the door and we pile in with the girls.

"*Sayonara* the fuck out of here," Cochran yells at the driver.

Spare Tire staggers out the door. "Hey! Wait for me." He lurches and falls into T. Harry's back.

"Aw, shorry 'bout that," Spare Tire mutters, shuffling around him.

T. Harry and Scar Arm go after Spare Tire who backpedals frantically, a losing effort because he's too snockered to stay on the sidewalk. He veers into the street.

"Turn around. *Muy pronto*," I yell at the taxi driver.

The taxi does a one-eighty. T. Harry and Scar Arm catch up with Spare Tire, drag him up against the side of a building and start pounding him. Cochran jumps out of the taxi and slams the gangsters' heads into the building. Spare Tire covers his eyes.

"I'll pay for the drinks, honest."

Cochran drags him to the taxi and pushes him in. He lands in the girls' laps.

"Oh God. I've died and woke up in heaven."

Cochran jumps in the front seat next to me and the taxi spins away.

"Escaped by the four skins of our teeth that time," Cochran says. "You cop a bottle, Yaeko-Sue?"

She pulls a fifth from beneath her skirt. Cochran gulps down a slug and passes the bottle around. Spare Tire can't believe his luck. First he thought Cochran and I made a fool out of him with the mental detector, then he got fleeced out of his Ko girl, and after that got beat up by the two gangsters, but now, in a miraculous turnaround, he's lying in the laps of two lovely Ko girls, and drinking Old Overholt whiskey straight from the bottle. Sitting next to them, Doc Hollenden nods to the music blaring over the taxi radio and, up front, Cochran and I stare through the windshield at the brightly lit streeets that turn into dark shadows as we zoom out of town.

Cochran looks like a demented madman with his flaming red face and hair charred from his temple to the top of his head. In the back seat Heroko-Betty laments the loss of her leather sleeve, and her job at the 500 Club.

"Don't you fret about that," Spare Tire tells her. "I'll get you the material you need to fix your jacket. You say you sewed that outfit yourself?"

She brightens. "Oh yes. Some day Heroko-Betty buy a dress shop and sell clothes she makes." Her face falls. "Soon as she save enough money." Tears spring to her eyes at the thought of her hopeless dream.

"Those crooks won't ever let you leave, honey. They tie you up like a sharecropper. You'll never make enough to get out of debt to the company store. But don't worry about that now. You got me on the case and I'll—"

The taxi lurches to a stop, dumping Spare Tire and the girls and the Doc onto the floor. The driver turns with a happy smile.

"Beach right here."

A family is camped on the sand. Tents made of blankets hang on ropes, and the kids are asleep inside. The old folks sitting outside at a low table are playing what looks like a combination of mah-jong, dominoes, monopoly, chinese checkers and go.

I wander to the water's edge and swish my feet in the ocean. Tiny creatures glow and flicker in the phosphoresent wake. Heroko-Betty grabs me from behind and hugs me tight. Not so hard, baby, I no feel so good. She lets go and claps her hands. What now?

Oh, good, just what we need. Cochran has bought a case of Asahi beer from the mah jong family. He plops the case on the sand and passes out bottles.

"They were willing to part with the beer for windfall profits. Now who do you suppose got the windfall, them or us?"

Doc Hollenden gulps happily. I fall on my back. Heroko-Betty pours beer on my face and licks it off with a slick puppy tongue. She fumbles at my clothes. I kick and splash. She wraps her spidery arms around me. The ocean roars. Salty tears flood my eyes. Heroko-Betty arches her back and squeezes me from root to tip, drawing a long tight knot out of my chest down through my gut and out my dick like a double ought wad from a ten-guage water-buffalo gun blowing sparklets into the black Japanese sky, goodbye you, *nos vemos más tarde.* I fall into a peaceful sleep. Two seals bark and laugh and roll in the surf. Chinese checkers race across the sky. Dominoes *clack clack* like wooden shoes walking on the top of my head. Water swirls around my legs.

I groan and try to sit up, but a heavy weight holds me down. Heroko-Betty is passed out on my chest. The seals are Yaeko-Sue and Cochran wrapped tightly together. Doc Hollenden sleeps with his head across their legs. Spare Tire slouches over the case of beer. Empty bottles clank in the surf. The taxi honks. The supply plane to Soc Trang is waiting. I crawl out from under Heroko-Betty and poke the seals.

"Let's go."

We stagger to the taxi. There's enough beer left to drown the barking dog that bit so bad the night before and it looks like we'll survive the ride. Suddenly the taxi skids sideways across the road. A big Mercedes sits crossways, blocking our way. The band members from the 500 Club form a line in front of the car. T. Harry and Scar Arm stand at the ends of the row, hulking punctuation marks in their ruined business suits.

"Uh, oh," Cochran says. "This is going to call for some creative Zen thinking. Anyone got any ideas?"

"Retreat," Doc Hollenden says. "The quality of a constructive withdrawal is not strained."

"Retreat, hell," I say. "Facing the Hammer's wrath if we don't make it back to the base on time will be worse than anything these creeps can dish out. Crash on through."

The driver's eyes widen.

"Oh no. Taxi not mine. Have to pay if it wrecked."

Spare Tire waves his wallet. "Buy them off."

Cochran rubs his head. Flakes of burned hair come off in his hand. "Not a bad idea," he says.

Cochran takes out his pocket knife and starts cutting up the taxi driver's phone book. The girls keen like mourning widows, in this case their own funeral. Ours too, probably. Forget that.

Cochran steps out of the taxi.

"Okay, okay, you win," he yells. "Take all our money." He holds up a big handful of cut up phone book pages with real money on top. "We'll just skeedaddle on out of here."

He hops in the taxi. The driver turns the car around and burns out, back toward the beach. Cochran holds the money out the window and lets the bills peel off into the wind.

"Get them," T. Harry yells.

The band members race forward, stomp on the bogus money, grab the ones fluttering in the wind, so intent on getting them they don't notice the Doc and me hiding in the bushes. The Doc is shaking like a dog shitting peach pits. T. Harry and Scar Arm scuttle past, exhorting the band members. "After them! We'll get their money and them, too. They owe us."

I lead the Doc along the bank of a ditch that parallels the road.

"Quit your moaning and start paying attention," I tell him. "This is your Vietnam snooping and pooping training."

"Pooping is right." Turds and garbage float on top of the water. The Doc shudders. "To think of it. Dying before I even get to that god-forsaken country. What an ignoble end. And me a professional man."

"Hush, we're there."

I peek over the edge of the ditch. The car is pointed toward the water. The Doc and I crawl up to the car and, just as we hoped, they didn't bother to lock up. I open the driver's door and slip the gear shift into neutral and release the hand brake. The last thing I do before we give the car a shove is tighten the Doc's necktie around the horn button so that as the car begins its descent down the incline, the horn is blaring.

Just as the 500 Club gang realizes what's happening and stops chasing the phony-baloney money to come rescue the car, the taxi roars over the hill. Cochran leans out the window.

"Chopper pilots, not B-29 pilots, *NYYYAAAAHHHH.*"

Doc Hollenden and I jump in the taxi and we skid around the rear of the Mercedes ahead of the gang band members rushing up to stop it from going in the ditch. T. Harry and Scar Arm arrive in time to see the car settle in a welter of bubbles.

"Guess if I hadn't left the door open it might have floated."

Cochran slaps me on the back. "Congratulations, my boy. Another fine example of your dry Texas wit."

"Never mind that. We got enough money left to pay the taxi?"

Spare Tire holds up a wad of bills and cackles delightedly. His eyes are black and his nose broken, his lips caked with blood.

"Man, this beats anything I ever saw in Korea. Even Mama Toko's. I got to hand it to you Gyrenes. You know how to have fun. Say, ladies, what are you crying about? It's all over."

"Maybe for you, but not us," Yaeko-Sue sobs. "You will go away but we have to stay. They will beat us and make us work on Four Corners with street creeps. Now we will never get enough money to get free."

"Hey, didn't I say I'd take care of you? You'll be making more dough than you'd ever get slaving for those bastards. I'm taking you gals to Kyoto and setting you up in that dress shop. Heroko-Betty, you can design and sew. Yaeko-Sue, you can be the sales lady. What do you say to that?"

"What about my little boy?" Heroko-Betty asks. "Can he live there, too?"

"Sure as you're sitting on your sugar daddy's lap. I know just the place. Got an apartment upstairs and another in back. It'll work out just fine."

The girls bounce up and down on Spare Tire, hugging and kissing him, kicking Doc Hollenden in their glee.

"Hey, the glasses. Watch out for the glasses."

Cochran gives me a thumbs up.

"Start your engines," he growls. "This launch is a go."

We leave Spare Tire and the girls waving goodbye from the taxi, and carry Doc aboard the plane. The rear door whooshes closed, the engines roar and a sickening tug presses us into the thin canvas seats. We break out on top and level off, props throbbing in a broken beat until the pilot finds the right synch and the throb settles to a lulling hum.

Cochran's asleep at last, chin bouncing on his chest. Doc Hollenden jerks like a puppy dreaming about squirrels. Too bad he left his gear behind. *Bueno, no importa.* They can ship it to him later. Nothing to do now but sleep it off. Those gangsters were real bastards. Forget them. The memories break into fragments. Little droplets joining with the great big sea.

8. Loss of Concern

It's not just my shoulder, Doc . . . my head hurts like hell . . . worse than any hangover . . . Daddy said there's no hangover like a hangover from drinking jungle juice . . . they made their own in New Guinea . . . distilled whatever fruit they could find and then soaked more fruit in the juice and then drank the mess . . . no habanero hot sauce like at home but that jungle juice did the trick . . . turned everything all cattywampus . . . sent funny signals to my brain . . . write with your tongue . . . read with your ears . . . listen with your eyes . . . please your toes . . . and it made the little kids sorting through the trash and singing "Pistol Packing Mama" sound like the heavenly choir . . . but you don't want to hear that noise the next morning . . . not when it's ringing like church bells in your head . . . I know it's all in my head, Doc . . . same thing your predecessor told me when I described the curly edges I saw on the building roofs after he gave me an opium pill . . . that was Doctor Eversham . . . you never met the man . . . they sent him home after discovering a discrepancy in the dispensary . . . too many opium pills were unaccounted for . . . I don't mean to be talking out of school here, Doc . . . forget the pills . . . I need a shot and not any jungle juice nor that Tennessee Jack Daniels, neither . . . hit me with the real thing . . . put me under, Doc . . .

Leaving Doc Hollenden asleep in the supply plane, Cochran and I go to our tent and change into flight gear. We're expecting an angry welcome when we walk into the ready room but the poker fiasco is buried in the turmoil caused by the rifle shot we heard in the enlisted men's area the night we flew to Japan. Corporal Randolph, one of the mechs, killed himself, and all the talk's on Randolph, why'd he do it, was it an accident, or was he under some kind of mental strain no one knew about?

Captain Rajah Beamus, the ops officer, begins the meeting before the Hammer arrives. "This is for the benefit of you gentlemen who have never been overseas before. You're going to see things and do things that would never occur back in the States. The important thing to remember is that what a man does here is his own business and is not to be discussed with others, and that includes what you say in letters to your wives."

"Uh-oh," Cochran says out of the corner of his mouth, "sounds like the old lecture on the loss of concern for the hallowedness and sanctity of marriage."

"We know now that Corporal Randolph killed himself after getting a Dear John letter from his wife. It didn't help that he was a moody man, given to brooding."

"As opposed to breeding," Cochran says, *sotto voce.* Not *sotto* enough.

"That's enough, Lieutenant. The last time I was overseas there was a married officer in the squadron who ranched in town with a local woman. One of the other officers wrote a letter to his wife telling her about the affair. The word was passed among the wives, and the rancher's wife, in on the gossip train, found out what was going on. She in turn wrote a very nasty letter to her husband and at the end of the tour the officer was faced with the prospect of a divorce."

"What are we supposed to do?" Cochran interrupts. "These abominable conditions are ripe for sexual explosions. There's no relief nowhere. I woke up this morning with a horrendous hard-on, one of those jack lever things. Push it down and it raises you off your feet. I knew if I so much as touched it, it would go off."

He hesitates a beat.

"So I touched it."

The pilots hoot and slap their legs.

Rajah Beamus glares. "Knock it off. This is serious. One more word out of you, Cochran, and you'll pull duty officer for a week. Now hear this. The officer who got the letter from his wife saying she knew about his overseas affair, that officer went to his Commanding Officer and complained about the harm the original letter-writer was doing. The C.O. called in the Puritan letter-writer and gave him the ass chewing of his life, warned him never to mention another squadron officer in any more letters home. Any questions?"

Ben-San, forever the class clown, makes a phoney yawn. Mouth gaping wide, he releases a long drawn-out moan, taken up quickly by the other pilots.

"I've got a question," I yell through the moaning. "What happened to that man? That dastardly letter-writer? Did his wife divorce him, too?"

"I have no idea, Lieutenant. I don't pry into other people's lives."

"Does this mean a man can't trust his wife to keep the things he tells her to herself?" Rob Jacobs asks.

"My advice is to not to tell wives anything about other men's affairs."

"Then do you recommend setting up a snake ranch and not saying anything about it?"

"I'm implying nothing of the sort, Lieutenant."

"A stiff dick has no conscience," Ben-San yells.

"Any port in a storm," Cochran bellows, setting the pilots off.

"Porthole." Followed by a fake laugh, *snorfglffff, gitchhhh, belly itches.*

"As you were, gentlemen!"

Too late. The dam is breached. What's he expect, lecturing us like we're college fraternity numbnuts?

"If one of us should happen to write the kind of letter you mentioned, about one of the married men . . ." Cochran says, ". . . then the nasty letter that comes back, the impending divorce. Are we to, ah, assume that the officer concerned . . ." black eyebrows rise up and down . . . "the one who caused the mess, would he be given the same treatment by our Commanding Officer, the treatment you mentioned, the royal ass chewing?"

"That's up to the C.O."

Before another fake laugh can erupt, Emmett stands up.

"Knock off the shit. It's okay to do your banging. Hell, everyone knows a man will have his nooky, but do it away from the squadron, for Christ's sakes. You can't trust anybody. It might be your bunkmate finking on you."

"Stick by your man," Ben-San sings.

"Don't pull that shit on me," Rob Jacobs calls.

"Kiss me on the way out," yells another pilot.

Fake laughs and joke sneezes go off simultaneously. *Har har no time off. Kachooie hog grease*. When they die down, Ben-San says, "Hey, if you're horny as a goat then go ahead and bang your brains out. Then admit it. Who cares if someone finks."

"You're forgetting the code," Cochran says. "You either got to be sneaky or you got to be pure. There's no common ground of good sense anywhere between. When have you ever heard a man admit he's a lecher, boozer, gambler and mean-tailed bastard? Especially to the woman he's tied on to for life."

"What about you?' Ben-San shoots back at him.

"Me?" Cochran asks. "I'm not considering marriage."

"I never told anyone this," Rob Jacobs says, "but when we first got here I had a rash on my pecker. I powdered it, aired it out, scrubbed it with dial soap every night in the showers, kept after it, and now I've got it licked. Hasn't come back for three weeks."

"Incredible," Cochran says. "There's a lot of space between my dong and my feet, but I'll give your treatment a try." He grabs a can of foot powder off the floor and pours it down the front of his flight suit.

"I've got a confession of my own," he says, rubbing his crotch. "Doris Day climbed into bed with me last night."

"Doris Day," Ben-San says. "I thought she was a professional virgin."

"Not last night she wasn't. Blowee, all over the sheet and my skivvies. It was a mess, but well worth it."

The pilots cheer and begin singing:

Rooty toot toot, rooty toot toot.
We're the boys from the institute.
We don't drink and we don't screw.
And we don't go with girls who do.
Nor fuck, nor fuck, nor fuck you!

Everyone's on their feet, stomping on the wood floor.

"Short arm inspection!"
"Whip 'em out!"
"Skin 'em back!"
"Clean 'em off!"

"Smegma smegma, raw raw raw," everyone yells, followed by a mass explosion of joke sneezes and fake laughs morphing into tongue thrashings of idiotic phraseology.

The Hammer enters the ready room tent, followed by the X.O., Major Lurnt.

"Attenhut!" Captain Beamus orders.

We snap to attention. The Hammer gives us a curious look.

"As you were, men."

He takes his place at the head of the tent, looks us over, and begins.

"Gentlemen, end of the month action reports are in and they indicate the Army helicopter squadron flying those ancient H-21 Flying Bananas have logged more sorties than us. I don't know if they are counting two-minute check flights and on-ramp run-ups as sorties or not, but this is an unacceptable situation. The Army will not, cannot, log more sorties than us."

He pauses and lets it sink in. We sit, waiting expectantly, pencils poised over our kneeboards.

"I've decided every flight we make will count as a sortie. Even instrument hops, which we will be starting today and continuing until everyone is caught up on their yearly requirements. Of course we will also be flying our regular support missions."

He turns to confer with the admin officer. I gather up my flight gear and head for the flight line. It's my turn in the barrel. I'm scheduled to fly with the Hammer. An instrument hop, no big deal, but I'm *muy nervioso.*

The pre-flight and pre-start checks are uneventful. Maybe it will be a pleasant enough hop after all. The Hammer presses the starter and flips on the mags. The starter grinds and as the Hammer fingers the primer, the engine coughs, catches, sputters and rumbles unevenly. The Hammer jockeys the throttle and nods his head. Interpreting the nod to mean he is ready, I ram the mixture handle forward. The RPM gauge zings through 2500 turns before the Hammer can back off the throttle. The engine sputters, then settles to an even roar. The Hammer glowers at me.

"What in god-forsaking hell did you do that for?"

I yearn to turn down the intercom volume, but respond clearly. "You nodded your head, sir. I thought you were signaling for the mixture."

Doubt dances in his eyes. "Maybe I did. I don't remember it. But maybe I did."

The fire in my gut dies to a respectable ember.

"Sorry about that, Huckelbee. I've got a lot on my mind."

He checks the instruments and fumbles with the warning lights. Overcome by a flash of compassion that neutralizes my good sense, I say, "Hell, sir, that's all right. I was just kidding anyway. You didn't really nod your head."

I must have lost mine.

"What? WHAT?"

The Hammer's face threatens to pop out of his helmet. His cheeks bulge against the sides of the plastic liner, his eyes are red-veined and distended.

"No. No sir . . ." I stammer. "I was joking, sir . . . only joking . . . you *really did* nod . . ."

"Out."

His arm reaches toward me like a long thin rapier in a nightmare death-dream, his finger extended, pointed at my chest.

"Out. Out of my plane. Out before I . . ."

I jump from the cockpit. My helmet rips the radio cords loose. I fall to the apron and run for the line shack, with the crew chiefs guffawing in my wake. An ignominious show but worth the embarrassment, considering I don't have to fly with the Hammer, flight schedule be damned.

"Send Warrant Officer Hastings out here," The Hammer yells after me.

Warrant Officer Chuck "Cool Beans" Hastings, taciturn, cigarette in the corner of his mouth, has been in the Marine Corps longer than anyone else in the squadron. As an enlisted aircraft technician at the tail end of World War Two he had to fly the planes when they were short of pilots so they made him a Warrant Officer and sent him to flight school. After flying fixed wings in Korea he transitioned to helicopters. He's seen it all—unflappable.

I go in the line shack and pass on the message, then get out of there. Walking to the ready room tent I spot an old, scraggly bearded Vietnamese laborer fishing around in a metal trash container. I nod and bow and he continues to root.

A stack of books and pamphlets are piled on the ground. I lift one and check the title: "Tactics Of Marine Corps Helicopter Operations." I check out the rest of the pile and then look inside the trash bin. Someone threw away his correspondence texts from the Marine Corps Institute. This could be a problem. Those books and pamphlets are outdated and worthless to us, but still. . . . I can see it now, *smuggled out of camp to a VC area, passed on up the line, Ho Chi Minh's eyes light up . . . this is top stuff, send message to old man, keep rooting in the trash . . .*

I hustle on over to the ready room tent and tell Captain Beamus. He goes out of his gourd . . . I picture him crazed, *rises out of his chair like a circus monkey performing for a peanut, three flips, two circles, then falls back on the ground, froth billowing around his mouth. . . .* He comes back in focus and says, "Who? Where? Take me to him."

He grabs my arm and hustles me outside, eyeing each worker like he's ready to shoot him on suspicion of dried fish farts.

"That one?" he says. "That one? That squinty-eyed bearded one? I've suspected *him* for weeks."

The Rajah is on the old fellow like a weasel on a rat, and the only thing the poor guy can do in defense is point at me, babble incoherently and nod his head, trying to signify I gave him permission to keep the books. I'm shaking my head, *no, no,* that's not the way it happened. Captain Beamus doesn't pay any attention to either one of us. Taking anything from the trash is a heinous offense. One that must be punished by the most fearsome weapon in the arsenal of the intelligence agent based on foreign shores—interrogation.

Captain Beamus drags the old man by his scraggly beard to the interpreter to uncover his ulterior reasons for taking the books.

I follow at a slow pace and, when they round the corner of the tents, I slip inside the camp reefer and pick up two cases of beer, happy to let the interrogation proceed without me.

Dos condenación, if Doc Hollenden doesn't spot me with the beer. The Doc, somewhat recovered from our Tokyo adventure, is making a valiant effort to be a responsible flight surgeon to make up for when he staggered, drunken and bleery-eyed, off the plane and an enlisted man had asked, "What in the hell is that?" and another had replied, "I don't know but it sure ain't no *Marine*."

"Lay off that alcohol, Huckelbee," he says, not realizing the irony of the statement, "you need a break to recuperate from your trip to Japan."

Yes, I nod, continuing on. "Don't you no nevermind, Doc, nothing to get excited about, the beer will calm my nerves, settle my stomach."

I drop the beer on the tent porch and pop a cap. The breeze rustles the tent flap and a cool wind riffles across my shoulders. On the other side of the path Vietnamese workers toil like bugs, digging and shoveling, mixing mortar; laying bricks and raising timbers. One floor and one wall at a time the buildings go up and as soon as they are finished we will exchange places with the Army. Their chopper squadron will be based here in the delta and ours up north in the mountains. Reason being those underpowered Army H-21 Flying Bananas—even though they have the same engine as our choppers—can't hack the higher altitudes along the demarcation line. But no tents for the Army pilots. They will live in brick buildings with running water and flush toilets.

Cochran and Ben-San, emulating the Vietnamese workers, are digging a drainage ditch in front of our tent, figuring they can divert the water that continually threatens to flood our quarters. They burrow a tunnel under the porch, scooping the dirt out with their hands, working from opposite sides.

Ben-San reaches under and grabs Cochran's finger.

"I've got some kind of creepy worm," he says. "Yack! It's pulling me under."

Cochran pulls until Ben-San's shoulder is jammed against the porch.

"That's good. That's good," Ben-San croaks. "I quit. We don't have to dig any farther."

Cochran turns him loose and Ben-San gets up and brushes the mud off his pants. Cochran looks over at the Army building construction. "Dig that."

Two Vietnamese workers are lined up one behind the other, swinging their picks. White bandannas circle their heads. Their backs are bare and the picks rise and fall in synchronized motion . . . like the beaks of primeval birds. . . *thunk!* . . . the picks hit and the pattern is destroyed as they stroke out of turn. Another worker sneaks around the side of the building and picks up a bamboo pipe. He takes a deep drag, puts the pipe down and goes back to work. Every few minutes another worker comes over and takes a drag.

"What do you think, Mike?" I ask Cochran.

"Hard to tell."

We watch a while longer, Cochran twitchy in his chair.

"I can't stand it," says Cochran. "I'm going to find out."

He walks over to the building and squats down. He points to the bamboo. "How about me? Little toke, huh?"

The worker hands over the homemade pipe, the bowl embedded halfway up the bamboo stem. Cochran wraps his lips around the end and takes a deep drag. He holds it in, then slowly lets it out, a thoughtful expression on his face.

The Vietnamese foreman comes up behind him.

"Not for Americans, " he says to Cochran, shaking his head. "Very strong."

Cochran nods and hands him the pipe then returns to the tent.

"Well?" I ask him. "Did you complain?"

"Complain? About what?"

"About them loafing."

"Loafing? Who gives a shit if they're loafing? I wanted to try out their smoke. Jesus, it was awful. I had a hell of a time keeping from gagging. I thought maybe . . . they just *might* be . . ."

He looks at me.

"What? Spies."

"No, not spies. Just smoking some god-awful tobacco."

A few minutes later the workers pick up their tools and leave. The PX opens and the line snakes inside. In an hour the movie will crank up in the hangar. *Guns of Navaronne*. We've already seen it twice. We go to chow and return to the porch for a nightcap. A friendly procession of events. Although a Vietnamese outpost might be overrun twenty miles away, it seems far removed from our slapadaisical porchfront where we lounge like lazy *braceros* sprawled across ammo cans and rickety-ass chairs.

I have the night duty. I'm supposed to sleep in the ready room tent in order to protect the maps and briefing notes from infiltrators, and to answer the phone in case Washington calls. It's hot inside the ready room tent so I move my cot outside. The choppers on the flight line glow like bulbous green bugs in the light of the humpbacked moon. I spray the mosquito net with bugbomb, crawl inside, listen to the night sounds and fall asleep. Sometime, in the early morning, Doris Day materializes out of the darkness and crawls into my cot.

I grab Cochran at breakfast.

"Remember what you said about Doris Day?"

He nods.

"Well, she was in my bed last night."

"What?" he yells. "You bastard. She's my girl. I didn't give her to the whole goddamn camp."

Cochran starts to walk away then comes back. He leans in close and winks. "She's pretty damn good, isn't she?"

9. Gesture of Good Will

I said it, Doc, but I didn't mean it . . . that thing about how a tidy war wound could be a stepping stone to a political career . . . when Hemingway's kid asked if he'd be catching a fish, his dad said, "Don't put your mouth on it, son" . . . double-barreled earnest advice . . . getting shot at is bad enough, Doc . . . getting shot is even worse . . . old Bautista, our handyman on the ranch, got tired of the big red rooster kicking the shit out of the little black rooster . . . so he blew some locoweed smoke in big Red's mouth and when the cock went limp, he turned him loose . . . you can guess the result . . . little Black started kicking the shit out of big Red . . . so you see it doesn't matter much whether you choose that side of a war or this side of the war, you got to go on the other side . . . the future side . . . when the kids take over . . . just like a young rooster takes over after the old ones end up in the pot . . . we Gyrenes are hard-hearted brutes, Doc, except when it comes to kids . . . no matter how fucked up the little bastards are . . . the skinny ones, the ones with open running sores, big heads, malformed legs . . . undernourished, dirty and continuously exposed to bugs and bacteria . . . they all have dysentery and probably always will . . . over half of them will come down with tuberculosis at some point in their lives . . . what's their future, Doc? . . . what does the future have in store for them, Doc? . . .

We're up on the board. Part of a two flight assignment. Capt. Beamus and Ben-San leading, Cochran and me on their wing.

Rajah Beamus's asshole is always puckered, but today it's tighter than ever. Where the hell did he get his flight suit cleaned and starched? It's got creases for Chrissake. He stands on tippytoes looking us over, scowling at our baggy, bloodshot eyes. He straightens Ben-San's collar, adjusts my pistol belt, glares at Cochran.

Why's he always the tight ass? Goes totally overboard about the regs and the appearances. That just doesn't work in a chopper squadron where, unlike the grunts, we're never on the drill field doing right shoulder arms, forward march, column left, hup two, hup two. The straight and narrow military life must be all he has, the only thing he knows, and he seems compelled to make believers of us all.

That'll never work with Cochran, he's too big to fit the mold, but he sees me as a likely prospect to be a lifer, one who will perpetuate the code. It's in my blood for sure, but why does he have to be such an asshole about it? Where's the human touch? He's going to get needled until something pops, then we'll see what comes out, blood or bile.

"This is an important run," he says. "We'll be carrying dignitaries of the highest order." He looks around, makes sure no one is eavesdropping. "Connected all the way to the top . . ."

"You don't mean the Pope?" Cochran interrupts.

"As you were, Lieutenant. Presidential relationship. Be on top of your game. Sharp. No screwing around."

He continues lecturing us as we walk down the flight line to the choppers, but stops talking at the sound of an approaching aircraft.

An SVN AD-6 Skyraider fighter-bomber lumbers in for a landing. A crosswind catches the plane and the Vietnamese pilot adds power to straighten out. He slams on the rudder, the tail slews around and the bird slides sideways down the runway. It skids past us and careens into a helicopter parked alongside the runway. The Skyraider crushes the chopper against the fence where they come to a halt with the fighter-bomber's wing imbedded in the helicopter's belly.

The emergency siren goes off and a crash truck heads out from the control tower. A jeep beats the truck to the crash. Three Vietnamese MPs jump out, pistols drawn. One jumps up on the wing of the plane and aims in at the cockpit.

The crash truck roars up, spewing foam. Up on the wing of the plane, the first MP pulls the pilot out of the cockpit and throws him down to the ground where the other MPs grab his arms and hustle him into the jeep. The driver guns the engine and they race down the runway toward the Vietnamese end of the field.

"Justice is swift and injustice merciless in the unsettled frontier," Cochran says.

"No time for lollygagging," Beamus says. "We've still got a mission to fly."

Doc Hollenden comes puffing up. "Any room for me? I gotta get out of here for a while, take a break."

"Sure. Hop in."

We lift off and fly east to My Tho, the ARVN 7th Army Division base on the Mekong River, forty miles west of Saigon.

Two Mercedes sedans sit alongside the runway. Resplendently attired Vietnamese big-wigs and civilian high muckity-mucks stand alongside generals weighted down with chestloads of medals. A bare-headed American, wearing dark pants and a white blazer, towers over everyone. When we've shut off the engines, he walks over to the choppers and motions us down.

"I'm Robert Greatheart, assistant to the Ambassador. You will be making a VIP run today, carrying several important people—and one very important person."

He gestures toward the group standing in front of the cars. In the middle, everyone around her posturing in proper deference, a tall, slender woman stands aloof. A traditional white *ao dai* hugs her body from neck to ankle. A small parasol embroidered with sea swallows sits on her shoulder. She gives it a twirl and the swallows flutter around her head.

"Madame Nhu," Greatheart says. "She's married to President Diem's brother and is the ex-officio first lady of the country, since the president is a bachelor. She's not to be trifled with. Her husband, Ngo Dinh Nhu is head of the Can Lao, what we would call their secret police. You'll be flying her to Sa Dec where she will attend a formal dinner and, afterwards, address the townsfolk. Then you'll bring her back."

He looks us over. "I needn't remind you how important this mission is, not only for the good of our Vietnamese American relationship but also for the building of good will between the Diem government and the people in the outlying provinces."

Captain Beamus surprises us with a click of his heels, a snap to attention and a crisp salute.

"In the tradition of the United States Marine Corps you can count on us to—" he begins, but is cut off by the embassy official.

"I'm sure. Shall we proceed?"

Madame Nhu and the most important officials climb aboard the Rajah's chopper with sprightly alacrity, considering the weight of the medals, the stiffness of the starched uniforms and the rigidity of their encrusted scowls. The lesser encrusted jump in with us. Doc Hollenden greets each one with a grin and handshake, his glasses slipping down his nose.

We land on a soccer field at the edge of Sa Dec. A cluster of houses hugs a canal. A dirt road leads into the village. The local dignitaries greet Madame Nhu and her entourage with bows and greetings, then escort them into the ville. Captain Beamus, having ingratiated himself with the official party, hops aboard the gravy train for the official dinner. Cochran and Ben-San and Doc Hollenden and I and Soonto and the other crew chiefs are left standing in the soccer field. We're quickly surrounded by a crowd of villagers. They're small. Even the adults are the size of kids, except for the very old, who look like shriveled midgets. For the first time in my life I feel like a giant, towering over everyone. Cochran, the six-two gorilla, they must find unbelievable.

The women chew betel nut, leaving their teeth red if they are young, or black if they have been chewing for a long time. The old men cultivate stringy beards, eight or ten meager hairs. Amazed by the profusion of hair on our arms and wrists, they yank at our fur when they get close enough to touch. They are also curious about the size of our plumbing and follow and gawk when we take a leak. Mothers carry babies perched on their hips. Whenever a baby screeches, mom whips out a breast and nurses the kid quiet.

A grizzled old gent steps forward. "My name is Trung Nhut," he says. "You, I, we are friends to visit and tour our village. Hie, shoosh," he yells at the kids.

The little shits are everywhere. Kids without pants. Kids without shirts. One wears a straw cowboy hat and looks just like a kid from Texas. A girl wearing a short white dress with flowers around the hem peeks out from behind the boys. They're like gophers popping out of burrows, big ones, tiny ones, some carried by middle-sized ones. Some dirty, others filthy and all barefooted. Feet that never felt the slap of leather. Feet that curl toes in soft mud. Feet that beat flat soles on hard-baked ground.

They wave their arms and yell, "Hello. Hello." They all know hello. And okay. Everything is, "Okay. Okay."

They are awed, curious, and scared, moving closer all the time until one boy gets close enough to find out that the giants are harmless. Then there is a rush to make sure they all get a chance to touch an American.

They surround Ben-San, pulling at his legs and arms and fighting to be the first to pull the hair on his arms, gawk at his boots, his knife, his pistol; a contest to see how much he will tolerate. He is engulfed and only manages to escape when Sergeant Soonto gives a kid a piece of candy. Then they are all over Soonto. They beg him for a can of C-rat peaches. They don't even like the peaches. It's the begging and the getting. They've gone too far too fast. Burned their cute cards. No more freebies. Sour grapes replace sweet treats. Soonto chases them away.

They turn to Cochran. Pull at his flight suit, screaming and scratching like crows working a roadkill. Cochran swings his arms and, furious, maddened, face contorted, he whirls around, lets out a mighty whoop and charges the pack.

The kids run screaming, a little guy falls, mowed under by the bigger boys. Cochran bursts out laughing and the kids, realizing they have been tricked, are immediately back on him. All but the kid on the ground. He twitches and froths, his eyes rolled back in his skull. Cochran leans over him.

"Soonto, you got a C-rat spoon?"

Soonto tosses it over. Cochran pries the kid's mouth open and presses the spoon down on his tongue. He holds the spoon in one hand and the kid's head in the other until the boy stops twitching. The kid's eyes come back and he looks around.

Cochran eases the spoon out. "There you go little feller, you'll be all right now." He helps the kid up and steadies him until he can stand by himself.

Doc Hollenden, who has been hovering over the impromptu treatment, nods his head. "Yes, a mild epileptic attack. He should be fine."

To draw attention away from the kid, I take off my hat and point at it and shout, "Hat," and the kids take up the lesson and shout back, "Hat."

In rapid succession I shout pencil, camera, gun, knife, head, hand, arm. Every time they hear a new word they set up a roundhouse football-game cheer. In the midst of the screaming, a procession comes by, led by two men carrying scrolled oriental banners. I point and shout, "Parade!" The kids yell and wave. Behind the banners four men carry a small temple with incense burning inside. That too is greeted with a cheer.

Bringing up the rear is a large container, carried by eight men. One of the men takes off his cap and waves it at us and the kids go into a frenzy, laughing and screaming and leaping and dancing, a great merry ball, and not until we look closer do we realize that what we are treating with such merriment is a funeral procession.

Three kids are splashing in a big puddle. A crew chief throws an empty C-ration can into the water and a kid whoops after it and retrieves it off the muddy bottom. The other two kids immediately set up a clamor, demanding their own cans. The crew chief wings two cans into the water and the scrabble brings more kids running. It becomes a free for all with fights and crying, the bigger kids getting the cans, the little ones missing out. Cochran yells at the men to knock it off.

"But Lieutenant," the crew chief says, "they're enjoying themselves."

"Sure," says Cochran, "like dogs enjoying a fight their masters sicced them on."

"That would be fun," he smirks.

"For dogs, maybe. But these aren't dogs."

Rather than argue about it, Cochran falls back on the easy expediency of ordering them to stop, a rarity, seeing's how he reacts when anyone pulls that ordering shit on him.

"We go now," Trung Nhut says. "I show you our village."

We walk along the road into town. The kids surround us and slow us to a crawl. A canal full of scum and debris runs alongside the street. Hordes of flies buzz around turds lying in the gutters. The road opens into a square with a marketplace in the middle. I stop at a stall and buy a bag of hard candy. The kids climb on me like I'm Sandy Claws. They crawl up my legs and, in order to get them off, I pitch the candies out in the street. I try to escape while they fight for the booty but they catch up and grab at my hands, unrelenting in their demands.

I use my remaining piasters to buy a short straw broom, perfect size for paddling, and begin slapping at the mob of kids. Like the president of the Skunk Works, I exude a mean sense of power. It doesn't do any good. No one even notices, but just then an emaciated, long-legged, black-and-white dog comes running past, and the kids chase after it. The dog runs in a big circle and comes back and scoots between Soonto's legs. One of the kids grabs at it, the dog yaps and snarls.

"Hey *perro*," I call, and reach out to pet him. He snarls and snaps at my hand. I pull back. All right, all right. No touchy-feely, I can dig it. Sergeant Soonto laughs. He holds out his hand, the dog looks at it warily, then sniffs Soonto's knuckles. He lets Soonto rub his muzzle and scratch his ears. A rotund man with a short machete fastened to his belt elbows us aside. He grabs the dog by the scruff of his neck, gives him a good shake and carries him away.

"Come now," Trung Nhut says. He leads us through the marketplace, past goods arrayed on blankets, stalls crowded with people sipping tea, chatting, smoking bamboo pipes, nibbling on *cu do*, puffed rice candy. The tour ends at a small house facing the square, where we go inside for our not-so-stately dinner.

The walls are bamboo and the ceiling a thatched roof. Stilts hold the wooden floor off the ground. There are no chairs so we sit on mats in a circle. An elderly lady prepares us tea.

"The hostess of the house," Trung Nhut says. "Green tea. We call," he struggles for the right words, "hook-shaped curly tea. The leaves curl up when dried."

The hostess pours the tea from a pot into a bowl and then ladles it into our cups. Young ladies roam the circle filling our bowls. Trung Nhut describes the dishes: "*Com*, rice. *Mam kho*, salted fish stew. *Nuoc cham gung*, ginger fish sauce. *Mien ga*, noodle and chicken soup. *Dua mon*, vegetables in fish sauce. *Thit cho*, meat." He doesn't say what kind.

I look at Cochran. He has a sickly smile on his face but gamely samples each dish. Luckily, they've provided spoons along with the chopsticks.

"Hey, not bad," Ben-San says. "Meat's a little tough, though."

"Special for you our honored guests," Trung Nhut says.

"Kinda stringy," Cochran says.

"Chew each bite thirty-six times," Doc Hollenden says, masticating vigorously.

Stringy and tough, it reminds me of something. That skinny mongrel. *Madre de dio*. My stomach does a flip. I get up and stagger outside and stand in the shade of the overhang. Hold my stomach, wait for the others to come out.

Trung Nhut performs the obligatory goodbye dance, graceful bows and mellifluous murmurings of appreciation. Enough with the thank yous already, I'm dying out here. He finally exhausts the requisite requirements of a proper departure and escorts us away.

A small pond, full of rushes and muddy water, sits in the center of the ville. Trung Nhut kicks off his sandals, rolls up his pant legs and wades in up to his knees.

"You see." He reaches with his hands, feeling along the bottom. "Aha." Spreads his arms, bends, grasps, starts pulling out a slimy python. Our eyes get bigger as the snake gets longer. At least eight feet in length with brown skin splotched with white markings, the python's flat yellow head lolls sleepily as it lies languorously loose in Trung Nhut's arms.

"Village pet. Eats rats, his belly is full, so no danger now." He gropes along the snake, showing us a lump halfway down. "He is grown too big. We scared he will eat a child. We would like you to have Dinh Lanh, a gift."

He holds the snake out, one hand behind its head, the other clutching him in the middle. The snake flutters its eyes. His tongue flicks out. Trung Nhut smiles. "Dinh Lanh is a friend. He will give you much happiness and remind you of hands clasping across Vietnam and America. A gesture of goodwill."

"Whoa," I say, backing off. "I don't think so, *compadre*."

"Ah, you chickenshit." Cochran reaches out. "Give me that sucker."

"Are you sure?" the Doc says, looking alarmed.

Trung Nhut feeds the snake to Cochran, like reeling out a thick rope, first the head and then the body. Dinh Lanh's eyes open wide and his body quivers, a pulse up and down its length. The snake winds around Cochran's back and along his arms.

"Take a picture, Huck."

Okay. Is that a smile, *Señor Gorilla Hombre Con Culebra?* I snap the shot. Gorilla Man With Snake, but no smile. Cochran's eyes get wide. Dinh Lanh has his tail wrapped around Cochran's chest.

"Hey, this fucker's squeezing on me. Get him off . . ."

The kids laugh and jump up and down. Trung Nhut looks on, nodding and smiling. I snap another picture.

"Make with the snake charm, Cochran," Ben-San says. "Sexy undulations. Exotic whistling."

"Ah, shouldn't we do something? Not just stand here?" Doc Hollenden says.

Cochran's face turns red. Dinh Lanh is wound around Cochran's arms and chest and clamping down. I drop the camera and grab the snake. It's like pulling on a fire hose pumped full of water. Unmovable.

". . . Can't breathe . . ." Cochran gasps.

I'm eyeball to eyeball with Dinh Lanh. Inside his orbs I see green determination as old as pond stones worn to pebbles . . . before his eyes suck me into his depths, my survival knife is at his throat . . . last chance, fucker, turn loose . . . what? No way Jose? . . . okay, if that's the way you like it . . . a quick thrust of my knife through his mouth straight into whatever tiny brain runs this sucker's outfit then out the top of his skull with all my might . . . how's that for a decision, motherfucker?

"Nnnnh, nnnh . . ." Cochran mumbles.

What the fuck. The snake hasn't let up.

"His muscles locked," says Trung Nhut.

"Now what?"

The dog butcher steps forward and slices with his machete, *whup whup*, up and down the the python, spraying blood, skin, bone and guts. It looks like he's slicing Cochran along with Dinh Lanh. Pieces fall to the ground. Kids scoop up the chunks. Cochran stands, arms outstretched, eyes bugged, nary a cut.

"You okay?"

He nods. "Gddbliggdd pyysthonnn . . . gttt piggure . . ."

"What?"

"Piggure, gddbliggd it, piggure . . ."

I step back, aim in and snap. Caption: Gory Cochran.

Trung Nhut is rather sad. "Dinh Lanh was good snake." He brightens. "Will make many good meals."

Doc Hollenden grasps Cochran's wrist. Peers at his watch. Raises his eyebrows. Looks over his glasses.

"What about it, Doc?" I ask him. "Is he fit?"

"Fit enough to fly, although his pulse rate is a little high. But I can't say his uniform will pass muster."

Captain Beamus comes striding up, the official lunch having ended. "All right, let's get back to the choppers, it's time for the speechifying . . . what in the name of Chesty Puller is going on here? Lieutenant! Get yourself cleaned up. The dignitaries will be along any minute and they better not see a United States Marine Corps officer looking like that."

Cochran leans over the pond, grabs handfuls of water, splashes his flight suit, squeegees off globs of snake with the side of his hand, gets rid of most of the goop, but the process leaves him sopping. No nevermind, it will dry fast in this heat. We head out to the soccer field, hustling to catch up with Beamus and Ben-San. Trung Nhut huffs along behind.

The townsfolk are lined up, waving small SVN flags and murmuring patriotic phrases. Madame Nhu steps onto a platform and bows. She straightens and begins speaking, slow and stilted.

"She not good Vietnam talker," Trung Nhut tells us. "She speak French mostly. Very strong person. Some call her Dragon Lady. Now she talk about Woman Solidarity Movement. Will help villagers with nurseries and maternity clinics and schools. Now she say there will be stiff penalties for adultery. Divorce is outlawed except by permission of President."

"Who just happens to be her brother-in-law," Cochran mutters.

"Vietnamese people are on purification road, she say. No more taxi dancers, no more prize fighting, no immoral entertainment of Trojan rubbers, beauty contests, fortune telling, gambling, bee-hive hairdos, fast western music."

From the looks on the villagers faces she isn't getting much support for the proposed changes.

"Now she talk about people who are opposed to government in Saigon. She say we will track down and shut up and vanish all those scabby sheep."

Her voice rises and she speaks slowly, emphasizing each word. Trung Nhut keeps his voice down. "She say, if one bows to madness and stupidity of immoral acts how can one find strength to fight atrocities of communists? We must unite under central banner."

Muted applause, mild flag waving. Madame Nhu bows and steps off the platform. An old bentover man, wrinkled and gnarly, mud-riven as the paddies, shuffles forward. Madame Nhu stops and looks at him. The old man stands up straight and hawks a big loogey right in her face.

A greatness of oohing and ahhing. A vastness of surging forward. *Caramba!* A quickness of a thrust between the old man and Madame Nhu. A bodyguard, gun out, barrel up the old man's nose. Madame Nhu shakes her head, no, and wipes herself with a silk hanky. She lowers her parasol so no one can see her face and glides away. The bodyguard clubs the old man and scurries after her.

The townspeople surge forward. Soldiers with rifles face off the crowd. The generals and high muckity-mucks make a hasty exit. I look at Cochran. He has the same notion. We sprint for the choppers. Doc Hollenden puffs behind.

"Let's crank it up, Soonto," Cochran yells, climbing into the cockpit. "We gotta book on outta here."

Soonto nods, climbs in, carrying something under his flight suit. No time to mess with that. I look at Cochran.

"Did you just say book on out of here?"

"Yeah, why?"

"Oh, nothing." Sometimes the Marine Corps rubs off on you and you don't even know it.

We lift off and turn east. I look down at Trung Nhut, standing by himself, waving. Soldiers are herding the townspeople along the road, toward town.

"So much for the gesture of good will," Cochran says.

We drop the load of morose and somber big wigs and their dragon lady at My Tho and head for home as the sky darkens. The flight line is ablaze with floodlights. The Vietnamese fighter-bomber has been yanked out of the Marine helicopter's belly. Mechs swarm around the mangled chopper. Doc Hollenden gives a wave and heads for the dispensary. We go in the flight shack to fill out the after-action report. Soonto edges around the side of the building, keeping his body between us and whatever he's hiding inside his flight suit. He bumps into the wall and there's a slight yelp, then he disappears around the corner. Cochran shakes his head.

"I don't want to know," he says. "C'mon, let's get a drink."

At four o'clock in the morning, the Sadec lunch explodes in my stomach, delayed-action fuse triggering the blast. I fight the full-up sensation in my throat and bowels then get up and dash for the head. My flip-flops slap wet against my goopy feet as I sprint past the tents and a surprised sentry.

On the toilet, wet from the rain, all hell breaks loose . . . frightening flickering shadows cross my sweated forehead . . . voices reverberate old warnings through my ringing ears . . . *"Don't eat the native food" . . . Captain Beamus, the self-ordained Oriental, poo-poos the warnings: "The natives eat it and they don't seem to suffer" . . . Cochran corrects him, "Bullshit, they all got dysentery. They're just forced to live with it"* . . . until done, weakened, washed out and exhausted, I stagger back to the tent, take two pills, eat a couple of soda crackers and punch the ticket to dreamland.

Workers pound and dig, laying cement across my chest . . . smell of rice paddies wafts through the tent on a hot humid breeze . . . sweltering tremulous drums beat a frenzied tune on the top of my head . . . a shower roars in from the southwest, drenching the tent . . . rousing me to get up and make an assessment. Seems the cure has taken. The pills, plus the C-ration John Wayne crackers. They explode in your stomach, not in your mouth. Old Corps glue for stoppering loose bowels.

With my body settled down, the next morning it's back to the regular routine of wearying hours in the cockpit, the radio blaring in my earphones, Cochran beating time on his leg.

10. The Silence of the Tropics

Slow it down, Doc . . . it slips away too fast . . . what was immediate, all-consuming, burned on my brain . . . slips away . . . I grasp at wisps . . . a Vietnamese home defense corps soldier lies on a stretcher with his eyes stuck open . . . bloodied body unnaturally sprawled . . . waiting to be lifted aboard the helicopter . . . lines of men and women pass sacks of rice, cages of chickens, boxes of canned goods from the chopper belly to the ground to be carried to huts, to be cooked on wood stoves to end up in people's bellies . . . a squad of ARVNs pile aboard . . . flown to a landing zone . . . kicked out into a paddy, rifles held high above waist-deep water, rotor wash beating down . . . strange bloated shapes move through the water . . . slippery eels . . . goopy sea slugs . . . a small fish with a barbed horny head rises and discovers a flow of piss splashing into the water . . . swims up the stream of piss and lodges inside the pecker, eating its way into the urethra where it dies . . . leaving an oozing infection . . . no known cure . . . it's not gonna happen on my watch, Doc . . . when that mancón *comes swimming up my pee, I backpedal as fast as I can . . . keeping just ahead until I'm pissed out . . . my stream spurts dead . . . the fish falls to the ground, mouth opens and shuts helplessly . . . there's danger everywhere, Doc*

. . . only way to avoid it is to fly higher . . . out of range . . . in the comfort of the clouds . . .

The silence of the tropics has been shattered by a line of cumulonimbus clouds that have cleared the air, watered the soil and awakened me from the doldrums. The mail has been sorted and delivered, and all over the camp Marines hunker down on cots, boxes, chairs or the ground to read their letters from home.

Cochran sits on a camp stool in front of the refrigerator. Hors d'oeuvres are spread out on another camp stool: mess-hall soda crackers, salami, pepperoni and cheese. He carves out spots of mold with his survival knife. A cocktail pitcher sits on the floor: a number-ten can filled with martinis and ice.

He raises his head and sniffs, makes a face. "Do I detect a malodorous odor in the air?"

"I'm not sure," I say. "You'll have to prove it. How do you spell malodorous?"

"Spell? I'm talking about smell, *muchacho.* This isn't an English class, you know. School's out. Have a drink."

We swig greedily. Out there is the war. Both sides feeling their way, evolving tactics, a prelude to the conduct of future wars, dragged out without ever really ending. The center comes undone. What rough beast slouches toward Saigon? Diem runs the country with an iron family hand, passing out officialdom to his relatives, keeping track of everything, keeping the country safe from degenerate activities, like dancing, for instance. No telling what secrets are being passed back and forth as, heads close, bodies rub together in communist conspiracy. Not that communists are such great dancers.

Balmy summer days are quietly tucked away with Aunty Kathy who was committed on the last day of August. Fall is right around the corner. Brings out the do's and the dont's. Bills, babies and new cars. Books to read. Coeds to cuddle. The turf smacks of frosty action. Gladiators unlimber their meathooks, swath their muscles in padding, and, with the roars of millions shaking the firmament, go at it with teeth, forearms, cleats and the piling of ons.

A North Vietnam citizen is handed a mortar shell. Carries it hundreds of miles down the Ho Chi Minh trail to a mortar crew on a knoll overlooking an ARVN outpost. A Viet Cong soldier takes the shell, drops it in the tube, it goes off with a thunk and whoosh, the soldier turns to the citizen, "Go get another."

Rob Jacobs perches on the edge of his cot, pours powder on his feet, the skin flaking and shredding with jungle rot. Cochran rummages through his clothes.

"Christ on a crutch, I'll have to wash some skivvies, these are all full of nicotine stains."

"Why don't you give up smoking?" Rob Jacobs asks.

"I would if I thought it'd stop the shits."

Cochran pulls off his shorts, holds the raggedy garment to the light, sniffs, grimaces and flings it in the wet pile under his cot.

Pom-pom girls unlimber their jigs and jounces for the first home game and coaches vow to make amends for last year's disasterous season. Trees bloom scarlet and gold and shed their mantles. Coeds lie on dormitory roofs. Metal sun reflectors provide the season's final tanning rays.

The sense of unity that first spread through the pilots and crew chiefs, extending even to the lowest enlisted ranks, still exists, although like Cochran's shorts, it's a bit tattered. We're a gaggle of men working in unison for a noble cause, our lives in jeopardy. Fly our asses off all day, accept a bullet or two in payment and put out a few rounds of our own; flat clips and scattered impact from the grease gun, a wild-firing, short-ranged, fast-bursting, fat-slugged automatic weapon. Then return to the tent; flaps dangling, ropes singing, floors buckling, beds damp and mildewed, shoes covered with mold, metal oxidizing into caustic red surfaces; our home where we gather every evening for drinks and bull roar.

In Bumfuck, Missouri, Miz Tildy slops her pet pig but unknowingly drops in a serving spoon and the pig chokes to death, all bloated and worthless, and it galls Miz Tildy so bad she comes up raging from a grog bender and blows out the TV with her double-barreled twelve-gauge when she catches Jonathan Winters doing his hog farmer bit, making *suwee suwee* pig talk.

The bubonic plague arrives in the Far East. Fleas transported through the Suez Canal, slipped tariff-free past Nasser's guards busy putting down a riot, have debarked ship somewhere in Formosa and from there scattered through the Phillipines, Okinawa and China, to North Vietnam and, following the Ho Chi Minh trail, to South Vietnam.

Americans are invulnerable, if not from the Viet Cong, then at least from the plague. For we have had our shots, adding a sore arm misery to the grumblings in the lower bowels where an occasional explosion disrupts even the most important of activities. The runny shits won't take a back seat, even for war.

In Pennsylvania, hunters get ready for deer season. In Southern California the first hint of rain builds over the Santa Ana Range. In Florida wisteria spreads its shoots in preparation for next year's display. And in Texas whirling miniature cyclonic dust storms dance across the grass prairies.

The word comes down from the top: don't have your film developed in Vietnam. The VC get copies of our pics and use them for training aids and propaganda. Nobody believes it and nobody sends their film to Okinawa to get developed.

When humor comes it is contagious, laughing and swinging up and down the rows of tents, into the mess hall, out on the flight line and even on the missions. Catches in a man's craw, tickles his gonads, sparkles among the ice cubes in his drink.

Cochran picks up his towel and soap and steps out on the porch to shower in the rain.

"Uh-oh," he yells. "Big trouble. The duty officer forgot to take in the Hammer's flag. It's soggier than one of my socks."

"Blah," says Rob Jacobs. "I wish the fucking flag would rot after the trick the Hammer played on me today."

He picks up the bottle of gin.

"There I was," he says. "Flying a nice tight wing when the bastard splits the needles and leaves me grabbing for the collective a thousand feet above the zone, not even a shout to tell me we've arrived. *Whoosh*, he's gone and I have to circle around and come back in. By the time I land he's already taken off, and when we get home I get my ass chewed for flying a sloppy wing."

Rob spills gin on his hand and wipes it on his flight suit. The metamorphosis of the Marine. From shit-kicking warrior to shit-faced whoremonger, sucked into the morass and mire of the Ugh American on the Far East Tour.

Daddy is proud I am serving my country, sure that I'll uphold the Huckelbee tradition. "Fight with courage and bravery, son. Never miss an opportunity to reap honor. Yours is a fighting man's world, one in which the strongest and most valorous always win."

There's nothing on the line for us over here, Daddy. Not as if we're fighting for our soil, our homes, our families, against a foreign invader. No, we're here to assist the SVN against the NVN, but who can tell the difference unless it's a slightly different accent and a different way of living in a slightly different climate and terrain, say like the difference between a Yankee trader—"I be from Milwaukee"—and a Kentucky tobacco farmer—"You be, huh? Down here we speak proper English; I am from Coon Lick."

The Vietnamese farmer is caught in the middle. The Viet Cong demand food and shelter and total submission. Night-time atrocities are common. In the daylight, huge buglike machines swoop out of the sky, spitting bullets and disgorging troops. The Viet Cong say the bug machines spread disease and death. They might have something there.

I have traveled and seen new places. Hawaii, Guam, Okinawa, Japan, Vietnam. In letters home, the names scrawl from my pen like drool from a baby's mouth. What I don't tell them is no matter where we go, I have discovered, lurking beneath the grinning surfaces of these so-called exotic places, a common reaction to Americans: suspicion. Concealed by a willingness to fleece the Yankee out of his dollar. Provide him with insidious delights: smut. Gala extravaganzas. The country prostituted to please the jaded tastes of the American visitor.

I take advantage of a day off flying so the mechs can work on the sick birds, and hop a ride to Saigon on the supply run C-123.

The capitol is a leisurely city far removed from the outposts, maintaining its French flavor with sidewalk cafes, pissoirs and flower stalls and French still the acceptable language. The shops are closed twelve to three for an after-lunch *siesta*, just when I arrive downtown. I forego the offer of a pedicab and walk along broad streets lined with trees and large stores. Exploring deeper, I turn down a narrow, shadowed side street, past crowded stalls, hustling vendors and brown-skinned, red-mouthed betel nut chewers. Tall, stained, brick and mortar walls hem me in, windows barred and dirty, tables and chairs and benches piled with cloth bundles and goods wrapped with string. A man in a pith helmet and short-sleeve khaki shirt, a glaring scowl on his face, pushes a wheeled cart carrying flavored drinks toward me. I sidle past, deeper into the shadows, along slime-drenched walls where laughing faces mock my own filth. There, a sign ahead, STEAM BATH AND MASSAGE, just the place to boil off the dirt and diarrhea crud encrusting my body.

I push the door open and go inside. A furtive look from an old man changes to an ingratiating smile, so happy to exchange my money for a towel. He points to a changing room. Once I'm bare-ass naked, my feet curling on the cold concrete floor, I balefully eye the steam room, empty and gloomy, a bare bench alongside one wall. The wooden door closes behind me with a solid thunk. A small opaque window in the door is the only break in the monotonous gloom of the room. Overhead, a bare bulb sways in the ghostly fog.

The hot mist crushes me, forcing the air from my lungs. A shower head sticks out of the wall. I turn on the spigot but it spins uselessly in my hand. The heat bears down on my head and shoulders, muggy sweaty oppressive steam. The room is too small and confining. My pores open, making me more vulnerable. Bodily fluids ooze from my skin. The close air constricts my breathing. I push on the door, but it is locked shut by an invisible catch, no handle on the inside. I push harder, a fringe of panic seeping in with the steam. The bulb sways crazily in the gray ceiling soup. Darkness and blurred reflections stare from the window. Thoughts of murder awaken forgotten warnings: don't go off the main street. Don't go anywhere alone. Intense stifling heat, suffocating air. The long-ago closing door. The missing handle. I bang my fist on the wood, muffled, barely discernible. Through the misted window a face watches with slitted eyes, grining mouth, white teeth. I knock desperately on the unforgiving door which suddenly swings open flooding me with fresh air. The steam room proprietor smiles helpfully.

"All done?" he says. "You shower?"

"It doesn't work."

He turns the spigot.

Water flows in needle streams, cool refreshing head-clearing lung-cooling water, splashing over my throbbing head and running down my back and legs in sparkling relief.

"No more steam?"

"No, no more."

"You like massage?"

After the steam room, anything.

We go into a small room containing a massage table. I relax and listen to the reassuring sounds of commerce and activity coming from the street. The massage pummels away the memory of being locked in the steam room.

Outside, the shops are still closed for the afternoon nap break but the bars are open and I go into the Texas Roundup. The front heavily screened to fend off grenades, a not so subtle reminder of the war. Young, dark-eyed, long-haired girls work behind the bar, serving drinks and playing dice or cards for the bill. I haggle with two girls and play liar's dice. I'm too spent from the massage to sample their feminine wares. A little girl walks into the bar. She pulls at my leg and asks if I want to buy some peanuts.

"No," I tell her. "Beat it." The standard phrase for putting the kids off.

She tugs again, very insistent, and once more I tell her to leave.

She looks at me and says, "Why you don't give *me* money? You buy them drink."

I stare at her unblinking dirty face, grubby clothes and tray full of peanuts then pull out some piasters. I hand them to her and then leave to catch a taxi and return to the air field, with the bitter taste of the *Bia La Rue* beer still on my tongue.

"Conned again," Cochran says, when I tell him about the little girl. "Americans are the biggest suckers in the world. Make them ashamed of being Americans and they can be conned out of their skins."

I'm too tired to argue.

The southwest monsoon simmers to a close. Three or four days of steady rain recede to afternoon showers of hard and fast duration. The nights are clear and a breeze rustles the tent flaps, but not enough to ward off the mosquitos. The morning sun bakes the runway and the water from yesterday's rain steams and dries. By noon a layer of wispy clouds boils in off the ocean and the muggy heat is at its worst.

Another month and the showers will end. The rice paddies will dry, the ground will be cracked and peeling, with dust rising and swirling on the fingertips of the wind. The hot season will be at its zenith and, along with the temperature, the war in the Delta will heat up.

Action and situation are muddled and confused, like a bowl of noodles. Politics and war. Impossible to move in one direction without a corresponding move in the other. What we get out of this depends on what we go in looking for. For some it is a medal, a badge of glory signifying so many combat missions. For others an opportunity to shoot up the countryside, let off pent-up frustrations

In Washington it is a study of new tactics and weapons. In Saigon, an accumulation of American money and supplies. At an outpost in the boonies, it's beer, C-rations and rice, dropped from the skies by a green whirley-bladed bird, huge and splendid with its tricks and capers, delightful to watch and touch, particularly the amazing giants who make it perform.

Much of it gives us a feeling of satisfaction. Hauling food and supplies to isolated outposts. Evacuating wounded to the comfort and safety of a hospital. And we feel better knowing we're not the complete barbarians Hanoi Hannah makes us out to be. Still, we're reluctant to trust the villagers, the families who are trying to keep their homes together, plant and harvest their crops, live a peaceful life.

You, who write to us, can you understand, does this make sense? Your letters are like messages from another planet. Does someone sitting in an office crank them out to perpetuate an American myth? A central morale building where families and towns and friends are invented and their activities chronicled? A vacation is planned—was it ever completed? Baby has a fever. Does the fever continue? Time stops and remains stationary until the next letter arrives, and, like a freight train on a siding, the pace picks up and the train jogs ahead to the next switch where it sits until prodded forward again.

Hello there. I send my answer into the void. Hello there. I, too, am an American. I am over here but still one of you. When you read this do you know that I am in the jungle, mingling with small brown people, passing out C-ration candy to their kids? Do I have depth, voice, body, a kiss? Or am I a picture hung on the wall, a projection on a piece of paper?

I write Rosey that I will comb the hills and the markets, peer into musty corners with my trusty jeweler's eyepiece screwed into my left farsighted eye, and search for the perfect piece of jade, the solitary gem, the translucent marvel, the only stone remaining in Vietnam that will fit into the final fine bracelet to emerge from the Orient. I hope it makes her happy.

The evening shower curtains down another Vietnamese sunset with its full Roy G Biv spectrum beaming through moisturized prisms. The wind whips the rain water under the tent flaps and skims a muddy sheen over the floor.

I feel better having talked to you. We will chat again. You are so many and we are so few. Who are the fortunate ones? I desire answers. *Adiós, hasta luego*.

11. Soc Trang Short Timers

It's not just my shoulder, Doc . . . there's other parts broke down, too . . . synapses misfire from my head to my toe all the way down to the very sole . . . slap me silly, Doc . . . Daddy would slap me with a roll of pennies . . . knock some sense into my head . . . where's the backbone? . . . who's got the glue? . . . can I ever be the man they'd like me to be? . . . dapper, suave, air of total confidence . . . I lean against a tent pole inside the ready room . . . cup of coffee balanced in my hand . . . raindrops fall on the canvas roof . . . at the front of the tent, Captain Beamus lectures on radio frequencies . . . what more could a man ask out of life? . . . the leaking roof, Beamus lecturing, muddy coffee, pilots stinking and unshaven in rotten flight suits and sweaty flak gear . . . till the emergency comes . . . warning light's on, Doc . . . BINGO FUEL . . . throttle back, set her on max cruise rpm . . . there's nothing but jungle down there . . . put her in a slow climb, get as much altitude as you can . . . if that engine quits, it's autorotation city, Doc . . . just hope we don't have to go into those trees . . . turn this chopper belly side up and give it a good shaking, Doc . . . scramble the codes . . . reprogram the helix . . . everything's out of order . . . the walls are crashing down . . . a bang-up job . . .

"Come on, Rob, you robust Panda Bear. Everybody's been back for an hour. Get into your civvies and grab some chow, this place is about to explode."

"Fuck you, Cochran. If you had to go through the shit I just did, you wouldn't be giving me a load of your odious ragass."

"Well, aren't your skivvies in a wad. Odious? How do you spell that? I thought you'd be hot to trot what with a blowout party on the line."

Rob Jacobs peels off his flight suit, baring his flaccid pale body. "Maybe, if I hadn't banged up the bird." An attention-grabber that brings the tentmates close. Rob rummages through his clothes. "I was flying Yankee Victor 84, that bullet scarred beast, it's got a jinx on it, I swear. No sooner had I lifted off a canal dike with twenty ARVNs aboard than the bitch lost her turns and I started settling into the ditch. I twisted the shit out of the throttle and got just enough manifold pressure to crawl up on the bank of the canal, but I scraped the rear end and ripped the tail wheel off."

He eyeballs us, glum look on his shiny face.

"I held the chopper on the main gear with the tail off the ground, kicked the passengers out and came on home. You'd have thought the bird was falling to pieces there were so many gawkers watching. I guess it must have looked hairy with the tail wheel gone and chunks of skin hanging off."

He slips into a clean pair of shorts and goes out on the porch, the rest of us trailing behind. He pours water from a jerry can into a steel pot.

"They'd set some sandbags in a pile and motioned me to hover with the tail over the sandbags. Circling around in front of me were two shirtless Marines playing harmonicas. Distracted me enough I got off center and there's the Rajah, waving the musicians away and guiding me to the left, then, easing me down, using his arms like he's the paddles on an aircraft carrier, bringing in a jet across the ramp."

Rob Jacobs scoops water, sopping and soaping.

"So I set her down easy, the Rajah gives me the cut sign and I bottom the collective. I don't tip over so I figure everything's okay and shut down the engine, leave the ass end of the chopper sitting on the sand- bags."

He dries off and troops inside the tent, leading a parade. "And who should come up and shake my hand and congratulate me?" He pauses a dramatic beat. "None other than the Hammer himself, telling me I did a fine job, excellent flying, a reassurance I can take to the bank —probably means the sand bank, coming from him—and I'm not to worry about the tail wheel, only a minor thing, then he has to get back to his report writing, adding new names to the qualified section leader list, now do you think I'm on that list?"

He looks us over. A fake laugh from Ben-San: *harfershugering fucking up*.

"Yeah, I'm with you on that," Rob Jacobs says. Pulls on his pants and shirt. "What's for chow?"

"You've caught the final skoshi minute," I tell him. "Barbecued steak."

We head over to the mess hall. Outside, along one of the walls, steaks are sizzing on the tops of fifty-five gallon drums cut in half. The smoke and smell of burnt Yankee meat rises in the evening air.

Out on the flight line the mechs have swung the tail end of Yankee Victor 84 onto the back of a jeep and are maneuvering the chopper toward the hangar. Rob Jacobs watches mournfully, waves goodbye to the mangled bird with a thick T-bone, black and charred on the outside, dripping red in the middle, reminds me of a Texas steak, so hot that when you wipe your mouth it burns a hole in your sleeve. He tears off a big bite and a gob of juice runs down his chin. He raises his sleeve to wipe, his last clean shirt before laundry day.

"No! Not tonight," I yell. I hold out my hand. "A cloth if you please."

The cook promptly whips a rag out of his pocket. "Here you go, sir, allow me." The rasty cook daintily pats Rob's mouth. Rob Jacobs slugs a large swig of beer and rips off another bite, cook at the ready with his rag.

We're Soc Trang short-timers. The camp has been rebuilt to Army specifications, the new brick barracks are finished and the exchange of bases that once seemed like a long ways off is suddenly here. Tonight we're all spiffed and cleaned, putting on the dog, a Soc Trang farewell party is in the works.

A wet wind wafts a dank primeval smell off the paddies. The tide is out and the water is low. A flock of herons flies by in perfect parade formation, heavy left, and the pilots bang their gnawed steak bones against the garbage cans, mutual admiration of a skill we share. On the horizon a fiery sunset blazes across the top of a towering thunderhead.

Inside the mess hall, the tables and benches are shoved against the wall. Doc Hollenden has liberated the medicinal alcohol from the dispensary and mixes a potent punch of Kickapoo Jungle Juice, half grain alcohol and half grape juice with chunks of pineapple floating on top. A high-topped chef's hat sits on his head and he has a white surgeons's gown wrapped around his body.

"Fill 'em up, lads," he calls out, pushing his glasses securely on his nose. Cups formerly containing chow-hall koolade now brim with jungle juice. The ice machine is cranked to the max, ensuring there will be cold drinks all night long.

The noise level in the mess hall rises as the evening darkens. Bawdy songs vie with tales of impossible flight. Down with the punch. Up with the party. After the tail-wheel debacle, Rob Jacobs is ready to cut loose and take on the world, but the world is too wrapped up in its own revelry to bother with him. By ten o'clock everyone is snockered. The crash of the door banging open startles the party into silence. The Hammer strides into the room, and before anyone can make the appropriate scream of hierarchical obeisance, he shouts out a pronouncement:

"Gentlemen. I give you . . . the *General!*"

General MacLeod, top ranking Marine in Saigon, marches in

behind the Hammer. Five-feet, six-inches tall, he's dressed in starched utilities, silver stars gleam on his collars, thick-lensed glasses fog his eyes. Before the General can say anything, a voice from the back screams a greeting.

"A hymn, men. A hymn for the General. Give him a hymn." Bolstered by drink, strengthened with love, bouyant in praise, we burst forth in off-key unison, *"Hymn . . . hymn . . . fu-uck hymn . . ."*

The General falls back as if hit with a magnum. Nervous laughter fills the chow hall. General MacLeod juts out his jaw, bristles his mustache and with his body crouched, his legs crooked and his fist clenched, he stands poised like a cocky bantamweight. He shoots open his fist and extends his middle finger. Fuck you!

The tension holding the room like a steel band is broken. Everyone cheers and raises their cups in salute. General MacLeod grabs a cup out of Doc Hollenden's hand.

"This," he yells, a Scot's burr to his words, "is the real Marine Corps. Not those stiff-necked pussy-whipped blabbermouths in Saigon."

Captain Beamus forces his way into the General's space, eyeball to eyeball. "Yes sir, General. I agree. One hundred percent."

The Rajah is face to face with a prime example of what a short snappy squared-away officer can accomplish—ascendence to the very top—and he's not going to let this opportunity go to waste. Before the Rajah can say a word, the General spears him with a glare and orders, "Straighten that gig line mister."

"What?" Captain Beamus is totally bumblefucked. He looks down at his shirt front. The military requirement of a perfectly straight line of buttons, from neck to belt, the so-called gig line, is askew. The Rajah tugs the buttons into a straight line and raises his head. The General is gone.

The Rajah looks around the room and focuses in on me. He heads my way and by the way he bears down, I can see I'm the one in for a good old-fashioned talking-to.

"Hucklerbee," he says, stentorian voice rising an octave from its normal sober low rasp. "I've had my eye on you. For some time now. For some time."

"*Como tan, Capitán?*"

"You've become most unmilitary, most unmilitary. Nothing definite, nothing I can put my finger on, but it's there."

Captain Beamus leans back and lays his finger against his nose, looks me up and down in a search for the clue lying somewhere behind the translucent curtain obscuring his vision.

"Not contempt. More a sign of disrespect. No, not disrespect either, not quite. You're getting more and more like that other Lieutenant, that . . . but never mind him. It's you. Questioning everything. Your back constantly up against the wall. No need to shake your head. You know I'm right."

Right about what, I'd like to know, but I keep my mouth shut. No sense in arguing with a career officer, not when it's ten to one. I'll be getting out as soon as this stint is over. So lay off the bullshit and leave me free to take this war one day at a time without getting hurt or killed or going bonkers like some shoot-'em-up cowboy riding the blood lust high.

He leans in closer.

"You may think I don't have the backing to keep you junior officers in line, but mark my words, before this tour is over, you'll have cause to respect me."

Captain Beamus teeters and nods knowingly.

"I've got good reason to say you'll be treating me with much greater respect."

He waits for me to take the bait, but I do the slow wait, wondering where his jungle juice loosened mind will lead him.

"Think on this for a moment," he says. "Colonel Rappler, the Hammer, as you call him, is sure to be relieved of his command some hungry day when a ribbon-starved officer will arrange to have him transferred. And who does that leave in charge? Major Lurnt. Can you imagine what that would be like? I'd give him two months before he went to the hospital with a nervous breakdown. Then it would be up to one person to carry the torch."

Captain Beamus pauses for me to identify the apparent successor. He nods at the dubious look on my face.

"Figure it out for yourself. I'll have my Major's leaves in a couple of months, just in time to take command. Then you'll see how a true commanding officer will handle you and your friend."

Captain Beamus smirks and throws down his drink, a triumphant gesture at the thought of running the show, no one to undermine his plans and ideas. He staggers over to the plank table for a refill. Doc Hollenden, having sampled his product often enough to ensure its delectability, sloshes the punch into Captain Beamus's cup and across the front of his khakis.

To hell with Beamus and his high and mighties, I say to myself. Fill 'em up and swill 'em down. The songs come faster and words shriek shriller. Smoke pollutes the rafters. Drinks puddle the floor. Feet slip in the goo.

Rob Jacobs, the pudgy Panda Bear, staggers toward General MacLeod. Rob Jacobs, the lieutenant normally the most pleasant, normally the most quiet, is a belligerent drunken lout. He gets in the General's face and sticks out his finger, his mouth distended, tongue wagging.

"Listen here, General," Rob Jacobs shouts, his finger pointing at the General's face. "I don't give a shit if you are a General. I don't care what rank you are. I still have a right to my say and what I say is . . ."

The Arkansas Razorback, Executive Officer Major Pappy Lurnt, catches sight of the finger pointing and the voice shouting, and he sallies forth, plowing through the crowd, knocking aside drinks.

"Goddamnit, General, even a Lieutenant with a slight tail wheel blemish on his record has a right to be section leader . . ."

The Arkansas Razorback smothers the Panda Bear with a neck-squeezing headlock. A ruffled sound from Panda Bear's mashed mouth blurts out from under the Razorback's armpit. "What the hell . . . ?"

"Listen, Jacobs. You can't go poking your finger at a General and talk to him like that. It just isn't done."

Major Lurnt wheels his bundle into the drunken melee, away from the General, then figuring it's safe to let him loose, releases Rob Jacobs, who, before this, merely trying to be helpful, merely wanting to set the General straight, is now pissed.

Ben-San raises a tenor air, "*In china they ne-ever eat chile.*"

Rob Jacobs overshouts the song, "I don't care if you are a Major, you can't do that to me."

He insists they go outside to rassle this point of honor to its logical conclusion. Major Lurnt argues for a minute, sees it is useless, and agrees. As soon as they clear the door, the Arkansas Razorback once again engages the Panda Bear in a headlock, and the two heavyweights lumber in one direction then another, a slow ponderous dance to the cacaphonic beat of the shrill pitched singing inside the mess hall.

So sing me another verse worse than the other verse.

Pappy Lurnt, face puffed and red, mouth close to Rob Jacobs's ear, drawls, "You know why they call Arkansas the Wonder State? It's because little shindigs like this are nothing compared to an Arkansas hogdown, where there's surf-fishing, back-flipping, knocking down mountains, blowing holes out of the ground and tying rivers into knots, the men range on one side of the room and the ladies on the other, the men snort, the women beller, the men leap and tumble, the women rear and kick . . . "

Pappy's mouth is slippery wet against Rob Jacobs's ear. "Then the hogdown dancers race around the room in couples until the razorback wrangler throws his hog prod into the middle and that's when the hogdown gets hot"—around and around, back and forth, Rob Jacobs prying at the soft parts of Major Lurnt's body; the Major squeezing his head—"chairs and tables get knocked over, lights are blown out, the whole bunch piles up in the middle with men and women tangled together, the whole mess not to get straightened out until morning when bosoms are bared and trousers torn open and there's a suspicion in the air that babies have been made . . ."

"I once knew a gal with a hole nice and tight," Ben-San leads the chorus.

Rob Jacobs sticks out his leg to trip Major Lurnt and they teeter, lurch to a recovery, then collapse in a heap with Rob Jacobs's mouth next to Pappy's ear. "You've been piling it on thick as pig tracks around the corncrib door. The only reason they call Arkansas the Wonder State is because it's a wonder anyone stayed there. I'm from I-O-Way, where we raise hogs and not hay and Gramps was the king of the whole fray. He was so hard he could knock sparks out of a rock with his bare toes. He could laugh the bark off of a tree. His dog Founder would run down the hogs and hold them by the ear till Gramps came up and skinned the hogs alive, then Gramps would let the hogs loose so they could grow another hide. It worked good in the summer but in the winter they all caught cold and died so he butchered them where they lay and stored the meat in the freezer for eating another day . . ."

"She packs it with alum at least once a night . . ."

A crash against the side of the building startles the General. He spills his drink on the Hammer. Ben-San is left hanging on a high note. The reefer door swings open untended. The tub of punch falls off the table. The party surges outside.

Rob Jacobs and Major Lurnt lie on the ground, arms and legs interlocked. The Major untangles himself.

"Come on, Jacobs," he says. "Now admit you're drunk and get up. That's enough for one night."

Rob Jacobs motions weakly with his hand. Cochran leans in close.

"Gramps's drinking habits is what killed him," Rob murmurs. "After a while the liquor didn't have any kick so he added strychnine and when that lost its effect he put fish hooks and barbed wire in his toddy and it rusted his stomach so bad it gave him indigestion . . ." Rob's voice grows weak.

"And then? And then?" Cochran says, nudging Rob with his foot.

"... oh, he wasted away to iron and skeleton and finally died."

"What a load of hog shit," Pappy Lurnt says. "He doesn't know a P from a pig's snout. What's the matter with him anyway?"

"At the end of his rope," Cochran says. "Exertion was too much for him. Good old Panda Bear."

A dark pool seeps out from Rob Jacobs' head. His hand sneaks up and touches the liquid, then rubs it as if he were trying to smudge out a spot, but feeling the spot grow quicker than the rubbing can get rid of it, the hand gingerly slips up under his face, explores for a second, then is hastily withdrawn.

"Ooooh," Rob Jacobs moans.

"*He's bleeding*," Ben-San sings.

Major Lurnt bolts for a drink. Doc Hollenden, after checking out the cut over the Panda Bear's eye, recruits two officers to carry Rob Jacobs to the dispensary. General MacLeod sounds off in praise of combat Marines whose stalwart contributions to the proud tradition of the service will never go unheeded, but his Scottish burr is so bad no one can understand a word. He gives up and searches for a junior man to fetch him more ice. The Hammer wanders away, finds a cot and collapses on it, mosquito netting draped across his chest, head resting on a sodden pillow.

Outside, the cloud cover parts and the moon shines through. In the operations tent the duty forecaster notes the hourly weather report and enters it in his log: scattered layer 1100 feet, overcast 5000.

Back in our tent, Ben-San hums the tune to "The Harlot of Jerusalem" and wishes he could remember the words.

Major Lurnt, asleep in his bed, doesn't feel his eye swelling and discoloring.

Rob Jacobs lies angelic and happy in the dispensary, five stitches closed the split over his eye, bandage fresh and virginal in the moonlight.

In the new BOQ barracks, built for the Army pilots, a drunk Marine staggers to a cot in the dark, finds someone already there and pushes him onto the floor, then curses the beer-soaked pillow.

The body on the floor sits up, rubs his head, and fumbles outside where he runs into General MacLeod sitting on the ground drinking a warm cup of jungle juice.

"Oh, I say, Colonel . . ." the General begins, but the Hammer shoves by without a word, splashing through the mud, slipping along the ditch.

"Well," General MacLeod huffs, but his indignation is cut short by a belch and a heave and the short snappy General blurts the evening's fun into the Hammer's retreating footprints. It's up to Doc Hollenden to get the General to a warm bed. There's one cot still unused in the dispensary—next to Rob Jacobs—and that's where the General snores the night away.

"Funny business," Cochran mumbles from his bunk. "Rob Jacobs is getting further and further out . . . more and more frantic . . . you watch . . ."

Cochran's voice lowers to a soft murmur. I strain to catch the words, but instead of Cochran, it's Captain Beamus talking in my head. "Don'tcha know, Huckelbee, you have a future in the Corps, you can be a senior officer" . . . "But sor, but sor, will the curse come on me, sor?" . . . "Consider yourself born to command, the man at the helm." . . . "But sor, will I be coarsened, will the head-butting make me dogmatic, pussywhimpering?" . . . "All part of the responsibility, Huckelbee" . . . "Oh, sor, spare me the mantle, ungird me the loins, I yam what I yam, sor . . ."

III
VIETNAM

September, October, November 1962

Da Nang
The Mountains

"We came out like Hell's Angels."

Shu Fly pie and apple pan dowdy
Oh I never get enough of that wonderful stuff

---

12. What Lies Ahead

There's a change in the weather, there's a change in me . . . pack my bags . . . strike the tents . . . dismantle the portable ice machine . . . Da Nang looms in the offing . . . Da Nang . . . an ominous sound . . . like the clang of a dissonant gong struck in the hollowed skull of a vulture-picked, fly-cleansed water buffalo. . .

See me as the duty officer, Doc . . . sitting in the ready room, the tent billowing in the harsh wind . . . I'm drinking hot coffee to warm these bowels ere they burst before the long windhowl night ends . . . morn's light brings Cochran to relieve me . . . he picks up the log book . . . turns to see the Hammer standing at the tent flap . . . grim-faced . . . sparks smoldering . . . he beckons with his finger . . . outside, in front of the ready room tent, the sign: HMM-188, THE HAMMERING EIGHTS with scarlet claw hammers and eggbeater props flying figure eights over a bright golden background . . . it lies flattened . . . splintered into plywood shreds . . . sand covers the remnants . . . it must be replaced . . . and replaced posthaste . . . the Hammer leaves it up to us . . . every officer knows how to handle these problematicals, Doc . . . pass them on down the line . . . Sergeant Soonto, front and center . . .

Da Nang . . . an echo like the memory of third-grade frolics . . .

dropping the chalice with a clang . . . a costumed pageant that Momma cried over and Daddy snored through . . . we're going to Da Nang and the soldiers are coming to Soc Trang . . . and in keeping with the spirit, the winds . . . the fickle tickle of the Capricorn highs and the sibilant sighs of the tropical lows . . . the winds will change, too . . .

The dry season arrives in the Delta. The wet Southwest Monsoon breeze turns into a hot humid wind, bringing steady heat and cloudless skies. Three months of sun, persistent as time, unbearable as fate. Hard-baked rice paddies and sticky skivvy drawers.

In Da Nang, low clouds cover the hills with mist and rain. The Northeast Monsoon, the mountain rainy season, is upon Da Nang. The Army will bring their heat and helicopters to Soc Trang. We will take our machines and wet weather to Da Nang.

But before the change, the Army had to finish a final job in Soc Trang. No canvas-tubbed, chemically cleaned, water purification system for the doggies. Their engineers dug a well, put up a water tower, stood back proudly and announced the changeover could now be made; flush toilets and hot-water showers are ready for use.

Two days before the move we wake up to discover the new aluminum painted water tower defaced with Army-baiting taunts. Across the front, a prankster has painted a Marine Corps globe and anchor. Beneath, in the same black paint, the letters: USMC. The decorators covered the rest of the water tower with taunting phrases: ARMY SUCKS. FUCK YOU DOGGIES. BITE THE HAMMER'S CLAW.

The Hammer strides out of his tent, sees the water tower and calls for his number-two man, "Major Lurnt!"

The Exec runs out in his skivvies and gapes while the Hammer bellows for him to By God get every bit of that black paint removed, and not after breakfast, but right now.

An hour later a working party has covered the black blasphemy with fresh aluminum paint. The Marines stare at the repaint job and mumble and sulk. The last item to disappear is the Marine Corps Emblem.

"That's a mistake," says Cochran. "The Hammer could have at least left the globe and anchor on the tower for the Army to paint over. Now the men will make sure they leave a message."

The next day someone has painted a crude drawing of a claw hammer striking an Army helmet. ARMY TAKES A MARINE CORPS POUNDING.

"I won't have it," the Hammer vows, striking his fist into his hand. "Gross insubordination, disobedience of a direct order. You'll put it to a halt . . ."

"Yes, sir." Major Lurnt hops in his jeep and drives to town and buys the last gallon of aluminum paint in the province, vowing this is the final repainting job he'll organize, tonight he'll put an armed guard on the tower.

Before dusk a sentry armed with rifle, bandoleer, flashlight and whistle takes up his position below the water tower. He remains on post until midnight when he is relieved by another Marine who an hour later, rather than suffer a knock on the head, is willingly led away and tied up by unknown assailants.

We are up before dawn for an early takeoff, baggage aboard the helicopters for the six-hour flight to Da Nang. C-123 supply planes will shuttle the heavy equipment and, following the Hammer's itemized schedule, the squadron will be moved and ready to begin flight operations out of Da Nang by dawn tomorrow morning.

Cochran and I preflight the bird. Sergeant Soonto hovers around the troop-compartment door. The belly is crammed with sea bags and footlockers.

"Good morning, Soonto," Cochran says. "All ship-shape, ready to fly?"

"Yessir, Lieutenant, *ichi ban*, number one."

We turn to continue the preflight. A little *yip* makes us pause. Cochran's eyebrows rise. We turn back. Soonto is busy tightening a strap around some crates. Cochran leans in the belly of the bird for a looksee. I peer over his shoulder. Soonto's catchall sits next to the door. It's not zipped shut and a black wet nose pushes at the opening.

"What have we here?" Cochran says, reaching in. The nose juts out, forcing the zipper open, followed by a white muzzle, snarling teeth, a fierce growl and a quick snap at Cochran's hand, jerked away an instant ahead of the sharp teeth.

"Here now," Soonto orders in a stern voice. "None of that. You mind your manners. These are *officers*."

"Yes, please do be a good dog," Cochran says. "Open the bag, Soonto, let's see what you've been hiding."

Black and white spotted, skinny and long-legged, one ear cocked, the other hanging down, we recognize him instantly: the cur we thought we ate when we flew Madam Nhu to Sadec.

"What the hell," I say. "You mean that wasn't the meat in the stew?"

"I'm sure he wasn't the only cur in the ville," says Cochran.

"Un-fucking-believable. You've had him here all this time, Soonto? How's come we never saw him before?"

Soonto shrugs. "Kept him in the hangar and the back room of the line shack. The men, you know, they sort of adopted him, our mascot."

The dog is suspicious; will Soonto let these strangers cart him off to the butcher? He curls his lip, narrows his eyes, tense.

I laugh. *"Un perro demenio,"* I say. "Oh, I am so frightened, *perro.*"

Soonto's eyes light up. "That's it, Lieutenant. You nailed it. A devil dog. A real Marine."

Cochran shakes his head. "You've kept him hidden this long, might as well bring him to Da Nang. We'll see how it plays up there."

"Yessir, Lieutenant." He pushes the dog into the catchall. "You stay there, now, and no noise, you hear?" Zips the bag.

Cochran turns to me as we walk around the back of the chopper. "That's not just Soonto's cur, it's his curmudgeon."

"For sure. Hope he has his rabies shot. Isn't a Marine devil dog a boxer?"

"Well, yeah, in true Corps lore, but we don't have to take it literal.

They call us leathernecks, you know, but now our shirts have soft collars. Let's get a move on, we're about to go."

The choppers are lined up on the runway. From where we sit the water tower shines clean of any painted blasphemy.

"Soc Trang tower," the skipper radios. "Hammer Flight ready for takeoff."

"Roger, Hammer flight. Have a good trip and happy hunting."

The round dome of the sun sprouts out of the horizon as we wheel in a lazy arc over town and descend toward the airfield for a final low pass. We cross the field at two hundred feet and I look down at the heads, the mess hall, the few tents remaining and the hangar, searching for something that will lock this place in my memory. It looks the same, as familiar and nondescript as ever. Except, unseen from the ground, a red Marine Corps Emblem covers the top of the water tower. Then, in front of us, tall white numbers appear: HMM-188 THE FLYING EIGHTS, painted across the runway in ten-foot-high letters.

No one breaks radio silence to comment, and the Hammer flies on, making me wonder if, unknowing, he thinks he has won the battle of the paint, or if, knowing, and not saying anything, he keeps us in doubt. Cochran chews his gum, noncommital, intent on flying a good wing. He glances at me, shakes his head and shrugs his shoulders.

I pull down my visor, fold my arms over my chest and close my eyes; snoozing, until Cochran nudges me to take the controls. I lock on the section leader, and while Cochran sleeps I say farewell to the Delta.

Goodbye I sing to the rice paddies. *Goodbye* I jig a dance on the rudder pedals to the farmers. I hosanna the canals, paddies and the binjo ditches. Transferring to a camp with permanent buildings, a BOQ, toilets and showers is anticipated with pleasure, getting there is a day-long flight.

The contour of the country changes, rolling hills replacing the flat delta as we climb towards the northern plateau.

"Look there," Sergeant Soonto calls over the intercom.

A big black beast thunders over the turf, raising puffs of dust.

"What the hell?"

Cochran banks for a closer look. A big bastard of an elephant, wide-eyed, huge-tusked and hung like the bull boss of the herd.

"Imagine that," Cochran says, "nothing but jungle and that big bull waving his trunk and bellering for some cow he can spend the day humping."

"Let's plug him," I say. "Drill the muthah smack dab in his loathesome head. Gotcha Dumbo. I'll gouge out his tusks with my survival knife and load the ivory aboard, sit around the fire every evening with my chisels, carving small images and goddesses in homage to the Elephant Bwana, the good tuskmaster. I'll use his scrotum for a tool sack."

"I don't think the tuskmaster would appreciate that."

"Ha ha. No ivory goodies for you, spoilsport."

"I do believe you are going native, Tomas. Time you had a little R and R. What do you think, Soonto?"

"That's a ten-four. We'll burn that town to the ground."

"What town's that?" I chime in.

"Hong Kong, Bangkok, Manila. Take your pick."

We make a refueling stop at Nha Trang. Shut down and heat C-rats on the engine manifold. Soonto sneaks his cur out for a pee and a dump.

"Load 'em up," and we're aloft again, four sections of six choppers each, strung out across the sky, our backs and bottoms stiff, the morning enthusiasm long-since vibrated into numb endurance.

"Check that out," Cochran says.

A long line of dark insectlike choppers passes on our left, the Army Flying Bananas heading for Soc Trang. The poor bastards will be operating tomorrow morning, fighting to keep those monstrosities in the air. We'll be doing the same, not missing a beat, peering ahead, eyes squinting until we give up, realizing we can't see all that far ahead.

What lies ahead is a seacoast city. Beaches with white clear sand stretch for miles. Breakers spank the sand. Mountain ridges nudge the seacoast like a resting dinosaur's tail, and clouds cover their peaks.

The slopes are thick with rain-forest growth. Waterfalls plummet down vertical cliffs.

We arrive at the Da Nang airbase along with an evening shower. The airfield, two long parallel runways capable of handling jets and large transports, is three miles from camp and we sit next to the helicopters waiting for trucks to haul us to our new quarters.

A jeep pulls up ahead of the trucks. Emmett jumps out. He was part of the team sent ahead to prepare everything for our arrival. He gets on the truck, a big six-by-six with planks along the sides to sit on. We follow him aboard and as we head out, he begins talking, our tour guide.

"You'll note, the road is a mess, a battle between the Marines and the flooded clay roadbed. It's a tossup which will win, but the Motor Transport boss has a heavy duty road grader to throw into the fray. The engineers build, grade, tamp, smooth and repair the road until they have it in good working condition. Then a single hour's rain floods the road and digs foot-deep rivulets across the crown, but Captain Road Grader clamps another cigar between his teeth, rousts his weary crew and once again roars to the attack."

Emmett points out a pile of dirt and a ditch running alongside the road.

"There's the water line, runs from the air base to our compound. When I got here we had no water. The grader had plowed up the line, flooded this whole area we're driving past. Drained the big water tank. Gave Captain Road Grader an excuse to build a new water line, and he had ditch digging equipment flown in from Japan."

We give the construction a desultory glance. How much longer is this going to go on? The whole damned ride it looks like. Emmett has the bit and isn't letting go.

"Colonel Swinn, the camp commander, had to curb the engineers' grand ambitions. They were beginning to take precedence over everything, so, once he was one grader blade ahead of rainstorm destruction, Colonel Swinn ordered Captain Road Grader to hold the line. Ah, here we are, our new home."

We pull off the road through a gate and into a walled compound. Brick-and-mortar buildings, a central courtyard, everything clean and neat.

"Enlisted men's barracks to the right, mess hall in the middle, senior officer's rooms in the building straight ahead. New home for the junior officers is here on the left."

We climb down, toting our duffel bags. Emmett stands at the door of a long building, windows lining the sides.

"These are the old barracks where the French Legionnaires lived when they were fighting their war. Unfortunately for them, Viet Minh guerillas snuck in one night and killed them all in their sleep."

He doesn't get the reaction he hoped for. Who gives a shit? But in honor of the history we dub our new quarters the Frog House. Where the ghosts of the Legionnaires drink pernod and nibble on truffles.

A hall runs the length of the building, down the middle. Cochran and I and Ben-San and Rob Jacobs grab a room across from the toilets and showers.

The water tank never refills. Not enough water in the well, or maybe the pump can't supply enough. When the tank runs low we go on water hours, and can only brush our teeth, flush the toilets and shave and shower two hours a day.

We have maids and a barber. We no longer wash our mess kits in the immersion heaters. Instead, real plates and knives and forks are cleaned by Vietnamese pot-wallopers hired to do the pearl diving. Liberty goes every night in a town full of booze and broads.

"If we no longer live like animals in tents, don't have to scrape stainless steel mess trays, walk half a mile to shit in a hole, then for God's sake why can't we have other good things too? Like some roundeye women?" Rob Jacobs complains.

"That's not going to happen, but you're right," Ben-San says. "In Soc Trang it was part of the game to go without sex—maybe in a moment of extreme horniness bang an ARVN camp follower snuck under the barbed wire, but in this regal setting, we're entitled to a higher class of damsels."

Doc Hollenden comes into our room. He's more nervous than ever, looking out the window, hefting the pistol he strapped on his belt that first day he arrived, bleary and acid-stomached, from his drunken layover in Japan.

"I asked them not to send me here," he mutters. He belches and fights down the rancid juice. "Look here." He shows us a piece of paper. "The VD list. It's distributed around the command to discourage the men from sticking their dicks in dirty holes. Colonel Swinn told me to do something about it, there's officers' names on that list. So, I've been treating the officers on the sly, scratching their names off the list."

"Good for you," Cochran says. "Think how it looks, the men getting the idea old Captain What's His Name is one of the boys. Why, he's got the clap, just like me. Man has his pleasures, the bill will come due and he'll have to pay up. Put my name on there. I'm not worried about anyone seeing it."

"But you don't have the disease," Doc Hollenden says.

"How they gonna know? It'll look funny if there's no officers' names on the list."

Doc Hollenden stares at the paper. "I'm not sure . . ."

"You never are. Take the bull by the horns, Doc. Make him roar."

He pushes the Doc out the door.

"Lights out, men," he says. "Tonight we sleep. Tomorrow we fly."

13. The Native Seers

Clean sweep fore and aft, Doc . . . sweep this shoulder rot right out the door . . . it's a stinking bleeding mess, fouling the whole deck and I want to be shunt of it . . . I know you can do it, Doc, if you follow the example of the do-gooders . . . those twinkling-eyed, firm-handshaking, stalwart, upright men who can spot a thirteenth-century boondoggle all the way from the heights of their rooftop tables at the Continental Hotel in downtown Saigon . . . looky there, one cries, how those poor unfortunate women are all bent over, using short-handled brooms to sweep out the dirt . . . no wonder they are so round shouldered, so crooked backed . . . put it on the hot wire to Washington, code red . . . and, in rapid response, fifty thousand American brooms with full-length handles are offloaded from the cargo jet at Ton Son Nhut airport . . . they will install some spinal rectitude . . . God knows the nation can use it . . . and the brooms go out to every hamlet, every ville, every outpost . . . while the Dudley Do Rights in Saigon sip their gin and tonics and gaze out over the land from their vantage point high above Saigon city and see . . . what the fuck! . . . Vietnamese women not grateful at all, are still bent over, still sweeping with short-handled brooms . . . while the cut-off tops of the American broomsticks lean against the walls . . . sad testament to another failed attempt to bring modern technical expertise to a backward nation . . . and if this pain is any indication, the emergency treatment on my shoulder is going the same direction . . . consult the native seers, Doc . . . they wink knowingly, nod heads, read the signs . . . the moon is full . . . time to plant rice and conceive children . . . make auspicious sacrifices to the Oriental gods that escaped the missionaries' purge . . . hang banners from overhangs and eaves of houses . . . mutter strange incantations . . . burn incense . . . smoke curls above the trees . . . babies are shushed . . . solemn rites begun . . . distant sound of thunder, muffled, unlike the usual thump of artillery . . . no night to wander the streets . . . get a prescription, Doc . . . jungle powders . . . dried yarbs . . . hootchie-kootchie dancers . . .

The morning breaks quiet and clear. The flight line is busy, twelve birds scheduled to carry troops to a mountain outpost sixty miles to the south.

Clouds and mist lying off the northern end of the runway seep across the field. The first drips of rain are gentle but denser drops quickly displace the wispy spray. The monsoon has arrived.

The ready room is cold and harshly lit. The walls are damp, and the clothing racks reek with the smell of sweat-stained body armor and musky gun belts. In the front of the room the map board is layered with enemy positions and friendly outposts, the whole picture a tangled mess.

"Be ready for anything," the Hammer warns. "We won't know what we get until we find out what we've got."

It's too early to mutter insidious responses to that meaningless statement and we file silently out of the ready room to preflight the choppers. Engines screaming and rotors clattering, we lift off in a welter of spray. We're doing the old-fashioned troop switcheroo. Shuttle a replacement group of ARVNs into a mountain outpost. Move in a hundred men and seven thousand pounds of supplies. Haul out the soldiers we're replacing.

Montagnards, mountain tribesmen wearing bead necklaces and brass bracelets, live in the village ringing the outpost. The women are bare breasted and sagging, the men taciturn and staring. The Montagnards are ancient enemies of the Vietnamese, who consider the mountain people barbarians. But in order to help combat the VC, the Montagnards are flown to the lowlands in small groups and trained to use modern weapons, and then carried back to the mountains to fight on the government's side. The Vietnamese are leery of the setup, figuring once the VC are destroyed, the Montagnards will turn on the government and establish their own mountain state. Necessity makes for uncomfortable bedmates.

The first trip to the outpost, Captain Beamus, leading the flight, gets lost. He goes up the wrong valley, makes a wrong turn at a river fork and we tool in circles for twenty minutes while everyone screams directions over the radio, confusing Wee Willie Weems, Captain Beamus's copilot.

Wee Willie, so named because of his short stature and good nature, often gets the short end of the stick, which means flying copilot with Captain Beamus a lot. Wee Willie is good at map reading, but Captain Beamus constantly doubts Willie's instructions. Thus we endure the endless circling.

We hunt for the outpost until we're low on gas and Captain Beamus decides to go back and start all over again. We make a long slow turn, everyone heading back except Emmett, the number one plane in our division. He goes on ahead, calling, "I think I see the place," and we follow him to a clearing under the clouds which reveals the landing strip. Captain Beamus catches up with us and barrels ahead to make a low pass over the field.

Cochran watches him go, then turns to me. "'Huck, old buddy. I don't know what the rest of the boys are looking at, but that's not the same field that's on my map."

Captain Beamus reaches the same conclusion. He turns back toward Quang Ngai, the coastal refueling strip. I ease off power to conserve fuel and it's a nut-clutching thirty-minute flight to Quang Ngai with bingo fuel in the tanks, too fine a calculation for my timid soul.

While we're on the ground refueling, Captain Beamus rails at everyone, first blaming Wee Willie for getting us lost. He then delivers a biting lecture on radio discipline and the unacceptable insubordination of pilots who go tooling off on their own. He looks at Emmett, who looks back, poker faced. Captain Beamus drops it but he exchanges copilots with Emmett, Wee Willie for Herbee Jenkins, a guarantee of success, for Herbee goes along with everything and doesn't argue with the aircraft commander, even when the pilot may be in the wrong.

The next trip looks like a lark. The route is familiar, the weather clear, and everyone is happy until Captain Beamus again misses the outpost, flying away from it in the wrong direction, eleven choppers following faithfully and silently, observing very careful radio discipline, everyone fully aware of our leader's mistake.

"He can fly us to hell for all I care," says Cochran, putting prevailing sentiment into words. We continue in the wrong direction until an anonymous pilot, not wanting to waste the entire day on the same dull run, chances a blast from Captain Beamus and calls, "Target bears thirty degrees to starboard."

Captain Beamus doesn't respond to the voice but turns the thirty degrees and heads for the outpost. Just as the short landing strip appears on a scarred and barren mountain top, Emmett's engine coughs, two black clouds pop out the exhaust like twin cannonballs, and the engine quits. Emmett plummets toward the strip, autorotating to the one open spot in thirty miles of jungle. Cochran guns after him, sure as the saints that he won't make it, but Emmett screeches in a tight turn, hits the middle of the strip, bounces over a mound of dirt, skips across a ditch, and comes to rest on a pile of bamboo poles. The Vietnamese troopers fly out of the cabin door like baseballs knocked from a batting cage.

"Clear the field. Emergency. Emergency." Cochran calls on the radio and there follows a wild chopper dance as everyone skitters clear of the strip. Finally we land and shut down and get out of the helicopter.

Mechs surround Emmet's chopper and open the doors to the engine. After a long discussion they decide it is a blown cylinder. Everyone agrees Emmett did a terrific job making it to the landing strip, testimony to his excellent flying skills.

Cochran and I visit the village, a collection of hastily assembled huts and tents built for a tribe of Montagnards who walked out of the jungle seeking sanctuary. Montagnard customs make the strongest occidental stomach quiver with anxious peristalsis. While still in the hairless stages of puberty they prepare for the trials and ordeals of adulthood by clubbing out their front teeth. High on betel nut, they file the stumps down to bloody gums before enjoying the first grown-up pleasures of marriage, hunting and sweet yam digging: full time jungle occupations.

The pain remains after the betel nut wears off. The chunks of teeth left imbedded infect their gums and they walk around for the rest of their lives hawking pus and gunk which gloms to bare feet like sticky patches of gum. U.S. Army dentists make the rounds of the villages, curing the infections by removing the old rotten stumps and packing the holes with antibiotics. The Americans are suddenly in popular demand around the mountains, possessing magic which can relieve some of the pain of primeval survival.

We're in the village on rice-distribution day and families are gathered around a large thatched longhouse. Old men in loincloths, women draped in brightly colored blankets, everyone bedangled with bracelets, neckpieces and huge earrings, some plain round hoops, others bent in wild elaborate designs. A soldier doles out rice from a large sack marked with the Hands Across The Sea emblem.

Cochran walks around, looking for something to trade. Crossbows are a hot item, going for pocket knives, cigarette lighters and other knicknacks, but the market has been so glutted the price of a crossbow is now hard Vietnamese cash. Cochran hopes to get around the inflation by dealing with the bare-chested women. Planning ahead, he went into Da Nang one day and bought some items to barter with.

He pulls wildly colored, delicately laced panties and bras from the pockets of his flight suit. Then he entices a shy woman to come closer, take a look, feel the material. Cochran holds a bra up to his chest and points to her breasts. She laughs, blackened stumps exposed, and the other women giggle and push her forward. Cochran turns his head and spits. A bright red gob splatters across the dirt. His teeth are stained dark purple. He hikes the straps over her shoulders, and fastens the snaps across her back. It's a red lacy number with a deep cleavage.

Cochran claps his hands. "Wonderful," he cries.

She is delighted and turns to the other women who cluster around, touching and prodding the strange new garment. In a few minutes Cochran exhausts his supply. The Montagnard women exchange their husbands' crossbows, arrows and wooden spears for the cotton-and-silk underthings.

Cochran gathers his booty and carries it to the helicopter, stopping outside to hawk a virulent plug at my feet.

"Pretty good haul, huh?" he says.

I stare at the wet mess spreading in the dirt. "What the hell is that? You taking up betel nut now?"

"Agghh," he grimaces. "Tried it but I can't stand the taste. Made up my own mixture of Mail Pouch and food coloring. Always said the only way to deal with the folk is get down to their level."

He spits again, another red glob.

The natives are hungry and grubby, but the American adviser, an unassuming Special Forces Major with the mild manners of a history professor, tells us this is the best they've ever had it and they like the treatment they're receiving. The Sneaky Pete Special Forces have taken on the Montagnards as their pet project, drawing from a seemingly unlimited supply of money to buy them weapons, supplies, vehicles and ammunition. Once a month the supply officer makes the rounds of the Sneaky Pete outposts. He carries a wooden chest full of freshly minted piasters, money he gives the Montagnards.

"You mean we're paying them to fight?" Cochran asks.

The supply officer winks. The Sneaky Petes have found a means of bypassing the rule stating we're here only to advise, not to take charge.

"If they take our money they'll also take our orders," he says.

Captain Beamus has been listening in. He revels in this kind of insider dirt. He steps into the conversation and adds his astute analysis of the current military situation, taking advantage of the opportunity to discuss it man to man, Marine pilot to Special Forces adviser. I wander off to investigate the dirty mud huts, village pets and scattered machine gun emplacements.

Ben-San follows a few minutes later, shaking his head.

"I can't believe Captain Beamus," he says.

"What now?"

"The Sneaky Pete Major was saying they have leopards wandering around the outpost. Last night one got blown up in the minefield. Captain Beamus couldn't get the picture. 'A leopard?' he said. 'A tame one?'"

Ben-San shakes his head again. "The adviser completely ignored him. Went on saying they have seen the Viet Cong using elephants to carry their mortars and artillery pieces into the hills."

Cochran walks up, the corners of his mouth stained, and I ask him if he was there.

"There for what?"

"When the Major said a leopard wandered into the minefield last night, Captain Beamus wanted to know if it was a tame one."

Cochran laughs. "Captain Beamus isn't the only one out of it."

"What do you mean?" says Ben-San, realizing Cochran is about to spring something on him. "Isn't it true?"

"It's true enough, only the Major was talking about lepers, not leopards. The villagers won't allow them in the compound and last night one wandered into the minefield."

"A leper," says Ben-San. "No wonder the Major ignored him. You mean a wild one? That's raw."

"Mount up," Captain Beamus orders. "We've got a load of passengers to take back to Da Nang before dark."

"Wild ones?" Ben-san yells back, but Captain Beamus stalks down the path as if he hasn't heard.

"Haw," Ben-San guffaws, mentally preparing the story for the evening playback at the bull roar session in the Frog House.

We lift off and fly out of the mountains. Captain Beamus is pleased. His perserverance has paid off. After three tries, he navigated us directly to the outpost and we completed our mission before dark. He voices a little braggadocio over his triumph: "My head may be bloody but I'm still unbowed. I was determined to find that place."

Although a broken chopper still sits at the outpost, a reminder that as soon as the weather clears we will have to return with a maintenance crew to repair and fly it out. Captain Beamus will avoid that chore, thank you, not his department. We arrive in Da Nang with low clouds hanging over the runway and slog to the Frog House.

We never know from one day to the next if we will be flying or sitting on the ground. October is an on-and-off month. Rains ten hours straight, then lays off two or three, or whimsically, will be clear during the day and then pour all night. The only consistent prediction is that it will rain, no telling exactly when. We get news of the Cuban Missile Crisis, half a world away, a world poised on the brink of nuclear destruction.

"There's a silver lining to this," Cochran says. "If the shit hits the fan and the missiles fly we're sitting in the safest place possible. No one's going to give a fuck about Vietnam."

14. The Old Pissing Contest

What could be worse than this, Doc . . . worse than getting all shot up . . . only one thing I can think of . . . but it's so much worse it's unthinkable . . . drop a Fat Man on the fuckers . . . that'll end this dirty little war and put the kibosh on the Red Horde . . . leave them crawling out of a radioactive hole . . . sounds muy estupido, *doesn't it Doc . . . the same thing came up in flight school . . . the instructor asked me if I had to make the decision in 1945 would I have dropped the bomb . . . I was stumped . . . what was I supposed to do . . . jump in a time machine . . . go back to 1945 . . . do I take my present-day knowledge with me or am I starting clean . . . if I'm there then with what I know now, hell no, I won't drop the bomb . . . but if I don't know the consequences then I might go with the party line . . . end the war . . . spare us invading Japan . . . save thousands of American lives . . . the instructor is getting impatient . . . I dip into the Cochran playbook and dissemble . . . I tell him, yeah, I'd drop the bomb . . . on an unoccupied island . . . pissed the instructor off . . . but it would work, I told him . . . when the Japanese saw what the bomb could do, they would surrender . . . and everyone could go home . . . were it only so easy, Doc . . . to get out of this mess and go home . . . but I have promises to keep . . . and there's miles to go before we sleep . . .*

Across the Song Han river from Da Nang, off the highway and over the sand dunes, the beach lies flat and white, glittering like a blanket of tiny crystals, soft near the dunes, packed firm where the waves spank the crystals flat. Each incoming slap followed by the whispering retreat of the backslipping water. The sky is clear, a blue dome pulled down to the sea and clamped in place.

A six-by-six truck drives through the sand to the water's edge and deposits a load of Marines. The men spread from the truck like flowers opening to the sun. The truck turns around and roars off. For the next six hours we are free, no claim laid on our bodies other than the sun, the breeze, the prickly sand and the salty sea.

"Why hasn't Henry Kaiser capitalized on this?" says Cochran, eyeballing the horizon from the mountains to the sea. "He could spend half his fortune turning Vietnam into a resort."

Instead of aluminum hotels the Vietnamese have constructed thatched-roof, flattened beer can siding shacks filled with tables and canvas back chairs, the structures shaded by scarlet and gold awnings. Kids hawk pop and *Bia La Rue*.

A party of Marines pours into a shack. Their portable radio is tuned to Armed Forces Radio Saigon and they begin foot-skipping and diddy-bopping to the thump of a loud electric bass. In the distance a thin black line stretches down the beach, extending from the dunes to the water, blurred shapes of human figures.

"Better check that out," Cochran yells.

We run down the beach past a group of Marines sitting on the sand with their feet cooling in the water.

"Where you off to in such a rush?" one of the Marines yells.

"Crazy beach scene up ahead," Cochran answers.

As we get closer a boat takes shape in the water, an oversized rowboat riding low in the trough of a wave, then it dances on top of a swell, the bow rising out of the water like a marlin.

Wiry Vietnamese men pull on a rope that stretches into the sea. The men lean into the rope, their legs muscled and bronze, their faces blank as the sand. As the sea breathes and a wave brushes the shore, the rope slackens and in unison the men pull, one step, then another. Then they wait.

"Fishing," says Cochran.

"That's it," I say. "They've got a net out and there's a buoy. That must be the end of the net."

The men take up a few inches of line and I watch for the buoy to move but it is too far away to tell. Cochran walks up to the line and pulls on it. The Vietnamese watch warily. One of the younger men gestures and Cochran wraps his arm around the rope and leans into it.

"Pull me hearties. Give her a good yank. Come on, you lubbers, lend a hand."

I catch hold and help pull. Cochran begins to chant: "*Yo-ho, here we go, with a hidey-hie and a hidey-ho, we pull with all our might, we pull the rope out of sight.*"

The rope begins to move, inching towards the dunes where a Vietnamese fisherman coils the rope in a circular pile. The head man stands in water up to his waist, feeling the rope, testing its strain. *Take it easy*, he motions, but we pull on.

"*Give her your heart, your throbs, your sway-backing best. Don't slack when a fish gets away and we have to pull in the rest.*"

Farther down the beach another group pulls on the other half of the net, a huge bow sweeping across the sea, trapping the fish in its ponderous path. Ponderous until now. The rhythm of the centuries is disrupted.

"*Now me hearties with the balls to go with your brawls. Fling your fists into the fray and put your back into the bay.*"

Not for us to pull with the motion of the waves. Not for us the long day's grind to net a passel of fish. We, by Jesus, got a man's hold on the rope and will have that net full of fish on dry land within the hour or eat humble pie in the coliseum at dawn.

The head man makes frantic waving motions, exhorting us to slow down, but Cochran sings out, unheeding, sweat pouring into his eyes.

My legs and back throb and the rope makes an indentation in my arm. The net inches forward, a slow pulsing movement. The waves help and we gain. The ebb hinders and we pull harder to make a profit when we should be content with saving a loss, and then, suddenly, the rope breaks.

"Son of a bitch," Cochran yells, holding the raveled end of rope in his hand. "Guess we got a bit too testy for her."

The head man screams at his crew. They stand on the beach looking bewildered. It is a catastrophe they weren't prepared for and while they moan and cry we roll in the sand laughing.

"You got to pull with the current," Cochran yells. "Just like I was saying. You can't rush these things."

The head man looks from Cochran to his net. How many years of pulling in that look? To have these foreigners bull in with their unasked-for help and botch everything?

Cochran leaps up, his laughing jag over.

"Don't sweat it, old man," he says, and, grabbing the free end of rope, he plunges into the water. I jump in behind him and we swim toward the wooden buoy. Even with our frantic pulling the buoy hasn't moved very close to shore and we attack the water with the same vehemence we used to break the rope. A quarter mile from shore, my breath stabbing like a blunt bayonet in my ribs, Cochran turns and motions. Ahead, limp as a petered-out dick, is the other end of the rope. Cochran mates the ends in a granny knot, "Everlasting and evermore till rot do you part," and we rest on the taut rope.

"That dumb son of a bitch. Did you see his face when the rope broke?"

Again Cochran laughs, the low sound rumbling deep in the pit of his stomach masking the silent panic that struggles for escape every time one of his booming deeds blows up in his face.

He lets go of the rope and we swim to the beach and collapse on the sand, luxuriating in the warmth until the Vietnamese bring in their net and catch of fish, the sun drops behind the mountains, and the truck grinds down to the water's edge to load us aboard and carry us back to the base.

Cochran and I decide to stop in town. We jump off the truck and wander the streets where we laugh at the kids, goof with the bar girls and mosey into a tapestry shop. Pete Alexander, the camp interpreter, is inside buying a green and red silk banner with Chinese emblems embroidered up and down its sinuous length. We look it over and Pete deciphers the story for us. The characters stand for good health, many children, big fortune and long life, the usual characterization of wishful thinking since the only one that ususally comes true is a houseful of hungry kids.

Another tapestry catches Cochran's attention. A large white silk bedspread with long tassels hanging around the edge. Four smoke-blowing dragons, eyes buggy, horny spikes along their backs, ears pointed and sinister. The dragons twist around a slant-eyed tiger, his ears laid back and mouth turned down, tooth hanging over a nasty-looking lip, head centered in a garland of flowers.

"Wonder how much this costs," Cochran says. "Hey, man," he asks the bowing owner. "How much? How many pees?"

The old man clasps his hands and smiles. Then he says something in Vietnamese.

"Huh? What's that? What'd he say? How much?"

Pete Alexander has been listening. "He says it's already been sold. He made it for a soldier in the United States Army."

"Ask him if he can make one for me."

Pete says something in Vietnamese and the owner answers, gesturing towards the bedspread, his face animated.

"It takes a very long time to make," Pete interprets. "He has to design each dragon and draw it out and then stitch it together. The tiger takes longest of all. Every one he does is different. He puts an individual effort into each piece of embroidery."

"Yeah, yeah, I get it," says Cochran. "Artist-type character. But don't get me wrong, I've got nothing against that. Can he do one for me?"

"He says he can make you one like this or he can put something else on the banner."

"This one is fine. No. Wait a minute. There's one thing."

Cochran scratches the burr of hair sticking out of his shirt cuff. "Those flowers surrounding the tiger's head. They're not right."

Pete mentions it to the artist who goes into another long story, drawing his hands in a circle and talking all the while.

Pete translates. "The tiger lives in the jungle. He is the king of all the beasts and these flowers are the real plants found in the mountains of Vietnam—"

"Yeah, yeah, I can see that," Cochran interrupts. "Perfectly obvious. He has to frame the tiger's head, can't have a disembodied tiger head floating around in the middle of the bedspread. But why the sickly-looking bushes. Can't he frame the head in something else?"

Pete relays the question. "He says the jungle plants are a necessary part of the story. They fit the setting—"

"I realize all that," Cochran interrupts again. "Tell him the way I see it these dragons are lackeys of the tiger. They sit around blowing fire and smoke, keeping the king's paws warm and his whiskers curly. He's the top boy, the head honcho. He doesn't need those weasely vines wrapped around his head. How about some flames instead? Yeah, that's it. Flames from the dragons. Surrounding him but they can't touch him. He's too regal to be burned. Ask him if he can do flames."

Pete attempts to imitate Cochran's description but has to settle for a question about the flames. Cochran watches the old man closely, gauging his reaction. The owner shakes his head.

Cochran pokes me in the ribs. "Oh, oh. The old boy doesn't like it."

Pete argues some more. Finally he turns to Cochran. "He says he can do the flames if that's what you want."

"Good deal. How much?"

"We'll have to go in the other room and decide. He has to draw it out and figure the amount of material needed and then his wife sets the final price. She handles the business end of things."

We go into the back room and sit down in front of a low table where the owner's wife and another old woman are manicuring the evening's potion of betel nut. They first grind the betel nut and mix it in a lime paste, then they spread the goo on young green leaves. The women chew a gob, grind it down to juice and shreds before they start spitting. The betel nut eases the misery of their backs and erases the rheumatism in their bones, making them easy headed on a chewing and spitting spree. It also stains their teeth a dark black color which the wife counters by rubbing her mouth with lemon.

The owner wants two thousand piasters, about twenty- five dollars American, but Pete has overheard the old man say he made the other bedspread for fifteen hundred piasters and when Cochran hears that he offers twelve hundred. The old man waves his hand and laughs silently, pantomiming the outrageousness of the offer.

"Goddamnit, Pete, tell him I won't go over fifteen hundred pees, not after knowing he sold the other one for that."

The old man smiles sadly and shakes his head. He sketches in his notebook, writes down some figures and says something to Pete.

"He says he is very busy now and to get this done he'll have to hire out some of the needlework which makes it more expensive."

"Well piss on that," says Cochran. "If he can do one for some other guy, I guess he can do it for me. Tell him fifteen hundred and that's final."

Pete tells him and the owner jabbers to his wife. She spits and bats the argument right back. Pete gets up and says, "Let's go. She's trying to get him to accept it. Maybe he'll call us back when he sees we're walking out."

We get up, thank the old man, and say goodbye to the ladies. The owner rises, presses his hands together, we nod and walk out.

He doesn't call us back so we keep going.

"I can't figure it out," Pete says. "His wife wanted him to do it for fifteen hundred, but he told her, 'Truly I do not want to do this job,' and she didn't force him."

"Why that little bastard," says Cochran. "That's your artistic temperament for you. Fuck your belly to feast your soul." He lifts his nose and sniffs. "What's that smell?

An old wizened man, thin as a scarecrow with clothes to match, wheels a cart toward us. The closer the cart the grosser the smell.

"Durian," says Pete, "a real delicacy."

The nearer the vendor the ranker his wares.

"Yuck," Cochran says, "smells like a feefool, something between a feedlot and a cesspool."

"I was thinking more of a binwall," I say. "Something between a binjo ditch and a hog waller."

The cart stops alongside and we get a good look. Some kind of evil-looking fuit, a yellow ball of spikes. Cochran reaches out a tentative finger.

"Yikes, sharp. You could kill a person if you hit him in the head with one of those things."

"Let's get some and drop them from the choppers," I say.

"The Cong would like that," Pete says, "as long as you didn't hit them in the head. They believe the durian has magic powers, keeps you looking and feeling young, and it heats your body so you don't need a blanket to sleep at night."

The old man whacks a durian with a cleaver. It splits in half and the smell wafts up, worse than ever. The old man slices off a chunk and offers it to Cochran, who leans away, leery.

"Go ahead, try it," Pete says. "There's an old saying, 'When the durians come off the trees the *ao dais* come off the ladies.'"

"I get it. An aphrodisiac." He takes the chunk, holds his nose and bites off a little piece.

"Sometimes they roll the fruit on the ground to cover the thorns with grass and leaves," Pete says. "Then let elephants eat the durian. It comes out the other end whole. Enhances the eater's experience."

"Aaargh." Cochran spits out the chunk. "Why'd you have to tell me that?" He wipes his mouth. "Actually, I'm glad you did. I was about to swallow the damned thing."

The old man holds out his hand. Cochran pulls some piasters out of his pocket and gives them to the vendor. The old man pushes his cart forward and we head for the highway and catch a truck going to the base. We squat out of the wind for the bouncy ride home. Cochran works his mouth and jaw, trying to get rid of the durian taste.

"Those guys, they're something," he says. "The fruit-seller was pretty laid back and the old fisherman was a load, but the tapestry artist takes the cake. You got to admire him for refusing a job when his heart's not in it. Did you notice when it happened, when the deal was queered?"

I shake my head.

"Right when I told him how I saw the scene, how the tiger and dragons looked to me. He didn't like my version one bit. The layout was his idea and if he had to change it to suit someone else, then that guy's going to pay through the nose.

"Except I didn't do it. After I found out how much he sold the other one for I couldn't pay any more than that, just like he couldn't do the job for less than what he asked."

"Yeah, right, more of the old pissing contest." I tell him.

Cochran scratches his chest and shakes sand out of his shirt. My back is burned from the sun and raw from the salt water, my arm sore from the rope. I lean against the sideboards and scratch my shoulders on the wood. No sooner do I close my eyes than I'm jounced awake by the truck slamming to a stop.

"Home sweet home," Cochran says.

We're parked next to the mess hall. I climb down and stagger to the Frog House. We've missed the shower hours but I'm so beat it doesn't matter. Covered with sand and salt and burn, I fall into bed. Gladys can sweep up the mess in the morning.

15. Sixes Sir

Some water, Doc . . . a nice cool drink . . . that's the ticket . . . abolish all fever spots . . . empty the ice machine . . . raindrops falling on my head . . . sweet balm of rapture . . . fly me to the moon, Doc . . . I need a reprieve . . . Cochran is a maniac . . . we fly eleven hours on a massive troop lift, he never turns loose the controls . . . with the bit in his teeth, he's a horse not a gorilla . . . we refuel at a dirt strip with big black gas bladders filling us up . . . choppers gulping gas, three at a time . . . rotors shut down but engines running . . . we're full up . . . bird in front of us still refueling . . . Cochran curses, what's the fucking holdup . . . engages rotors, twists on turns, pulls the collective up and lifts off . . . raises a big cloud of dust and sends pebbles flying and the gas jockeys ducking . . . we fly across the runway five feet off the ground and sit down to wait . . . well, that was uncalled for, I tell him . . . he scowls and I don't touch the controls all day . . . he pays the price the next day. . . we sit waiting to be called for a supply run . . . Cochran, all worn out, sleeps in the shade of the chopper belly and when we're finally ordered out I fly every run . . . some kind of payback, there, Doc, or is it a reconciliation? . . . pffllff *. . . this water tastes like blood, Doc . . . what kind of service you offering here . . . fill your hand pard . . . hard to pander when you're potted . . .*

The officers kick in twenty-five bucks each for the pleasure of dickering with the Ice Queen. All base construction is conducted through the Ice Queen, a slinky, black-haired, English-speaking Vietnamese, who, even after taking her cut, still gives us a good deal. She'll build us a thatch-roofed and bamboo-sided officer's club that will be the envy of the compound. Not that that's much of a challenge. The Staff NCOs already have a club. They quietly built their own out of scrounged and moonlighted materials right after we arrived.

The first month here we drank in our rooms, hoping for an officer's club to magically appear. Then, no sooner do we start dickering with the Ice Queen, than the Hammer stands up at the morning meeting and announces we need an O club. We take that to mean he'll take on the job, so we back off with the dickering.

What it really means is that there's an immediate halt to the whole thing. The Hammer is too involved in operational planning to do anything about an O Club. He is ordered to Saigon for a conference and in his absence we hold an O club meeting in the Frog House and elect a board of governors with Emmett as our president. The resolution is passed that the club will belong to the men who built it, to run as we please with our rules and our policies. In the couple of days the Hammer is gone we get the working parties and committees organized, liquor is ordered and the Ice Queen is given the go-ahead to build.

When he returns, the Hammer surveys the lumber and bricks, retires to his room to run a private study of the plans and intentions, then reappears to okay the construction. The building materials are quickly assembled into a snazzy little hut with a thatched roof, brick and bamboo sides, a solid wall at one end, the other three walls screened waist-high to the roof. Liquor cabinets; rattan furniture; reefers leased from the Ice Queen; a suave Vietnamese bartender; two slinky waitresses; and the place is good to go.

We cool off with cold beer in the club after our touch football games. Following a long day in the cockpit, we drop in for gin and tonics. Poker games go until late hours. We have daylong gatherings when the rain puts a damper on the flight schedule and there's nothing to do but fill up on spirits and ride the high of a bottle of courage until some drunken shavetail tells a Major to go fuck himself and the place clears out.

But even during the carousing and the false courage of the bottle, a worm burrows in the backs of our minds: take care, take care. The heavies are watching.

We make a move before they strike. Call another meeting. The incubation period is over, the club has come of age. The initial investment is paid off and enough money has been made to declare free drinks one night a week. Now it's time to get serious. Before the heavies stomp on our free-wheeling antics we have to come up with some bylaws, a written creed of respectability.

"Yes, and about time," cry the malcontents, the prudes, the disapproving members who have been quietly watching the unbridled revelry. "We are still officers and Marines. We still carry the sword and the banner, ride the ball and eagle into backward illiterate nations. It's up to us to maintain tradition, provide protocol, uphold impeccability. We demand shirts and ties. Class Alpha uniforms, rules for behavior, an opening and closing time. Plus, of course," said demurely, "proper respect for age, infirmity, deformity and rank."

"Rank on this, you fuckheads," a member of the loosey goosey contingent fires back. "Take your namby pamby to the library. Here's where we let down our hair. Burrheads we may be but we sport handlebar mustaches waxed to sharp points. Stick ourselves in the bloodshot eyes. Down with your set of rules."

"Cop some couth," a rulemaker retorts. "Pay attention to what Miss Manners has to say."

"Señorita Manners can *chupa mí verga*, Jose; this is bandit country and that's cop my dick to you ignoramuses."

"Lay it on them, Tomas," Cochran says.

I bow, appreciatively. The opposition flashes lightning, roars thunder. Tigers and VC hide in their caves, wondering if a rabid herd of animals is running loose in Da Nang.

When the wrangling lulls, a general rule evolves: To each shall be left the discretion to dress properly and behave in a manner commensurate with the company and the crowd. A mission statement for the ages to include the aged. An opening and closing time is decided upon, and the meeting breaks up, the loosey-goosey core group assuaged, having salvaged a semblance of freedom. No ties required. Drinks all around.

The champagne taste of victory is soon barfed up in the form of sour bile. The Commanding General of the First Marine Aircraft Wing flies in from Japan for an official visit, and a party is held in his honor. We got a club, we got couth, and this time, instead of a knock-down, table-breaking, liquor-spilling, no-holds-barred brawl like we threw in Soc Trang, the Hammer orders up a classy cocktail party, starting at five in the O Club and ending at six thirty, after which the Heavies will attend a gala dinner, and when dessert is done, they will retire to their rooms with full stomachs and healthy belches, war and death having taken a backseat to the amenities of social decorum and witty repartee.

In order for everything to go smoothly, a notice is nailed to the O Club door. Shirts and ties are required for the cocktail party. This goes against our by-laws that require any changes to be okayed by a vote of all the members, but no one is there to cast a vote. The junior officers spend the day in the blue, turning the screw, and don't get back until after dark.

We jump off the bus and, still wearing our grubby flight suits, flock to the club. Notice on the door? What notice? Inside, the place is empty, the heavies having already departed for dinner. We belly up to the bar and call for drinks. Mai Duc, the Vietnamese bartender refuses to acknowledge our orders, falling back on the inscrutable Oriental bit, can't understand a word we say. He points to the door. *"Hui là."* Read the notice, numbnuts. So much for a drink. Too much trouble to change into the proper attire.

We drag over to the mess hall to eat and find it secured. The junior officers ate at five-thirty and now the dining hall is reserved for the General's party. The mess sergeant throws a case of C-rations out the door and we take it back to the Frog House and eat cold turkey in our rooms.

The next morning at the all-pilots meeting, Grits Emmett, our elected president, announces that from now on T-shirts will not be allowed in the club. We must either wear civilian shirts with collars or else our dungaree jackets.

T-shirted and unheeding I call out, "When did we vote on that?"

"We didn't . . ."

I start to shout, "Then who says so?" when I feel two laser beams of shut-your-mouth rays boring a hole in my forehead. Our father who art in command glares, a deep down meltdown that clams me totally.

It's the same old simple story. A fight for love that turns gory. Build a club the Hammer says. Finance it. Run it. Be the manager, secretary, treasurer and purchasing agent. Let's see some management ability out of you junior officers. Keep having your meetings and continue voting on your policies. For you are the ones in charge. Tiny tinkles of laughter.

I decide to boycott the club and drink in our room in the Frog House. Cochran is there haranguing our Vietnamese maid. No one can pronounce her name, so we call her Gladys. Cochran has on a pair of black Vietnamese pajamas with the legs way too short and a cooking pot lid on his head that's supposed to look like a coolie hat.

"Leave my stuff alone," Cochran says. "I don't need anyone making my bed, putting my clothes away. I can't find a damned thing."

Gladys, upset by his rant, covers her face. Pete Alexander, the camp interpreter, pulls her hands away and tells her Cochran isn't depriving her of a job, he is simply cuckoo and wants to make do for himself. Pete makes the circling squirrelly finger motion next to his temple, but she doesn't get it. She leaves to take care of another foursome down the hall. They will laugh and tease and make her job more enjoyable.

Out in the hall there is a crash and tinkling of broken glass. The light goes out. There's cursing, followed by laughter. The frisbee game that runs the length of the hall breaks up, an automatic forfeit when someone smashes one of the neon lights hanging from the ceiling. Pete Alexander goes out to see about cleaning up the mess.

Emmett comes in. He holds up a bottle of whiskey and tells us this stuff is so expensive you can't drink it, you can only suck on the cork. Cochran takes the cork and smells it. Emmett tells him to wipe the cracker crumbs off his mouth before he sucks the cork. Cochran stares at Emmett for a second and throws the cork out the window.

"What—" Emmett starts to say but Cochran interrupts, "That's a damned lie that I have cracker crumbs in my mouth and they're gonna contaminate your cork. Cork this, Grits." He gives him the finger.

"Don't call me Grits, you gorilla."

"Okay," Cochran says. "We both know gorillas cook their grits before they eat them."

Cochran holds out his hand. The cork is lying on his open palm.

"Here you go. The one I threw out the window I found on the floor. Suck on that."

"Suck this, asshole." Emmett grabs the cork and stomps out the door. Cochran turns to me.

"You can be a martyr to the cause," he says, "and sit in the room and drink, but I'm going over to the Club."

He spins his coolie hat on the floor with a clank, pulls a pair of pants over the pajamas, slips on a shirt and leaves me sitting in the chair I traded off an Army sergeant for a K-bar knife he could give to his C.O. who was being sent back to the states.

One time I came in the room after a long day of flying to find Rob Jacobs sprawled in the chair, his leg hanging over a chair arm, head lolling on the back cushion. He laughed when I told him to get up. I grabbed his leg and spun him out of the chair. Before he could go on the attack I was sprawled in his place.

"You can sit in it when I'm not here," I told him, "but when I want the chair, it's mine."

He didn't like it but he let it go and I'm thankful we didn't have any more problems about the chair. I can laugh about it now.

Outside, the sergeant of the guard chews out the sentry for lingering too long in the shadows of the building. On the other side of the concertina wire, the shrill voice of Hoang Dong, the famous Vietnamese singer, serenades the ARVN barracks. On our side of the wire, music booming out of the EM housing provides a rhythm and blues counterpoint. I stare at two drinks, a major decision facing me. With a Bloody Mary, various hot licks, with a double scotch, a cool elevated headcloud. I'm going for the heat.

I take a slug of Bloody Mary, turn on the tape recorder and add my musical offering to the mix. *Fight with the captain and I land in jail; ain't nobody around for to go my bail . . .*

In response, the enlisted men on the other side of the compound pump up the volume: *You got me working, boss man. You won't let me stop. You big boss man . . . you ain't so big. You tall, that's all . . .*

I scrunch my shoulders and swig down the scotch. I'll ignore the ramped-up music. Those bastards will never jump a man who doesn't give them cause. Is ignoring them a cause? Shit, I better let them know I know they're out there. I crank the volume to eleven, stare at the broken knob in my hand: *Well lawdy, lawdy, Miss Clawdy. Girl you sure look good to me. You like to ball every morning. Don't come home till late at night.*

OH, HOT DOG! I'm riding a blind hot streak of luck. Turned it around, drowning out those *patatas calor*, and I burst into song. "The Hawks and the Doves." *To shoot or not to shoot. Some say yea and some say nay. When the moment comes you have to pick your way.* And yes, oh Sweet Jesus, thank the Lord, they dig it . . . or do they? What's the vision? How does it look through the third eye. . . ?

It looks like a tiny postage stamp of an outpost sitting on a cliff edge I'm bearing down with a full load in the belly my right hand a grip of death on the stick my left hand a full throttle power drive to the deck and hit the ground with a thud kick the gear out Emmett peels my fingers off the stick says you punched out the ASE punched it out on purpose says I who needs Automatic Stabilization when he's got the bird under total control I'll fly it home says Emmett you get an up on your flight check by the way and what a relief that is but it sounds like they're not happy with my choice of music over in the EM quarters *big brawl man, can't you hear me when I whack you with a wooden cot stake* that starts a big fight with not much damage inflicted but every jarred head that comes out shaved from the barber shop will be covered with battle dressings maybe I'll shave my head in solidarity to show them one officer's copacetic, but does anybody care?

Better drink on it. I pour another combination, scotch murky in one glass, Mary bloody in another, her head stuck on a celery stalk. The walls are peeling, globs of effluvium slide to the floor . . . red like ketchup, red like tomato juice, red like a Bloody Mary . . . I belch out of the room, stagger down the hall . . . call for help, "EARL, EARL" . . . plunge my head in the toilet . . . "Earl" . . . spray the name into the bowl . . . *Yes-a, I, oh I'm gonna love you . . . Come on let me hold you darlin'. 'Cause I'm the Duke of Earl.* Flame out. Crash and burn.

A banging on the door pounds on my hungover head. Light streams through the window. I put the pillow over my head.

"Go away."

Captain Beamus stomps into the room. "What are you doing in bed? Don't you know you're the duty officer?"

Hangnailed feet dangling from the bed, sheet pulled under my chin, I push the pillow aside and give him a bleery look. Captain Beamus is disgusted. Forced to deal with the duty officer flat on his back at ten thirty in the morning. "Get your ass out of the sack and get outside and get those ball games stopped before church services go down at eleven hundred. Wing Headquarters flew in a preacher from Japan. We will not have games competing with God."

"Yes, sir," I mumble. "You're right. It's the proper thing to do."

"Get them stopped, Fuckelbee. That's all I want from you. Nothing else. Just get them stopped."

I get up, dress, brush my teeth, borrow a whistle from Ben-San's dresser, and at two minutes to eleven, dressed in inspection starched utilities, pistol strapped to my waist, sunglasses dimming the molten sun, I march outside the Frog House, stomp to the basketball court and blow the whistle. Once. Twice. Then to prove I'm not fooling, one last long lingering blast.

The men stop, wondering what the fuck this lunatic wants. I'm out of wind from whistling and can't speak. My first thought is that I've lost my initial advantage, but the wait turns out to be as effective as a dramatic pause on the speaking platform.

"All right, you people. Break it up. The C.O. desires you to haul ass off the courts and into the church before eleven o'clock. I'm here to see that his wishes are followed."

I pull out the railroad pocket watch Daddy passed down to me. It's attached to my belt loop with a braided human hair chain I traded away from a Montagnard tribesman for a C-ration can opener.

"You've got exactly one minute and fifteen seconds to make it."

They stand unmoving, sullen.

"On the double. GET moving!"

There is a slow moseying to the mess hall where the religious services are being held. PFC Alvin Sneedly stops on the edge of the concrete court to pick up his shirt. He's pushed aside and knocked down the steps.

I help him to his feet, brush off the dirt.

"You all right?"

"Sixes sir."

"It's after eleven o'clock," I tell him. "Get cleaned up and turn yourself into the First Sergeant. Tell him you were late for church."

"Yes, sir," he says. "Thank you, sir."

"Not at all. Not at all." Sarcasm does not affect a man fucked up from a night of drink.

I look out across the deserted basketball courts, the bare backstops, the jagged metal backboard poles. I slap the whistle against my thigh, relishing the slap and the sting against my leg. Takes my mind off the jackhammer in my head.

Coffee, aspirin. Sergeant Soonto moves out of my way as I turn to go back to the Frog House. He shakes his head. "Lieutenant," he says sadly, his brown eyes morose. The cur snarls at me from between his legs. I walk away, chastened.

Oh me. Big boss man. I've become the same old turd I'm always railing against. Can't you hear me when I call?

16. Grog All Around

Howsabout a taste of the good stuff, Doc . . . some of that Kaintucky Jack Daniels . . . like the song: long dong from Kentucky . . . long dong ain't he lucky . . . long dong what I mean . . . he's long dong gone from Bowling Green . . . until his luck runs out . . . then he's long gone cong from Mang Buc ducky . . . long gone cong, he's unlucky . . . like a string run out to the end . . . remember, son, Daddy says, when it comes to Bull Roar a little parody can go a long ways . . . yes, Daddy, I know . . . Marion Morrison was either a joke or a hero . . . big, slow, and, yeah . . . deliberate, for sure . . . he's a Hollywood Marine . . . his real name is known only to Marines in the know . . . what the hell, Doc, I'll share it with you . . . his name is John Wayne . . . and he said lots of people say the only reason anyone goes into the Marine Corps is because they can't make it on the outside . . . well, that's their personal bull roar and they're talking too fast . . . slow it down, Doc . . . lay off the hotdogging . . . give it to me straight . . .

"No more hotdogging on the deck trying to flush out the Cong."

Colonel Hammer glares us to attention. A few pilots sit up, ready to take notes. The rest of us sprawl across the ready room chairs. We're grizzled, jaded. Outside, the first hints of rain are building in low hanging clouds. If the clouds stay below the mountaintops we'll scratch, if they rise, we'll itch, those who itch to fly.

"They're catching onto us," the Hammer continues. "They've learned that one round, in the right place, even from a paddy farmer's blunderbuss, can bring a chopper down."

Then the Hammer lays down the catechism again, holy and infallible: "In the interest of safety and longevity no one will fly below fifteen hundred feet unless absolutely necessary."

No shit. Can't argue with something we've already been doing for months.

"Get in quick and don't mess around on the ground. Climb out fast and stay out of small-arms range."

The C.O. slaps his pointer against the mapboard and paces the front of the ready room, his back stiff, stomach taut. He's tense. We're tired.

"Make sure you know where you are at all times. We don't need any more border incidents, wandering into Laos."

He smacks the map again, slapshot of attention.

"Knock off the idle chatter on the radio. Keep the channel clear for important messages."

I stifle a yawn. Fungus creeps across the walls. The maps and schedule boards are splashed with grease pencil scrawls: squadron notices in black, artillery ranges crosshatched in red; friendly outposts blue triangles, Viet Cong positions boldly outlined in orange; ribald comments etched in green: *Tower monkeys screw ripe mangos and feed the mush to the birds*.

"If the weather stays clear we go. Stand by for launch."

The colonel steps down and takes his seat in the first row of chairs.

I'm flying with Cochran, per usual. We're on a two-chopper mission, resupplying Mang Buk, an outpost sixty miles west, on our side of the river from Laos. After we drop off our cargo we're supposed to bring back a load of ARVN soldiers. They get the lackadaisicals when they're away from home too long, and they have to be rotated out every couple weeks.

Captain Beamus will lead the flight. He's as serious a VC hunter ever come six-gunning through this yere neck of the jungle, and once again his copilot is Wee Willie Weems. The perfect assistant, quiet and serious, a good map reader, which is essential on these flights, so that we don't do anything stupid that might get us a bullet up the ass.

The clouds rise. The weather clears. It's a go. We walk out to the line shack where we read the airplane gripes and sign off the birds. The enlisted men watch from behind the counter. A door opens in the back of the room and there's a flash of black and white. Soonto's cur. The nearest guy slams the door shut, the other men bustle around, drop clipboards, yell questions at one another, a catastrophe of distractions. Soonto's walking fast toward the chopper.

Outside the line shack I tell Cochran what happened.

He laughs. "They must think we don't know about the cur."

"Yeah. Hiding him. I was glad to see the mutt again."

The chopper is loaded with crates of live chickens and pigs, sacks of rice, bundles of clothing, cases of beer and crates of ammunition. Sergeant Soonto gives us the thumbs up. Everything all stowed.

Cochran pops in a wad of gum and walks around the chopper. "You want some gum, Tomas? With enough chewing gum we can change the course of time."

"Knock it off," Captain Beamus yells from the other chopper. "Let's wrap it up and head out. Did you check the turn and bank indicator, Lieutenant Weems?"

"Yes, sir, and it was straight and level, all the way."

"Gentlemen," Cochran says, sticking his gum over a bullet hole in the side of the chopper, "Lapsong Chung says the secret of the indicator is to think of the soul and not the ego. It took the Vietnamese centuries to discover swallowing seadragons by the dozens does not make for effective contraceptives."

He kicks the tire.

"Forget the tires and the wiseass," Captain Beamus yells. "Get in and crank her up."

"A quick check of the oil, sir, it could probably stand a quart."

"Cochran, start that bird or you're grounded for a week."

We spin up and lift off in a welter of spray. Forty-five minutes out, forty-five back. Time to kill. I fold the map so it shows the route we'll be following. Piece of cake, long as the weather holds. We follow a river valley into the mountains, skirting the clouds and ridge lines. I fly while Cochran reads a book, but he can't concentrate. He is too busy eyeing the mountains, the clouds and the altimeter, listening to the steady rumble of the engine, his ear attuned to the slightest wheeze, belch, fart, hiccup or other hint of internal disturbance, but the Wright engine churns steadily, oblivious to the weather, the proximity of the earth's surface, the possibility of enemy fire and the necessity to complete the mission.

I tune the AM radio to pick up Hanoi Hannah. She's always good for some entertainment. "U. S. Marines, are you full of blood and death this morning after killing more of our freedom fighters and eating their livers raw for a satisfactory breakfast as befitting barbarians from the other side of the world? I see you are now in the air trying to hide from our eagle-eyed freedom fighters. They are excellent shooters you know." Funny how she always knows when we've launched.

"Turn back, turn back, let's go home," Cochran sings softly over the intercom, the altimeter needle locked on eight hundred feet, the cloud layer showing no sign of rising even though the ground slopes unrelentingly upward, toward the close finite point where earth and cloud meet, blocking our path.

"Neither bullets nor clouds nor mountains shall stop the helicopter pilot on his appointed rounds," says Cochran. "The pigs must get through."

He reaches over and sets the pressure altimeter needle on one thousand feet. That makes him feel better and he ignores the radio altimeter blatantly signaling "liar" at him, its needle now locked on seven hundred.

Cochran goes back to his book and I stay close on Captain Beamus's tail. We sneak up the valley and cross a ridge, sliding over the top in front of a cloud too old and too wispy to be a threat, then we fly up another valley where Cochran disturbs himself enough to say, "Keep track of the way out in case we lose him."

We arrive at an impasse. The valley peters out and we are walled in by hills. The outpost sits on a ridgeline dead ahead, a flat spot hacked out of the jungle. There's only enough room on the pad for one chopper at a time. We tighten our shoulder straps and shut down the AM radio. No distractions now.

"Keep circling," Captain Beamus radios. "I'll go in and land."

He dips down and aims for the landing pad. We are in a hole with barely enough room to turn, hemmed in on the sides by mountains and on the top by clouds. Cochran takes the controls and puts us in a sharp bank to avoid a low cloud.

"We made it in all right," Captain Beamus crackles over the radio, "but the people down here are saying something about fire."

Cochran and I look at each other. Taking fire or is he on fire?

"Say again," Cochran transmits. "You're breaking up."

"I said . . . urp . . . squawk . . . gurk . . . fire."

"That's it," Cochran says over the intercom. "He's talking gibberish. We'll have to play the tape backwards to figure out what he's saying. Sergeant Soonto, check around and see if we're on fire, will you?"

Cochran heads into the dip between the ridges where the other chopper snuck through.

"No smoke down here, sir," Soonto says.

"The trouble is," Cochran says, tightening his circle, "the instant the tape runs backwards it explodes in negative time."

"Sir," Sergeant Soonto calls over the intercom.

"What is it?"

"There was a pig got loose down here."

"He's running around?"

"He was, but when you broke off like that he went out the door."

"Food for the tigers," Cochran says.

"I'm on my way out," Captain Beamus radios. "Do you have me in sight?"

A green shape zips past. "Roger that." Cochran turns the bird on its side and angles in.

"Time," Cochran growls, boring through the edge of the clouds, "it can't go nowhere without you, jes' sets there and twiddles its thumbs."

He lines up on a red scar showing between the trees.

"Landing zone in sight," Cochran radios. We continue along the tree tops and flare for a landing. Beneath us three figures scurry on the packed-dirt pad, waving their arms and signaling us not to land. They point to a hill farther ahead. Cochran pours on the coals and we pass over the clearing.

"They're waving us off," he radios Captain Beamus. "Did you take fire in the zone?"

"Negative on that."

"There's another pad on top of that hill," I tell Cochran. "I think they want us to land up there."

"For Christ's sakes. They must be crazy."

The top is only fifty feet above the other pad but it is in the clouds. Cochran wraps on the turns, pulls in fifty inches of manifold pressure and we creep up the side of the slope, wheels brushing the trees and bushes. He flies along the branches and leaves until the pad is under our wheels and then eases the chopper down. Cochran sets the brakes and pulls the mixture handle back to normal. A fire smolders in a fifty-five gallon drum next to the pad.

"There's your fire," I tell Cochran. "I bet they were trying to tell Captain Beamus the fire marked the zone. He must have landed on the lower pad."

Beyond the drum, wooden hooches sit next to reinforced bunkers. We slow the blades but don't shut down.

"Kick the cargo out and let's get going. Hey! Make them wait till we unload, goddamnit."

I peer between my legs into the belly. ARVNs have mobbed the helicopter. Thirty or forty, each carrying a pack full of bedding and mess gear and clothing. Lowland soldiers, they hate the mountains and can't wait to go home. They smother Soonto before he has a chance to unload the cargo.

Cochran waves out the window. "Get away, you bastards! Damn them! YOU ABOARD, SOONTO?"

He rams the mixture forward to full rich, intending to take off before the Vietnamese can overload us. I pull the handle back and hang on tight. Cochran sits astonished, red knob immobile in his great hairy fist like a wild rose plucked from an amazed bush.

"GODDAMN," he yells, turns loose of the handle, pulls off his shoulder straps and jumps out of the cockpit. He leaps into the mass of soldiers, rice, chickens and back packs, beats on the soldiers with his fence post arms, throws them aside like wheat shocks ripped by a tornado. The ARVNs run from the helicopter like a rack of pool balls blasted by the cue.

Two are trapped in the belly. Cochran reaches in and tosses one out by the seat of his pants. The soldier lands on his head, rolls to his feet and comes up running. Soonto throws the other soldier out. Cochran belts him on the side of the head as he flies by. The ARVN stumbles like a man coming to grips with the land after a wild ride on a centrifuge. Soonto starts throwing out the supplies.

Cochran walks over to the soldiers and smiles, intent on settling the ARVNs down. He points to one wearing sergeant stripes. "All right now, we do it my way, *hieu bit*, get it?" He motions him toward the chopper. The soldier approaches warily but Cochran is still all smiles and he personally ushers the sergeant in and points to the bulkhead.

"Sit him down, Soonto."

He points to another soldier.

"You. *Hai.* Number two. Come here." He helps the soldier in. He pats another on the shoulder and begins pushing them forward, one at a time. "Seven, *ocho*, nine, *diez*, 'leven, *muroi hai*." Stops and holds up his hands.

"That's it. No more. *Muroi hai.* Twelve only. You get it?"

The remaining soldiers look on impassively.

"You wait here," Cochran points. "I'll take this load out." Motions and whirls his fingers *put put put*. "Another chopper will come in and get the rest of you," *flutter flutter flutter*. They nod solemnly. "Get it? *Hieu bit?* Sure you do."

Cochran climbs into the cockpit. "Just hope those fuckers don't know there's no more choppers up there. All set, Soonto?"

"Roger."

"Take her away, Huckelbee."

I pour on the turns and lift out before he can strap in.

"What the hell were you doing down there?" Captain Beamus radios.

"Had to sort the wheat from the chaff," Cochran answers.

"Say again."

"Too many passengers, not enough space."

Captain Beamus lets it go. "Stick close," he says. "We've got another stop."

Cochran looks at me. They didn't say anything about that in the briefing. He clicks the intercom.

"What's going on, Soonto? You know about another stop?"

"Scuttlebutt has it Captain Beamus made a deal with a Green Beret to trade a Marine K-bar knife for an Army Springfield aught-three rifle. The Green Beret told him there's an outpost closer to the border that's got hundreds of them."

"Whooee," Cochran says. "Always a surprise. Okay, Huck, I've got it."

We enter the river valley and instead of turning right towards the coast, we turn left towards Laos. Cochran tucks in close on Captain

Beamus's port side. We're flying up a ravine with steep tree-lined slopes on either side. The river below narrows as it rises to the top of the V where the ravine comes to a point. Winds gust, shaking the helicopter and a heavy rain sleets against the windscreen. A black cloud blocks our way.

Captain Beamus turns away from the cloud, forcing us to turn with him. Cochran, flying in the right seat, eyes glued on the other chopper, can't see what's happening on our left side. A branch reaches out to grab us. A green-and-red parrot erupts from the tree, its *bawking* buried in the thump of the rotors. That's *demasiado proximo* for my Texican skin and I do the unthinkable and take over the controls.

"I've got it." I yank the stick over, drop full collective, jam left rudder and key the radio: "Breaking off." Autorotate in a spiral away from the other chopper, away from the tree-covered ravine, down to the river below.

"Roger," Captain Beamus calls. "I'm right behind you."

I ease the stick back, pull up the collective and add throttle, merging engine and rotor, then nose over and skim along the river. I pour on the turns, following Grandaddy Huckelbee's hunting maxim: a moving target is hard to hit, adding little Tommy Huckelbee's in-country corollary: a fast-moving target is even harder to hit.

"No lower, please," Cochran calls out over the intercom.

The river widens, giving us more room.

"Chopper two, this is chopper one," Captain Beamus calls. "I'm taking the lead. I'll pass on your right and climb."

I double click the radio button and ease off the throttle.

"I've got it," Cochran says, taking the controls and pulling into position on Captain Beamus' flank. "Good work back there. That was a tough spot. I couldn't see what was going on. If you hadn't . . . "

". . . I know, if I hadn't, we'd be eating C-rats on the side of the mountain."

"Two," Captain Beamus calls, "the mission is scrubbed. We're going home."

"How'd those troopers do down there?" I ask sergeant Soonto.

"They bounced around off the bulkheads a time or two but no one shit their pants."

The clouds are anvil-topped pillows, ranging high above us. The pointed mountains, once so close, are now round humps, and the tangled forest has given way to terraced fields. The sandy beach lies ahead, our landing field a thin black line.

In a lot of ways, coming in is the most dangerous time; relax too soon and that's when you prang — but Cochran stays on it all the way and we make a smooth landing and roll safely into the chocks. We shut down and lock the rotor. The ARVN troops bail out on the double and form up on the runway, then march away.

A small crowd is gathered around the other chopper, pointing at the tail. We walk over and take a look. A bullet has punctured the tail cone. Captain Beamus is elated. Action. Just what he craves. He pokes his finger in the hole.

"Seven-point-six-two, looks like to me," he says.

"At least," Cochran says. We walk toward the line shack. "By supper time it will be the size of a rocket." He shakes his head. "I guess I'm supposed to say I'm getting too old for this shit. I could pack it in and become a recruiter, suck in the hometown tough boys. Harps and halos standard issue. Pitchforks optional. Into the fray you go. Uh, sorry, lads, I can't come along, but duty calls. Oval office. Rose Garden. Cabinet meetings. All that, you know. But carry on and God go with you. You're going to need Him."

He opens the door to the line shack and we go in.

"All hail, good warriors," Cochran greets the pilots and crewmen. They turn and look, poker faced. "Come gather at the troughs, good friends. We need relief and relief is close at hand. No farther away than our well-stocked party hooch. There's grog aplenty there. Enough grog for everyone. Grog all around. What do you say?"

"Walked away from another one," I reply.

Cochran laughs. "I'll drink to that."

He starts filling out the after-action report. The other men return to their paperwork. I lean on the counter. My flight suit is sweaty wet. The helmet has left a red line around my forehead. The flak vest on my shoulders feels like a fifty-pound weight. Soonto's cur lies on a pile of rags in the corner. He snores softly and his eyelids quiver and his leg twitches, as he chases a rat in his sleep. Time for that grog. Let's have it. Grog all around.

17. Peer Out the Window

Help me up, Doc . . . gotta see what's going on . . . is it dawn yet . . . how's that song go, Doc . . . up in the morning . . . out on the job . . . work like the devil for my pay . . . my great uncle Toby, Grandaddy's brother, never did a lick of work he could get out of . . . he was too lazy to hunt his own meat . . . he ordered a Venus Fly Trap from some magazine after he read how the plant caught and ate its food simply by holding its mouth open and looking inviting . . . when the bug flew in, that sweet moist mouth closed gently around the dinner and digested it down . . . if it could do that to a bug, once that plant grew up to its full Texas size, it could trap all the meat Uncle Toby would ever want . . . rabbits, raccoons, squirrels . . . he jest had to sit and smoke his pipe and keep an eye on the plant . . . snatch the animal out before Venus shut her trap . . . whew, smell of that corncob pipe makes you think he reaped the bowl from behind the two-holer . . . ye reap what ye sow . . . and that lucky old sun got nothing to do but roll around heaven all day . . .

Mother couldn't stand it when Daddy went off to war and left her all alone with me and Grandaddy and mi abuela *on an endless chunk of Texas scrubland that seemed ages away from her native Austin, so she left and Grandma took me over . . . over the border most of the time*

. . . she preferred living with her family rather than staying in Texas fetching for my rasty old grandpa . . . Daddy caught the malaria and was medically discharged from the Army with the shakes and fever so bad that when he came home it scared me nearly to death until he ate a whole bottle of atabrine and it cured him . . . Mother never did come back, we got the divorce papers in the mail . . . a heartbreaking story, huh, Doc, for all the good it does . . . but, Doc, I implore you . . . do me some good, will you . . .

Up in the morning to the sound of the wailing camp whistle and peer out the window. If it is clear, we fly. A short hop we're back for lunch. A long hop, the healthy, not necessarily tasty, C-rats to tide us over. After supper, a drink, maybe a movie. If the movie is too old, or too bad, then it's to bed. Up in the morning peer out the window. Grey, overcast, still too dark to tell.

The duty clerk sticks his head in the door.

"Lieutenant Benson, you're on Tiger Flight. Get to the airstrip on the double."

Grousing, Ben-San grabs his gear and hustles out to the waiting jeep. Cochran turns on the radio. President Diem says the tide is turned, the government is on the offensive. The senior United States Army adviser agrees, the South Vietnamese are winning the war. The Commandant of the Marine Corps says another four or five months will show a marked improvement.

"I don't know what war they're talking about," says Cochran, "but if we don't get those outposts resupplied before the rain socks us in, the heavies will be sucking rotten eggs out of the other sides of their mouths."

An explosion shakes the barracks. Rob Jacobs sticks his head out the door, turns back and yells, "MY GOD THIS IS IT, the VC are hitting the camp!"

We grab our pistols. What was that defensive plan? Where the hell are we supposed to assemble? The sweet smell of an electrical fire wafts into the room. I'm about to break out the window screen and jump outside, when someone hollers that the junction box has shorted out and blown up.

Cochran is poised at the door, ready to bolt. He hasn't shaved and his stubble is a black mask. He won't grow a mustache even though most of the pilots sport bushy hedges, thin slivers or waxed handlebars. It's either his ordinary obstreperousness or his refusal to be a dues-paying member of the pack. Why should I cultivate something on my face that grows wild on my ass?

"False alarm," he says. "Back to bed."

I peer out the window. "Clearing up, *compadre.* Today we fly."

The ready room is the usual mix of pilots strapping on their pistols, writing on their kneepads, folding their maps, the routes in and out; low voices assessing the terrains, the loads they'll be carrying, the murmuring preparations interrupted by Ben-San crashing through the door.

"We were too late with the Tiger Flight, as usual," he says. "The VC hit a train coming around the mountain on the Hai Van Peninsula, right at dawn when there was barely enough light to see."

"I thought that area had pillboxes to cover the level stretches," Emmett says. "How did it happen?"

"It was right where the tracks go around a curve and down a grade where it crosses a gully. The VC blew the bridge when the train was crossing. The ARVN guards were in the last car and it went down in the gulley, putting them out of the picture. The engine kept going but the back cars were off the rails and they dragged the whole shebang to a stop."

Ben-San sheds his flak vest and flops down on a chair.

"By the time we got there the VC were long gone. But not before they lined everyone up, gave them a lecture: look how well your government protects you, they can't stop us from wrecking the train, best to join up with the VC. Or else. Then they shot a woman. The ARVNs we carried in did a halfhearted search and their platoon commander told the passengers not to worry, they will get to Da Nang safely. The government will destroy the political criminals who blew up the train. After that we packed up and got out of there."

"Hmm, both sides well represented, stating their useless cases," Cochran says.

Grousing and grumbling all around. Scratching of stubbly chins and shakes of wondering heads. Ben-San goes in search of a Coca-Cola and the rest of us continue prepping for our flights.

Cochran and I are flying wing on the Hammer. A platoon of Viet Cong has infiltrated Tien Phuoc, a village twenty kilometers south. They are conducting propaganda lectures in the school and village square. A government agent snuck away and alerted the nearest outpost which radioed Da Nang for help.

The regular forces are in the field, so the SDC, Self Defense Corps troops, irregulars from the villages, are the only ones available. They carry four different colored scarves in their pockets and every few hours, following a pre-established plan, change scarves. Anyone not wearing the right color is shot on the spot, for the Viet Cong also wear black silk outfits and the secret scarf change can put the finger on an infiltrator.

We brief, preflight and load the troops. They are dressed in black shirts and trousers and carry bandoleers of ammunition across their chests. They wear bright-red scarves and are armed with M1s and BARs. They have no boots or helmets, instead they wear cloth caps and sandals.

After a short flight to the village we orbit overhead and wait for air cover. The Hammer establishes radio contact and we rendezvous with two T-28 fighter-bombers.

"Slowing it up," the Hammer calls, and we flare, drop the power and settle onto a cultivated field. The T-28's fly race-track dummy firing patterns on both flanks. The Hammer will call them on the radio if we start to take ground fire and then the dummy runs will go live.

We're on the ground for only a few minutes. The troopers jump out and run toward the village, the red scarves a gaudy contrast to their black shirts.

"All clear," Soonto calls over the intercom.

We lift off and bank into a right turn.

"I'm ready for that G and T," Cochran says, the stick light in his right hand, left fist squeezing the throttle and holding the collective steady.

Fifty feet off the deck, Soonto calls, "We're taking fire, Lieutenant."

Cochran looks at me. "Grab your gatling gun, Tomas, see if you can spot them."

"We're getting a lot of oil, down here," Soonto says. Then, "Oh shit, I think I got hit."

"How bad is it?"

"No blood showing but it hurts like hell."

"Hang in there."

"Transmission oil pressure dropping," I say. "Temperature gauge rising."

"Yankee Victor Two under fire," Cochran reports over the radio. "We've got a bad transmission leak."

"Roger that, you going to try for home?" The Hammer answers.

"Negsville, I'm setting down as far away as I can get from those shooters."

"I'll cover you."

Cochran lowers the collective and drops the nose. We angle toward a bare spot. "How's it looking down there, Soonto?"

"Transmission oil is spraying me like a race horse pissing blood. Hot, too."

Cochran eases up the collective, pulls back on the stick and sets us down. He disengages the rotors and applies the brake, keeping the engine running. Soonto jumps out of the belly and climbs up on the roof. He opens the transmission inspection hatch and peers in, rubbing his bottom.

"Keep an eye out for the bad guys," Cochran tells me. He switches to the radio. "We're checking out the tranny, Yankee Victor One. Keep us covered."

"Roger that. Everything looks clear from up here."

"What's going on with Soonto?" Cochran says.

"He's stoppering the hole with pieces of his jacket."

Soonto gives a thumbs up, closes the inspection hatch, jumps down and hops in the belly.

"Winding her up." Cochran engages the rotor. "Keep an eye on those gauges," he tells me. Then he calls on the radio, "We're coming out, going to try for home."

He lifts off and heads north, gauges on the redline. "What's it looking like down there, Soonto?"

"Normal seepage, sir. Maybe a little on the heavy side."

We slap down at Da Nang on the roll and don't stop till we reach the maintenance shack.

"Good work, Soonto," Cochran says, after we're shut down and standing on the ground. "What the hell did you say about being hit?"

Soonto grins sheepishly. "Got me in the ass, sir, knocked me off the seat."

"You okay? Let me see."

Exposing his left buttock, Soonto reveals a bulge the size of a tennis ball, brilliant as a star going nova, red and purple and emitting a shitload of heat.

"That's significant," Cochran says. "Where are your bulletproof panties?"

"I was sitting on them." He holds up fingers. "Two pairs."

"Saved your ass."

No one wears the flak pants any more. Scrunches your nuts into mashed potatoes. We put the pants on the seats and sit on them.

"Go see Doc Hollenden," Cochran says. "I'll put a note in the after-action report. Maybe you'll get a purple heart out of this."

"Yeah," I chime in. "The purple of the medal on your chest

will match the purple of the welt on your ass."

Soonto gives me his Samoan look, deadpan, eyes dark pools.

"How poetic," Cochran says. "At least we were spared your stupid purple heart on joke."

"*Cállate tu boca*. Oh, what's this?"

The cur is peering intently at Soonto, eyes probing, one ear cocked. Soonto makes a small gesture with his hand. An almost imperceptible wag of a tail, and the cur sits and nestles its muzzle in Soonto's hand. The dog has filled out. His legs are still too long for his body. He'll only let Soonto touch him unless Soonto gives the okay—then the cur will deign to be patted on the head.

"He's not a cur," Cochran says. "He's a curmudgeon."

We go in the line shack and fill out the after-action report, then write up the transmission leak—one round, one hole, no apparent gear damage.

"Walked away from another one," Cochran says. "Knock on wood."

"I'll drink to that. Bottoms up."

18. Neatness Matters Most

Put it to me straight, Doc . . . no gilding the lily now . . . I had a little gelding on the ranch . . . when I got older I rode the horses we kept in the remuda, just like the rest of the cowhands . . . later on I was able to put my equine knowledge to good use . . . I had the weekend off from flying one Saturday during our desert deployment in Yuma, and went down to the stables to check out a horse for an overnight camping expedition . . . I figured something was up when the Gunny Sergeant in charge of the stables led out a big brown gelding all saddled and ready to go for a check ride around the inside of the corral to make sure I wasn't some greenhorn who didn't know a cinch from a stirrup, and all the enlisted men who worked in the stables had hoisted themselves up on the top rails of the corral for a gander at the upcoming show . . .

I climbed aboard the gelding, the Gunny let go of the bridle, I nudged the horse with my heels, he turned and glared at me with a wild red eye, then bolted for the fence, figuring to scrape me off before we even started around the corral . . I pulled the reins and yanked his head alongside my boot, holding him in a tight turn . . . he spun around a time or two then saw it was no use, and stopped, his head pressed against his flank . . . I leaned over and grabbed his ear with my teeth and chomped down . . . the horse let out a wail, the enlisted men broke into shouts and laughter, I turned loose the ear and whispered in a soothing voice, "You and I are going to get along just fine, aren't we" . . . he whinnied, shook himself and walked, trotted, cantered and galloped through his paces and, with the check ride successfully completed, we spent a companionable two days wandering around Mexico, camping under the stars . . .

Another rainy afternoon. I write letters, filling the empty pages with my wide tracked, webfooted trail. Study "shy man shitting in the woods," the wood carving Cochran traded from the Montagnards, an ape squatting on his heels, legs crossed, arms and hands covering his face. The wood is green and unfinished and Cochran sands and stains the carving, rubbing its ass and flanks.

I check out my crop of crabs. The little devils are in a pilgrimmage around the Frog House, visiting every man in turn, delivering an itchy message, much like the religious zealots back home who pass out fear-mongering pamphlets: Are you AWAKE? Read the WATCHTOWER. WHAT DOES GOD HAVE IN STORE FOR YOU? CRABS?

They are "little friends" to the Japanese, come to visit and mooch but the Nipponese are too hairless for the crabs to hide and they are soon spotted and dispatched, migrating to the furry jungles of a visiting American.

Now a new visitor. A blister bug on my elbow. No one has ever seen a blister bug. They light on your skin and a water blister pops up and breaks, leaving a goopy rash. The worst is to squash a blister bug at night, blisters spread wherever it is mashed. Looks like your shoulders and chest have been burned after you roll around atop a blister bug all night. Head for the shower, and, if the water is on, you hose the blister bug down the all-consuming drain.

If we can't fly we have ground training. We muster in the ready room at 0800. Ben-San, back from five days R and R in Japan, plunks down next to me. His eyes are puffed and red rimmed. Back bowed.

Hands shaking. Brain tremored. I pass him my notebook with a question written on the open page: *You look all fucked up. Feel okay?*

He fires it back. *"Jo-to Ichi-ban. Daijoubu,"* and adds a poem:

Now I lay me down to sleep
With a Jo-San by my side.
If I should die before I wake
She fucked me to death.

Ben-San was not going to have anything more to do with Yoshika, the Japanese girl he fell in love with and asked to marry, not after being called into the squadron office and have Pappy Lurnt tell him, "You marry that bar girl and take her home, by the time you get there you're married to a nigger."

"But she's Japanese."

"Same difference. You're as horny as an Arkansas milk snake."

Pappy Lurnt sails the marriage request form across the desk. "Deep six this piece of trash. The skipper won't sign it. Get out of here."

Ben-San left the office and jumped on the R and R flight to Japan.

"First thing off the plane," he whispers, "I picked up two Jo-Sans and took them to a hotel. One was a fatso, the other a slim-hipped beauty. I humped the beauty and didn't find out until afterwards that she was a he and I'd been compromised by a sister-boy. She had tits. That's what fooled me."

"How'd you like that, making out with a boy?"

"Blah. I didn't do that. I never make out with whores. First off, I was drunk. If it weren't for that I probably wouldn't have been in the room."

"Wasn't she naked?"

"She had on a half slip hiked around her hips, hiding her cock, which she had taped to her crotch in some weird way to make it look like he didn't have one."

"How do you know he did?"

"Old fat mama-san told me."

"God, forgot about her. What was she doing all this time?"

"She was lying on my back, the top slice of a Chinese sandwich."

"But how did you do it?"

"I couldn't figure that out. Fatso explained it to me. Showed me rather. The sister-boy reached around under his ass and cupped his hand to make a cunt out of it."

"Sounds like an old Mexican trick."

"He sure fooled me."

"Must have left a bitter taste."

"Blah. Not until I found out. Pretty good screwing up to then. Old Fatso was laughing her jugs off so I bugged her to find out what the joke was. I found out all right. The thing that pissed me off was I paid for that piece of ass. Can you imagine that? Paying ass price for a hand job?"

"She had nice tits."

He scowls and scribbles in my notebook:

I'm the sheik of Koza BC.
My love say she belong to me.
At night when she at work,
Butterflying with some Air Force jerk,
I'll sneak to her pad and sleep,
Across the habu grass she'll creep,
Someday she'll be my love for free,
I'm the sheik of Koza BC.

"That's when I went back to Yoshika," Ben-San whispers. "She was working nights at the Temple Bar caging drinks and making appointments, but while I was there, she remained true. She was taking a course in hair care during the day, hoping to get a job in a beauty parlor. When things got too hectic, she told me, she'd slip into the head at work and snort some powder from the bartender, kept the girls chipper and hustling.

"The last night there I told her that the Marine Corps wouldn't let us get married and we'd have to split up for good. I had already paid her month's rent, plus food and drinks and I convinced myself there's only so much a man can do.

"'Get another job. Get away from the Temple Bar before you burn yourself out,' I told her. 'Find a nice Japanese boy and get married.'"

"'Yeah, sure,' she said. 'And maybe you find nice roundeye girl and get married. I once had good job working at Staff NCO club at Kadena Air Base and Sergeant set me up in a snake ranch, promised he'd get a divorce and marry me, allatime keep me busy with laundry and cleaning and he never did get divorce, instead he go back to the States. He write me letter, say when he come back, he knows Yoshika waiting for him. He in for big surprise. I no big fish. I fish him.'"

"The next morning I flew back here," Ben-San says.

He bends over my notebook and writes with a shaky hand:

Four o'clock comes slowly
Ever so slowly
I sit in silent solitude
Awaiting my Jo-San
And curse the coming day.
Four o'clock comes
Along with my Jo-San.
I turn to her with a scowl
I mention the rack
She turns her back
Say she love only me.
'Then why you butterfly?' I ask.
'I no butterfly,' she say
'Just checko-checko'
'But Jo-San,' I say.
'I pay your rent
Buy you food

Buy you booze
Why you checko-checko?'
'Someday you go home,' she say
'Your Jo-San left all alone
No man to share the rent
No money for abortion in case of accident.
I checko-checko for the day to come,
When you pack bags and stateside run.'

"What traits identify the successful leader?" Captain Beamus intones. "To whom in history can we look for great examples of leadership? Catherine the Great. Moses. Genghis Khan, the man who led the hordes to the edges of civilized Europe. And what about one of the greatest leaders of all time?"

He pauses but no one answers him.

"Rommel. Rommel is the only officer I know of who was a Captain longer than me. For eleven years he was frozen in rank but he didn't waste his time. He read, wrote and studied. Prepared himself for the day when he would be promoted, when he would take command. And we all know what happened. He became one of the greatest armored cavalry tacticians the world has ever known."

Ben-San is gripped by the emotion of the talk. Or in the grips of something else, for he is sagging and moaning. Viewed from the lectern he appears interested in the talk, so interested he is taking notes.

Listen me buckoes
And you shall hear
How to be a lead-eer.
Notice my poise
My dress, my manners,
Especially the
Front of my trousers.
The open fly

The gaping void
And the lack
Of a man-sized peter.

"An officer is a gentleman," Captain Beamus lectures, "and that means he exhibits all the qualities of a gentleman. Dress, manners, wit, intelligence and *savoir faire*—the ineluctable tidbits that no one can define but everyone can recognize."

"What's that mean? He can't run for office?" Rob Jacobs yells out.

"As you were, Lieutenant. Consult your dictionary and expand your vocabulary. Your word is your bond."

I take the notebook from Ben-San.

Your Word Is Your Bond
I am a laughing hypocrite
That is to say I'm full of shit
But according to my outward show
I believe in everything I appear to know.
And who around can give me the lie
When my icy demeanor freezes his eye?

Captain Beamus brings the ground training session to an end. Before we can escape, the Admin Officer, Captain Miles "Standish" Briggs stands up and annouces that the Commandant of the Marine Corps is coming for a visit. The Commandant doesn't want us doing anything out of the ordinary. The dispatch from headquarters says it will be a working-day inspection. He'll walk around and talk to the men and get his own opinion of what we're doing, and we're to treat it like any other day.

Which means we'll scrub and clean and wax and hide our garbage and worn-out equipment in preparation for the inspection.

"Remember, this isn't really an inspection. Normalcy is the SOP. But have your top NCOs stationed in key locations so if the Commandant stops to ask questions he won't be talking to some yo-yo who can't tell the time."

Hops are cancelled. Work on the helicopters ceases. Every man turns to and polices the shops and the offices. Captain Beamus orders the metal shop to construct racks in the ready room where the pilots can hang their flight gear and flak suits. He numbers every slot on the clothing racks and assigns each pilot a number.

"You will hang your flight gear and flak suits on the proper hook. If you want to use hangers you'll have to supply your own."

Everyone ignores him. So, early the next morning, Captain Beamus picks up every piece of gear—helmets, pistol holsters, map cases, kneeboards and flak suits—that isn't hanging in its proper niche and hauls it all to the equipment cage and dumps it in a pile in on the floor. That will show those insubordinate cretins.

The Commandant arrives right on time. The NCOs man their posts as if it is a normal working day, while the goldbrickers are hidden behind shelves or sent to the mess hall for an early all-day chow. The ready room is clean and tidy, a tribute to Captain Beamus's zeal. The floors are swept and the benches are in precise rows. Comfortable canvas-backed chairs are lined up for the Commandant and his covey of officers.

The monsoon rains seep into the hangar and the ready room. The air is heavy and funereal, and, in the line shack, we the pilots, banished from the ready room, wait morosely for the visit to end.

Only Cochran is excited.

"Is he here yet? Dammit, don't block the door."

Cochran jumps in and out of the rain, camera poised, waiting to snap the Commandant, capture his presence, devour his visage.

Cochran hasn't shaved—never shave on a rainy day, might have to go back to bed and it would be wasted—and the stubbles on his face are as thick as scrub elms along a farmer's fence. He has thrown his absorbent Marine Corps raincoat around his shoulders, and his misshappen baseball cap, shrunken and faded from rain and sweat, gloms to his head like a limp rag.

The Commandant's arrival is heralded by a throng of newspapermen and photographers pushing into the line shack. They too are barred from the ready room briefing, but after being shuttled about for weeks they don't feel any animosity about being shunted aside. One shack's as good as another. Soonto's cur raises his hackles at the intruders. He growls and slinks behind the counter—never trust a stranger, might turn you into meat for the table.

The press corps includes a woman. She is short and squatty, hair streaky and stringy, glasses covering puzzled eyes. A Leica hangs around her neck and a photo bag is draped over her shoulder. A torn trench coat covers a man's shirt and a pair of dirty slacks. Wet sneakers glom to her sockless feet.

"Oh, man," Cochran says, "look at that. Real roundeye ginch but what a butch-looking babe."

He edges away from the door. The woman stands apart, warily casing the pilots.

"She's got her eye on you, can see you're *un hombre grande,*" I tell Rob Jacobs, who has taken Cochran's place at the door. She gives Rob Jacobs a casual glance. Rob looks rastier than Cochran.

"Yeah, I think she has at that. Do you suppose she wants to take my picture?"

Not so very long ago Rob Jacobs was a very dapper young man with his large smiling mouth, curly lion's mane and smooth tanned skin.

"I'm the most handsome man around, including Cassius Clay," he would say to himself in the mirror, but that was before he was hooked on the booze and the bars, and before he got eighty-sixed at the blackjack table in the O club. He was at the table every chance he got, doubling and tripling his bets until he was tapped out and borrowing money from everyone in the squadron.

It started out as fun but he became obsessed and, ultimately, possessed, a demon raging within, and when he was barred from the table, the demon howled for release. Gone are the joke sneezes. Gone are the fake laughs. Gone is the shipshape Lieutenant. Gone is any pretense of holding it together, his manners slopped so low they wallow with the hogs. He's been kicked out of the O club, he's a social pariah in the Frog House, he spends every spare minute in town, drinking, until the MPs throw him in the bus, for the last ride to the base.

The alcohol benumbs and benigns. Everything is loose and all right. There is no longer a war in Vietnam, the smiling brown bar girls click into full frame beauty and Rob Jacobs is riding on top, his demon at peace. But only for a while. His behavior in town gets so outlandish—tabletop dancing, grabbing the microphone from the vocalists, mooning the Air Force officers, spilling trays of drinks—he gets barred from every bar in Da Nang.

No matter. He crawls through a hole in the perimeter fence and crosses Highway One into Dogpatch, a ratty-ass slum-jumble of huts and hooches nailed together out of flattened beer cans, where piss-warm *bam bai bao* beer can be had for five piasters a can, and where the sleaziest whores, too pock-marked for town, put out for 20 pees. Rob Jacobs' demon is at full-bore roar.

His outlet is sex. Sex which is more than the normal dorking. Inhibitory commands are deafened as deep briney excursions are logged in the big score book. Horniness whips him to the max. He'll outdo every stud ever come cock swollen and nut throbbing through the fence. He's singing the long dong song, meanwhile his *chinga* is savoring the thought of the new blouse she will buy with the piasters she's earning. For Buddha's sake can't you hurry up, Yankee dolt? She pulls his hair, *come on*, *you*, and he is gone, gone around the bend and over the edge of the last cliff to nowhere.

"I'm deep, I'm down deep," he tells us. "I can't control myself. Unspeakable forces at work." He holds his head in his hands.

Cochran recommends an exorcism, or if not that, a counseling session with the chaplain. Seeing these suggestions have no effect, Cochran gets down to the bone.

"Rob, don't you have any willpower?" Cochran asks him.

"Yeah, I've got lots of willpower, I just don't have any won't-power."

"Ask yourself, Rob. What would your daddy think?"

"Oh Lordy, why did you have to bring him into this?"

"Because a strong daddy is a force that sticks in your craw. My dad told me one time to sit in for him in the poker game that went on every afternoon in the Molten Iron Club. He gave me ten thousand dollars to play with. I was shitting blue bricks, sitting at the table with men who would break your kneecap if they thought you were looking at them funny. They cleaned me out in two hours. Then I had to face Papi. He surprised me by clapping me on the shoulder and congratulating me. Turned out it was dirty money he had to get rid of."

He pauses.

"And all the time I was trying to win."

Poppa power prevails. Rob Jacobs cleans up his act. The normal daily routine helps. He still has to roust out with the rest of us at reveille. He still has to fly. He's still a Marine. Cluching the symbolic globe and anchor he treads the straight and narrow. He still looks like shit. The photographer lady is the first thing to arouse an interest in feminine pulchritude since his reclamation effort began.

Cochran jabs Rob Jacobs with his elbow to pry him away from the door.

"Beat it," says Rob, not giving ground. "I've got something going here."

"You?" Cochran is incredulous. "No way."

"Guess again," I say. "Check him out.

Rob Jacobs stands up straight, stomach in, shoulders back. He spits on his hands and slicks back his hair. For all the good it does. His pistol hangs half way out of his shoulder holster. His camouflaged flight suit is ripped under one armpit, exposing dirty skin and a grungy shirt.

"Okay," says Cochran. "I get it. He's trying for svelte. Good luck, Marine."

The photographer holds up her camera, idly focusing around the line shack, ostensibly getting a light reading. Rob Jacobs turns so he is in half profile. His hand slides up and fondles his pistol butt. I stand aside so the rip and dirty shirt are in plain view. The camera clicks.

"Hey," Cochran yells. "You think that picture will come out, dark as it is in here?" He leans over her shoulder. "What setting are you using?"

"No pictures inside. Not enough light."

"How's about letting me shoot one of you?"

Cochran backs off and points his brownie. She stands rigid as though the camera were a gun. Rob Jacobs bellies up.

"Mind if I have a copy of that picture you just took of me?" he asks. "I can give you my name and address. You can drop one in the mail."

"Get the hell out of the way," Cochran says "You're blocking the light."

"I think inside is too dark," the girl murmurs, pulling her coat tighter.

"I'll just grab a pencil and piece of paper."

"Hold still, dammit—"

"Here he comes, Mike," I interrupt. "The Commandant is here."

Cochran elbows his way out the door into the rain. The Commandant, heading an entourage of Generals, Colonels, Majors and a couple of weary looking Captains, strides around the corner of the line shack, the Hammer marching at his left, one proper pace to the rear.

"Hold her, General." Cochran plants himself in the Commandant's path and aims in.

"Got it. Thanks a lot, sir." He steps aside and salutes. The Hammer stares ahead.

"Your public information man, Colonel?" the Commandant asks.

"Ah, not exactly, sir."

"Fine boy. Out in the rain doing his job, I like that kind of attitude. I didn't catch his rating. A corporal, I imagine."

"No, sir. That was one of our pilots."

"Oh?" The Commandant glances around.

Cochran has climbed on top of a pile of lumber. When the Commandant spots him, Cochran waves and grins. Points to the camera and makes a round O with his thumb and forefinger; everything's okay.

The Commandant goes into the ready room for the Hammer's briefing. Cochran climbs down from the lumber pile and hunkers under the eaves of the hangar. I join him there. Rob Jacobs stays in the line shack, he'd rather study the woman.

After the briefing, the Hammer leads the Commandant on a tour of the hangar and working spaces. Staff NCOs stand at attention in every office and every shop. There isn't a sound of a tool being used or a machine at work. A Marine begins pounding a nail in the supply cage and the Hammer motions to the First Sergeant. He scurries away and puts the kibosh on the whang bang.

At every stop, during every talk the Commandant has with an average-picked-at-random-during-a-normal-working-day Marine, Cochran is close by, snapping pictures. I pretend I'm his assistant. The entire inspection party having ascertained through whispers that the Commandant made a favorable comment about the madman, ignores Cochran's wild antics. The Hammer endures Cochran's presence, reluctant to leave his favored spot to the left, one pace to the rear, confident that he'll get Cochran later. We circle back to the line shack and the reporters file out, the inspection over. The Leica lady darts out. Rob Jacobs follows, calling out his name and address. He stops, despondent and miffed.

"Probably some cheap foreign bull dyke anyways," Rob says.

"You could tell that from her trench coat," I say.

Cochran runs up to us. "One picture left. Where'd she go?"

"Gone," says Rob Jacobs.

"Gone? Why that no-good German. She *was* German, you know."

"How do you know that? By her accent I suppose."

"Accent? What accent? All photographers who wear trench coats, slacks, and follow wars are Germans. Besides, her hair was streaked, wasn't it?"

Rob Jacobs and I nod our heads.

"Proves it. You didn't want to fuck with her. She wears M-80s for tampons. Piss her off and she raises her leg, points her crotch at you and lights the fuse. Hold that."

He takes a picture of us. There's a snarl at our feet. Soonto's cur stands at the door, hairs on his neck bristling, tail stuck straight out. He sniffs and steps outside to piss on a rain-soaked plant.

We plod over to the ready room and scarf down the donuts and lemonade the Commandant's entourage left behind. The Duty Officer announces all flying is scrubbed, and we go outside and catch the bus to the Frog House, leaving just before the Hammer returns to the ready room. He finds the place empty and the lemonade and donuts gone. Rob Jacobs is still there and he tells us later that the Hammer seemed pleased with the impression he made on the Commandant, the neatness of the area, the appearance of the men and their prompt correct answers to the Commandant's questions, but Rob could tell the Hammer was also pissed at Cochran, the nerve of the man, in a thousand places at a thousand times with his goddamned camera. Only Cochran would have thought of a camera.

The Hammer zeros in on Rob.

"What are you gawking at Lieutenant? Get that flight suit replaced, it's a disgrace."

Then, Rob tells us, the Hammer roared off in his jeep, blowing past Private First Class Alvin Sneedly who stepped out of the line shack just in time to come to attention, snap a salute and catch a shitload of mud across his clean starched utilities.

19. Time is a Tightrope

What time is it, Doc? . . . can't you get this show moving? . . . fooling me all the time . . . like the time Daddy and I went to visit mi abuela *. . . with my little dog, Dingo . . . white with brown spots, bristly hair . . . goes everywhere with me . . . up early, time to go home, where's Dingo? . . . he had to go out,* niño, *I thought it was all right . . . Dingo, come here, boy . . . where are you, Dingo . . . Daddy is impatient . . . Tomas, we have to go, we don't have time to look now . . . not enough time for Dingo . . . we never found him, Doc . . . time, she run out on Dingo . . . where does time go, Doc . . . stretched so thin, does it break and then end . . .*

We're going to the dogs, Doc . . . ever since Soonto got his cur it opened the doghouse doors . . . seems like every enlisted man in the squadron has his own dog . . . they are all over the compound, the hangar, the equipment cage . . . the pilots stick to walking the Dawg . . . what we call the helicopter . . . we're sitting on a pad of an outpost we just resupplied, and an American all dressed in jungle gear demands we take him to some spot over on the Laotion border . . . he can't believe it when we say nothing doing . . . he says this is a dog mission . . . what? . . . he gives us the wink, we still don't get it . . . "dog," he says again, "you know, oh for Christ's sakes do I have to say it out loud" . . . he looks around, leans in close . . . "CIA," he whispers, "special orders" . . . "a dog mission is the code that gives me clearance" . . . Cochran laughs, shouts for anyone to hear: "CIA my ass" . . . "if you don't go through our operations section and get an ops order, we don't take you on any mission, secret or otherwise" . . . "but we will give you a ride back to Da Nang" . . . the secret agent declines and stomps off fuming . . . after first promising regal retribution from offices on high . . . a lot we care . . . we leave the dog man behind and fly back to the base . . . that's where the relief is . . .

We muster in the ready room. The maps, pencils, flight gear, flak vests and pants usually spread all over the place are missing. A few things hang neat and tidy on Captain Beamus's clothing rack. We thrash around the racks and behind the mapboards looking for our equipment, recalling the Rajah's warning: *We've built these racks and assigned every pilot a hook. The hooks are numbered and your number is on this list. Everyone start using them.*

"If you're looking for your gear, it's in the equipment cage," Emmett says, walking in the door with his flak vest.

A mad rush to the equipment cage, paw through the pile in the middle of the floor, everyone frantic to find their gear, except for a few who stay in the ready room, not wanting to get enmeshed in the mess. I walk over to the rack and lift off a set of vests and pants. These will do. So what they're not mine.

"That son of a bitch," says Cochran.

"Which one?"

"Beamus. What the hell he have to do that for?"

"Yeah," says Ben-San. "Who gives him the right to fuck with our gear?"

"I'll fix his ass," says Cochran. He walks over to the rack and searches around. Captain Beamus and the Hammer are huddled together over a map in the front of the room. They ignore the abuse running in rivulets under their feet, a backwash of anger swirling around their ankles. Cochran opens the ready room door and throws a set of flak pants and vest out in the mud. A murmur of laughter. Captain Beamus looks around suspiciously. He and the Hammer split up, the pilots gather in small groups to brief for the day's runs. The duty officer writes the plane assignments on the acetate schedules board.

Cochran groans. "We're flying again. I was hoping the weather would cancel us out."

A three-plane flight to Duc Pho, an isolated outpost at the bottom of a deep river canyon forty miles from home base. Captain Beamus and his copilot, Wee Willie Weems, are leading the flight. Cochran and I are flying on their wing. Ben-San and Rob Jacobs are piloting the third bird, and they grouse over our chances of getting home early. Practically nil with Captain Beamus leading.

Bennett walks up. "Before you get through briefing I've got something to pass out," he says.

Bennett hands Cochran six bullets for his pistol, tracers that leave a red trail when they are fired.

"What are these for?" Cochran asks.

"In case you go down you can use them for signaling,"

"All six? My, how generous."

Everyone laughs, remembering how Cochran had his pistol taken away for firing it whenever he felt like it. He got it back but he still shoots at animals, rocks, trees, bushes, anything, saying that a pistol demands to be fired, it's inherent in its nature.

"Now you're going to be really dangerous," I tell him.

"What are you worried about? I never hit what I'm aiming at."

"With these you might hit something when you miss," Ben-San says.

Cochran inspects the red-tipped bullets, pulls out his revolver, ejects the cartridges and replaces them with six tracers.

"No," Emmett says. "You're only supposed to use one tracer every six rounds."

Cochran ignores him, shoves his pistol back in his shoulder holster. Captain Beamus comes over to brief us for the hop. We'll follow the

Song Cau Dai River to the outpost. Stay tight on him, maintain strict radio silence and keep on your toes. The weather doesn't look too good and we may have to squeeze in low.

Cochran and I exchange a look. What about the fifteen-hundred-foot rule?

"We'll drop our supplies one at a time, join up and follow the same route home."

Captain Beamus roots around the flight gear hanging on the rack, paws through the gear lying on chairs or dropped in corners, the ready room once again messy.

"What are you doing?" Rob Jacobs asks him.

Captain Beamus glares. "My flak vest. Some clown has—"

"Why not check the equipment cage?" says Ben-San.

By the time Captain Beamus locates some gear and arrives at his plane, Cochran and Soonto and I are fired up and ready to go. Time and tide wait for no man. Ben-San and Rob Jacobs also sit waiting. Tides are timed, you know, right down to the very second. The ebb and the flow, the old in-and-out game, *respiración.* Captain Beamus doesn't waste time preflighting, he doesn't have to, Wee Willie Williams did it for him. The Rajah straps in and starts up, comes on the air for a radio check, and we taxi and take off, leveling at fifteen hundred feet, over the wide flat sandy delta where the river meets the South China Sea, then we turn inland, following the river west, into the cloud-covered mountains.

We can't get above the ridge lines on either side of us, which makes for a nervous tingling in the belly. At this altitude the VC can shoot down at us from above or catch us in a cross fire from across the valley. A squall line forces us closer to the river. The valley pinches into a narrow corridor, walls steep and menacing. High winds and bucking turbulence snap and bang the rotor blades, and we slow down and wrap on turns to prevent blade-tip stall.

"Christ," Cochran moans over the intercom. "Here we go again. The man won't ever turn back. Damn the torpedoes."

"Give him a call on the radio and suggest we abort."

"And eat radio discipline shit for a week? No thanks."

The Rajah bores on. There's too much turbulence to hang in tight and we drift apart. Over the radio we hear three other flights have aborted. Captain Beamus plows on.

We follow him around a sharp bend in the river, Ben-San and Rob Jacobs behind us. Captain Beamus disappears into a rain shower. We surge through the shower and break into the clear. Captain Beamus is ahead of us, his running lights flashing against a dark storm layer lying close to the river.

"We'll never make it through that," Cochran says.

It's a hundred to one that Ben-San and Rob Jacobs will agree, but the Rajah continues on and his lights vanish in the dark cloud. Cochran approaches the storm line and breaks off, pulls a one-eighty and heads back out the river canyon, Rob Jacobs right behind us.

"Looks too bad up here," Captain Beamus calls over the radio. "I'm heading back. What's your position?"

"We've already turned around."

Captain Beamus breaks out of the storm cloud, a hundred feet below, down on the river.

"Where are you?" he calls.

"I'm ahead and above, leading the flight."

"Like hell you are. I'm the flight leader. Get your ass back here where you belong."

"Roger that."

We circle in a tight turn and come up on Captain Beamus's flank.

"If it hasn't socked in downriver we've got it made," Cochran says over the intercom. I nod. My hands inside my flight gloves are moist and cold. Another rain squall lies dead ahead. It gets darker. I squeeze into the seat pan and concentrate on Captain Beamus's bird, his running lights dim in the mist. We enter the squall and his lights disappear.

"I've lost contact," Cochran says over the air. To our right, Rob Jacobs hangs in close. The mountain looms on our left. Cochran drops the collective and we dive toward the river. The radio altimeter registers seventy-five feet.

"No lower, baby. No lower," I tell him.

Tree tops flash past on either side. Cochran pours on the coals and speeds up.

"What's your position, Cochran?" Captain Beamus calls over the air.

"Seventy-five feet over the water, heading downstream."

"Roger that. I'm through that bad spot but I had to get down on the water to make it. Looks good up ahead."

Click click, Cochran keys the mike in response. We're flying through patches of ground fog and rain. The narrow walls of the canyon reach close as we hurtle down the narrow gorge.

"Number three," Captain Beamus calls on the radio. "State your position."

No answer. I lean out the window and peer back into the soup but there's no sign of Ben-San and Rob Jacobs. The cloud bank rises and we climb off the river's surface.

"We have to get out of here," Captain Beamus radios. "We're starting to draw ground fire."

"Great," Cochran says over the intercom. "That's all we need."

"If you read, number three, we're heading out," Captain Beamus radios. "I repeat, if you read, we're heading out."

"I'm going back, take another look for them," Cochran transmits.

"Negative on that, we're too low on fuel," Captain Beamus answers.

Cochran turns the chopper and heads back upstream.

"If we came through once we can go through again," he says over the intercom. We skim along the surface of the river.

"Smoke ahead," I say. "One o'clock."

"I think we've got them," Cochran says over the radio. "We're going in for a look."

"What's the weather like?" Captain Beamus answers.

"Shitty. Clouds are low on the hill but I think we can get under them."

"I'm coming back. Don't do anything till I get there."

Cochran clicks the mike to acknowledge, then says, "Fuck that," over the intercom and heads toward the smoke. We get lower and slower, staying just above the tree tops. The chopper lies burning in a small clearing, blasted out where they crashed. Cochran noses in closer.

"We've got company, Lieutenant," Soonto says over the intercom. Cochran banks to the right. "Got 'em," he says. "Hose them down."

The M-60 barks, short spurts.

"There's someone down there, lying on the ground," I say.

"Is he moving?"

"Yeah, he's waving an arm."

Cochran continues the turn and straightens out right into the muzzle of a VC pointing his AK-47 at our nose. Bullets smash into the engine and cockpit. The windshield splatters and a round zings past my head. Cochran bottoms the collective and the chopper drops, smoke billowing out of the engine.

"Tranny's gushing oil," Soonto says.

"Pressure's dropping fast," I say.

The engine clunks, bangs and clanks, chopper jolting with every misfire.

"Strap in, Soonto, I'm taking it down," Cochran says.

"Where?" I say. "There's no place to land."

"Right there," Cochran says.

He drives the chopper into a narrow space between two trees, a hill rising sharply on our left. Cochran holds his airspeed long enough to plow through the treetops, shredding branches and leaves with the rotors, then, as the blades start to break up, he cuts the engine and lays the chopper on its left side with a jolt that throws me against the door. Our right side is open to the sky.

"Everyone okay?" Cochran asks. My head is ringing but no damage done. Soonto says he's all right. Cochran shuts everything down.

"Let's get out of here before she blows. Bring your rifle and magazines."

The smell of AV gas fills the cockpit. Cochran goes out his door, carrying his Armalite. I climb over the center console and jump down. Soonto is rummaging around in the belly.

"What you doing, Soonto? We got to skedaddle."

"Just grabbing my catchall." He throws out a duffle.

"Get the M-60," Cochran says.

Soonto lifts it off its carriage and hands me the machine gun, with the ammo belt trailing, then jumps down. Cochran hefts the duffle.

"What the hell you got in here?"

"Emergency gear, sir."

"Okay, let's go. The other chopper's over this way."

Cochran carries the duffle and his rifle. I cradle my weapon and follow behind. Soonto loops the ammo belt around his shoulders and, M-60 at the ready, joins in line. Cochran stops and motions us out of the way. He takes out his pistol and aims at the chopper. He fires a tracer into the gas tank and the helicopter explodes. Black smoke rises to merge with the clouds. The heat washes over us and we turn our backs and head out, leaving nothing for the VC to salvage.

We struggle through the tangled undergrowth, and hike along the curve of the mountain until we get to the other chopper. Cochran motions us down, signals for me to go left and Soonto right. Crouching, we peer through the foliage. Ben-San and Rob Jacobs' helicopter lies smashed and burning. Five VC, standing at the other side of the clearing, have paused to look at the smoke rising from our burning chopper. Cochran points to me and Soonto, levels his Armalite and nods his head. We open up and drop two, but the other three run into the jungle, bullets splattering in their wake.

"Shit," Cochran says. "Come on, Huck, let's see who that is on the ground. Soonto, you cover us."

Ben-San lies in a crumpled heap, flight suit charred, arms and shoulders of the material burned away, his skin black and cracked. Inside his flight helmet his burned face is covered with big blisters. His chest heaves.

The M-60 clatters. I lean down. "Ben-San, can you hear me?"

His lips move. I put my ear to his mouth.

"Rob's dead," he whispers. "Took a bullet in the head. We plowed in before I could grab the stick . . . crew chief gone . . ."

"Come on," Cochran tells me. "We've got to get out of here. Grab my rifle."

Cochran hoists Ben-San on his shoulders and shuffles into the jungle. Soonto keeps up the fire. When we are deeper in the foliage, Cochran lays Ben-San down. "Hate to do this but we have to get that helmet off."

Soonto comes hustling up. "Ah," he says, "that's the shits."

A rising gorge seeks frantic relief in my throat but I slam it back into the hell from which it sprang and slide his helmet off. His hair comes with it. The skin is peeled and raw.

"They say not to do this but we've got to cool him down."

Cochran pulls out his water bottle and dribbles water over Ben-San's head and face, then across his shoulders and arms and hands.

"We need some cloth. What you got in that bag, Soonto?"

Soonto pulls out a wrapped up parachute. He opens the bundle and cuts strips with his knife. Cochran lays the cloth over Ben-San's head and face and along his shoulders and arms. He dribbles the water over the cloth.

"Okay, let's go."

He hoists Ben-San up. Slinging the rifles over my shoulders and carrying the duffle in my hand, I take the lead. We struggle deeper into the jungle, smashing through the bushes and leaves, can't worry about the noise now, or try to hide our way, the important thing is to get some distance between us and the VC.

"They're coming," Soonto says from the rear.

"Find a good spot and slow them down," Cochran says.

Cochran is hunched over, lifting his feet high to keep from getting tangled in the roots and branches. Behind us there is a burp of M-60 fire. The jungle opens and some light streams in. We stumble onto a game trail, a narrow flat shelf running alongside the hill. The ravine drops sharply to our right and a stream crashes and burbles down at the bottom.

Soonto comes puffing up. "That won't hold them for long. I'd say we're fast getting into a position what they call untenable, Lieutenant."

Cochran grunts. "How many rounds you got left in that ammo belt?"

"Bout all used up. Hundred, max."

"Hey," I yell. "Here's something might help us out."

A big tree, three foot in diameter, 300 feet tall, has toppled across the ravine. Its root wad, full of dirt and rock, blocks the trail. The top, thick with branches and leaves, is jammed against the opposite hill.

Cochran looks at the tree. Back down the path. Up at the sky. "Not a hell of a lot of daylight left. We've got to find a place to hunker down. We don't have enough ammo to hold them off here, but the tree can still work for us."

I get it. As a bridge, not a fort. It's a long ways over and the branches are a major hindrance, but something to grab hold of in case you slip. Don't want to think about that.

"Got any rope in that catchall, Soonto?"

"Parachute cord."

"That'll do. Tie the Lieutenant to me so he won't fall off. Huck, you slip on back down the trail and keep an eye out for the Charlies. They should be leery of catching up with no cover anywhere. Give me a two minute head start then come on back."

Soonto rummages in the duffel. I head back, come to a curve and lean against the hill, rifle ready. Check the selector, full auto. Remember, short bursts only. Sweat stings my eyes. I swipe at it with the back of my hand. Makes it worse. Fuck this shit. I step around the corner and let loose a burst. Then another, until the magazine is empty. Eject it and slam in the spare. That should hold the *hijos de putas.* I beat it back to the tree.

Soonto is halfway across, reaching under the trunk. He's wrapped parachute cord around a limb and under the tree and back over the top. He ties the ends together, pulls a package out of his flight suit and jams it under the cord. The package has a long hunk of what looks like string sticking out. He slips the string through the parachute cord so the end is pointing up in the air. Then he hustles back and jumps down off the tree.

Cochran turns to me. "What happened back there."

"Nothing. I thought it would slow them down."

"Okay, let's do it."

Soonto gives him a boost and Cochran gets up on the tree with Ben-San across his shoulders. He sways till he gets his balance and starts out.

"Lose the M-60," he calls over his shoulder. "You carry the duffle, Huck. Soonto, you bring up the rear with the rifles."

Soonto throws the M-60 and the belt into the ravine. He gives me a leg up and I crawl onto the tree. The duffle is around my back, held by a strap across my chest. Not as bad as a tightrope walk but no stroll across a plank, either. One slow step at a time, I come to Soonto's lashup. It's not a piece of string at all. It's a fuse.

"Keep moving, Lieutenant," Soonto says from behind me.

If that's a fuse then that package has got to be *una carga de enorme importancia.* I grab a branch for support, ease around Soonto's lashup and keep going. Behind me I hear a cigarette lighter click and a soft *fizzzzz*. Up ahead, Cochran continues across. I want to pass him and get over to the other side. How much time did Soonto give us? More than enough, I hope. We're not racing the Cong, we're racing against time and time is a tightrope, a lift of a foot up and a foot down, a drop of sweat plopping on a tree branch thick with leaves. Cochran makes it to the ground on the other side. I jump down alongside him. AK rounds shatter wood, splatter splinters, rounds zing, then a booming explosion drowns the AKs, obliterates the sound of the wind in the trees, kills the gurgle of the water in the stream, and leaves our ears ringing.

Soonto slams into the dirt next to me and we fall to the ground and cover Ben-San with our bodies. The top of the tree angles up, its mangled bottom tips downward, and the leviathon hurtles in a growling, debris spitting, headlong rush down the steep ravine, limbs and branches scrape our backs and shred our flight suits, rocks dirt and underbrush cascade madly along with the tree to a spectacular resonding kerplash in the water below where the massive giant smashes into its blown-apart other half that careened just as crazily down the equally steep opposite hill, trunk, limbs, root wad and all, the tree's top and bottom abruptly crashed to a stop with their conjoined ends rudely stoppering the stream in its madly scampering tracks.

The stream swirls and muddies below the newly created dam. On the other side of the ravine, a big gap is carved out of the hill and the trail is obliterated. No VC in sight. A bird shrieks, our watches tick, the hands spin, and time that was stretched like a tightrope . . . loosens . . . our yammering hearts sledgehammering against our rib cages . . . are stilled . . . our ragged, shallow breathing is . . . now . . . calm.

20. Paper Scrawl Torture

What's with the noise, Doc? . . . can't hear anything on the radio . . . where's Soonto? . . . there, standing by the engine . . . Lieutenant, the gripe sheet says there's a shudder in the rotors, I fixed it best I can, how's about cranking her up, make sure it's okay so I can write it off and clear the bird for flying . . . sure, no hay problemo, *oh my, that will never do . . . sorry, Sergeant Soonto, this bird is definitely down . . . heavy as an elephant, never get off the ground . . . I rode the elephant, Doc . . . when Daddy came home from the war still shaking with malaria and took me to a circus, a small ragtag outfit . . . but they had an elephant . . . he was walking behind the tent, led by his handler . . . he stopped and reached out his trunk and snuffled me . . . air holes breathing in and out . . . he smelled of hay and something moist and rheumy . . . the elephant knelt . . . I was boosted up on his head . . . ears like huge wings flapping . . . he walks . . . I rise up and down with the movement . . . the leathery skin of elephant between my legs . . . his vibration rising to my head . . . it's all about the vibration, Doc, the whole chopper is vibrating . . . but can't you do anything about the noise, Doc?. . . the rotor blades are clattering . . .*

The clatter of rotor blades brings us to our feet. Ben-San lies on the ground. His breathing is ragged and he moans softly. A helicopter circles, farther down the hill. Soonto rummages in his duffel.

"Pop that sucker," Cochran says.

A red plume rises from the smoke grenade, and we wait, willing the chopper closer. The clatter gets louder and Cochran fires his pistol, five tracers arcing like stars falling backwards. The white YV painted on the nose of the chopper gets closer and the bird hovers overhead. The crew chief looks down at us from the belly door, Doc Hollenden hanging over his shoulder. The crew chief hooks a harness to the hoist cable and lowers it.

"Get Ben-San ready," Cochran hollers over the noise.

Brush and tree branches whip around us. Dirt and rocks pepper our faces and arms. Soonto and I slip the collar under Ben-San's arms. His eyes are open, but his face is a grisly mess. His mouth gapes in a blackened grimace. I take it for a smile, a good sign. Up he goes, spinning slowly. The crew chief and Doc Hollenden pull him in.

Cochran motions me to go next. Once inside, I fall against the bulkhead. The pilot looks down from his perch. Emmett. He nods to me and turns back to the instruments, holding the chopper steady. Soonto comes aboard and then Cochran. Emmett turns the chopper, points the nose downhill and we follow the stream to the river. He pours on the turns and we race for the coast. Two other helicopters circle the spots where the crashed machines smolder, smoke wisping skyward.

The crew chief takes off his helmet, points at the pilots, mimics talking, hands the helmet to Cochran who scowls, shakes his head, closes his eyes and turns away. The crew chief looks at me. What the hell. I put it on.

"How come you're here?" I ask over the intercom.

"Beamus radioed for help," Bennett says. "You're in a shitload of trouble. When we get back to the base, they're going to ream you a new . . ."

I hand the helmet back to the crew chief.

We land in Quang Ngai and taxi up to an Air Force C123 with its ramp down. An Army doctor and two medics wait with a stretcher. Doc Hollenden helps them lift Ben-San on the litter. He lies limp, shot full of morphine. Props turning, ramp closing, the plane hits the runway on the roll and takes off for the Nha Trang Army hospital.

Back at the chopper Emmett is having an argument with a Vietnamese Army Major. In his awkward English the Major is ordering Emmett to fly him south to Quin Hon but Emmett is having none of it.

"This bird is going north, back to its nest."

Emmett turns and stalks away.

"Watch it," Wee Willie Weems yells.

Emmett wheels around. The Major is fumbling with the straps on his holster. Emmett whips out his stainless steel Colt Python and in a slick smooth draw fires three quick rounds into the asphalt, the first one a tracer. The Major's eyes widen, he mutters something and beats a hurried retreat across the tarmac.

"What are you lame brains staring at?" Emmett says. "Let's mount up before any other asshole wants a piece of this."

"Is that a peace maker?" Willie asks me. "Just the size of it makes me sue for peace."

"By the look on that Major's face, I'd say what he needs is a pacemaker."

We haul up the coast in fading light to Da Nang, land and shut down and face a waiting clatch of pilots. Doc Hollenden shoos them away and hustles us to the dispensary. He lathers fiery disinfectant across our backs, then orders up some hot chow followed with double shots of whiskey before we stagger to our room and collapse in the sack, alongside two empty beds.

Grilled relentlessly. Why did you go back on your own? Why didn't you maintain radio contact? Why did you expose yourselves to ground fire? Why did you leave the downed helicopters and force the search aircraft to look all over hell for you in disintegrating weather threatening even more lives and equipment? Questions bang a putrid drum, but the bottom line is we got Ben-San out of there. If the Viet Cong got him they'd have killed him.

"Well, there's that. You have anything else to add?"

"Yes, sir," Cochran says. "I'd like to recommend Sergeant Soonto for a medal."

The Hammer scowls, non-commital, then motions us away.

The grilling over, we run into Emmett. I look at Cochran. He nods, *let's take him on*. Emmett. Cock of the walk. Belligerent as a tomcat. Let's talk to him, *mano a mano,* see if his back's bent out of shape from all our shenanigans, going all the way back to the poker game fiasco.

"Hey, Grits, what went down out there?" I ask him before Cochran can start in.

"I was in the air carrying ARVNs to an outpost that had called for help when we got diverted to the crash scene. Luckily the Doc was with us."

"Don't think we aren't appreciative. We thought we'd have to spend the night out there and you know what that would've meant for Ben-San."

"We didn't know what we'd find. I was able to get low enough that I didn't run out of cable when I lifted you out because with that tree gone there was enough room to hover. It was still a tight squeeze."

Emmett doesn't say anything about it but we know it took an expert hand on the controls. Cochran gives me the nod and we break it off, forego any kind of big head-butting confabulation. There's already enough rancor swirling around the ready room. The deaths have hardened the faces, hardened the talk. ARVNs have become gooks, slant-eyes, slope-heads, sneaky bastards. And to think, they asked us over here to help. And what about Rob Jacobs is the question on everyone's mind. He still hasn't been found. The crew chief was thrown out of the chopper in the crash and his body has been carried off the mountain and flown to Quang Ngai where an identification and burial team takes over.

Captain Beamus organizes the administrative tasks. Establishes an accident board. Grabs Cochran and tells him, since he is the squadron Career and Welfare officer, to start writing letters of condolence.

"Hey, that's the C.O.'s job. I can't write his letters for him."

The Hammer is out at the site, directing operations. He's hoping Rob Jacobs's body will be found, squashing the rumors he might still be alive, that he was thrown clear, wandered off into the jungle, maybe captured and killed. Cochran sweats and agonizes over scrawled pieces of paper, determined not to fill them with meaningless bullshit.

"How can I capture his essence?" he asks me. "The pride Rob Jacobs took in his cavernous mouth that could chomp an apple in half in one bite, his joke sneeze, his sordid trips to town to prove himself alive?" He answers his own questions. "Impossible."

Cochran searches out Captain Beamus to volunteer for the team searching at the crash site.

"What for?"

"So I can help. I used to be on a mountain rescue team when I worked for the Forest Service. I assisted on lots of rescues."

Captain Beamus eyes him suspicioulsy. "Can't do it. We've committed enough pilots to this operation. Something might come up where we need everyone. We're still a functioning squadron."

"Yeah, yeah, I know, contingency situations." Cochran stalks off.

Beamus calls after him, "Keep working on those letters, Lieutenant."

Instead, Cochran goes to the ready room and flops down in a chair. He flips a bullet in the air and catches it, looks at the red tip.

"At least these were good for something," he tells me.

"Yes, Emmett's generosity paid off in aces. When were you ever on a mountain rescue team?"

Cochran puts the bullet in his pocket. "I just said that to get out of this shitty job."

Colonel Swinn, the base commander, orders the operation halted, so we can get everybody out before the VC hit us in strength. It is certain, he says, that Rob Jacobs's remains were consumed in the fire.

Back to the paper-scrawl torture. Cochran flings pencils and erasers around the desk, applying the mental, gnashing the dental, mashing the mind, heart and body of a friend and now-deceased squadron mate upon an empty page.

Three days later, the letter still not finished, Captain Miles Standish Briggs, the Admin Officer, takes over, follows the letters of condolence format in the Marine Corps Personnel Manual, gets Beamus's okay, takes the typed sheets to the Hammer who inks in a few changes and an hour later signs the smooth draft.

Cochran arrives at the briefing the next morning to find Captain Ed "Ramshackle" Pomfrey, the squadron Safety Officer, asking if anyone has any suggestions that would help out in case of another incident or accident.

"Yes, now that you mention it, I have something," Cochran says. "We've had radio discipline beaten into us so much that when we get in a dangerous situation, and should say something, we don't, for fear of catching hell."

"Yes . . . ah . . . a good point," Captain Pomfrey says, glancing from the Hammer to Captain Beamus. Neither comments so Ramshackle says, "If there's nothing else . . ." then lets it drop and sits down.

The Hammer gets up and briefs the day's hops as if everything's back to normal. Were it only so. That evening the special services movie projector is grinding out a skin flick on the wall of a darkened BOQ room. Cochran goes in to see what's going on.

"Where'd that come from?"

"The First Sergeant found it in Battern's gear," Lieutenant Ted "Too Tall" Tolliver says.

"Sergeant Battern? The crew chief who . . . ?"

"Yeah. The First Sergeant figured the movie shouldn't be sent home with Battern's stuff but it was too good to be thrown out."

"How the hell did it get in here?" Cochran says.

"I confiscated it," Emmett says. "Who cares, anyway?"

Cochran leaves and walks down the hall into our room. "I can't believe it," he mutters. "I can't believe it."

There's more to come. At the all-pilots meeting the next morning we get hit up for a donation.

"What say we chip in and buy Ben-San a radio?" Emmett says. "There's a nice model in the PX. Portable, AM, FM and shortwave band. It will make the time pass faster in the hospital."

Nods and agreeing noises.

"I don't think it's such a hot idea," Cochran says. "Sure he's lonely, who wouldn't be, and it could happen to any one of us, but if we're really concerned about the man himself, let's all write him a letter. Fifty letters would cheer him up a lot more than the radio."

That shuts everyone up, a real damper. No one wants to write a fucking letter. The Hammer jumps into the breech.

"Good point, Cochran. I agree one hundred percent about the letters, but in this case I think we should do both. How does that sound?"

No arguing with the Hammer. Everyone murmurs their assent. The Hammer gives Cochran the eye and when the hat comes around he drops in a dollar.

"Let's see how many letters get written," Cochran says.

Word comes from Ben-San he wants to talk to me so operations lays on a chopper and assigns me to deliver the radio and letters. Cochran can't go. He's gotten roped into another job: helping build an orphanage in town.

One night Cochran was playing folk music on the tape recorder, and the chaplain, Father Sam, the chaplain what am, paused at the door. He stood, listening to the clear female voice:

I had an old dog and his name was Blue,
Betcha five dollars he's a good dog too.

"That's my cousin Joan," he said, a big grin creasing his face. He joined in on the song:

Old Blue treed and I went to see,
Blue had possum up a tall oak tree.

Cochran added his voice:

Old Blue died and he died so hard,
Made a big dent in my backyard.

They sang together, voices clashing horribly:

Shook so hard shook the teeth from his head
Shook his clothes to pieces, to the very thread.

"Come on in," Cochran said. "I never could carry a tune."

"And are you, my son," Father Sam asked, walking into the room, "a follower of the true faith?"

"Lapsed, Padre, or is it prolapsed, definitely not relapsed. Now I'm a follower of Lapsong Chung, the ancient Chinese philosopher, you know, he-of-the-best-laid-plans-of-planting-too-early-in-the-is-nipped-in-the-bud school of thought, so save your breath, Padre."

"And is that the great man's image?" Father Sam asked, pointing at Cochran's wooden statue of Shy Man Shitting In The Woods.

"The very same."

"Ah well, then that's that."

The chaplain started talking about the orphanage he was working on. It started out as an Ice Queen project. What was once a shack with some beds and a dirt floor became her pet project and she espoused its needs to an American journalist and pretty soon, women in the states, having gotten wind of the chirrun's plight, sent, *mas dineros*.

The Ice Queen loved getting the cash, thank you, it allowed her to buy milk, for instance, canned in America, labeled with the Hands Across The Sea logo, sent to Vietnam, stacked on shelves of every grocery store shack in the country, even in Dogpatch.

"Hey, that shit is supposed to be free. Why is she buying it?" Cochran wanted to know.

"That's not important," Father Sam said. "What's important is that we are helping these unfortunate war orphans."

"What a laugh. You know as well as I do that cold bitch is taking a big bite out of the money."

"Bite your tongue, young man. I won't put up with that kind of language. This is a noble cause. Don't you denigrate the good intentions of those who are concerned enough to do something for these poor kids."

"Your mouth runneth over, Chaplain. You want to help those kids and make sure they get what they need, then it's not money that's pocketed before they ever see the benefit. Here, hold this."

Cochran rummaged around inside his seabag. "I had this stuff saved for an emergency but it will probably go bad before I ever use it." He pulled out syringes and bottles of pills and ointments, boxes of medicine and dressings and antibitotics.

"Where did you ever . . . ?"

"Won it off a corpsman in a friendly game. Never can tell when you might need some personal treatment, you know what I mean, Padre; don't want to get it logged in the old record book." He gave the chaplain a wink and ripped the blanket off his bed. "Here you go."

"But that is goverment property."

"Naw. I fleeced it off the supply clerk. It's free bait and belongs to whoever has it wrapped around his scrawny limbs." He dropped a parachute on the floor. "Good clothes- making material."

Five pounds of hard candy, hoarded for trade at the outposts, joined the pile. Canteen cups. Soap, toothpaste, razors and shaving cream. Books, pencils, paper, talcum powder, toothbrushes, shoe polish, brasso. All wrapped up in the blanket, toted on Father Sam's back and deposited in his room.

Word got around and the stack grew so large it spilled outside, where it was covered with a tarp. Cases of nonperishable food. Lumber and nails and building materials. Enough, Father Sam pleaded, enough. The pile was getting too big. They loaded it all in the back of a six-by-six truck, and lumbered into town followed by a weapons carrier full of Marines who gave the orphanage a face lift. New roof, paint job, partitions, inside plumbing and a kitchen. The orphan kids pawed through the packages, clutched at the Marine's legs, dodged Sisters' clutches.

Word of the work made it to the Ice Queen and she hustled over to encounter a beaming, pleased nun whose demeanor underwent a quick change under a barrage of questions. What of the plans we made, the Ice Queen demanded, my committees, the ladies we were recruiting to help? Father Sam pointed to the building and the kids, and that was explanation enough.

While Cochran is tied up with the Chaplain and the orphanage, Wee Willie Weems and I fly to the Army hospital in Nha Trang.

We land and shut down and catch a ride from the flight line to the hospital buildings, and find out where Ben-San is, then head that way. We're a couple of rasty-looking characters in our dirty flight suits and wrinkled fore-and-aft caps, clomping past starched white nurses and orderlies, doctors with stethoscope necklaces, clipboards like shields, ball-point pens sticking out like spears from their shirtfront pockets.

"You look a lot better than the last time I saw you," I tell Ben-San, our winsome old roomie whose head and arms and hands are swathed in white bandages, his eyes black chunks of cinder stuck in the snow.

"Yeah, that was grueling, but don't let this fool you. They're ripping me to shreds."

"Ha ha, I bet," Willie says. "Those roundeye nurses?"

"No, the fucking doctor. Every day, when he peels off these bandages, cheery as a bar girl caging drinks, he tears off the scabs with them. New way to treat burns, he says. Doesn't leave such awful scars. Hurts like a bastard, though, so screw the scars, I'll take them over the treatment. He thinks that's a great joke. What have you got there?"

"The guys chipped in and bought you a radio," Willie says. "Plus we got a whole passel of letters. How many are in the bag, Huck?"

"Uh, I don't know. Twenty some. Hey, go find out where we can plug the radio in, Willie."

He leaves and I pull a chair up close to the bed. "What's going on, Ben-San? I heard you wanted to talk to me."

"Huck, what are they saying?"

"The crash? Hell, everyone knows that wasn't your . . ."

"No, not that. What about Yoshika? Any of them think I still have a chance with her, you know, messed up like this?"

"God, no one's even thought about that. We just want you back on your feet."

"I want to marry her, now more than ever. I'm not staying in the Marines, even if they'd have me. Will you help me out?"

"Me? What can I do?"

"I just need to know someone is . . ."

Willie comes in the door, carrying an extension cord. "They said there's a plug-in on the wall, under the window."

He scurries around, sets the radio on the table next to the bed. "You want to try it out?"

Ben-San looks at his hands in their bandaged mitts. "Not now, thanks."

"What've you guys been talking about?" Willie asks.

"Nothing," I say. "We were just yakking about how long it will be before Ben-San gets out of here."

"They're saying it will be a few days," Ben-San says. "As soon as the fever stabilizes, then it's back to the States."

"It's great seeing you," Willie says. He looks at his watch. "The guys will be glad to hear you're doing so well. We better hit it, Huck, long flight home."

"Yeah. Shake it easy, Ben-San, I'll be in touch."

"Thanks for what you and Cochran and Soonto did, Tomas. And don't forget what I said, you hear?"

"Roger that."

On the flight back, my mind's churning. Sure, Ben-San wants to marry her, now anyhow, but what about when he's back in the States, and what about Yoshika? Is she going to want to hook up with him after he kissed her off? And what's it going to be like when she sees him, all burned up? *Estoy rechenado mis dientes*, gnash my teeth, I'm at a loss here, and no one else in the squadron is going to deal with this shit.

21. Spirit of Reconciliation

Where's the protection, Doc? . . . rounds are zinging in nastier than hornets . . . they promised us more armor plating for the cockpit . . . what you talking about, cockpit, Cochran says . . . what you need is an armor-plated jockstrap, protect your most vitals . . . is that protection from infection? . . . in 469 BC Hippocrates discovered one of the oldest infections known to man, but his mistake was thinking it was an involuntary flow of semen . . . somewhat on the order of a wet dream . . . the name he gave the disease stuck . . . gonorrhea . . . the flow of seed . . . I don't know who discovered the rubber, Doc, but I'll always remember what Cochran said . . . just roll it on until you either run out of rubber or you run out of pecker . . . what we really need is a reinforced rubber . . . yeah, a rubber mallet on your head, I tell him . . . any violence, it'll be on your head not mine, he says . . . inch-pay, e-may if you've heard this one, Doc . . . there's no excuse for violence except when making love . . . at least according to that old razorback, Pappy Lurnt . . .

"Son," Pappy Lurnt says, puffing on his cigar, "don't you be taking this any further. By the time Lieutenant Benson is back in the States the memory of that Jo-san will be shaved so thin it could sit on a dollar and give you fifty cents change."

Pappy taps the ash from his corncob pipe into a dried wild boar snout sitting on his desk.

"Remember this, young Lieutenant, you don't take a hog to market in a Cadillac. The only thing that's going to make your friend feel better is a drink of virgin's piss and you'll never find any of that out here. Now vamoose and deep six any notion of bothering the skipper with this marriage blather."

I shuffle back to the room, any chance of helping Ben-San squelched. I'm out of my element here, totally at a loss, and I put the whole thing aside, hoping some brainstorm will come up later. Our room is spanking clean, all of Rob Jacobs and Ben-San's gear gone, their beds made up, and we're awaiting the arrival of two new replacement pilots. On the other side of the room Cochran is covering the wall with pictures and clippings, part of his disinformation ploy to confuse the enemy. He's suspicious of the maids. How many of them are passing on info to the Cong? . . . *One American, he slouch like ape and his underwear, whooeee, bad enough he didn't change more than once a month, now he not change at all, wears skivvie briefs till they shred to pieces then puts on another pair over the top—four, six, eleven elastic waist bands all piled on each other, filthy dirty.*

He cuts pictures out of magazines, pasting together a collage. Screaming, gesturing Bertrand Russell, glorying in a peace fit, is glued atop austere, skeletal Isak Dinesen, Bertrand shouting, "DON'T LET THE BASTARDS PUT YOU DOWN," Miss Dinesen quietly retorting, "Don't Break The Cool," and now Cochran's new addition to the collage is a newspaper clipping that claims the Buddhists, who are in conflict with the Vietnamese Government, believe the Americans have sent a spy, "to look us over." When asked to describe him, the Buddhists tell the reporter, "Well, he was tall and had a very long beard and his hair was very long in back and curly. He said he was a poet and a little crazy and he liked Buddhists. We didn't know what else he was so we decided he was a spy." The clipping went on to say that the newsman burst out laughing. 'That's Allen Ginsberg, the Beatnik poet.'"

The door to the room opens and a cavernous face peers in. He introduces himself. "Lieutenant Jonathon Merkle, from Paducah, Tennessee. Blessed are the pacemakers," he says, "for they shall keep the beat."

He's a Bible thumper, he's proud to admit, for he comes from a staunch Baptist family that believes full immersion is necessary, talking in tongues is okay, snake charming is entirely possible and hot coal walking totally acceptable. Bible quotes are a requisite, no matter how badly mangled, and heavenly ascension is a perquisite for those who talk the talk.

I glance at Cochran. *Madre mío*, what hath God brought? Cochran waggles his eyebrows. More grist for the mill.

"You want to go over to the O club and hoist a few?" Cochran asks the newcomer.

"No, thankee, I'm going to stow my gear and hit the sack, and, God willing, get some sleep. I've been traveling for days."

"Old Baptist John there, he's stuck on that train," I say, after Cochran changes into regular duds and we head out for the club.

"Bound for glory," Cochran says. "Faith is the conductor, belief is the engineer, it's rapture on the rails. Forget going to the O club. I yearn for greater delights. Let's swing in here."

He knocks on the Rajah's door and peeks in. Captain Beamus looks up from some papers. The look on his face goes from quizzical to a grimace.

"Hey Captain," Cochran says, "Why don't you get your glad rags on and let off some steam with us in town?"

Captain Beamus shakes his head, "No, I've got work to do. You go on without me."

"Okay, but you'll be missing out." Cochran hesitates at the door. "Say, since you won't be using it, mind if we borrow your jeep?"

The Rajah looks us over for a moment, then says, "Go ahead," and turns back to the papers on his desk.

Cochran pulls the door shut. We hesitate, waiting for a crash, an ashtray, say, against the door. All quiet.

"You know," I say, "in the spirit of reconciliation maybe we ought to cut the fucker some slack, *da chance al cabrón,* as they say down on the border."

"Yeah but the border we're working on is the DMZ."

We're in our civvies, not all that different from our Marine khakis—chinos, short-sleeve shirts, penny loafers, white socks—two Yanks on the town, usually with guns and bullets strapped around our waists, but not tonight, not while we're walking in the spirit of reconciliation.

"So, maybe we ought to ease off fucking with the Rajah's flight gear," I tell Cochran.

"Yeah, cutting off the pants legs on his flight suit might have been topping it a bit. After all, he did make the call that spared us a night on the mountain, which probably saved Ben-San's life."

We drink to that, and decide to forego our previously churlish behavior, not in keeping with our status as officers and gentlemen. We're splurging, eating lobster, drinking white wine and nibbling Camembert cheese at a pretentious French restaurant where it's business as usual, despite the war. As oddball luck would have it, Emmett and Too Tall Tolliver are also eating in the restaurant and they clomp down at our table for after-dinner drinks.

What's with this new friendly Emmett? He has adopted a proprietary air, probably because he rescued us from that mountainside hellhole. Since Cochran and I are mellowed out in the the spirit of reconciliation, we abide his drunken gusto and Germanic bluster. Emmett is in rare form, yakking exuberantly, bumping his gums in glee over the blissful rapture of the well-known hummer.

"It's a honk house pleasure, and you ought to get to know it. Sweet Lips is famous for giving the best hummer in the Far East. The Army boys taught her to hum 'When The Caissons Go Rolling Along,' which is worth its weight, but nothing compared to the treasure, er, I mean the pleasure you get from 'The Marine Corps Hymn.' You'll be seeing stars, Fourth of July fireworks, the old red white and blue cascading in streamers across a rainbow colored sky."

Cochran and I raise our eyebrows. Pretty flamboyant prose from old Emmett.

"Yep," he says, "far as I know there's only two authentic Vietnamese contributions to international folk art. Betel nut and the hummer."

Cochran gives me the eye and we edge out of our chairs.

"Hey, where you going? Don't you want her address?"

"Some other time, maybe."

"No, no. You've got to give it a try." He writes the directions on a napkin. "It's out on the fringes, in the dark side of town, very private."

A knowing wink from Emmett. Or was it a lewd leer? The light isn't very good in this room. When we get to the jeep, Cochran pauses and looks at me. Like it or not the bastard has put a bee in our bonnet.

"What do you say?" Cochran asks. "Want to check it out?"

I'm dubious, mighty dubious. But temptation is twanging. I shrug. "Still early, what's to lose?"

We drive through the center of town, Cochran at the wheel. I've got the napkin opened on my lap. Brightly lit streets and gaudy storefronts give way to potted dirt roads, stalls with charcoal fires and kids playing on dirt roads in front of tin-siding shacks open to the street. I'm trying to read street signs and find the right house numbers.

"There. That looks like the place."

We park down the street and walk back to an open-fronted shop. An alley runs alongside. We go down the alley and knock on a door. An older woman, wearing black silk pants and a long white shirt, opens the door. She looks up and down the alley and motions us in. Holds out her hand. We know the drill. Two hundred and fifty piasters each. The money disappears under her shirt. She leads us down a hallway and motions us inside an austere room.

A woman rises from the bed. Sweet Lips. She is young and clear skinned with hooded eyes. Barefooted and wearing a short smock, she is all business. She nods to Cochran, indicates for him to lower his pants. *Diablos y qué?* Am I supposed to stand here and watch? I turn away. She gasps. Must be those shredded layers of filthy BVD waistbands.

A banging and shouting and scuffling in the hall interrupts the proceedings. That doesn't sound like an impatient customer to me. Sweet Lips puts her finger to her lips, glides across the room, pulls back a curtain and opens a window. Come on, she motions. Cochran, limp as a wet noodle, pulls up his pants and hobbles to the window. I go out first and he follows after. We tumble to the ground, get off me you fucking gorilla.

We struggle to our feet, Cochran buttons up and we look around. This isn't good. We're in a small yard, enclosed on three sides by a high wall and behind us by the house. The voices in the bedroom rise in angry shouts, then are followed by a crash. Flashlight beams pierce the dark yard. If they catch us out here we're fried. We hunker down next to the house. Harsh demanding masculine voices cry out questions. Questions wanting answers, and wanting them right now. Shrill feminine voices shriek in response.

"It's a raid," Cochran whispers.

"No shit, Dick Tracy."

That's sure as hell not the Shore Patrol. Probably a Vietnamese vice squad, hopefully not the Can Lao secret police. Any way you look at it we're in deep shit. If we get hauled in they'll fry our asses all the way from Beamus to the Exec right up to the Hammer, maybe even the base C.O. While I'm fretting, Cochran crosses the yard and checks out the walls. Eight feet high with broken glass glinting on top. He takes off his shirt and throws it up on the wall.

"Give me a leg up," he whispers.

What now? Out of the frying pan?

"Come on," he says. "They'll be looking out that open window next."

Okay. I boost him onto the wall.

"Oooch, owww." He's getting acquainted with the broken glass. He leans down with a hand. In for a peso. I grab his hand and he hauls me up, introducing me to a skin-shredding welcome.

"Yow, that rankles."

We slide off the wall and land in soft dirt on the other side. Yank out our hankies and daub at the bloody spots on our hands and bodies. We're standing in the flower garden of someone's home. The rooms in the house are lit up and people are moving around inside.

"Here, rub this all over you," Cochran says. He holds out a blob of evil looking muck.

"What the hell is that?"

"Just dirt and stuff from off the ground. It will hide your smell."

"My smell? Who gives a rat's ass about my smell?"

"We stink like skunks to the Vietnamese. Anyone comes outside they'll smell us right away."

Cochran rubs the muck all over his chest. Gives me the look. I take a glob from him. He's right about one thing. It doesn't smell American to me. Filth, dirt, rotten vegetation guck, honey bucket glop, putrid rotting stuff. I close my eyes and rub it on my stomach and chest and arms. The door opens and a kid steps outside and looks around. I stop rubbing and hold perfectly still. This is it. Showdown time. Something rubbing against my leg starts a shiver that runs up my spine and explodes in my head. What catastrophe now?

I glance down and stare into the piercing green eyes of a cat. The kid calls, the cat slaps my leg with its tail and, meowing, runs to the kid. The kid picks him up and they go inside. My heart rate slows down to a few hundred beats above normal. After a while the lights go out in the house. After a longer while, after counting the stars peeking through wispy clouds, after absorbing the smell of smoke from a million charcoal fires, after our legs have gone numb, after the mosquitos have drained us dry, Cochran says, "They gotta be gone by now."

We shake some feeling back into our legs, then it's up and over the wall, more bleeding, more hanky pats, then cross the yard to the window, locked, but Cochran has had it with all this hiding and he smashes the window and yanks it open.

The bedroom is dark and empty. We slink down the hall to the room where we first came in. The older lady and an older man and Sweet Lips are sitting on a couch. We walk in. The trio cowers, terrified at the sight of two bloody monsters in shredded mud-caked clothes. But then, realizing it is only the barbaric Americans, their frightened looks change to disgust.

As far as I'm concerned, it's over, let's amscray before something else happens, but no, Cochran rubs his finger and thumb together, the universal sign for moolah. He wants our money back. The old guy rushes up to Cochran, yakking a mile a minute, waves his arms and hands, makes emphatic no-no noises, points to the door, makes a sound like a siren, waves bye bye, makes the same finger thumb moolah motion, waves bye bye again. Okay we get the picture, they had to pay off the police, and now all he wants is us out of there, out of their lives. He shoos us out the door. We are reluctant but compliant, what are you gonna do? *La realidad es una chinga,* or as they say in a Texas whorehouse, reality is a bitch.

Outside, Cochran considers his arms, the bleeding, his ruined shirt, his ripped and blood-stained pants, his face grimy with sweat and dirt. Shit-muck smell all over him. He looks at me.

"Go get the jeep. You're not as fucked-up looking as I am."

Is he serious? The way I feel, I'm a sawed-off replica of his garbage heap mess.

When I pick him up he is laughing. "What's so funny?" I snarl. "Losing the money, is that what's funny? Or is it our arms like barb wire whipdown? Or maybe our clothes throwaway trashed. Or is it this smell making my throat gag?"

"None of the above. I was just thinking about how it all went down."

Cochran's face contorts into a piratical smile. "It's like a Vietnamese TV cop series. Eliot Ness and the Unsuckables." He chuckles grimly. "They had to have been tipped off, coming in right on our heels like that."

"What are you implying?"

"They weren't after Sweet Lips and her pals, or they would have hauled them in. Not mentioning any names but who else knew about that place?"

I look over at Cochran. Is he implying what I think he's implying? Memories can be simmering, payback a long time coming. Is Emmett holding a grudge? We don't really know what's going on behind that blunt Teutonic forehead. Anger, we've seen that. Antipathy toward the Red Horde, that's a fact. Maybe what it's really all about is those fucking communists are fucking atheists and Godlessness must not be allowed to spread. Well, that will never happen, not with us on the case, just look at Cochran and me, bleeding and beaten, clothes torn and covered with shit. How could anyone think these two miserable specimens could be anything but total winners in the fight against the world communist takeover?

Cochran is ready to crash, slumped in his seat, brooding. He glances over, picks up on my quizzical stare, smiles, and his face comes alive. There's the Cochran I know and love, although I'd never tell the bastard that.

"Just shifting gears, Tomas, that's all, just shifting gears."

Back at the Frog House, Emmett sticks his head out of his room. He must have been waiting up for us.

"I see you made it home okay. How was it? Whoa, looks like you did some tussling." He makes a face. "What's that smell?"

"How was what?" Cochran says, his voice flat.

"You know, 'From the halls of Montezuma to the shores of sweet lipsaree.'"

"Don't know what you're talking about. Here, make sure these get to Captain Beamus." Flips him the jeep keys.

We continue down the hall to our room.

"Emmett didn't tip the cops off," Cochran says. "That would be too devious for him. He's a straight-ahead guy."

"I'll sleep better knowing that."

Cochran turns off the light and we undress in the dark. I rub myself with my clothes and throw the stinking mess in the corner. That's where you can put your spirit of reconciliation.

22. Axes of Responsibility

I can see, Doc, by your Hippocratic oath you are a learned man . . . well versed in Latin . . . that must be the indecipherable inscription writ upon your script . . . the very prescription . . . I am not a total ignoramus, you know . . . of all the pilots in the squadron I was the only one familiar with the name, Tregaskis . . . I did a book report at Texas Military Academy on "Guadalcanal Diary," *his first-hand account of a World War Two battle . . . a Marine flyer came wandering in . . . he'd been in the jungle for seven days, dodging Japs and existing on red ants and snails . . . medics used a penknife to amputate a Raider's arm . . . Marines singing "Blues in the Night" with a chorus about how my mama done tol' me a woman was two faced . . . then the shouting of a man in trouble . . .* yama yama *. . . then machine-gun fire . . . the shouting stopped . . . enemy landing parachute troops . . . snipers popping from all sides . . . one man wounded in the leg . . . suicide attack with bayonets . . . mortar and artillery fire ends the attack . . . this same Richard Tregaskis . . . of gangly frame, slouched shoulders, eyeglasses slipping down his nose, clothes wrinkled and awry . . . has come to visit our squadron to research material for a new book . . . and the other pilots don't recognize the learned man, Doc . . .*

He stands in the back of the ready room, notepad in one hand, pen in the other, scratching away. After the briefing we break into individual groups and Richard Tregaskis walks over to Cochran and me and Emmet and Wee Willie Weems. We're hauling rice to a coastal village, an hour down the coast, and he'd like to come along. He's cleared it with the C.O., he says, and it's fine with us, glad to have his company.

"You go with Cochran and Huckelbee," Emmett tells Tregaskis. "I'll take the larger load of supplies." Emmett turns to us. "That'll give you more room in your chopper."

Tregaskis sports a floppy hat, work boots, brown pants and shirt. His safari vest pockets are jammed with pens, a small flashlight, knife, first-aid kit and other protruberances. Calm and reticent, he writes our names and hometowns in his notebook, pauses at the door of the helicopter to get Soonto's info, "Somoa, that's interesting," straps in, we fire up and take off, circling over the North China Sea, then head south, the beach on our right, fishing boats beneath, teardropped fishing nets visible in the shallow water.

"Check that out," Cochran says over the intercom. He banks the chopper so I can get a look.

"Shark, alongside that fishing boat."

A big one, as long as the boat. Cochran straightens and flies a loose wing on Emmett. Overhead, wispy cirrus clouds skim by. Inland, where the ocean spills over the dunes, fishing nets droop above the water like hammocks hanging on willow poles.

"Take her, Huck," Cochran says. "I'm going to snap a pic. When I give you the word, bank it to the right."

"Aye, sore." I shake the stick, let him know I've got it. I glance over. He has his camera in one hand and in the other, *Díos bendito*—he's got a grenade. What's that nutcase up to? He pulls the pin, throws the grenade out the window, keys the intercom, "Now, Huck," I lay the chopper on its side, there's a thump and a big flash. "Got it," he says.

"What was that, for Christ's sakes?"

"Willie peter. Pretty great, huh?"

Yeah, real great. White phosphorous. If that grenade didn't make it out the window we'd be melted toast.

"Number Two, what's going on?" Emmett calls over the air. "Are you taking fire?"

"Negative," Cochran answers. "Just taking a picture."

"Lieutenant," Soonto comes up on the intercom. "This reporter just keeled over down here."

Cochran keys the radio. "One. Our passenger is having a medical problem. He's passed out. We're returning to base."

"Roger that. We'll carry on."

"Pour the coals to her, Huck."

Doc Hollenden is waiting on the apron. When he gets to the chopper, Tregaskis is sitting up, groggy. The Doc checks him over.

"What's the prog?" Cochran asks.

"Nothing too serious. He's diabetic and didn't take his insulin this morning. It's in his bag in the ready room."

They head off in that direction. Soonto secures the chopper. "What about this rice?" he asks.

"Leave it for now," Cochran says. "I'll find out if we're delivering it or not."

We go over to the line shack and write up the hop. Cochran calls the ready room and, after checking with the schedules officer, goes to the door and yells, "Sergeant Soonto, the flight is scratched. Someone will come and get the rice."

Soonto's cur pokes his nose out from behind the counter.

"Oh, he's coming, don't get your paws in an uproar," Cochran says, then turns to me. "No joy on flying for us, Tomas, let's get shunt of this gear and revel in a G and T."

When we get back to the Frog House, the other new guy is in our room, stowing his gear. He looks up, sets his clothes on the bed and walks forward, extending a hand. A T-shirt is glued to his skin, and his abs are like xylophone keys. He's a buffed-out burrhead, sleek as a bullet.

"Daryl Dumbert from Queens," he says, out of the side of his mouth like a Cagney gangster. His extended hand forms a pistol, "Pow pow, and what's youse guys monikers?" A bone crushing shake. "What's the action, do I hang around this joint all day or do I get to mount the sky, show old Charlie what's for?"

"We just got bounced so we're going to change and go over to the club and hoist a few. Want to come along?"

"Sounds like a plan."

"Better wear a shirt," I tell him. "We've got a dress code forced on us."

He rears back, exaggerated look of surprise. "Check weapons at the door? Sounds like home. What the fuh, when in Rome . . ."

His short-sleeved shirt is covered with illustrations of New York Yankees baseball caps. He walks with a heel-and-toe bounce, points his gun finger at Mai Duc, our Vietnamese barman. "Set 'em up my man, this round's on me."

We no sooner get settled than a clerk sticks his head in the door.

"Lieutenants Cochran and Huckelbee, you're wanted in the squadron office. Pronto."

"Maybe that's our good conduct medals finally arrived," Cochran says. He gulps his drink. "Sorry to abandon ship but duty calls."

"Hey, don't let it rattle yer cage." He makes with the gun finger.

"That Dumbert's a head job," I say.

"Yep, a real Dum Dum."

We go in the office and stand at attention in front of Captain Beamus. He looks up. "Not me, this time. The Colonel wants to see you two." He motions with his thumb. "Go on in."

The Hammer is writing at his desk. He keeps us waiting for a minute then turns in his chair and looks at us, pressing the fingertips of his hands together.

"Have a seat, no sense in standing."

He pulls his chair around the desk and faces us. I shift nervously; what's he up to? This isn't his usual method.

"I'm sure you know what this is all about." He holds out a pack of cigarettes. Cochran and I shake our heads. He lights one up. "Things have gotten to the point where we need to have a talk, nip this situation in the bud." He blows out a mouthful of smoke and lifts his eyebrows, waiting. When Cochran and I don't say anything he abruptly snuffs out his smoke and points his finger at me.

"I'll take care of you first, Huckelbee. I don't know what part you played in this hand grenade business but any more tricks like that and I'll have you standing the duty for a month, you understand?"

This is the old familiar Hammer. I leap to my feet. "Yes, sir." Standing stiffly at attention.

"Sit down for Christ's sake, sit down." He turns to Cochran. "As for you. Frankly I don't know what to do. You've got the ability and the brains, there's no doubt about that, but you can't seem to put them to proper use. Don't you realize you're not the only one involved when you pull some crazy stunt like today? There are other lives at stake besides your own. If you want to go off by yourself and fool around with grenades that's one thing, at least you're not dragging along your copilot and crew chief. Plus the fact you were carrying a passenger, a very important passenger I might add."

The Hammer slams his hand on the arm of his chair.

"I realize that, sir," Cochran says.

"You damn well don't show it." The Hammer gets up. "We'll never get anywhere this way." He walks over to the refrigerator. "How about a beer?"

"Sure, why not."

"Huckelbee?"

"Thank you, sir."

He opens three cans and passes them around. "I know you think I'm a heartless old fart," he says, sitting down, "but I used to have the reputation of being a rebel, doing things my own way, pretty much as I pleased and having a good time while I was at it. But that all had to change. Just as it will for you."

He leans forward in his chair. "Don't get me wrong. I didn't lose my individuality. But I realized what it meant to take on the mantle of responsibility, and that's what you'll have to do. You keep pulling borderline stunts, right on the borderline, keep it up you'll get in so deep you can't back out."

The Hammer goes to the refrigerator and opens more beers. I swill down the dregs and take a new can.

"You're always pushing. Pushing the Operations Officer, the Schedules Officer, the Supply Officer, and pushing me too. Well, one day, you'll push too far." He gives Cochran the glare eye. "This might have been the day."

"Colonel, you've got me all wrong. You figure I've got it in for you, a personal grudge, that I set out to deliberately provoke you."

"Not just me. Anyone who gives you orders."

"No sir, that's not right. I do things completely without malice. I don't hate anyone so much I go out of my way to aggravate him. Things that happen to me happen completely on their own."

The Hammer snorts. "You behave just like a little kid who thinks only about himself, disassociates his behavior from others."

"More like the way the Chinese behave, sir."

Uh-oh, I'm thinking, now it's coming. I never should have hipped Cochran to that Lapsong Chung shit.

"Chinese? How's that?"

"They believe the spook of misfortune is constantly dogging their heels, so they make a special effort to dislodge him. For instance, whenever they cross the street they purposely dawdle so cars will pass close by, the closer the better, figuring the car will knock the evil spirit off their backs. A rough way to lose the evil spirit because the car has to pass close enough to hit the clutching spook but not so close the Chinaman gets banged up in the process."

"I've never heard such a load of horseshit in my life. What's that got to do with your childlike behavior?"

"Chineselike behavior, sir. You can imagine those people piss off the car drivers to no end. How'd you like every person walking past your car to dawdle and invite you to carom him into the gutter? You'd love to but you know it would be your ass so you honk and swear and take it out by banging your hand on the steering wheel."

Cochran leans forward.

"I've got a bigger spook on my back than any Chinaman and I'm trying to knock it off every chance I get. You're like the driver of that car, who's shit sure I'm in your way on purpose, expressly to give you a hard time. Not true. Everyone's got his personal evil spirits bugging him and most of us aren't trying to compound someone else's. Unless the person driving the car just happens to have an extra fifty or sixty pounds of foul-smelling, stomach-rumbling, tongue-lathering evilness he's trying to unload on me. If that's the case, then I am apt to raise a deliberate hassle."

Babbling sweet tongue better you should bite off before it's your head, I think. The Hammer remains calm.

"Wait a minute," he says, "I'm not sure I understand all this."

He fetches more beer. I've lost sensation in my legs. When did we last eat? My thoughts spiral on. Piddling jobs wear a man down with their grindstone efficiency. Triviality kills the spark. Mother dear, am I to quit doing anything and just sit on my ass complaining? No, son, how can you expect to get a better grip on life if *no pegar o dar ni golpe,* you've done fuck-all?

The Hammer's voice intrudes on my mental prattle.

"You attack the military system as being wrong, but what about yourself? What have you done that's so wonderful, what have you shown . . ."

"But those jobs are meaningless, they're nothing . . ." Cochran starts to say.

"I know I seem hard to you," the Hammer interrupts, "but I've preserved my individuality, while at the same time taking on a responsibility for all I have to live up to."

"I can't be two people, the real me I'm saving up for the future, and the other me putting up a front until that golden day," Cochran retorts.

"You get the responsibility, you have to act differently," the Hammer says.

Cochran jumps to his feet.

"Don't let the bastards keep you down," he hollers, close to the edge. Shit, he's always on the edge, and the heavies are both fearful and at the same time egging him on, the hangman's noose is waiting. Beer cans clutter the floor. Cochran starts to fall forward, steadies himself on the arm of the Hammer's chair, they are bleary-eye to beery-eye.

"Which all due respeck, sir, could I suggestion a making?"

"What are you trying to say? Spit it out, man."

"When we flying back from squadron full up troop lift whyn't we make a victory pass over the runway, let the men huzzah the op a success?"

"That's kid stuff, Lieutenant."

Cochran stiffens. "If there's nothing else, sir, I think I better get something to eat."

The Hammer waves his hand, *get out of here*. Cochran hauls me up and we kick through the beer cans, sending them spinning. I turn around.

"*Con su permisso*, Colonel?"

"Beat it. I don't want to hear any more of that Mexican *peon* crap."

Got it. We walk out the door, leaving the Hammer sitting in the rubble.

"The word, *peon*, means pedestrian, you know," I tell Cochran.

"So, what's your point?"

"Just shows to go you the gringo's superior attitude. Big cars, they look down on pedestrians, to the peril of the *peon*. Tell that to Lapsong Chung."

Cochran stops and glares.

"All my life I've had some old molded fart, paunch-bellied and secure in his sinecure, lecture me, and I've had to listen. Someday I want to laugh in that old fart's face. All this bullshit about responsibility."

He smacks his hand with his fist. "I tell you, Huck, a man, a real man, has the hot blood surging, he can outdo anyone, he's the number one stud bull of the lot. Head high, he sings out, dances, plays great licks on his sound box, bops like no else. Life's a keyboard with a limitless number of songs waiting to be played. And you know something? I figure my best bits are stoppered. I've learned the scales, now it's time to start playing my tunes."

He looks at me suspiciously bleery-eyed. "You're not fooling me, you runt. You're like the rest of the moles. Covering up the thing you'd really like to do because you're afraid of the ridicule, figuring it's better to let a dream die untried than chance having it fail."

He stares, out of focus. "Why the hell you so dry and wizened, anyway?"

"Because I'm from Locos, Texas, the driest, scrubbiest, most desolate patch of scrub and sand in the world."

He shrugs. "Well, I guess every man has the right to be as big as it's in him to be."

"Thank you, kind sor, for your astute observation.That's not a right, that's an obligation. But when the ding-dong bell of knell tolls, it's not just for me and thee but for all of humanity."

"You lost me on that one, slick tongue. Let's hit the sack."

23. Topping It The Max

Doc, can't you cool the yammering . . . why don't you answer, Doc? . . . you being an obtuse goose or a plain ignoramus?. . . there was a newspaper clipping stapled to the Hot Scoop board . . . our son came home from Vietnam and has done nothing but sit around the house and teach our parrot to swear and every time a visitor comes to the house he makes the parrot swear while he sits there and laughs and now I can't ask the parson to tea, what should I do . . . get your parrot a mate, lady, once they start fucking they won't bother talking, but as for your son, have you tried paregoric, it blasts you right out of your skull, I've used it for years after answering these stupid questions . . . ha ha . . . Daddy's deliberately evasive . . . harping on that bull roar again . . . it's all bull roar, son, and the sooner you know it the better . . . but, Daddy, it can't be ALL bull roar, can it? . . . well, maybe not all bull roar, son, but so much so that you might as well call it all bull roar . . . okay, he says, I'll hedge a little . . . cut through the bull roar and maybe you'll find a tiny kernel of the nut of truth that ain't been crushed or spoilt or burnt in the fires, but you got to dig real deep, boy . . . or else you'll be a shallow garcon, *like the frogs say: knee-deep, knee-deep . . . Daddy was of the 4-F generation . . . find 'em, feel 'em, fuck 'em, forget 'em . . . those days are gone, Doc, we're the Get It generation . . . get it on, get it up, get it in, get it out . . . whatsamatter, you don't get, it, Doc . . . well, you're a medical man, and that's what's important . . .*

The club is decked out like an Oriental whorehouse. Chinese lanterns hang from the ceiling. Streamers crisscross the beams like kaleidoscopic spider webs. The walls are adorned with scarlet and gold flags. Behind the bar, a big banner proclaims: HAPPY BIRTHDAY USMC. The biggest day of the year for the Corps, a traditional full dress dinner at the mess hall followed by an all-night party in the club, replete with live entertainment, the whole shooting match overseen by Mai Duc, attired in white pants and shirt with a black bow tie. He gives rapid-fire instructions to the nervous bar maids, resplendent in *ao dais*, then he rushes over to harangue the band, a Vietnamese jazz trio called The Self Defense Corps, electric bass and guitar, full drum set, one microphone, the musicians dressed in black with bright-red scarves tied around their necks. They noodle on their instruments, adding a light din to the preparations.

Tables are set up with the chairs facing the bar. An aisle runs down the middle. The first pilots arrive, laughing and chattering and smoking stogies. They sprawl on chairs and call for drinks. The trio breaks into song, "*Somewhere there's music, how faint the tune. Somewhere there's heaven, how high the moon,*" in high plaintive voices, the guitar on full vibrato, bass line a solid thunk, rimshots and cymbal clashes, giving the song a Far Eastern slant.

The new pilot, Baptist John, surveys the scene from the door, beams and exclaims, "Truly the light is a sweet and a pleasant thing for the eyes to behold, the meek and the strong meet together and our Lord is master of all," evoking handclapping and, "Amen, brothers," and, "Set him up," and, "Lest the meek take a tumble."

Baptist John is shoved aside by Herbee Jenkins—"Make way there"—with Wee Willie Weems hard on his heels. Then a mob fills the club, grabs the chairs, and pounds on the tables. The barmaids are flustered trying to keep up. Mai Duc mixes and pours drinks fast as a dribble of fat skipping across a hot skillet.

I'm hunched near the bar, nursing a gin and tonic, eyeballing the room. Again the door swings open. Stepping proudly through, dressed to the nines in a sport jacket and pleated pants, light-blue shirt with a red tie, is our esteemed Admin Officer, Captain Miles Standish Briggs, and on his arm one of the four Army nurses flown in from the hospital at Nha Trang for the occasion. She's dumpy, but sashays happily on her ample hips, a bright smile on her face, mascaraed eyes behind big rimmed glasses. *"Somewhere there's music, how near how far. Somewhere there's heaven, that's where you are,"* the words drowned by handclapping and wolf whistles, banging of drinks on the tables, and then, entering the din, burning cigar leading the way, face puckered in mountainous valleys and craggy ridges, Pappy Lurnt, and on his arm the tiniest, the chippiest, bounciest bird to ever grace the club. *"There is no moon above when love is far away too."* They are no sooner seated than stern-visaged Captain Beamus makes a stentorian entrance, impeccably dressed as always, and towering above him, an immensely tall, black-maned horse-faced woman, with a bray to match and a set of chompers Man of War would envy. *"The darkest night would shine if you would come to me soon."* And finally, at the parade's pinnacle, as befitting his rank, our esteemed commander, Colonel Arthur The Hammer Rappler, enters to raised glasses and, "See him," and, "Call upon him," and, "The mantle be upon his shoulders," and, "Splice the main brace," and other nautical inanities picked up from hanging around with squids at the Neptune Bar in town. The cries go unheeded by both the C.O. and his female companion, the Nha Trang Head Nurse, who is of similar age and rank as the Hammer, her militant shape covered with an austere skirt, blouse and jacket. *"How still my heart, how high the moon."* The Colonel holds out her chair, and they take their places at a reserved table on the aisle.

The din rises to full pitch. Cigar smoke fills the room. Colored lights pulsate. The drum starts a Hawaiian beat and eight pilots wearing grass skirts dance into the club to a boisterous welcome for the *autentico* Hawaiian song and dance number. Doc Hollenden gyrates in the middle of the dancing line. Coconut-shell and parachute-cord phony bras dangle on hairy chests below phony fabric leis. Monkey fur hangs over their eyes. Garish red-painted mouths pucker in kisses blown to the audience, and the pilots respond with cat calls, guffaws, joke sneezes, laughs and foot stomping. Drink glasses are banged on the tables as the dancers gyrate wildly with their arms and hips, a fitting rendition of the obligatory dance ritual demanded by every party held on any island or land west of San Francisco. The hula line breaks into song. Doc Hollenden, standing in the middle, leads the chorus:

Hiu me ka nihi poi
Hiu me ka big-a-opu

A crushed lime splats against a hairy chest. Undeterred, the hula line repeats the song, in English, for the edification of *el vulgo, la gente sin educación,* those ignorant jerks, the uneducated hoi polloi:

Give me some poi, boy
Pass the seaweed, sneed
Give us some love, joy
You know what we need

The dancers hula down the center aisle toward the door. Hands grab at their skirts, pulling off chunks of fronds. Ignoring them, the dancers lean in and leer at the nurses, *Hiu me ka big opu.* Pappy Lurnt stabs them away with the lit end of his cigar, and they sashay out the door, *Pass around the poi,* to a standing round of applause and long lewd cheers.

The cheers no sooner die than a swaggering New York gangster bursts through the door. He's sharp as a punji stake in his snap-brim hat, wide-padded shoulders, dangling key chain and pegged pants, *Díos bendito,* more of a cross between a hoodlum and a hipster, with a mean scowl on his face. Dum Dum Dumbert, in the Queens flesh. He grabs the microphone, "How's it going, ladies, yah need anyting, youse jest give me dah woid, and as fer youse gents, back off der, mind yer manners lessen youse wants yer kissers bashed in." With the jazz trio keeping pace, Dum Dum throws a hand sideways, and in a false Italiano accent belts out a romantic song:

In Napoli where love is king
When boy meets girl, here's what they say

A pause, then he's off, rollicking into the chorus:

When the moon hits your eye
Like a big pizza pie, that's a-mor-ay

He drops to a knee, implores with outstretched arm:

When your balls hit the floor
Like a B-54, that's a-mor-ay

The pilots jump to their feet and shout, *A-mor-ay,* Dumbert coming in over the top:

Bells will ring, ting-aling-aling, ting-aling-aling

Captain Beamus stands up and waves his arms, where's your couth, you louts, he tries to stop them. What a laugh. If he's worried the women will be offended, why doesn't he clap his hand over the ears of the nurse sitting next to him, but no, she is laughing her ass off along with the others, except for the Head Nurse who watches stoically. She's heard this kind of shit before, seen men making assholes out of themselves, have your fun boys, you'll come crying to me in the morning for your pills, your potions, your enemas.

Dum Dum presses on:

When your cock is the size
Of a mama-mia's thighs, that's a-mor-ay

The guitar whangs, the bass thumps and the pilots sing along, but Dum Dum's voice is stilled. He looks around with a belligerent glare, sees Mai Duc with his hand on the volume control. Dum Dum rushes the bar, but I grab him by the coat tail and yank him to the floor. Before he can get up, Emmett and Too Tall Tolliver have him by the legs and shoulders and are hustling him down the aisle and out the door, Dum Dum screaming.

Scuzza me, but you see,
Back in Napoli, that's a-mor-ay.

The pilots salute with glasses raised, *That's a-mor-ay,* down the hatch boys, followed by resounding crashes as they throw their glasses to the floor. Dum Dum's back in a wink, "Gimmee a drink," grabs one out of Baptist John's hand.

"Crown ourselves with rosebuds," Baptist John says. "Women may be the strongest but truth beareth away the victory."

The trio plays a light instrumental number while drinks are replenished. I meander down the aisle, exchange insults with the pilots, nods with the heavies and smiles at the nurses, and stop up short, for, there, making a surprise appearance, is the Ice Queen, stone faced, hair piled high, long white *ao dai* embroidered with gold thread, and, alongside her, the biggest surprise of all, our old Tokyo friend, Spare Tire, dressed to the nines in a silk suit and shirt and tie, his black shoes a bright sheen. He gives me a wink as they pass by, making the rounds of the senior officers and nurses. After Spare Tire settles the Ice Queen in her chair, he joins me at the bar.

"You're the last person in the world I thought I'd see in this place," I tell him.

"And a very elegant place it is," he says. "Kinda reminds me of Mama Toko's in Pusan, except I never saw any American women in that dive. Where's your buddy?"

"I don't know. Probably off somewhere putting the finishing touches to his poem. What happened after we left Japan, anyways?"

"I set those gals up in Kyoto and they're doing great. I had to procure them though."

"Procure? You mean, like buy them for sex?"

"Nothing like that. I had to pay T. Harry at the 500 Club a pile of yen to guarantee the gals their freedom. He was none too happy about his car, either, but he accepted the BMW I liberated from a company I sometimes do business with in Japan."

"I knew you did okay but, holy shit, your job pays that much?"

"Ha. This pissant war is bringing in beaucoup bucks for me and it's only gonna get bigger. As a procurer I'm in a prime spot. The military needs something from the natives, they come to me. Same goes for American companies setting up business. They need housing, transportation, shipyard docking, women of a higher class than the bars, they know who to contact."

"So the Ice Queen isn't just your date for the evening, eh?"

"That lady has her finger in every slice of pie in this country, so she and I are mutually beneficial to one another."

"Say, just between you and me and the Chinese lanterns, I've got something you might be able to help me out on."

"Sure, thing, Huckelbee. I owe you big-time for that outing we had in Japan. That was *ichi ban* in my book."

I give him a quick update on Ben-San. The crash, the rescue, the hospital, and finally, Yoshika.

"Wait a minute." He pulls out a notepad and pen. "Let me write this down."

I give him the particulars, closing with where he can find Yoshika, if she's still there.

"Okay. When I get back to Japan, I'll see where she's at on this thing, and get back to you."

"Better if you deal with Ben-San himself. I don't know how much longer he'll be in the hospital before they fly him home."

"Don't you fret, I'll . . . well, look who's here."

Doc Hollenden, changed from his Hawaiian rig into his party duds, walks up.

"Well, hidey, Doc, how come you aren't packing that gun you were so scared of back in Japan?" Spare Tire asks.

"Ha ha. The only thing I'm packing is my scalpel."

We're interrupted by a long drum roll.

"Looks like the show is starting," Spare Tire says. "I better get back."

He puts the notebook and pencil away. A quick hand clasp.

"Oh my God," says the Doc, staring at the door.

Cochran goose steps into the club, his arms swinging high, the band picks up the beat, *thump*, *thump*, *thump*, and the pilots join in, "Ay ay ay," as he marches the length of the club, does a flamboyant about-face and gives us the flat hand to the forehead salute. He's wearing a gold flight suit, crosshatched with scarlet paint. One pant leg is cut off at the knee. On his feet are high-top sneakers, one painted gold, the other scarlet. He hasn't shaved for three days and his black beard is a bristle brush with a red glow in the middle from a cigar sticking out of his mouth. He has blackened both eyes and they punctuate his face like gun muzzles. A rubber basketball cut in half and painted scarlet and gold sits on his head like an inverted mixing bowl. A cluster of American and SVN flags stick out of the holes.

The jazz trio pounds, the pilots chant. Cochran raises his hand and holds it until the hubbub dies. He takes the cigar out of his mouth and bows to the women, the flags on his head dipping in respect. "Good evening, lovely ladies, our honored guests and my fellow comrades-in-arms," hands extended, fingers pointed. "Happy birthday, number one hundred and eighty-eight to our glorious Marine Medium Helicopter Squadron One Hundred and Eighty-Eight, what you might call an auspicious numerical occurrence of the highest mathematical order, a congruence of digits never to be seen again on the planet, one I would like to honor with a little number, writ from the heart, with respect and insubordination to all, entitled, 'Topping It The Max.'"

He reaches inside his flight suit and pulls out a thick sheaf of papers. "What are these? Frag reports, how'd they get in here?" Sheets flutter to the floor as he paws through them. "Ah," he squints at a page, and wades in:

"In days of old when men were bold
And rubbers weren't invented
They wrapped their cocks in dirty socks
And screwed until contented.
'Balls,' cried the Queen. 'If I had two I'd be king.'
And the king laughed because he had two
As she lamented . . .

No no no, wrong poem, my 'umble apologies."
He crumples the page and flings it at the band.
"Here we go then:

The blades they were a-clattering
The peace they was a-shattering
Keep up your airspeed Harley
That farmer's name is Charley
And don't let his buffalo fool you
One just like it is the one that blew you
Full of holes and broke your window glass
With an RPG hid up its ass."

"Har Har," Cochran laughs, then scowls. "This is a tough crowd. I know, all this written shit is too stilted." He throws the pages in the air and erupts in a spontaneous ejaculation, "I see Safety Officer Ed Ramshakle Pomfrey has finally accepted the reality of the transmission and its relationship to the rest of the chopper. He has discovered that all flights of imagination should be grounded in anchors of reality. Gives him an opportunity to be one of the boys, a good ol' fella, here's snot in yer eye."

Cochran turns to the Chaplain. "Tell me, Father Sam, why did the Irishman wear two condoms? To be sure, to be sure, yas, better to be safe than to be Protestant. What kind of meat does a priest eat on Friday, anyways? None is the answer. Just remember, it all happens in the revival tent and what happens in the tent stays in the tent, held down by tent stays, of course."

Ka-blam, bang of the drum.

"Thank you thank you. Reminds me of a rifle-powered grenade flying up your fuel tank, bound to increase your air speed by mach one or two. Remember, fruit flies like a banana but time flies like a greased winged weasel. The thread holding the scimitar is unraveling. Save yourselves. Take deep yogic breaths. I see my cigar has gone out."

He whips out a stick match, strikes it on his flight suit zipper and holds it to the cigar. Flames shoot up his nostrils, the smell of burnt hair wafts across the room. "That's the way you trim your nose hairs when you're hunkered down in bandit country," he shouts. "No time to mess with pussy-wimp scissors when Charley's knives are slicing your balls."

"Oh my, non sequitor," Baptist John cries out. "The jungle is full of bones. Can those bones live? Weigh the balances."

"Yes, and separate the clavicle from the neck bone, Reverend, you be speaking the word and the mama-sans are on the lookout for some stuff and believe me, they have the muff that's tuff enuff to do the snuff. Make like the whale, it's no fluke when you slap the water and scoop up the fishies. Where are the loaves, man? When the rapture occurs the choppers will be bouncing off one another like ten pins in a Tasmanian devil-dog bowling-ball tournament.

"I see our supply officer, Captain Samuel Squints Bigelow is wandering around the battlefield picking up detritus and reflecting upon the stuff of immortality, filling both his mind and rucksack. Wait! Hold your applause," he cries, as the restless and antsy crowd rise to their feet and shout, "Shut the fuck up," and "We've heard enough of this shit," only to be hauled down by their tablemates eager to hear more of the heady stuff.

Thus reassured, Cochran plows on. "Captain Beamus failed celestial navigation in flight school, you know, but he can still locate true north by using a bolo knife and a scared Filipino shedding chicken feathers out the ass end of the helicopter while the good Captain bangs on a Vietnamese clapper drum and naked Montagnard women do the Charleston in the belly. Or is that the sound of Carl Emmett charging up Montezuma hill, sabre in hand, screaming through his meerschaum pipe, 'I shall return!'?"

Waving his cigar in the air, spittle flying out of his mouth, eyes red-rimmed and bugging out of black sockets, Cochran strides down the aisle. He stops at Pappy Lurnt's table and gapes lewdly at the bouncy nurse. She titters. Cochran points his cigar at Major Lurnt.

"Pappy's no chump
Not when he's caught in nature's way
And has to take a dump
He does it right in the Zone
Even when there's hell to pay."

Cochran leans back to avoid Pappy Lurnt's swipe at his cigar, then skips to the Hammer's table and picks up the verse.

"You wake in the morn' to the sound of the horn
And the smell of the binjo ditch
To the taste of the mold on the side of the bread
And the coffee that's blacker than pitch
You grab your gear and zip it up tight
And make damned sure your flak vest fits.
On every last mission it's been your division
That's been taking all of the hits

The engine is popping and the right mag is droppin'
About a hundred and fifty or so
But you'd go on report if you tried to abort
So out on the runway you go.
Skipper leads us aloft in a welter of spray
Everyone wondering if this is the day
When the guy in the sky throws a great fit
And the weather turns completely to shit.
Your co-pilot looks and sings the refrain
We can't see squat in this fucking rain
With a grunt and a start, he checks the chart
And suddenly studies the ground.
'Tell One Dash Zero,' he says like a hero
'If we hold this track we'll never get back
The colonel, that hound, has us Laos-bound . . .'"

Cochran flings his hand in the air. The cigar flies out and sticks in the thatched ceiling. The crowd, oblivious to the move, yells, "He's a hound dawg." "Turn this puppy around." "Back to the dawg house." "This flight is curtailed." Then all eyes turn upward. Cochran jumps on the table and reaches for the cigar just as the thatched roof bursts into flame. Cochran loses his balance and crashes to the floor. Shouts of "FIRE! FIRE!" fill the club.

The senior officers assist the women out of their chairs, around Cochran and out the door. The pilots rush to the flames and throw their drinks at the ceiling. *Whoosh*, a Chinese lantern disappears in a fireball.

"Calm. Calm. Everyone remain calm," Cochran shouts. No one pays any attention. The pilots have liberated the booze and are drinking big gulps and spitting mouthfuls at the ceiling. The hundred-proof alcohol flares up, smoke fills the club, the floor is swamped and the pilots slip and fall trying to get out of the way of a water buffalo being shoved through the door by six shitfaced Marines who fumble with the valves and struggle with the hand pump; one of them points the hose, there's a few feeble spurts, then a powerful gush rips through the roof; pilots grab at the hose, "Let me, No me, Turn loose you fucker," water sprays everywhere, and up in the front of the room, Wee Willie Weems grabs the guitar, Too Tall Tolliver liberates the electric bass, Herbee Jenkins shoves the drummer off his stool and Dum Dum shouts into the mike:

"She calls her daddy Big Boots
And Big Boots is my name
It takes a big man to wear big boots
That's her daddy's claim to fame
She's the gal in the red blue jeans
She's the queen of all the Gyrenes
She's the woman that I know
She's the woman that loves me so
She can handle my armored tank
She can drive it fast or she can drive it slow."

Emmett grabs Cochran by the arm and spins him around.

"Hey, Emmett, what's happening?" Cochran shouts. "A *pfennig* for your thoughts."

"I've had it up to here with you, Cochran. Of all the shit you've pulled, this tops it the max."

"Well, thank you, I did work long and hard on that—"

"Not your stupid poem or whatever. You came within a whisker of burning down the club."

"Well, that. That was really not intended and if I could do it over, I'd—"

"That's just it, you can't, you numbskull. You can't undo your asinine fucking stunts. First the poker game, then that grenade, now this and who knows what else you've gotten away with."

"Now hold it right there mister lily white, your hands aren't so clean. What about that blackjack game you've been running, taking money from your fellow officers?"

"You're full of shit if you think I'm getting anything out of that game. All the money goes back to the club, or did you think we paid for everything on drinks alone?"

Water is dripping everywhere. The stink of wet charred wood permeates our clothes. We're soaked in the filthy goop. The music has petered out. Everyone stands waiting, gathered in a circle around Emmett and Cochran who are locked in a staredown.

"I know," I blurt in, gotta inject some humor here, defuse this time bomb. "We're not here for the fucking around, right? Hey Emmett, can you say that in German? *Sprechen zie deutsch?*"

Emmett turns on me. "Keep your wetback face out of this, wiseass." He pushes me in the chest. Before I can come back at him, Cochran steps between us.

"Pick on someone your own size, fuckface," he yells.

"Wait a minute," I yell back. "I don't need your help to pop this doodle bug."

Cochran ignores me. "Come on," he says to Emmett. "I know you can do it. Give us the word, your favorite infantile phrase in your native tongue."

"I'll do it," I holler. "We don't need his phoney baloney. *No estamos aqui para hacer el capullo.*"

So what, it's Spanish, not German. Still means the same thing. It's way too late for humor. Emmett ignores me. Glares at Cochran.

"C'mon, bring it on," Cochran says.

"That's it, you fucking Gorilla," Emmett yells back, and the long dormant volcano that's been seething beneath the surface erupts with a big roundhouse swing that catches Cochran with a resounding wallop on the side of his head and sends the basketball helmet flying. Cochran steps inside Emmett's next windup and punches Emmet in the nose, snapping Emmett's head back and spewing a big spurt of blood.

"Gentleman, gentlemen," Baptist John calls out. "Have mercy. How many times must you forgive your brother his sins?"

"Shove it up your ass, you imitation Bible thumber," Emmett mumbles, holding his hand to his face, blood spurting between his fingers.

"Judge not, lest ye be tasting the slough of depression the rest of your days."

"Oh yeah," Emmett brandishes his fist. "Taste this and you'll be wearing false teeth the rest of your life."

"Not another word," Cochran says, brandishing his own fist.

Emmett waves him away. He pushes through the circle, stops and turns. "I don't know what's the matter with you idiots. I was going to say it before you started hammering on me. *Wir sind nicht hier um zeit zu verschwenden.*"

The German at last, accompanied with spitting blood. Emmett stalks out. The pilots are glum. The bunting, the streamers and the Chinese lanterns are a sodden mess, the club is a wreck, but, looking at the bright side, the building is still standing with four walls intact, nothing so bad a good cleanup and a new thatched roof can't fix.

Spare Tire steps forward. "I gotta hand it to you Gyrenes. You really know how to party."

"Well," Cochran answers, his ear swelling big as a cantaloupe, "as Grits so succintly stated, we're not here for the fucking around."

24. Surprise is the Key

Is it more bull roar, Doc, or should I say buffalo roar? . . . it swirls all around the line shack where we read the gripe sheets and then sign off on the choppers. . . in the background the bull roar soars . . . a ground-pounder Staff Sergeant waiting for a ride to Khe San says, I shot the water buffalo . . . I was riding security for convoys up and down Route One and started carrying a .22 rifle . . . I'd see a water buffalo with a kid sitting on top and I'd plunk the water buffalo in the ass and the beast would rear up and throw the kid off, and up ahead the bridge crossing the river would blow up, leaving the kid standing with wires dangling and the water buffalo hightailing it out of there . . . you have to give the man credit, Doc, he didn't kill the water buffalo, nor the kid either . . .

And then one of the crew chiefs, after hearing the story, says, My brother was in Phu Bai, working as an MP . . . he drove a jeep to Da Nang hauling prisoners and they were being sniped at by guys hiding behind water buffalos in the fields next to the road . . . one time he decided to let loose with a preemptive strike and he blasted the water buffalo with an RPG round . . . the buffalo went Kerboom *and so did the little old gentleman hiding behind it . . . the crew chief pauses to let that sink in . . . then says, My brother felt kind of bad, he didn't know if the old guy was a sniper or not . . . he didn't even know that he was there until the guy went flying through the air . . . Soonto yells at me from the door . . . come on, Lieutenant, we're ready to go . . . I scrawl my name on the bottom of the gripe sheet . . . I'm ready to go, Doc . . . write me off on your gripe sheet . . . turn me loose from this pain . . .*

Shit on a shingle, that old military breakfast staple served in heaping mounds of meat and white gravy piled atop toast hours before first light. Everyone is up, fifty pilots, dressed in camo flight suits, high lace-top boots, Hammering-Eight baseball caps with a cartoon figure eight logo hammering at a cloud, fire-resistant gloves sticking out of pockets. Some are wearing their leather flight jackets with fur collars to ward off the chill, a patch with name, rank and gold naval aviator wings sewn on their chests. On the backs, the old World War II- type blood chit: an American flag and beneath it in Korean, Chinese, Vietnamese, Laotian, Thai and Cambodian scripts, the promise of a hundred-thousand-dollar reward for the safe return of the pilot—in case you're shot down and wandering in the jungle.

"This shit will stick to your stomach," says Wee Willie Weems, shoveling in a mouthful.

"Verily," says Baptist John. "Your belly is like a heap of wit set upon by lilies."

"It's a frog dish original," Pappy Lurnt says. "Beef day la cream, or some such delicacy. Back in the first war, they cooked it up one night as a treat for the Army doggies but the Marines, out in front of the main body didn't get any, so next morning the Frogs sent it up cold. First Sarnt ordered it heated, put on slices of bread and handed it out for breakfast and that's when shit on a shingle was born."

And borne well it is, everyone chowing down with gusto for we know it's going to be a long day and the next hot meal will be many hours away.

"Been a military staple ever since," Pappy continues. "Cep'n where the Army uses chip beef, the Marine recipe calls for a higher class of meat—ground beef."

"Is that an example of Arkansas hogwash?" Wee Willie Weems says out of the side of his mouth.

"I heard that, wiseass," Pappy Lurnt says. "You remind me of a member of the Twisty Mouth family. Their mouths were twisted all which ways except for the youngest, and his being straight they sent him to college. He came home for dinner and afterwards they tried to blow out the candles but their twisted mouths couldn't blow straight, so the youngest gave it a try and blew the candle out."

Pappy takes a forkful of S.O.S. and chews slowly.

Wee Willie looks around. Getting no help, he says, "I don't get it."

"Shows the value of a college education," Pappy says.

Outside the mess hall the buses wait with engines idling. They are painted dark green and have wire mesh across the windows to keep the stray grenades out. As soon as the bus is full, the driver shuts the door and takes down the sign hanging in front: SSSRO, Standing Sitting and Squatting Room Only. He heads out, headlights piercing the dark. Everything is quiet across the fence in Dogpatch. The 5 P lady tending her water buffalo stands barefooted in the shallow water next to the road. The object of whistles and requests for sexual favors by the passengers, she will honor the request—if the driver opens the door and someone throws out a five piastre bill—by pulling up her blouse and displaying her breasts, but not today, not this dark morning. The bus roars implaccably onward, its destination the airfield and ready room.

The Hammer is already there, ensconced in his chair. He writes in his notebook, ignoring the bedlam of the pilots checking their pistols out of the weapons cage, putting them in their holsters, slipping on flak vests, making sure they have their emergency packets and medical supplies.

The Hammer stands up and faces the room. He waits for everyone to settle down. "As you know a major operation has been ordered on. A large VC force has been spotted coming out of the mountains to indoctrinate the villagers and exact their annual rice tribute. We'll load 2nd ARVN Division troops here and carry them to the drop zone at the base of the mountains and seal off the VC escape route." He points to the map on the wall. "25th ARVN Division troops from Tam Ky will attack from the East." He indicates their positions. "They are the hammer in this case," chuckles from the pilots, "and we're providing the anvil. If all goes well, this will be a very successful operation. Surprise is the key.

"For greater mobility we'll use three plane sections instead of four. The first wave will consist of nine aircraft and as soon as they lift out the second wave of nine will be landing. When they lift, the final wave of six will come in. The last aircraft in the flight will carry the corpsmen, mechs and spare parts, and will circle overhead. Maintain radio discipline and get in and out as fast as you can."

Emmett is standing on the other side of the room. His eyes are black and his nose is swollen. Cochran flops down beside me. One ear is twice the size of the other and the side of his face is an ugly black and blue, mottled in yellow.

"I can't believe it," he mutters.

"What?"

"They left-seated me."

"You're kidding."

"No. Beamus just gave me the word. My HAC's been revoked. Orders from the top. Lessen I straighten up and fly right, both on the ground and in the air, I'll be a permanent copilot. You're the Helicopter Aircraft Commander on this run, Tomas."

He gives me a wry grin and starts copying the radio frequencies and call signs on his kneeboard. *Que desorden.* A fine kettle of fish, as my mama would say, a real hie-dee-ho. Least ways Cochran and I are still flying together. We're on Pappy Lurnt's wing, with Wee Willie Weems his copilot. Emmet, with Herbee Jenkins, is leading the three-chopper section next to ours.

Briefing over, we hike out to the choppers. All twenty-four birds are available for the mission, the mechs having worked all night to fix every gripe, get every helicopter ready. The ARVN troops stand lined up on the edge of the matting, waiting for the orders to board. Cochran and I go to our assigned bird, Yankee Victor 23, and start the preflight.

"You take that side and I'll take this," I tell Cochran, then stop and stare. "What the hell happened to you, Sergeant Soonto?"

He gives me a hangdog look and points to his sleeve. "Corporal Soonto, sir." His lip is swollen, and he has stitches over one eye. "After the birthday party a few of us snuck over the fence to Dogpatch and found a bunch of Air Force jokers having an all- night blast at the Monkey Mountain Bar. Everything was amenable till they started ragging on us, 'Whatcha scratching at, Jarhead, got the itchy crotch from jungle bunny poopin and snoopin?' and making disparaging remarks about whitewall haircuts and shiny boots and flying-outfit Marines lacking the courage of the groundpounder Marines, which led naturally enough to a loud ruckus complete with fisticuffs which led to the Shore Patrol arriving which culminated in a trip to the doctor for certain Airmen and an appearance at Captain's mast for certain Marines and as a result I get busted a pay grade and a warning that from here on in I watch my step or face the greater consequences."

I'm very impressed. That's the longest outpouring of words I ever heard from Soonto. Still waters running deep welling up to the surface in a flood.

A surreptitious kiss of the Saint Chris, then it's up and into the cockpit and strap in. Cochran eases his helmet over his swollen ear and we run through the prestart check list. He reads off the items and I toggle the switches. A very different experience. I've flown right seat before but always with some other pilot, Wee Willie or Herbee or Too Tall or poor old Rob Jacobs—but this is the first time with Cochran as my copilot.

I hit the starter and the engine fires with a puff of black smoke then settles into a comfortable idle. The mech standing by with the APU moves farther down the line. Below us, the ARVNs climb in and squat on the floor.

"All green," Cochran says.

"Engaging rotors." I release the rotor brake and run the rpm up to 2000. The Hammer calls for a radio check. "Yankee Victor Two Three," I respond in my turn. We are ready to go, and taxi forward and lift off into the dark, running lights blinking.

The Hammer climbs at a slow 85 knots, so everyone can catch up and take their places in the formation. We level at fifteen hundred and make a sweeping turn south. Below us, a glimmer of white waves break and roll to the beach. To the right, cumulus clouds rise over the mountains and reflect the first rays of sun. We're flying dark with only the fuselage lights on, and I'm glued tight on Pappy. The old razorback has a steady hand on the stick and I need only slight corrections to keep my position. Cochran fools with the radios. We're on the VHF band for communication with Da Nang. The FM band is for squadron chat and now the AM comes on as Cochran finds Hanoi Hannah.

"Good morning Marine pilots of Colonel Arthur Rappler's number one eight eight squadron. I hope you are enjoying the cool flying weather because according to forecast it will be very hot later on and you should be taking your pleasure at the beach and not terrifying Vietnamese people who want to be left alone to live their lives under the peaceful protection of the only true government that has their welfare at heart, not the evil American puppet Diem in Saigon but the benevolent party leader, Ho Chi Minh, who implores you to refuse the illegal orders of your Generals working with the deluded armies in the south of our country to keep our peoples enslaved by capitalistic doctrine . . ."

"Whoa up there," Cochran says over the intercom. "Too much information, too early in the day, where's the music?"

". . . so turn back, Marine pilots, return to your base, spend the day repairing your burned-out drinking and gambling den, fill your cannibal hunger in your messy halls, forsake this useless attack that is doomed for failure . . ."

"Yeah," Cochran says. "Tell the Hammer to shove it up his ass, right?"

"You didn't hear that, Soonto," I say. He clicks the mike in response.

Hanoi Hannah continues on, letting us know what a waste of time this mission is, how we're only making things miserable for ourselves, wasting time and material while accomplishing nothing.

"Shut your trap, lady," Cochran says. "Don't you know surprise is the key to this operation?"

We wheel into our approach with enough light showing to see the clearing below with mountains on each side, a brush line in front and an open field sweeping to the sea. A solitary water buffalo stands in the field. Two T-28s flash past, guns firing.

"And now, Marines, a song from when we were allies working together to defeat the Japanese."

The Hammer noses over and the first division heads in. *Pistol-packing mama lay that pistol down.* Pappy is dropping fast and I autorotate like a rock to stay in position. *She kicked out my windshield and hit me over the head.* "Hot hot hot," someone yells over the air. "Taking hits," another calls. "Get in and out quick." "Shit, that's a machine gun." Off to the side a T-28 noses in and cartwheels across the ground in a fireball. *She cussed and cried and said I lied and wished that I was dead.*

I pull up collective, squeeze on turns and flare for landing. "Stay with me, Mike," I say over the intercom.

We touch down and I look out the window. The ARVNs pile out and hit the deck, one kneels, sets his rifle butt on the ground and points his rifle grenade in the air, "No, wait till we're clear," I yell , but he can't hear me. He fires and the grenade shoots up into the rotor blades, there's a clunk and explosion, metal bangs against the side of the chopper and we start vibrating like crazy, *we're a rooting tooting shooting trio,* I pull collective to lift and the cockpit explodes, a round tears through my shoulder slamming me into the seat, I lose my grip on the controls, but Cochran, riding them with me, keeps us going, not lifting but driving straight ahead, wheels never leaving the ground, *we're a terror make no error,* the chopper bucks and pitches, more hits coming, blood sprays over me, Cochran's flight suit and flak vest are ripped to shreds, flesh torn and bone mangled, but he bores ahead into the machine gun emplacement, crushes the VC gunners and silences the machine gun as we crash to a stop, blades flapping crazily, explosions all around us, *down Texas way they don't like the way we play,* the sound of choppers circling overhead, M-60s rake the tree line, someone appears at the cockpit window and yanks my shoulder straps loose, *pistol-packing mama lay that pistol down.*

"I've got you Lieutenant."

Soonto pulls me out the door, a helicopter thunks down behind us, Soonto drags me to the waiting chopper and throws me in, the crew chief pulls me over to the bulkhead. I hear a voice, "Here's your buddy." Another form is lifted in and thrown down next to me.

"That's it," Soonto yells, and, with the engine screaming, we rise out of the zone.

"Hang in there, Lieutenant."

Soonto jams a wad of cloth against my shoulder and wraps me round and round with a dressing like a trussed turkey its feathers due for a plucking and what about old Barney the Buffalo watering away in the zone is he stew for the pot or will rice pudding be on the menu no dogs anything but the dogs this whole fucking outfit has gone to the dogs the doggies have no sense and Daddy smacks me with a sack full of pennies to knock some sense in my head I'm sorry Daddy but it's the Marines for me and four generations of Huckelbee Army alligators tear at my bootheels I'm running for all I'm worth with a full eagle ball and anchor pack heavy enough to make a man fall over with thirst *ah, that's good, slurp it to me* "Come on, Lieutenant, don't fade on me now, we're almost there." I'm running down paths where faces are faded photographs of Huckelbees in New Guinea jungle fatigues and World War One helmets and Rough Rider Sam Browne belts and gray rebel uniforms, pictures that I carry out of the muck free of the misery but never free of the pain *owwwwwwwllll don't do that . . .* Soonto drags me off the metal deck of the chopper and onto a canvas stretcher.

"Slow down, we're bouncing him around," someone says.

I squint and make out shapes. "Soonto," I whisper. He bends down. "Hold up my head."

I'm being carried across steel matting, behind me there's another stretcher, a big body sprawled on top. Behind him walk men swathed in bandages and off to the side, watching us go past, the crew chiefs, and then, closer, faces looking down at me. The Hammer, "Good work, Huckelbee." Pappy, "You got as much sense as a sow that won't nurse her young but you did good this time, son." Captain Beamus, "All squared away now, Lieutenant." Emmett, "Filled an inside straight, *amigo*." Wee Willie, "Next round's on me, jarhead." Baptist John, "Hell from beneath is moved, a lion is in the streets." Dum-Dum, "Yah gave 'em dah Bronx cheer, spiking dat rat-a-tat-tat gun." Each face in focus, then a red haze covers my eyes and I drop my head, oh *madre mía* I wouldn't wish this on anybody, rich or poor, Private or General, President or slave. I'm carried into a black cave where it's too dark to see anything. I hear the sound of voices, coming from a long distance.

"You're in the C-123 . . . we'll be at the hospital in Nha Trang before you know it . . . destruction of the machine gun allowed the squadron to haul in more troops . . . ARVNs cleared the zone and set up positions . . . waited for the VC who never showed up . . . mission a victim of bad intell . . . on the plus side no civilian casualties . . . no one knows who shot the water buffalo" . . . *no one's saying anything about Cochran, Doc . . . where's Cochran? . . . is that him on the other stretcher . . . fill me in, I'm going under . . . did he make it or not . . .* "He's fading, they both need blood, can't the pilot squeeze any more speed out of this crate?" . . . *like trying to talk to a rock . . . what's a poor man to do but lie here like an old brokedown horse that wan-*

dered out in the sagebrush and fell down and can't get up again all's he can do is lie on his side and stare unblinking through one encrusted eye into the sky as far back into the workings of time as he can manage and wonder at the wonder and, if he can, wonder what the fuck happened . . .

AFTERWORD

After a thirteen month tour in Vietnam, with everyone back in the states, HMM-188 was broken up and reformed with new personnel. The pilots and men from the old squadron were scattered across the Marine Corps and civilian world.

Commanding Officer: Colonel Arthur "The Hammer" Rappler

His next assignment was the Planning and Development School at Quantico, Virginia, where he passed on the helicopter tactical knowledge he picked up in Vietnam. After that he retired.

Executive Officer: Major Bert "Pappy" Lurnt

Pappy retired after his Vietnam tour to his ramshackle home in the Arkansas Ozarks where he sat on the porch in his hickory rocker, smoking his corncob pipe, sipping white lightning and regaling his numerous kin and friends with tall tales gleaned from his travels in exotic lands.

Administration Officer: Captain Miles "Standish" Briggs

Captain Briggs put his admin skills to good use in the civilian world as head of the personnel department of a large nuts and bolts factory.

Operations Officer: Captain Ralph "Rajah" Beamus

The Rajah made it all the way to Lieutenant Colonel before his age and 30 years of service caught up with him and, after his last stint as the ops officer of the Third Marine Air Wing, he retired and opened a military-style camp for boys in the Catskills.

Supply Officer: Captain Samuel "Squints" Bigelow

Captain Bigelow, after leaving the Marine Corps, went to work for Sikorsky Aircraft, a honcho in their procurement department.

Safety Officer: Captain Ed "Ramshackle" Pomfrey

Captain Pomfrey put in his twenty in the Corps and retired to his hometown in Pennsylvania, where he raises beagle hounds.

Lieutenant William "Wee Willie" Weems

After Vietnam, Wee Willie was assigned to the Training Command in Pensacola, Florida, where he was a T-28 instructor. Afterwards he resigned his commission and became a crop duster.

Lieutenant Ted "Too Tall" Tolliver

Too Tall Tolliver got out of the Marine Corps, went back to teaching high school, but later rejoined the Marine Corps and lasted the full twenty before retiring, then became a marriage counselor and mediator.

Warrant Officer Chuck "Cool Beans" Hastings

Warrant Officer Hastings retired from the Corps after the Vietnam deployment and lived in Cherry Hill, North Carolina, close to old friends from his service days.

Lieutenant Basil "Herbee" Jenkins

Herbee Jenkins did three tours flying helicopters in Vietnam, later transitioning into the CH-47 Chinook, the large twin-rotored workhorse, then flew fire-retardant bombers for the Forest Service when he got out.

Lieutenant Stephen "Baptist John" Merkle

Baptist John couldn't resist the call and left the Marine Corps to become a fire-and-brimstone revivalist preacher, traveling all over the southeastern United States, mangling the scriptures so badly he got a huge reputation as a speaker in tongues.

Lieutenant Daryl "Dum Dum" Dumbert

Dum Dum did two tours in Vietnam, got out and became a policeman in Queens, working his way up to detective.

Lieutenant Carl "Grits" Emmett

Emmett left the Marines, flew for TWA, then went back to Milwaukee and bought a riverboat gambling casino that rakes in beaucoup dough which he uses to finance a halfway house for recovering gambling addicts.

Lieutenant Ben "Ben-San" Benson

Ben-San recovered from his burns, which left him badly scarred, and was engaged to marry a law clerk in San Francisco when Yoshika showed up. She quickly figured out what was going on, "Goodbye you," and hooked up with others in the Japanese community where she found work in a beauty parlor. Ben-San, meanwhile, continued studying law and became a member of the bar.

Lieutenant Rob "Panda Bear" Jacobs

Rob Jacobs is one of the earliest names on the Wall. An empty casket was buried in the family plot in Iowa.

Lieutenant Tom "Tomas" Huckelbee

Lieutenant Huckelbee, his shoulder scarred, barely functioning, left the Marines after Vietnam and became an English instructor at the University of Texas in Austin, spending summer vacations prowling the family ranch on the banks of the Rio Grande while working forty years, on and off, writing a novel.

Lieutenant Mike "Gorilla" Cochran

It was touch and go. His upper body was a torn-up mess. They lost him a couple of times in the operating room but he fought back. One morning, after his recovery was assured, he pulled a fade and left his hospital bed empty. He has no address or phone number. He never applied for a credit card. He never returned to his hometown. He never touched his social security. Rumors abound. He's living on the streets, he's running an orphanage in Laos, he's following the crops, he's a diamond trader in Beirut, a smuggler in Marseilles, yak breeder in Mongolia, Bhuddist monk in Nepal, a practitioner of Lapsong Chung . . .

Sergeant Soonto

Soonto put in his twenty, got out, still a buck sergeant, and returned to Samoa, a hero.

Soonto's Cur

When the Hammering Eights left Vietnam, the cur stayed behind and was adopted by other Marine Corps chopper squadrons. He ruled the hangar area and the living compound and sired many litters from Dogpatch bitches snuck through the fence. When he died of old age he went out as he came in: lean, aloof, wary of strangers, still aware of the perils of the Vietnamese cooking pot.

ACKNOWLEDGMENTS

Many thanks to squadron mate Gordon Gunter, without whose help this book wouldn't exist. I first wrote the novel in 1962 but lost the manuscript and Gordon send me a copy I'd given him. Jack Whipple send me a scanner and software that allowed me to scan the book into my computer, saved me having to retype the whole book. Another squadron mate, Bob Fritzler, filled in my memory gaps with helicopter workings and flight maneuvers.

Old friend David Stanford tuned me up the first time through the book. My agent, Sterling Lord, pointed me in the right direction when I digressed. Editor Aaron Schlechter was a guiding light with his suggestions and corrections. Thanks also to copy editor Ben Farmer and assistant editor Stephanie Gorton for their assistance.

Many thanks to my wife, Eileen, for her careful readings and for spotting inconsistencies in the manuscript, and for her constant encouragement and support.

Finally, thanks to our daughter, Liz, for her proofreading skills and fluency in Spanish.

author photo: Brian Lanker

Ken Babbs graduated from Miami University in Ohio and was in Wallace Stegner's Graduate Writing Program at Stanford University. Later, as a Marine Corps Captain, he flew helicopters in Vietnam. A founding father of the Merry Pranksters and a working partner of Ken Kesey, he helped Kesey write the novel *Last Go Round*. He contributed to the photo journal *On The Bus* and wrote and edited *The Cassady Issue*, a famous small press publication. He has worked as a filmmaker, sound engineer, farmer, writer, performing artist, builder, teacher, musician, actor, and bus driver. He and his wife live in the foothills of the Cascades near Eugene, Oregon.

www.skypilotclub.com

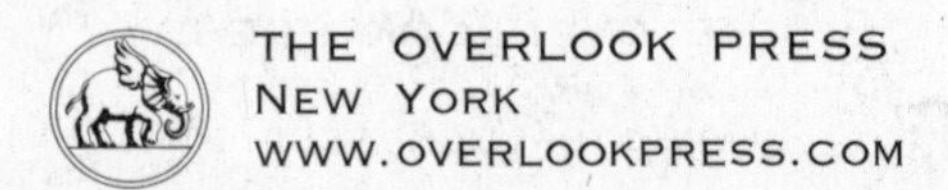